Freda Lightfoot was born and brought up in the mill towns of Lancashire. She has been a teacher, bookseller and small-holder but began her writing career by publishing over forty short stories and articles and five historical romances. She has a flat in the Lake District and a house in a small mountain village in Spain. To find out more information, visit Freda's website on www.fredalightfoot.co.uk.

Praise for Freda Lightfoot:

'Charming and exciting . . . A lovely story by an author with extraordinary feeling in her writing'
Bangor Chronicle

'Freda Lightfoot's talent for creating believable characters makes this a page-turning read.'
Newcastle Evening Chronicle

'The kind of character-driven saga that delights the Catherine Cookson and Josephine Cox audience'
Peterborough Evening Telegraph

Also by Freda Lightfoot

Luckpenny Land

Wishing Water

Larkrigg Fell

Lakeland Lily

The Bobbin Girls

Manchester Pride

Polly's War

Kitty Little

The Favourite Child

Gracie's Sin

Ruby McBride

Daisy's Secret

FREDA LIGHTFOOT

Dancing on Deansgate

CORONET BOOKS
Hodder & Stoughton

Copyright © 2003 by Freda Lightfoot

First published in Great Britain in 2003 by Hodder & Stoughton
A division of Hodder Headline
First published in paperback in 2003 by Hodder & Stoughton
A Coronet paperback

The right of Freda Lightfoot to be identified as the Author
of the Work has been asserted by her in accordance with the
Copyright, Designs and Patents Act 1988.

5 7 9 10 8 6 4

A CIP catalogue record for this title is available from the British Library

ISBN 0 340 82007 1

Typeset in Plantin Light by
Phoenix Typesetting, Burley-in-Wharfedale, West Yorkshire

Printed and bound in Great Britain by
Mackays of Chatham Ltd, Chatham, Kent

Hodder & Stoughton
A division of Hodder Headline
338 Euston Road
London NW1 3BH

To the memory of my Dad who died during the writing of this book, aged eighty-two. At twenty, as a new recruit in the Manchester Regiment, he was digging bodies out of the Christmas blitz. He spent every leave at the dances and fell in love with the big band sound. He will be greatly missed.

For information on the dance halls of Manchester I am grateful to the books of Phil Moss published by Neil Richardson. I recommend them to anyone with happy memories of that time.

1940

I

It was dark in the cellar so the girl felt quite safe in not pulling down the blind, despite blackout restrictions. At least the darkness within helped her to see better what was happening outside in the street, although the light was fading fast on this grey December afternoon. The gentle brown eyes were just about on a level with the pavement as she peered up through the grimy window set high in the wall. Had anyone taken the trouble to look in, they would have seen how huge they appeared in the pale oval of her face; a face which bore the marks of her mother's beauty yet with none of its brittleness. These cheeks were round and soft, the chin square and firm, giving an air of strength to the wan features. Even in the semi-darkness, light glimmered in the long strands of shining brown hair. Looking for all the world as if it had been cut with a knife and fork, the girl made no attempt to keep it tidy but allowed it to sweep carelessly about her face, as if the tumbling curls could shelter her from the world and hide the fear which filled those wide, startled eyes.

Her vision was limited through the grille that covered the window, and what little she could see was obscured by booted feet as shoppers dashed along in search of last-minute presents, turning the snow underfoot to a grey slush. War or no war, it was still Christmas.

Somewhere, beyond the periphery of her vision, she could hear a band: the Salvation Army playing 'Hark the Herald Angels Sing', and despite her fear that the raids might start again at any moment the sound brought a sensation of strange excitement, a quickening of her pulse. The soft, rose-pink lips broke into a wistful smile for, at fifteen, Jess Delaney wanted to be out amongst the crowds listening to the band, to be a part of the festive scene instead of missing all the fun, confined as she was in her own private hell-hole night after night. At first she'd made little complaint, not seeing it as important, simply another of Lizzie's eccentricities.

But now it was all too serious.

They were calling it the Christmas Blitz. It had started a few nights ago and in no time the whole of Manchester had seemed to be in flames, making everyone fear for their life. Enemy bombers had come again the next night, following the line of the canal system right into the heart of the city, pounding the life out of it for hour upon hour. Amongst others, Piccadilly had been hit, the Victoria Buildings destroyed, as well as damage done to the famous Free Trade Hall. A landmine had even fallen on Victoria Station. Who would know if one small house were bombed and a young girl lay buried beneath it? Who would trouble to come looking for her? Jess would much rather have gone to an air-raid shelter along with the rest of Deansgate Village, but her mother wouldn't hear of it.

'Don't lock me in,' she'd protested as she'd watched Lizzie apply the scarlet lipstick to her full mouth, frizz up her hair and generally attempt to make herself as appealing as possible. Lizzie had a weakness, several in fact, but the main ones came, as she herself was fond of saying, either in a glass, or a pair of trousers.

'Don't you start yer fratching. I've no time to listen, not now. I have to pop out and do a bit of business. Anyroad, you'll be safe enough in the cellar. No jerry bombs'll get you here. Solid as a rock is this house.'

Had she offered these words of comfort in any tone of voice other than careless and disinterested, Jess might well have believed her. She always wanted to. If you couldn't trust your own mother then who could you trust? But in Lizzie's case, Jess had learned from long experience that it simply wasn't wise to do so. Lizzie never put anyone's needs before her own, not even those of her own daughter, as her behaviour showed all too clearly.

Now, all Jess could do was listen to the street door bang shut and with a sinking of her heart, watch her mother's feet in their inappropriately high heels trip by the window above.

'Off out with yer latest fancy man, arta? What about that lass o' your'n, poor bugger?'

'Shut yer face, you. Keep yer nose out of my business Cissie Armitage, if yer know what's good for you.' Lizzie Delaney tossed her hennaed curls and, nose in the air, swung her hips more provocatively than ever as she sashayed down Back Irwell Street towards Deansgate. 'At least Jess doesn't make a nuisance of herself on other folks' doorsteps, unlike some I could mention.'

Cissie Armitage bridled visibly at this dig at her own offspring who were playing a relatively innocent game of making slush pies, although their favourite pastime was tying dustbin lids to doorknobs before knocking and running away hell for leather. Nonetheless she clipped her youngest boy's ear, making him yell out loud; more out of annoyance that her hated rival had scored a valid point over her than a belief that he deserved it. Cissie was furiously envious of Lizzie Delaney. Her own sagging figure in its wrap-around pinny could not be compared with her neighbour's slender curves, and the hair pins rolled into greying hair didn't hold a candle to the luscious curls that fell upon Lizzie Delaney's shoulders, for all the colour came out of a bottle. Was it any wonder she hated her?

'It's the poor chap what I feel sorry for. Who is it this time, poor bugger? Does he know he's likely to get the clap going wi' you?'

'Shut yer noise, yer nasty old cow.'

Cissie opened her mouth to add further invective about married women who were no better than they should be when their husbands were away fighting in the war. Never the quickest of thinkers, being more malice than wit, by the time she'd thought of a suitably killing remark Lizzie had vanished round the corner, leaving only the clack of her high heels and the lingering scent of cheap perfume in her wake. Incensed at being so thwarted, Cissie shook her broom handle and shouted after her in a big loud voice so that any one of the several other women listening with avid curiosity from their doorsteps could plainly hear. 'Tha'll cop it one day, Lizzie Delaney, when your Jake comes home. See if you don't.'

Hearing these last words quite plainly, Lizzie smiled to herself, tucked her bag under her arm and made her way along Cumberland Street, fully aware of both admiring and condemning eyes following her every step. It was slippy underfoot and the rapidly fading light of afternoon reflected eerily on the grey snow but she was used to walking in semi-darkness and every step she took seemed to lighten her heart, as always when she was off out to meet Jimmy. She heard the sound of a ship's hooter from down the docks and a shiver of delight trickled down her spine. That could be his ship calling to her, telling her he'd be with her soon. She could hardly wait.

When Lizzie reached Deansgate, she turned sharp right towards Castlefield Wharves, not even glancing in the direction of Finnigans, the smart leather goods store from where she'd purloined said handbag earlier in the day. Lizzie had no qualms about doing a bit of shop-lifting now and then. One had to keep body and soul together after all, and everyone knew shopkeepers made a fortune out of their customers with their over-pricing and exploitation of rationing. Anyroad, serve 'em right for not keeping a proper eye on their displays.

'If 'n you see something worth taking girl, take it. And if it don't suit when you get it home, I'll help you get rid of it, and make it worth your while.' This from Bernie, her oh-so-wily brother-in-law. Lizzie knew that she hadn't always made the right choices in life and allowing Bernie Delaney to take any sort of control over it had perhaps been the biggest mistake of all.

But then ever since that soft husband of hers had volunteered for service right at the start of the war, she'd been like a lost soul, unable to get a proper grasp on things. Why couldn't Jake have borrowed some of Bernie's native cunning and got himself a nice little job that avoided call-up? Trust him to do the noble thing, bloody fool. Being left to cope alone with a child had hit her hard. Was it any wonder she'd turned to his brother for support and comfort?

Trouble was, there were times when she got more than she bargained for. Bernie thought nothing of giving her a smack round the mouth if she stepped out of line. Lizzie had tried objecting to this treatment, loud and long, not that he took a blind bit of notice.

'You don't appreciate how valuable an asset I am to you,' she'd tell him, shaking her fist in his grinning face.

'Course I do, love. Don't we have a nice little trade going in the coupons you procure for me.'

'Aye, which you sell on at a bob a time while I get less than nowt for me efforts.'

'Nay, tha does well enough, and live rent free in a nice little house I provide for you. Nor do I make any objection to your other little sidelines, like stuffing the odd bits and bobs in your bag whenever you pop in Lewis's or the fancy shops on King Street, now do I?'

Lizzie gasped. 'Are you suggesting you take a cut from that too?'

'I take what's due to me, girl, and don't you forget it.' At this point the pale grey eyes with their short, stubby eyelashes would narrow to slits, the fleshy mouth tighten and the flabby jowls shake with such fury that there was no mistaking the warning signs and Lizzie had learned to keep quiet when he was in one of his moods. Bernie Delaney was no oil painting; a big bruiser of a man with a beer belly on him that made him look eight months gone, and with his own way of doing things. It didn't pay to be too critical. Lizzie had discovered that arguing only made matters worse, that pushing him too far would only result in another clip round the ear, or worse.

But rough diamond or no, he could be soft as putty when the notion took him, and a right card after a jar or two, so Lizzie always made excuses for his short temper. She liked to imagine that he was jealous of the fact other men found her attractive. Despite their frequent and furious rows and disagreements, he only had to smile at her and her insides did a little flip, and her knees turned to water. She couldn't help it. They'd had a bit of fun together over the years, largely because he had a way with him that Lizzie simply couldn't resist. She wouldn't describe it as charm exactly, more a certain edge to him, an excitement which convinced her, deep down, that she'd married the wrong Delaney brother. Her only disappointment was that he wasn't prepared to leave Cora for her. In Bernie's eyes, his wife was only one step removed from the Virgin Mary herself. Which must make Lizzie some sort of Mary Magdalene, or worse.

He would most certainly object to her trip out tonight. She was meeting Jimmy at the Queens on the corner of Potato Wharf. After a drink or two they'd go on to the Opera House which was putting on some sort of review for servicemen. During the interval they'd probably pop across to the Crown on Byrom Street, where he'd buy her a few port and lemons.

He knew how to keep her sweet did Jimmy. Usually, after a few dates, Lizzie would grow bored and be eager to catch the eye of the next good-looking male who happened to show an interest in her. But she'd been seeing Jimmy regularly for some weeks now and had grown surprisingly fond of him. She might even be sorry to see him go when his ship sailed.

Later in the evening they might go on to a dance, call in at the Globe on Gartside Street, or settle for a kiss and a cuddle down some back alley. Lizzie didn't mind which. She wasn't averse to a bit of slap and tickle, wherever she could find it. Life was too short, in her opinion, to deny herself such treats. Not that she admitted as much to Jake. She always replied to his letters with assurances that she was saving herself for him; for when the war was over and her reliable, caring husband returned home for good. Boring husband, more like. In reality she thought Jake a fool for imagining fidelity to be remotely possible, particularly in wartime. She wasn't cut out to be a flaming nun.

Lizzie pushed open the pub door and made her way down the lobby to the small room where she could get a quick snifter while she waited for Jimmy. She wouldn't dream of going in the vault where the men were playing darts, though she probably knew every last one of them. That was a rule even Lizzie wouldn't break. Jess would be furious to know she'd ventured this far through the portals of sin.

'Yer usual, love?'

'Ta Betty. Turned out nippy again this evening.'

'Aye, get that down yer neck and it'll warm you up grand. Though I fancy you might find a better way of keeping warm afore night's out.'

'A girl can hope,' and giving the cheery barmaid a wink, Lizzie picked up her glass and took an appreciative sip of the gin. This was her favourite tipple at the start of an evening, though an increasingly rare treat in these difficult times. She let it slide slowly over her tongue, feeling the glow of it radiating through her. Pure nectar. Ooh, what a wicked woman she was!

Miserable old sods like Cissie Armitage might call her a tart but Lizzie had her standards. Tarts stood on Tonman Street and charged for their favours, whereas Lizzie was particular who she went with, but if her latest fella liked to bestow little gifts in return for her favours, what was so wrong in that? Being a bleeding mother wasn't the be-all and end-all in life.

But then having children had never been a part of her plan and she'd been shocked to find herself up the duff with Jess. If she hadn't fallen with a baby at the tender age of sixteen, she might never have married Jake Delaney in the first place, and would still have been free to enjoy life. She half blamed Jess herself for this perceived misfortune, and also Jake for being so quick to march her down the aisle. He'd insisted he was pleased, that he loved her, that he liked kids and wanted four at least and had been disappointed when no more had come. What he didn't realise was that she'd taken precautions ever since, determined not to repeat her mistake. She'd felt a bit guilty about that at first, but how would she have coped with more kids? She couldn't even bring one up properly.

It galled her that Cissie Armitage, of all people, should accuse her of being a cruel and neglectful mother. Kids were a nuisance, everyone knew that, always demanding summat or other and never giving you a minute's peace.

At least she made sure that Jess was safe before she went out of an evening, not bundled off to that smelly old disused canal tunnel they called a shelter which stretched under Camp Street and Grape Street. Big it may be but it was like a dosshouse down there, running with water and no doubt infested with rats. She was much more comfortable in their own cellar. Now who could say fairer than that?

Lizzie wiped a smear of scarlet lipstick from the rim of her glass and took another long swallow of the gin, mellowing nicely and becoming increasingly certain with each ensuing sip, that no one could do any better in the circumstances. Anyroad, what other option did she have? She had to keep bringing in the money somehow and if sometimes she sailed a bit close to the wind, how else could she have provided for herself and her child? She'd never have done half so well on the scratty army wage Jake sent her. No, she must keep on hoping that Jess didn't enquire too closely into where the money came from, and that nothing went wrong. Lizzie knew for certain that if she ever ran out of luck and fell foul of the law, Bernie wouldn't stand by her. He'd made that plain enough.

'What good would it do for us both to be put through the wringer, eh?' he'd say, in that Cheeky Charlie way of his. 'Do as yer told and you'll be right enough.'

'And what if I'm not? What then?'

'Are you questioning my judgement, eh? Would I let my best girl suffer, I ask you?'

Ooh, she just loved it when he called her his best girl. That put her one up on Cora.

Lizzie glanced up at the clock on the wall. She'd ten minutes to finish this drink, then Jimmy would be here, full of swagger and with cocky mischief sparkling in his blue eyes. It made her go all funny just to think of how gorgeous he was. She might just abandon their plans for the evening altogether and take him straight back home. They couldn't have much time left before his ship sailed. Might as well make the most of it.

Another woman came in and sat beside her with a half pint of mild set on the circular table before her. 'Hello Dorrie love, how's your chap? Due any leave is he, or are you hoping he stays away for a bit longer, eh?' Crossing her legs and smoothing her skirt over silk-stockinged knees, Lizzie settled down for a cosy gossip with her friends.

The liquid notes of the bugles and trumpets were making Jess ache with the need to get out, filling her with a deep longing to be a part of this festive scene. Music always affected her so. But although this would be the second Christmas Eve in the war so far, not forgetting the countless other nights she had spent incarcerated in the cellar while her feckless mother went out on the town, Jess didn't feel any more resigned to her fate than she had on all those previous occasions.

She began to scratch and scrabble with her fingertips, desperately trying to prise open the window so that she could breathe the crisp cold air. If she were a butterfly or a bird, instead of a girl with dark brown hair and long, gawky legs, she could fly out through the grille, spread her wings and be free.

Jess pressed her cheek against the cracked pane wishing that her best friend, Leah, would materialise out of the gloom, yet knowing it to be unlikely. Leah would be fully occupied serving toasted tea cakes to pretty ladies in smart hats at Simmons's Tea Room on the corner of Deansgate where she lived with her parents. She frequently complained about the long hours she had to spend serving tea and washing up, though she would at least be warm, as well as certain of a good meal when she was done for the day and climbed up the stairs to the flat above.

There was never any such treat for herself. No doting mother standing smiling at the cooker, ready with a hot plate of home cooked dinner the moment she walked in through the door. No one to listen to her woes, or sit quietly knitting while she slept soundly in a warm bed.

Jess shivered. She'd tried to provide what comforts she could for the hours she must spend locked in here, a bed of sorts, blankets and a hot water bottle which quickly went cold. Yet, as always, it felt cold and damp in the cellar as well as dark. But once she lit the lamp, she would have to close the blind and then would feel shut off from the world outside, from the people in the street and the hustle and bustle of Christmas. She'd be quite alone, save for her books and her mouth organ, and one miserable Tilley lamp, at least until Lizzie returned to let her out. She always promised to be no more than an hour, two at most, yet would stagger home in the early hours, roaring drunk and more often than not with a sailor on her arm.

Jess dreaded those occasions the most, when she could hear the distant squeals, gasps and screeches of her mother in the throes of a drunken passion. She didn't care to imagine what went on behind the closed door of her bedroom, but the close proximity of a young daughter never stopped Lizzie making an unholy row about it. Not that Jess lacked too many details on the great mysteries of love and passion. Lizzie had made sure of that, brutally explaining to her daughter how to keep a man happy. And she'd also seen the messy results: the bruises and bites from her mother's more ardent suitors, the furtive applications and doses. It all seemed most unsavoury and not in the least Jess's idea of love and romance.

She realised suddenly that the music had stopped, that a certain hush filled the air. There followed the penetrating wail of the siren which brought a chill to her spine and set her heart pounding like a drum. When she heard the low drone of enemy aircraft approaching, Jess knew it was going to start all over again.

The house shook with the clatter of bombs falling, the crack of explosions, the rumble of buildings collapsing all around. The sky turned blood red as, down by the canal basin, warehouses were set on fire. Even here in the cellar Jess could smell the burning, see great balls of greasy cotton flying about, spreading the fire at lethal speed. Feet were running by the grille in panic now, Christmas shopping forgotten as survival became the only consideration. There were screams and cries as people fell, or lost touch with loved ones.

From her worm's eye view, Jess could see it all. One elderly woman was knocked flying, bags and basket catapulted from her arms, gifts trodden underfoot as others with less patience pushed past. Jess felt sure it must be the end of the world, that any second the roof of her prison would fall upon her head and squash her flat like a fly.

She turned away from the tiny grilled window to cower in the farthest corner, wrapping her arms tight about her head, blocking out all sensation, save for that of raw terror.

2

The all-clear sounded just as it was growing too dark to see anything. How long had the raid lasted, she wondered? A couple of hours at least, so it must be after seven, maybe eight by now. Not that it made any difference to Jess what time it was. She was still locked in the cellar with no sign of Lizzie, who hadn't come rushing home to see if her daughter had survived. No doubt she was safely holed up in a shelter somewhere with her latest fella. Jess uncurled herself from her cramped position in the corner and made her way over to the window.

Outside, there was activity of a different sort now, people starting to pick up their lives and go about their business again simply because they were able to. Back Irwell Street, so far as Jess could tell, had got off lightly this time. Who knew what tomorrow might bring but for now she could hear laughter somewhere, loud chatter, and even a few flippant notes on a bugle. Her neighbours were clearly counting their blessings and resolving to carry on, like the stalwarts they were. Patriotism ran high here in Manchester. Not for a moment did they mean to weaken. It was then that she heard a voice calling her name.

'Jess, is that you? Are you down there?'

'Leah?' Peering up through the gloom and grime she could just make out the pale outline of her friend's face grinning down at her through the pavement grille above the cellar window.

Leah was as fair as Jess was dark, with soft blue eyes and a pretty, heart-shaped face. She was a year older and quite sophisticated at sixteen. Nothing ever seemed to get her down as she positively bubbled with fun and laughter. Much as she loved her friend, Jess envied Leah her ability to laugh at life. She'd quite lost the knack of it herself.

'Cheer up, it's Christmas,' Leah said, as if reading her thoughts. 'We need to get you out of there. Where's the key?' She didn't ask why her best friend was spending Christmas Eve locked in the cellar, having seen her in a similar situation too many times before. She understood about Lizzie, and wouldn't dream of intruding on Jess's family affairs unless information was actively volunteered.

'Hanging on the hook behind the kitchen door.'

'Right, hold on a tick.'

The face vanished from the grille and Jess felt lonelier than ever, an aching pain of want somewhere below her ribs. How would Leah get into the kitchen? Lizzie would surely have locked the door before she left. Or she might have forgotten to put the key back on the hook and taken it with her, out of carelessness.

The minutes ticked by, seeming like hours as she waited for rescue. Any last shreds of hope had quite gone when suddenly there came a scratching at the lock and then the cellar door swung open and Leah was right there before her, looking mightily pleased with herself.

'Sorry for the delay. Nearly got caught by old Ma Pickles when I climbed over the backyard gate. Well, don't just stand there. Mother has mince pies for supper and you're invited.'

'I thought you'd all be staying down in the shelter.'

Leah gave a little spurt of laughter. 'On Christmas Eve? Ma wouldn't allow even Mr Hitler to ruin her Christmas, not when she's spent so many hours preparing for it. We must fly the flag, she says. So come on, shake a leg, we've even got some of Mr Ruggieri's ice cream to go with them.'

And suddenly, as so often with her friend, Jess felt as if a great black cloud had lifted, that the sun had come out and life was worth living again.

Carefully closing the cellar door behind them and putting the key safely back on the hook, the two girls slipped out of the house with much helpless giggling at their daring and swung, arm in arm, along the street singing loudly to the strains of 'There's a Bluebird on my Shoulder'.

Jess sat, pink-cheeked, in front of a blazing fire in the crimson and gold living room with its fine mahogany furniture and solid Victorian piano just as if she were a part of this family. She marvelled in silent wonder as they teased and joked with each other, shared amusing stories from their working day and generally seemed to enjoy each other's company. Even the usually stiff and formal Mr Simmons looked surprisingly relaxed, sitting in his wing chair smiling benignly upon his offspring, making jolly remarks as he smoothed his bristly moustache.

Robert, Leah's older brother, lay sprawled upon the rug, looking even more handsome than usual in pale grey slacks and a sweater, if rather quiet and sulky. He'd said little since she'd arrived, but then Mr Simmons praised the excellent food they were enjoying and Robert made a barbed comment about not everyone being so fortunate.

His father's jaw tightened disapprovingly, 'I understand your resentment at not being in the armed forces, son, but you perform an essential service here in the bakery, make no mistake. And folk must have bread, even in wartime.'

'If I could at least do something genuinely useful as well, be a fire watcher or something, then it wouldn't be so bad. Anybody can bake bread, even Jess here.'

For a second Jess held her breath, thinking perhaps this whole, lovely picture of family unity was about to be shattered, but no, the Simmons weren't like that. Very politely, though with a marked sternness, his father responded.

'Do not bring our innocent guests into this petty squabble. I've told you before, when I consider you to be old enough I shall allow you to join me as an ARP.'

'I'm twenty, old enough now for God's sake.'

'It wouldn't be appropriate for you to join at this juncture. We can't both take time off from the bakery. Better I take the risks and not you, a young man with all your life before you.'

'What about all those other young men with their lives before them, those who weren't rejected for service? What choice do they have but to take whatever risks are necessary?'

'Please dear, let's not quarrel, not on Christmas Eve,' Mrs Simmons intervened, looking anxious. 'And do listen to Daddy, darling. He really does know best.'

'Quite.' Mr Simmons glowered at his son from beneath bushy eyebrows. 'Hopefully the war will be over by next Christmas and further sacrifice will not be necessary. In the meantime let us enjoy this one, into which your dear mother has invested a great deal of time and effort. Now, perhaps Leah will entertain us on the pianoforte. Come along, my dear, and cheer us all up.'

Mrs Simmons clapped her hands. 'Oh yes, that would be lovely.'

. Jess hadn't quite understood all the implications of the small spat between the two men, or the shiver of animosity which had flickered briefly between them, but instantly dismissed it as no concern of hers. She was having far too good a time to worry about such minor matters. She felt as if she was in paradise. Earlier, they'd all listened to the

King's College choir on the wireless, and Jess had been utterly enthralled. It had seemed amazing that you could simply turn a knob and hear such beautiful sounds coming out of a box.

Now they all stood around the piano while Leah played a medley of carols for them to sing in loud, happy voices. Mr Simmons with his deep baritone and Mrs Simmons straining slightly at the high notes. Robert proved to have quite a robust, pleasing tone to his voice, and at one point Jess very daringly brought her mouth organ from out of her pocket and accompanied Leah as she played 'Silent Night'.

Mrs Simmons was delighted. 'My dear girl, that was lovely. You see, we shall enjoy Christmas, in spite of Mr Hitler's efforts to the contrary.'

Afterwards, tea was served by a maid in a white apron, and the mince pies, as with all the Simmons' baking, were utterly delicious. Jess savoured every mouth-watering morsel. How they managed to get the fat to bake such wonderful tarts, let alone the fruit and sugar that went into them, Jess couldn't imagine but instinctively knew that in no respect would Muriel Simmons have broken the law. However difficult procuring the ingredients for a good Christmas for her husband, son and daughter might be, it would be entirely proper and above board.

Unlike the Delaneys, Jess's own family. Uncle Bernie and his progeny of good-for-nothing, lay-about rogues were forever seeking a way to get around regulations, looking for the quick scam and an easy way to make a bit of brass. Aunt Cora did her best to control those sons of hers, with no support from their father, for, roughnecks, hooligans, spivs, call them what you will, every last one of them was a Delaney to the core.

Jess missed her own father badly, and not counting her scatterbrained, pathetic, hopelessly inadequate mother who

was a huge embarrassment to her, there was really only her
aunt who Jess cared anything about. A big, jolly woman, she
was a bit of a card was Cora, but then she needed a strong
sense of humour having married into the Delaneys, who, as
the whole of Deansgate was well aware, spelled Trouble with
a capital T.

The Simmons family on the other hand were famous with
the mill hands and dock workers for their hot pies and
currant buns, generously filled and sensibly priced. One step
up from the Co-op, many a new bride had enjoyed her
wedding reception within its cream and burgundy
surrounds, and any number of people had been 'buried
with ham' at moderate cost, served by suitably unobtrusive
waitresses.

'And how is your dear mother?' Mrs Simmons politely
enquired in her soft, carefully modulated voice. Plump and
matronly but supremely elegant with her swept-up hair,
pleated skirt and powder blue twinset pinned at the collar
with a tasteful brooch, she was so much the kind of mother
Jess would have loved to have, despite Leah complaining
about her high expectations and strict rules. Caring and yet
perfectly controlled, and with such exquisite taste.

'Very well, thank you.'

'Is she in employment at the moment?'

This was a question Jess was accustomed to and she
answered with smooth, if ambiguous, dexterity. 'She helps
me Uncle Bernie from time to time.'

'Ah, down at the docks. How useful. And yourself, are
you still working on the Market, dear?'

Jess agreed that she did still work at Campfield but was
keeping an eye open for something better. It was lively and
fun, in a way, working on the indoor market but Jess was
ambitious, keen to better herself, though she wasn't quite
sure how.

'Have you thought what you might do next?'

She shook her head. There was something about the very kindness of the woman which often left her tongue-tied. Even the scent of her Lily-of-the-Valley perfume made Jess feel very slightly grubby and unclean, not really fit to be seated on plush velvet cushions in this rarefied atmosphere of gracious living.

Muriel Simmons seemed to understand and merely smiled more sweetly than ever. 'Well, do come and speak to Mr Simmons before you make any final decisions, won't you dear? He is sometimes in need of help in the shop since girls come and go with alarming frequency. He may well have a position at some time in the future, for a fine young lady such as yourself.'

'Thank you. I'll remember that.' It troubled Jess that she had no clear vision of what she wanted, how her life might turn out, or where she was heading. Deep down was the fear that she might end up like Lizzie, wasting her life completely by turning into a feckless tart, or drinking herself into a stupor to blunt the reality of failure. Did she even have the brains or the talent to do anything worthwhile? Jess knew that she longed for a bit of lightness and fun, of which she'd enjoyed precious little in her life thus far; and that her heart cried out for independence and freedom. Getting away from Back Irwell Street and that dreadful cellar would be a start, what she most yearned for at the moment.

'Another mince pie, dear?' Mrs Simmons asked, breaking into her thoughts.

'No thank you, I couldn't eat another thing. Besides, I'd best be off.' Jess glanced at the clock on the mantelshelf, a solid gold piece with a pendulum that swung ponderously to and fro, the fingers pointing to half past nine. There would be hours yet before Lizzie came home but she didn't like to intrude further on the Simmons' generosity. She got up to go, carefully folding her napkin and placing it by her empty plate.

'As you wish dear. Leah, show your friend out. I expect we'll see you tomorrow. You must pop over after your Christmas lunch and show us your presents.'

Jess almost laughed out loud. Christmas lunch? Presents? That would be the day. No doubt Lizzie would be in the Donkey till closing time. A sharp pain of disappointment stabbed under her ribs at the prospect of the bleak Christmas Day ahead but she ignored it. Where was the point in fretting? Things could be worse. At least they didn't starve. Lizzie always made sure there was food on the table, even if it was basic fare and Jess the one to cook it. They certainly wouldn't be having goose as the Simmons family were. But why worry, the war would be over soon, everyone said so, then her dad would come home and everything would be different. Lizzie would have to behave for a start.

Remembering her manners, Jess smiled at her hostess. 'Thanks for inviting me. Those mince pies were delicious.'

'Well, there's still time to buy some for your dear mother. The shop will be open till ten tonight.'

'I'll mention it to her when I get back,' Jess lied, backing to the door. It was never wise to linger too long or Mrs Simmons might start getting curious and asking awkward questions.

More aware of what went on at the house opposite than she let on, Muriel Simmons slipped four of the remaining mince pies into a paper bag and handed them to Jess. 'Perhaps she's working late tonight and won't have time to call in. Give her these from me, with the compliments of the season.'

Jess blushed bright pink but was not so foolish as to refuse this act of kindness, charity though it undoubtedly was. These mince pies might be the closest she got to pleasure this Christmas, and again she expressed her thanks, more fervently this time.

Leah led her down the stairs to let her out through the shop, 'I can't wait for Christmas, can you?' The shop bell clanged when she opened the door but the two girls behind the counter were still too busy serving to take much notice. 'See that you pop over *before* lunch if you can.'

Jess willingly agreed in the hope she just might be asked to stay. She never had been invited to anything other than tea at the Simmons' house in all the years she'd known Leah, but she lived in hope that this might change as she grew older and proved herself to be both polite and well mannered. Jess always paid careful attention to the way Mrs Simmons held her napkin or used a cake fork. Such niceties might well come in useful one day.

She waved goodbye and set off quickly across the now silent, dark street. There'd been no further air raid warnings, no more sirens to send folk scurrying back to the shelters, thank goodness. The Sally Army Band had stopped playing and were standing around chatting and drinking hot tea from their flasks, their faces glowing like pale ovals in the soft light from their carefully shaded lanterns, instruments set aside while they took a breather. Intrigued, and reluctant to return to the confines of the cellar on this night of unusual and precious freedom, Jess wandered over for a closer look. There had been many nights in recent months when the sound of her mouth organ's plaintive notes was the one thing which had kept her sane. She loved music, a passion she shared with her father.

This thought brought a sudden vision of him to mind. Jess could smell the fresh scent of the Lifebuoy soap he used, the Woodbine cigarettes he smoked. She could hear the rap made by the toecaps on his clogs as he came up the lobby each evening after work, feel the vibration of his cheerful laughter as he held her in a great bear hug; but most of all she recalled the hours he had spent teaching her to play the mouth organ, and even allowing her to try a few tunes on his piano accordion at which he was an expert. These sweet memories brought a funny sort of tightness to her chest and Jess had to take a few quick breaths in order to ease it before worry over his well-being quite overcame her and she dissolved into tears right there in the street.

As she crept nearer, her toe knocked against something hard, so that it fell over with a clang. Bending down she scrabbled about in the darkness till her fingers closed about an instrument. A bugle, she guessed, by the shiny feel of it.

She glanced about her. The band members were happily gossiping as they made inroads into a huge mound of sandwiches. No doubt they'd be playing for some time yet. Then, as the pubs closed, they'd collect up the worst of the drunks and take them to the mission hall to sleep it off till morning. Jess smoothed the flat of her hand over the instrument, savouring the seductive shape of it, the smoothly polished surface. It was a miracle that such a small, insignificant object could make such marvellous sounds. She put it to her lips and blew. The note rang out, pure and clean and true, echoing along the darkened street, instantly bringing the gossiping band to a stunned silence.

'Who's there? Who's playing that bugle?'

Jess dropped it with a clatter and fled, desperately aware that someone had set off in pursuit after her.

She was in such haste to avoid being grabbed and leathered for her cheek in blowing a Sally Army bugle, that she didn't notice the chink of light creeping out around the blackout blind in her mother's room. She ran around to the back, let herself in and was halfway down the steps to the cellar when she heard the scream. She recognised it instantly as Lizzie's and, coming so soon after the sweetness of the bugle's call, it seemed all the more horrific, making the hairs stand up on the back of her neck, freezing her to the spot and chilling Jess to her very soul. Then without pause for thought, she called out her mother's name, turned and flew back up the stairs.

3

Jess stood at the open bedroom door, paralysed with fear, uncertain whether she should intervene or run for help. To her utter shock and dismay she found there wasn't one man but two in the room, each punching hell out of the other. One moment they were clasped together in a macabre dance, the next rolling on the floor, fists flying, pummelling each other like fury. The night light that usually sat by the bed had got knocked over and gone out and little could be seen beyond shapes and shadows. The smell of blood and fear was palpable, the sound of loud grunts, the crack of fist on bone, and over all the echo of Lizzie's screams. Both men seemed oblivious to her desperate efforts to intervene as she flopped between them like a rag doll, at times suffering the brunt of the blows. But then, without warning, one shook himself free, like a dog ridding himself of drops of water, and fled from the room.

Lizzie called out a name which Jess didn't quite catch, probably because the word was cut off by another blow from the remaining assailant, one that sent her mother sprawling.

'*You stupid whore!* Have you no sense? You don't do nowt without my say-so. Right?'

If Lizzie made any response, Jess couldn't make out what it was. For several more terrifying seconds she remained rooted to the spot as the man again turned his fists on Lizzie. Her mother was lying curled up, whimpering on the rug while he slapped her this way and that, each crack splitting the air like a thunder clap. It was the force of the blows which finally galvanised her into action.

'*Leave my mam alone!*'

Jess flew at him, punching her own pathetically small fists into his broad back, her fingers desperately trying to get a grip on his jacket to drag him off Lizzie. He rose up on a roar of rage, tossing her aside so that Jess fell back, cracking her head on the floorboards while he thundered down the stairs to vanish into the night.

For some seconds Jess lay stunned and dazed, before the sound of Lizzie's sobs brought her round, and she struggled to her feet to go to help her mother.

Mother and daughter clung together, Lizzie weeping softly while Jess attempted to mop up the blood and tears from a face already turning purple with bruises. She had a bust lip and one eye so swollen it was nearly closed and already turning black. Somehow Jess got her into bed but the next twenty-four hours was a nightmare as Lizzie drifted in and out of consciousness. Jess did her best with cold compresses, blankets and hot cups of tea, leaving her mother alone only as long as it took to nip round to Ma Pickles and ask her to send young Josh to fetch the doctor.

Doc Lee finally arrived late in the evening on Christmas Day. He pulled up Lizzie's eyelids, checked her for broken bones, prodded her with his stethoscope and offered little more than two aspirin and a few strong words of advice. 'She'll live, though whether she deserves to is another matter. Do try to keep your mother off the booze, Jess, if you can. It'll kill her if she goes on in this fashion.'

'It wasn't the booze what made them bruises on her face,' Jess hotly protested, unexpectedly feeling the need to defend Lizzie. But Doc Lee already had his hand on the door latch, his mind moving on to his next patient as if he'd no time to waste on feckless no-hopers without the wherewithal to pay his bills. Jess saw there'd be neither sympathy nor help from this quarter. She wanted to tell him that Lizzie hadn't always been this way. Couldn't he see that? 'How can I stop her?'

He paused to smile down at her, revealing himself as a kindly man if perhaps somewhat inured to misery by his chosen profession. 'Because you're made of sterner stuff, Jess Delaney, and despite your exasperation with having such a mother foisted upon you, you love the old besom. No, don't deny it, I've seen it in the way you care for her. Have you any idea who did this to her? One of her drinking cronies, I'll be bound.'

Jess had not got a clear view of Lizzie's assailant in the shadows of the gloomy bedroom. And she'd been too wobbly on her feet from her own injuries to attempt to chase after him, but in her own mind, she was quite certain who it was, utterly convinced as to the identity of the culprit. Uncle Bernie was the one who beat up Lizzie, though who the other man had been she couldn't even begin to guess. None of this, however, she had any intention of revealing to the doctor. She shrugged her shoulders helplessly, 'I wouldn't know. I saw nowt.'

Doc Lee frowned down at her for a moment, as if sensing some prevarication in the dismissal, but then recalling his busy schedule he shrugged and turned to go. 'Get her along to the Mission Hall. The Salvation Army are experts at salvation, even if you're not. It might not be too late. Lizzie is her own worst enemy and if you don't put a halt to this hell-bent ride to destruction she's on, then look to yourself at least. Otherwise you'll sink with her.'

Jess let him out the back door, thinking that if she hadn't just dented one of the Sally Army's bugles, she might well have acted on this advice. What a Christmas this had turned into! So much for the hope of lunch at the Simmons'. She slid the bolt into place after the doctor had gone, then rested her forehead on her clenched hands and sobbed her heart out. Why did she have to bear such burdens? Why didn't her mam look after *her* instead of the other way round? How was it possible to love her mother as a daughter should when much of the time Jess felt exasperated and infuriated by Lizzie's stupidity? Oh, why couldn't she be like any normal mother?

When the hiccuping sobs finally quietened, she brushed the tears away with the flat of her hand and went to build up the fire so she could brew a pot of tea. She longed, in that moment, for her dad to be here; couldn't seem to stop thinking about him. Why didn't he come home to help, or at least come home on leave to see them now and then? She hadn't even had a letter this week, or last, come to think of it. So far as she could remember there'd been nothing since that Christmas card in early December.

There'd always been a certain amount of jealousy and rivalry between the two brothers. Jake was the good-looking one. He was honest and hard-working with a good job at a local sawmill. Bernie always claimed his brother would never have done so well had it not been for the care he'd given him when they were growing up, keeping him out of a home for one thing. In a way that must be true for having lost both their parents in an epidemic of smallpox while still quite young, Bernie had made himself responsible for his younger brother, and fed them both, largely by living off his wits. Family legend had it that he'd tried everything from running errands, cleaning windows and washing up, to packing and loading down at the docks as well as scrubbing decks. Jess was only too aware, however, that this honest endeavour hadn't lasted long before his true nature had asserted itself and he'd found easier ways of making a living, by nicking the stuff rather than packing it.

But although Jake appreciated Bernie's efforts on his

behalf, he strongly disapproved of his brother's methods. He liked to believe that he was different and took great pride in saying so. A fact which always irritated Bernie since no one could ever quite pin down what sort of work he himself did for a living.

'Bit of this, bit of that,' he would airily remark, should anyone be unwise enough to enquire. Certainly his wife had more sense than to ask any such thing.

Lizzie had once explained to Jess that one of the greatest sources of rivalry between them came over their choice of wife. Bernie had opted for the easy-going Cora Garnet, a homely, anxious-to-please type. Making no claims to beauty, Cora was simply grateful that someone as lively and go-ahead as Bernie Delaney had ever looked her way. Lizzie, on the other hand, had been far more attractive with long, curling hair and a shapely figure, eager to enjoy life to the full. An 'I'm as good as any man' type of woman, which Jake quite liked. Her flirtatious grey-green eyes had once positively sparkled with fun and mischief, eager to taste life, inquisitive about everything. But despite her robust refusal not to be taken for granted, she'd been a good wife, and a loving, caring mother, at least in the early days.

And then Bernie Delaney had pushed his oar in and everything had changed. Jess could pinpoint the date exactly. The last Christmas before the outbreak of war. Christmas 1938.

The two families had made a point of always spending Christmas together and, apart from a few minor squabbles over who was to cook the turkey or provide the pud, it had always passed off pleasantly enough. Until that day.

Jess was never too clear over how it had all started to go wrong, she being only an awkward adolescent of thirteen at the time, wrapped up in her own concerns. Perhaps the adults had got a bit too merry, the women partaking of too many glasses of sherry, and too many glasses of beer for the

men but suddenly the laughing and joking began to get out
of hand.

Her mother had been wearing a new dress, a rose pink satin
rather shorter than her usual style, and with it a pair of black,
silk stockings which showed off her long shapely legs to
perfection. Bernie had already made one or two ribald
remarks about her new saucy look, and then for no apparent
reason suggested she show off 'those glamorous pins, so we
can all admire them. We could have a competition. Come on
Cora, you start the ball rolling. Lift up your frock, let's have
a look.'

'Nay Bernie lad, who'd want to look at mine, great lumps
of lard that they are, but if you must, who am I to spoil yer
pleasure,' and good naturedly, Cora had indeed raised the
hem of her plain navy skirt to reveal a pair of plump knees
topped by even chubbier thighs encased in thick lisle stockings. She beamed at everyone, as if proud of her girth and
some of the children sniggered and giggled behind their
hands, quite used to their mother's silly capers.

Jess could remember glancing anxiously over at her father,
seeing how tight and set his face had become. 'Leave the poor
woman alone, Bernie. You treat her like dirt. What right have
you to insult your own wife in this fashion?'

Bernie's face darkened to a dangerous hue. 'I reckon you're
the one insulting her by insinuating she isn't good to look at.
As it happens, I think she's a cracker. And at least I know
where she's been, which is more than some can say.'

Jake leapt to his feet, breathing hard. 'And what the hell is
that supposed to mean? Are you implying I don't know where
Lizzie's been?'

'Well, do you? She's a good-looking lass with an eye for
flirting. Who knows what she gets up to when you're working
down at that sawmill you set such store by.'

'Damn you, Bernie, you'll take that back or I'll knock your

teeth down yer flaming throat. You've a mind on you like a sewer.'

Bernie shrugged his great shoulders as if brushing the insult aside and snorted his derision. 'Flamin' Nora, what other sort would you expect me to have, after a youth spent in the gutter? Aw, come on Lizzie, be a sport. Cora has shown us hers, how about giving us a dec at yours.' And reaching forward he lunged at the hem of Lizzie's skirt, making her squeal in surprise and bat away his great hand with a playful giggle.

Jake's voice crackled with fury. 'Leave off, you dirty minded lump of muck. She'll do no such thing.'

'It's all right, Jake,' Lizzie intervened, struggling to calm the situation, 'I don't mind. It's only a bit of fun.' And she'd started to edge up the hem of her satin frock very slowly, giggling rather self-consciously. Jake tried to stop her by giving her a little push to make her sit down again but Bernie, revelling in the rise he was getting out of his brother, roared with laughter.

'Tek no notice of him, Lizzie love. Go on, dazzle us all. Mek us eyes pop out. We're all gagging for a gander,' then before anyone realised what he was about, he'd grabbed hold of Lizzie around the waist and tipped her upside down, swinging her up in his arms with her head inches from the floor. Jess and her father had stood transfixed, appalled, for not only could everyone now see all of Lizzie's legs but also her stocking tops and suspenders, the strip of bare thigh above and all of her frilly French knickers. Lizzie squealed in surprised protest but was utterly helpless to free herself, while Bernie continued to laugh uproariously and shake her up and down, as if it were all some huge joke.

The instant Bernie had set Lizzie back on her feet again, red in the face with embarrassment and very flustered, Jake had launched himself at his brother. Jake was tall, a well set up man with powerful shoulders and arms but Bernie had more bulk, was not an easy man to take on even had Jake been prepared to beat the daylights out of his own kith and kin.

Instead, he grabbed him by the collar, pulling his brother's face to within inches of his own and spat fury into his face. 'If you *ever* pull any more tricks like that, I'll kill you. Do you understand? Brother or no flaming brother, I'll kill you with me own bare hands.' Then he'd collected Jess and the now weeping Lizzie and taken them both home.

Thus had ended family Christmases for ever. Sadly, what had also ended that day, was the trust between husband and wife. Jake was livid that Lizzie had been prepared to show off her legs, saying she must have given Bernie some encouragement for him to imagine she'd even do such a thing. For her part, she accused Jake of overreacting and thus provoking Bernie into taking the action he had. Jess was packed off to bed but she could hear them arguing furiously long into the night.

From that moment on the marriage slid steadily downhill. Jake began to watch his wife more and more closely, to question her every move: why she was late home from the market, who she'd seen or talked to that day, where she was going of an evening; even if it was only for a bit of a crack in a neighbour's house. Lizzie would scream and yell that he was finding her guilty without even a trial, believing the worst because of Bernie's uncouth behaviour. Then Jake would be full of apologies and beg her to forgive him.

And in her defiance, Lizzie went out all the more.

But no matter how hard Jake tried, he couldn't seem to get the idea out of his head that the elder brother whom he'd always looked up to, who'd fed and cared for him after their parents were both dead and gone, had kept him out of institutions as a nipper and been his saviour and mentor, did, in some mysterious way, know more about his own wife than he did. And, once planted, suspicion that there was something going on between his brother and his wife, began to grow and fester.

By the time Jake went off to war, the accusations, the blame and the misery had done their worst. Since she was deemed to be guilty, Lizzie had made up her mind that she might as well be and given up the fight. Coldness and increasing distance had chipped away at whatever affection she'd once felt for the man she'd so hastily married, and she was a woman who needed warmth and easy comforts. Finding herself alone, she'd let Bernie into her bed and revelled in the excitement, the danger of it while the drink she consumed to blot out the few remaining pangs of guilt, gradually robbed her of every last shred of self-esteem and the remnants of her judgement. Bernie had said that she was no good. Jake had believed him. Therefore it must be true. Between the two of them, they had destroyed her.

Jess lifted the spluttering kettle from the hob, poured a drop into the tea pot, swirled it about to warm it then emptied the water down the sink before brewing the tea. Next, she fetched Mrs Simmons's mince pies from the tin in the larder where she'd put them for safe keeping and laid them carefully on a plate, setting this, with the two mugs, on a tin tray: the one with the picture of the funny little Bovril cow on it. If ever they'd both been in need of summat tasty, this was the moment. They'd had nothing to eat all day save for a slice of toast and dripping, and Lizzie had hardly touched hers. If Jess had the time and energy to think about it, she'd probably find that she was really very hungry indeed. She didn't even dare to imagine how wonderful roast goose might taste, never mind the home-made Christmas pudding Mrs Simmons would have been sure to provide, smothered in brandy sauce.

'Here you are, Mam. Can you sit up? Do you want me to hold the cup for you?'

Lizzie looked upon her daughter with brimming eyes. 'Eeh lass, what would I do without you? I'd be like a bobbin wi' no thread. I'm not fit to be a mother. Nor to kiss the ground you walk on.'

'Don't start getting maudlin, Mam. Yer stone cold sober, remember? Buck up and see what Mrs Simmons has sent you, with the compliments of the season.'

Lizzie looked at the mince tarts in wonder, then her mouth went square and she began to cry in earnest, nose running and words spluttered out between gasps of tearful self-pity. 'Look at me, forced to take hand-outs now. What a failure I am! No bloody use as a mother. I could never manage to bake such delicious pies meself if I lived to be a hundred.'

'Well you don't have to when Simmons's can do it for you. Come on Mam, eat one at least.'

Lizzie was thinking that no doubt Jess could easily manage to bake such treats but then that lass could turn her hand to anything she'd a mind to. For all she was a quiet, unassuming sort of girl who lacked confidence in herself, she was no fool. Intelligence shone out of those soft brown eyes of hers which so silently and shrewdly seemed to weigh up what was what in the world, and a stubborn strength in the way she'd taken over the running of their little house, preparing the meals as if she were the mother and not the child.

And if sometimes she adopted a sharply moralising tone, making Lizzie feel even more incapable, at least she possessed her father's warm, loving heart as well as a natural charm. And fortunately the lass wasn't plain but quite attractive, in a quiet, unadorned sort of way. Lizzie thought that she could have the chaps buzzing about her like bees round a honey pot, if only she'd put her mind to sparking herself up a bit. A dab of lipstick and powder would do wonders for that pale complexion for a start, and she could tidy that messy bird's nest of a hairdo for another. But then Jess wasn't the sort to show off or be flashy. Unlike her mam, Lizzie thought with a self-satisfied smirk; the guilt she'd been suffering from seconds before now all but gone as she began to worry about the state of her own face following Bernie's mishandling of her, the silly old bugger. What a temper that man had. What passion!

How much had the lass seen? Did she know who the two men were? Unsure how to handle the situation, Lizzie snatched up her grubby handkerchief, hung her head and took refuge in more tears.

With great patience and diplomacy, Jess finally calmed Lizzie down sufficiently to persuade her to eat half of one of the tarts. Lizzie loudly protested that her face ached too much to manage any more, so Jess finished off every last crumb of the remaining three without a trace of guilt. After that, she settled her mother down for the night, refilling her hot-water bottle, fetching Lizzie a glass of water and another couple of aspirin, tucking in the bedclothes before finally falling into bed herself, utterly exhausted. No doubt Mrs Simmons would have done much the same little acts of kindness for Leah.

4

The afternoon after Boxing Day Bernie came round, clearly on his way back from the Donkey, and, having consumed a skinful, was even more full of himself than usual. He deposited himself with a bump in the only decent chair and let out a great burp, patting himself on the chest as if he'd achieved something momentous. Then with a carefully composed expression of innocence on his brutish face, he enquired after Lizzie's health and on being told she was a bit poorly, insisted she get up and go out with him to do 'a bit of business'.

'The fresh air will do her good.'

He was dressed even more flashily than usual, it being Christmas, in a loud, lovat-green checked suit with a white silk muffler about his neck in place of a tie, which exactly matched the handkerchief that flopped, dandy-fashion, from his breast pocket.

Jess instantly protested. 'What sort of business? She's not well enough to go out.'

He hooked his thumbs in his waistcoat pockets and glowered at her from beneath bushy brows, spiteful little eyes taking in at a few darting glances a quick inventory of every item in the room before settling reflectively upon Jess herself. A smile crooked the corner of his moist mouth, causing a dribble of spittle to trickle down onto his chin. 'Are you suggesting that I don't have your mother's best interests at heart?'

Jess wanted to throw up whenever she looked at him, and

wouldn't have been in the least surprised had a snake's forked tongue flickered out from between those thick, blubber-like lips. His skin always appeared shiny and slick with sweat, and he was fond of combing thin strands of brown hair that curved over his bald pate with short, stubby fingers. He was doing it now as he watched and waited for her reply. 'Well, do you?' Jess challenged him. 'I've seen precious little evidence of it.'

'What did you say?' he enquired mildly, cupping one hand behind his ear. 'Tha'll have to say it again. I'm not sure I heard right.'

'You heard right enough.' Jess could feel her heart pounding behind her ribcage. She really didn't know where she was finding the guts to stand up to him like this. She must be mad, or happen her brain was turning to mush. And then she recalled how it had been this man's great, podgy fists which had battered poor Lizzie to a pulp, and she knew where she found the strength. She'd need every ounce of courage to do it, but perhaps now was as good a moment as any to tell him to leave her mother alone; to follow Doc Lee's advice and warn Uncle Bernie that if her mam continued drinking and carrying on in this fashion, she'd be a goner. Surely then he'd see sense and let her alone.

Unfortunately, she managed to say none of this as Lizzie chose precisely that moment to make an appearance. She'd no doubt heard Bernie's voice from the room above and thought it best to come down. She'd put on her best frock and done her best with her face and hair but she still looked as if she'd gone ten rounds with her hands tied behind her back.

Her brother-in-law glanced up at her and raised twin bushy brows in an affectation of surprise. 'By heck, that's a proper shiner tha's got theer. Which of yer lover boys give you that then?'

Lizzie judiciously made no comment. Jess moved at once

to the hob and poured boiling water into the waiting tea pot. It was a poor solution to their troubles, but tea was all they had. That and a dried up half loaf fit only for toast.

But obviously Bernie wasn't in the mood for such niceties. 'Get yer coat on,' jerking his chin in the direction of the understairs cupboard where he knew it hung behind the door. 'Don't pour one for us, we've to go out. Like I say, there's a bit of business I want yer mam to do for me.'

Lizzie put a hand to her face. 'But me bruises. What'll folk say?'

'They know to keep their noses out of my business. Put some pan-stick on, it'll be reet enough.' So saying, he picked up her handbag from the table and tossed it to her, and Lizzie did as she was bid. By the time she'd caked her face with the orange tinted powder and daubed her lips with scarlet lipstick, she looked like a sad and garish circus clown. But her eyes warned Jess to say nothing and do nothing as she meekly followed Bernie from the house.

He led her up Dolefield and along Bridge Street towards Deansgate so that he could avoid passing his own house on Cumberland Street, where he might be spotted by Cora. He kept a firm grip on her wrist, just as a reminder of who was in charge. Not being too sure about how much of events from the other evening Lizzie could remember, he'd already decided to make no further comment about it. Least said, soonest mended, wasn't that what folk said? She'd probably been too drunk to realise who had hit her, though there was still one small matter to be cleared up.

'I reckon you've stepped a bit out of line, Lizzie girl. And need a nudge back like. Wouldn't you say?'

'You know I meant no harm, Bernie luv. I were only having a bit of fun.'

'Course you were. But we can't have you going off at

boggart and pleasing yerself when and where you have it, now can we? Tha seems to forget who's in charge here. This chap what you've been seeing, Jimmy is it? Quite a generous sort is he?'

Lizzie cast him a sideways glance through spiky lashes gummy with sleep and the Vaseline she'd quickly put on to tart herself up for him, and waited to see what he would say next. She feared Bernie the most when he sounded at his most reasonable.

'Brought you presents, I shouldn't wonder. Paid for your tricks, eh?'

'Only the odd packet of fags, Bernie, nowt special.'

Bernie gave her a fierce shake, making her teeth rattle, shoving her down a back alley where he could lay into her without fear of being disturbed. His grip on her arm was tenacious and Lizzie was whimpering with fear. 'If'n you don't want any more bruises to add to the ones you've got, you'll let me be the judge of what's special, right? He could've been useful to me, had you shown the good sense to introduce us. These sailors get about, pick up stuff from foreign ports. But you kept him to yourself, which disappoints me greatly. I thought I could rely on you better than that, girl.'

'Oh, you can Bernie, you can. Like I say, we were just . . .'

'Having a bit of fun. Aye, so you said. And like *I* say, I'll decide when you can trip the light fantastic, assuming you deserve to, right? It comes to summat when I'm forced to follow you to find out what you're up to. That's not good, Lizzie, not good at all. I don't like it, you know what I mean?'

'Oh I'm sorry, Bernie. I really am. I meant no offence by it. I'd've seen you all right, you know I would, if'n he'd given me owt worth sharing like.'

'*You'd* have seen *me* all right? That's a laugh. Would you indeed? The boot's on the other flaming foot, you daft tart.'

'But you'll not hurt me no more, will you Bernie luv?'

'We'll have to see just how sorry you are, won't we? Whether you're going to be a good girl from now on.' Well lubricated with beer, he was feeling a bit randy so after a quick glance to make sure they weren't about to be interrupted, Bernie unbuttoned his flies, pushed up her skirt and thrust himself into her, giving her a good pounding, telling her to stop whining when she complained he was banging her head against the brick wall.

It gave Bernie malicious satisfaction to see his brother's once gloriously attractive wife brought so low as to beg; to do as he pleased with her skinny, worn out body and know how it would enrage Jake if and when he ever found out what he'd got up to. Loyal as Bernie was to Cora, he greatly resented the fact that it was his wimp of a brother who had nabbed the beauty. At least, Lizzie had been a looker in her day even if she wasn't any longer. He was the one who should have had the best-looking girl, just as he should have the most money and the best of everything, being the eldest and the one who had suffered the most. He deserved it.

He was quickly finished and while Lizzie fussed about making herself presentable again, he lit up a fag, drawing the smoke deep into his lungs as he considered the situation. It'd been hard graft for years keeping body and soul together. Mind, he'd soon recognised that working for others was a mug's game and had started siphoning off a bit extra into his back pocket here and there, though he'd been careful not to overdo it so that he didn't get caught. They'd managed to survive due entirely to his clever skills but Jake had never shown proper gratitude, not in Bernie's opinion. He'd taken it all for granted, even daring to criticise his style of operation, making himself out to be whiter than white. Now he'd turned himself into a tinpot flaming hero by volunteering to join up, and was apparently in line to be made sergeant.

But what did Jake know about anything? He could barely

remember the hard days before his parents had taken sick. Being only six at the time, ten years younger than himself, Jake could barely remember the beatings their dad had given them, the days when they'd lived on scraps from other folks' dustbins because there was no work to be had, or the times Mam had taken the two boys out begging on the streets. Bernie had wept very few tears when they'd died.

Since then, everything had always seemed to fall neatly into Jake's lap. He'd done well at school, was liked by all his teachers and never got the strap. What's more, he had a stunning musical talent which won him any number of friends and applause, then he'd landed himself a good job before marrying the best-looking bird around. Serve him right if she'd turned out to be the most troublesome.

He watched with interest as Lizzie bent over to adjust her stocking tops and suspender for she still had a nice pair of pins on her, even if the rest of her did look a bit well used. He licked his lips in anticipation at what lay ahead at the end of the evening. He'd have her again later, at a more leisurely pace this time. Lizzie was always more imaginative after she'd been knocked about a bit. Women needed to be sharpened up now and then. Did 'em a world of good. In the meantime, he dragged his attention back to the business in hand. 'Na then, this Jimmy, he frequents the Top Hamer on Byrom Street, did you say?'

Lizzie smoothed down her skirt and nodded.

'And he's worth a bob or two. He does usually carry a wad, right?'

'I don't know. Why d'you ask, Bernie luv? What is it yer going to do?'

Bernie shook her again and this time his grip on her wrist was so tight she thought it might cut off the blood supply to her fingers. 'When it's your turn to ask questions, I'll let you know. All right?'

'Yes Bernie.' She wondered if she dare tell him he had a smudge of her scarlet lipstick on his cheek, and decided against it.

'It's time this Jimmy character paid for the bother he's caused, and I hope you've learned your lesson to do as you're told, girl.'

He took her straight to the pub and there was Jimmy, sitting with his chums as usual. Lizzie heartily wished that for once he'd stayed on board his ship and got on with the maintenance work or whatever it was they were berthed here for.

'Now all you have to do is get him on his own and persuade him to buy you a drink. Bernie slid a small packet into her hand. While he's getting it, you slip this into his. It should quieten him down nicely. Got it?' He tapped the side of his nose with a nicotine stained stubby finger and winked at her. 'Tha can leave the rest to me.'

Lizzie wanted to ask what it was exactly, what effect it would have on her lovely Jimmy, and what Bernie intended to do after that, but she didn't dare. One glance into the frost pale eyes and she could only silently nod. It'd be a broken cheekbone next time if she disobeyed him, she knew that for certain.

'Put on yer best smile, girl. We don't want him to suspect owt, now do we?'

It all worked with terrible predictability. Jimmy was delighted to see her, instantly offered to buy her a drink and didn't notice as she slipped the powder into his beer while he was away at the bar. He drank his Mickey Finn without a trace of suspicion, too occupied in showing his concern for the state of her face and explaining why he'd thought it best that he make a run for it the other night, in the hope of saving her further suffering, and before the police were called and things turned really nasty.

Lizzie smiled and nodded at his excuses, thinking how

weak men were and feeling a nudge of regret that Jimmy should be as much of a let down as all the rest. It didn't take long for him to lose the thread of the conversation and Bernie came in just as he slid into unconsciousness. The pair of them half carried him out the door, laughing and joking as if he were simply the worse for the booze. Once safely around the corner in a back alley, Bernie propped him against a wall and stripped his pockets bare. He was indeed carrying a thick wad of notes, along with a gold watch and a cigarette lighter. Bernie stowed them all away in his own pockets, then as Lizzie bent down to check if he was all right, grabbed her arm and pulled her away.

'Leave him. That'll larn him for interfering in my affairs. Now we need to put as much distance as possible between us.'

Lizzie made no protest as he dragged her along the street, glancing back only once at the figure still slumped on the cobbles. But not for a moment did she imagine that Bernie had done this out of a fit of jealousy. Oh no, it was the fact she'd not shared her winnings with him, not given him his cut that had got his dander up. She realised what she should have known all along: that he didn't give a toss about her, that all his sweet talk about fancying her rotten was just so much flannel. And didn't she have the bruises to prove it? 'Can I go home now, Bernie? I've a right bad head on me tonight.'

But he wasn't done with her yet. 'No, you flipping can't. Just one last trip around the shops then you can have your Christmas after all, even if it is a bit late.'

'What do you mean? What d'you want me to do now? Have I not done enough?'

'There you go again, allus asking bleedin' questions. You owe me, Lizzie Delaney, right? So get cracking.'

She tried to object, saying how she thought it was too busy.

'It's too risky, Bernie luv, what with the Christmas Sales there are too many people about.' She didn't say, 'and I stand out like a sore thumb with this face on me,' though that's what she really meant.

Bernie took no notice of her protests. 'Button yer lip fer God's sake and do as I say without any argument for once.'

He led her from shop to shop, methodically working his way along Deansgate, down King Street to St Anne's Square and the routine was always the same. He kept the assistant occupied with his chat-up lines, while Lizzie filled her pockets with whatever little items took her fancy. Sometimes he told her exactly what to take and she mutely obeyed. In Lewis's, she tucked two pairs of leather gloves into the inside pockets of her coat, and slid some nice costume jewellery into her bag. From Taylor's, she purloined a few packets of Passing Cloud cigarettes. Last but not least, she grabbed several tins of salmon from a stack tucked neatly behind the counter in a small grocer's shop near Shudehill while Bernie waited outside.

Lizzie had almost begun to enjoy herself by this time, savouring the excitement, relishing the thrill of the risks, as she always did. She hurried out of the little shop, about to suggest they nipped back to Kendals as she was in need of some new shoes but could see no sign of Bernie anywhere. It was at this point that she came face to face with the policeman.

It had been all over the local papers. 'Woman gets three months for stealing six cans of salmon,' followed by some caustic comments on the failure of the government to stamp out black-market profiteering.

It didn't feel like profiteering to Lizzie. It seemed like a lot of fuss to make about nothing. It wasn't as if it were best red, only the common pink variety but she'd been nabbed the

Freda Lightfoot

minute she stepped outside the shop. Who'd have thought the stupid man would be so sharp as to notice and quietly send his lad off to call the police? God knows where he'd got the salmon from in the first place. Nowhere legal, Lizzie was certain of it.

Now she stood in line before the prison warder patiently waiting to be divested of her last remaining dignity. Not that she had much of that left anyroad, much of anything worth writing home about, point of fact. Lizzie knew that she'd long since lost the voluptuousness of her youth, the curves having shrivelled and wizened. All evidence of her former glory leaving in its wake a thin, string bean of a woman with a pale fragility about her; the kind that appealed to the bully in a man. Her cheeks were flattened and sunken, making the nose seem too prominent and bony. Her once richly coloured, wavy curls hung in greasy strands on her shoulders, all straggly and unkempt, badly in need of a wash. Even her eyes seemed to have lost their grey-green sparkle, looking pale and lifeless as a washed out dish rag. Where was the glamorous allure, the flashy bravado and the flirtatiousness she'd once been so famous for, and which Jake had accused her of sharing with all and sundry long before that was the case? Good job he wasn't near enough to see what had happened to her now. She didn't even have a daub of lipstick or pan-stick to put on as the authorities had taken every sodding item off her, though what did it matter here? Who would even notice, let alone care?

Having, by some miracle, survived the thrashing Bernie had given her, here she was facing three months in Strangeways. Her eyes filled with a sudden gush of tears. Her mam had beaten her when she was a nipper, over and over on her backside with the scrubbing brush, although half the time she never knew what she'd done to deserve such punishment. Now her husband had abandoned her, his nasty brother had taken over, and it was happening all over again, despite her being a grown woman. Didn't seem right somehow.

Lizzie edged along the line and when her turn came, sat on the toilet with the door wide open so the prison warders could see that she was not trying to abscond. Though how she could make a run for it with her knickers round her ankles was hard to imagine. Oh no, Lizzie hadn't lost her sense of humour. Not quite, anyroad.

Next, she was stripped and thoroughly investigated in every orifice, given a bath with a large dollop of disinfectant in the water and yet more dumped on her hair till she stank to high heaven.

Accept your lot, that was the answer, Lizzie told herself as she tentatively scraped the rough bristles of the bath brush over the bruises that covered her back and skinny ribs. Even the warders had asked a few awkward questions about them but had quickly lost interest. No doubt they were used to such sights. Where was the point in trying to make things different?

It was sad that this was what she'd come to, after all her hopes and dreams. She'd once imagined that she'd fallen on her feet proper in marrying Jake Delaney, but then it had all gone wrong and her world had fallen apart, all over a bit of nonsense one Christmas. She'd been relieved at first when he'd gone and joined up. At last there'd be an end to the constant bickering and arguing between them. He could go and fight in a real battle instead of a nightly one over the lack of trust he showed in his own wife. But then she'd found herself all alone and had felt utterly bereft. What was she supposed to do? Work on the docks, in a mill, or a munitions factory, for God's sake?

When they were first married, Lizzie had worked at Gatrix's but once she'd had Jess, she'd never needed or fancied getting a proper job again, and flogging herself to death doing war work wasn't her idea of fun at all. No Delaney worth their salt believed in wasting unnecessary effort unless it was absolutely necessary, not if there was an easier way to make money, so why should she? None save for Jake that is, her tosspot of a husband, and the saintly Cora who seemed to spend her entire life cleaning up after all those kids of hers. No doubt she'd be chortling with glee to see her rival brought so low.

After the bath, the prison warder brought out a pair of scissors and began cutting Lizzie's hair into an unflatteringly short bob. 'Hair to be kept off the collar at all times. We have enough vermin in here.'

Lizzie sank silently into abject misery as she watched the shreds of her former glory fall to the ground about her feet. It had taken years to grow it so long and it near broke her heart to lose it. What Jake would have to say when he saw it, she didn't dare to contemplate. But then he'd be furious anyway when he heard she was in jail. This would only offer further proof of her inadequacy as a mother.

Not a single week from the first day he'd joined the army had Jake failed to write Jess a long and loving letter. He also wrote regularly to Lizzie from France or Italy, or wherever he happened to be. She thought he might be out East now. Singapore or Africa. Not that she paid much attention, and cared even less. His letters told her little about what he was doing as they were generally filled with questions about his precious daughter. 'Is she doing well at school? Does she ever get sick? Are you getting enough rations and managing to keep her warm and well fed? Watch over my little girl, Lizzie love. She'll go far will our sweet lass,' and she could imagine the tears of pride brimming in his soft brown eyes as he wrote the words. 'See you take good care of my girl while I'm away.'

'It'd be easier if I had more money coming in than a

private's pay,' she would respond tartly. 'What did you have to go and join up for?'

And back would come the next letter written in a tone which echoed the hurt he felt because she couldn't understand his motives. 'I'm sorry you blame me for volunteering but it's my duty, surely you can see that. You wouldn't want me to be a coward, now would you? And I'm in line for sergeant soon, that'll help a bit, happen.'

Always had an answer for everything did Jake.

He seemed to think she didn't care, which wasn't true at all. Lizzie worried a good deal about Jess. Every time she looked at her, the girl had her nose in a book, was studying a sheet of music, or playing that dratted mouth organ. She might agree with Jake that their daughter was special and not want her to repeat her own trail of misfortune, yet Lizzie had no real idea how to go about achieving this seemingly impossible ambition; not in this neighbourhood, even if there weren't bombs dropping every five minutes, or so it seemed.

Nor did she have sufficient faith in Jess's ability to escape the inevitable downward slide which seemed to be the lot of all women: marriage, babies and total slavery with no happy-ever-after. Some women might think they'd escaped it by getting exciting jobs because of the war, working in factories, on the Ship Canal, on buses and trams, but come the day when the men returned home again, they'd be chucked back on the dung heap, back to the kitchen sink.

'Mind you don't get too serious. Fellas don't like girls who are too po-faced, and you want to catch yerself a good one,' Lizzie had warned her daughter, quite forgetting how they might never have survived if Jess hadn't proved quite so capable, so well organised and mature.

What would happen to poor Jess now?

Admittedly the girl was bright, sensible and practical, so much so that there were times when Lizzie felt herself to be the encumbrance, thinking the lass would probably do better on her own. Well, she was on her own now. Having a convict for a mother wouldn't help her get that good job she'd hoped for. So far as Lizzie could see, there'd be no hope for either of them after this.

In complete silence the warden handed Lizzie a nightshirt and toothbrush. Dressed in regulation cotton dress, woollen stockings and flannelette underwear, she was led up a metal staircase, along a landing to where a door stood open. Lizzie was ushered inside.

'Not quite the Ritz, is it?' she remarked drily but as she turned to check if the officer would give her an answering smile, she found the door of her cell banged shut in her face. Lizzie thought she would never forget the sound of it closing, or the rattle of the key in the lock as it turned, no matter how long she lived.

5

Jess had been living with Uncle Bernie and Aunt Cora for a whole month and, despite her aunt's efforts to make her feel wanted, absolutely hated it. Every morning she would prepare breakfast for her three cousins, Harry, Bert and Tommy before they went off to work down at the docks, as well as for Sandra who was nine and went to Atherton Street School. This must be the first honest work the three lads had ever done in their lives, and the older two at least, were only doing it in preference to serving in the forces for which at twenty-two and twenty they were eligible. Strangely it was skinny little Tommy who, at sixteen, was itching to be called up, much to his poor mother's dismay.

'Tha couldn't push an 'ole in an echo,' she'd say, 'let alone fight Germans,' and poor Tommy would flush and protest.

'I might not have put on much weight, Ma, but I'm fair strong.'

'Eat yer breakfast then and shurrup. Tha's legs on thi that a linnet would be proud of.'

It was proving handy for Bernie to have his sons involved in loading and unloading at the docks where they could keep an eye open for broken crates and other goods that chanced to go astray. One never knew what might fall off the back of a 'lurry'. It was also easy enough to overload a van with more meat or other rationed goods than had been accounted for, and send it off on a slight detour. Bernie had a growing list of shopkeepers glad enough of what they could get not to ask too many questions.

While Jess was seeing to the older boys, Aunt Cora would slop about in her carpet slippers and tatty old blue dressing-gown, happily chivvying her family to 'look sharp and get on yer way. No dilly-dallying allowed here.' Most of her attention was given to attending to the five-year-old twins who had just started school and were referred to by Bernie as the result of pilot error, which Jess didn't think was very nice. She liked the twins, again both boys, Seb and Sam, and would sooner have made breakfast for them rather than those hulking great lumps. If she ever spoke to nine-year-old Sandra, the girl would glower at her and sulk or make spiteful little comments.

'We don't want you here. Who said you could come and live with us?'

'Your dad, actually.'

'Well, don't think he can be your dad too. He's mine.'

'Don't worry, you're welcome to him.' And Sandra would flounce off in a huff.

Harry, the oldest, greediest and biggest show-off of the brothers, would shovel porridge into his mouth at record speed along with several slices of bread and whatever else was going, washed down by copious amounts of tea. He also complained loudly if Jess didn't have his snap tin and brew can ready the minute he was ready for off.

'And put more sugar in it this time lass,' he instructed, making a double decker sandwich comprising a cream cracker plastered with syrup wedged between two thick slices of bread. Jess watched in horrified fascination as he took a huge bite and managed to talk as he chewed, dribbles of butter and syrup running over the stubble on his unshaven chin.

'We don't have enough points. You get what we can spare.'

'Nay, don't talk to me about points and ration books,' he said, spitting cracker crumbs all over the tatty oilcloth that covered the kitchen table. 'Me dad allus has plenty.'

Bert chipped in, 'Don't be so mean, our Jess. I like it sweet too. Ladle it in, we can get some more,' and taking the spoon from her, did just that, scattering sugar everywhere and knocking over the milk bottle in the process. Snatching it up again, he emptied what remained of the milk into both cans, leaving Jess to mop up the puddle spreading over the table. It made her wonder, not for the first time, how the Delaney family managed always to have so much food in their larder and be so careless with it, when everyone else was making do with a dab of marg or an ounce of corned beef. She wasn't so innocent as to put it all down to Cora's skilful house-keeping. No wonder poor Lizzie had ended up the way she had, having been dragged into Bernie's nefarious schemes.

Of Bernie himself at breakfast there was never any sign. Cora always made him a bit of a fry-up later, once she'd got everyone out of the house and he had time to eat it in peace. Lucky Bernie, Jess thought, as she managed no more than a few spoonfuls of the porridge and a quick slurp of tea before dashing off to work herself, at the last minute as usual, gritting her teeth and slapping tears of self-pity from her eyes.

It might well be true that her uncle's life had been hard. Not that that was unusual on the streets of Manchester, particularly during the depression years and yet not everyone had turned into a petty criminal. He was fond of reminding them how he'd acquired his skills at the school of hard knocks, bragging about how the amount he earned in his wage packet had only been half the story and a quarter of the profit.

But none of that excused the way he'd treated Lizzie. This shop-lifting episode was simply the latest in a long history of abuse, and the worst to date. Jess had told him so in no uncertain terms as they'd come away from the magistrates' court after seeing Lizzie sent down. Jess had felt so aggrieved and concerned for her mother, she hadn't been able to help herself. 'She'd never be in Strangeways at all if it weren't for you. She should've been home with me that night, safe in her own bed, not picking pockets and shop-lifting. It's a wonder you have the gall even to look me in the eye after what you've done.'

'*I* didn't teach her to nick stuff. She learned that little trick all by herself. Made her feel good.'

'But you encouraged her. You took your cut.' Jess had felt all hot and bothered, terrified about what was going to happen next. To Lizzie, and to herself.

Bernie had simply smirked. 'Eeh, I do like a lass wi' a bit of spunk who knows how to speak her mind. I admire thee for sticking up fer yer mam but the problem with our Lizzie is that she doesn't think big. She's not clever enough, bless her, not like me. She's like a magpie lifting a few pretty trinkets and knick-knacks here and there. Complete waste of time, as she's bound to get nicked in the end,' quite forgetting that he'd actively encouraged her, even instructed her on what to steal. 'And where would you be today, little lady, without me? You'd have no home for a start. Come to think of it, you can't stop in Back Irwell Street on yer own, not a young girl like you. Not now yer mam's in t'clink.'

'I'll be all right on me own, ta very much. I'm fifteen, nearly sixteen. I can manage to look after meself well enough, as I have been doing for years.'

'Nay, I'll not be accused of child cruelty on top of everything else, so I'll have no more lip from you madam. Get yer bags packed. You'll have to come round to ours.'

Jess was certain she could actually feel her stomach plummeting into her boots, and a sort of giddiness washed over her. The prospect of moving in with Bernie and her Delaney cousins filled her with dismay and horror. She couldn't do it, she really couldn't. It should be him in the clink, not her mam.

And so the worst period of her life had begun. Bernie had let out their old house and she'd moved into the overcrowded little house on Cumberland Street. But Jess had made up her mind already that this was only temporary. Once her mam was released, they'd find another house, or a room to rent somewhere. Then they could make a fresh start. She meant to take much better care of Lizzie in future, keep her out of pubs, and away from sailors. And Jess would make absolutely certain that her mother had nothing whatsoever to do with Uncle Bernie and his nasty schemes. How she would achieve this seeming miracle she'd no real idea, but she'd certainly try. Hadn't he done enough damage already?

As the weeks slipped by Jess came to resent the fact that everyone seemed to go out of their way to keep Uncle Bernie happy. What was so special about him that he had to be given such special treatment, so that his entire family tiptoed around him as if he were some sort of god?

One afternoon when she and her aunt Cora were enjoying a warming cuppa after she'd got back from the market half frozen, Jess risked asking her why she'd married him.

'Because he were a reet bobby-dazzler in them days. And I weren't. Truth is love, I were bullied by me schoolmates summat shocking for being a bit on the plump side like. One day two girls tied me up with their skipping rope and sold ink pellets at ha'penny a time for the other girls to throw at me.'

'Oh, but that's dreadful.'

'Yer right. It weren't very nice at all. Me mam give me gyp when I got home, I don't mind telling you. Anyroad, Bernie spotted what were going on and he went for 'em. You should have seen them girls run.' Her plump jowls shook with laughter as she recalled the moment. 'He med it clear that if anyone had a go at me in future, they'd have him to deal with as well.'

'I see.' And Jess did indeed understand, even if she did think it dreadfully sad that Cora had been fooled into seeing Bernie Delaney as some sort of hero. Ever since then Cora had been his adoring slave, accepting all he told her as gospel, content to devote her entire life to waiting upon him, hand, foot and finger, without complaint.

But what about his sons? What caused them to be so meek and mild?

Even Leah was mystified when Jess explained it all to her as they sat together by the Irwell near the old Botany warehouse. 'He's always given the largest share of pie or portion of meat and them big lads of his never say a word despite the fact they're both working at hard, physical jobs down at the docks.' She explained about Cora, how she buttered his bread for him, tied his tie, fetched his *News of the World* or *Manchester Guardian* whenever he wanted it.

'Heavens!' Leah giggled. 'Does she scrub his back for him on a Friday night as well, do you think?'

Jess nodded, then her eyes twinkled as she added, 'Not that we're allowed to witness it, mind. She shoos everybody out while Bernie does his ablutions, so who knows what they get up to. Happen she gets in the bath with him,' and both girls fell into fits of giggles at the very idea.

'I don't think women that old can have sex, can they?' Leah wondered out loud, and Jess laughed.

'Lizzie seems to manage it without any difficulty,' and then slapped her hand over her mouth as she realised what she'd said.

'It's all right, Jess. I won't say anything wrong about your mam. I don't believe half what they say about her anyway. Go on with telling me about your uncle, and these cousins of yours. What are they like?'

Jess knew only too well that more than half of the rumours about her mother were indeed true. Leah might be a year older than herself but she was years younger and a sight more naïve than herself in *that* department. Muriel had protected her daughter well, perhaps too well some might say. Not wishing to consider Lizzie's current situation Jess gladly continued with her tale. 'You'd like Tommy. He's about your age. He's grand is Tommy. Desperate to join up, unlike the rest of them Delaney lads, dozy cowards that they are. There's big and boastful Harry, and daft Bert. I suppose there's more to them both than that, but it about sums 'em up. The twins, Sam and Seb, are lovely but Sandra seems to have a permanent scowl on her face. I don't think she likes me being there. She sulks a lot and rarely speaks to me, not even to pass the time of day. She doesn't say much to anyone, come to think of it, but then she's not expected to, being only a girl.'

'You could try setting her an example of what a thinking woman can achieve in life when she sets her mind to it.'

Jess giggled. Leah made her laugh sometimes with her fancy, middle-class way of looking at things. Thinking woman indeed. Jess knew she was neither of those things. Untalented, unintelligent, useless fifteen-year-old with an absent father and an inadequate mother, that's what she was. 'Fat chance. She's spoiled rotten by her dad, whom she worships, and even Aunt Cora will do anything to stop her going into one of her moods. But I still can't understand why no one ever disagrees with Uncle Bernie, not even his sons so far as I can see. You'd think they'd want to challenge him now and then, wouldn't you?'

'Perhaps they're a bit afraid of him too, so pretend to do as he says and yet quietly go their own way,' Leah shrewdly suggested. 'No matter what his family does, you must stand up for yourself at least. We can't let chaps have things all their own way.'

'Oh, I do stand up to him, don't you fear,' and they grinned at each other, as always in perfect accord.

'Are you very unhappy living with your aunt and uncle, Jess? I could always ask Mother if you could stay with us for a while.'

Jess looked at her friend askance. 'What, the daughter of a jailbird bunking up with Leah Simmons? Oh aye, I can see her approving of that one. There'll be no more mince pies from that direction now.'

Leah protested vigorously. 'Mother isn't at all snooty or toffee-nosed, though admittedly she does fuss at times. But she understands about Lizzie, about her . . . problems. I could ask her about the possibility of a job for you after Easter. Would that help?'

Jess gave a little nod, flushing with shame in the face of such generosity. 'That'd be grand.'

'Consider it done. I know what's wrong with you,' Leah said. 'You need cheering up. Isn't it your birthday soon, that should liven you up. You'll be having a party, I expect? You don't turn sixteen every day of the week.'

'Don't be daft.'

'Oh Jess, that's awful.' Leah fell silent for a moment, stunned that any family could choose to ignore such a significant event. Then she brightened, 'I know, we'll celebrate on our own, and what better way than to go dancing.'

'Dancing?' Jess gazed at her friend wide-eyed, even as a bud of excitement burst within. She'd never been to a dance before, nor even listened to a real dance band but she decided that Leah was right. Turning sixteen was something special which should indeed be celebrated. 'But I can't dance. I don't know how to.'

'I know a few steps. I'll teach you.'

And she did just that. Leah and Jess practised a few dance steps night after night in Leah's bedroom over the tea shop on Deansgate. Neither of them were particularly adept although what they lacked in style, they more than made up for in enthusiasm. Besides, they only had use of a very old wind-up gramophone playing a cracked record of indeterminate vintage which had once belonged to Muriel in her younger days. With a real dance band, they were both quite certain it would be much easier.

With her usual thoroughness Mrs Simmons stepped in to arrange for the two girls to have a few proper lessons at Winters Dance Academy. Mr Simmons stoically agreed to act as dance partner each evening to help them practise the basic steps while his wife offered endless instructions on the etiquette of the ballroom: such as how a girl was not obliged to accept an invitation but must sit out a dance completely if she should refuse a prospective partner for any reason.

Leah and Jess certainly listened most attentively, for all they were desperate to laugh, knowing that Mrs Simmons's real motive was that she believed this to be an excellent opportunity for her daughter to find an attractive husband, preferably a rich one.

As the big day drew near, Leah announced her decision. 'We'll go to the Plaza on Oxford Street.'

Jess gasped. 'But isn't that a very grown-up sort of place?'

'So what? With a bit of lipstick on, and a ribbon tied round that wild hair of yours, you'd pass for eighteen any day. You could be a real stunner, Jess Delaney, make no mistake.'

Jess giggled. 'You sound just like Mam. She's always saying I don't make enough of myself.'

Mrs Simmons gave her blessing to the idea, together with her carefully considered opinion that the Plaza was most respectable. If all went well, perhaps next time she might allow the girls to try the Ritz. 'You meet a much better class of partner there. But do watch your posture my dears, and always listen most attentively when a young man talks to you.'

'What if there's a raid?'

Leah shrugged. 'So what? How do you reckon everyone else is getting through this dratted war? Largely by ignoring it. We'll be safe enough. Why shouldn't we have a bit of fun? Stop thinking of excuses not to come. What's the problem anyway?'

'Uncle Bernie,' Jess admitted ruefully. 'He'll never let me go.'

'Oh, leave him to me. I'll fix Uncle Bernie.'

And she did that too. Once all the arrangements had been made, Leah gazed up at him with those entrancingly blue, innocent eyes and asked if it would be all right for Jess to stay at her house the following Saturday night. 'Mother's invited her to supper, to celebrate her birthday, and doesn't feel it would be safe for Jess to be wandering home in the dark on her own afterwards, with the blackout and all,' Leah lied without a flicker of guilt. Jess was quite certain he'd refuse to allow her to go, or even offer to come and fetch her home himself but Leah's charm held good, and he grudgingly agreed.

Robert, of course, escorted them, faithfully promising his parents that he would keep an eye on them and bring them safely home. They caught the bus, collecting Robert's fiancée on the way, each girl carrying silver dance slippers (in Jess's case an old pair of Leah's), wrapped in a brown paper bag. Once inside, they slipped them on, depositing their outdoor shoes in the cloakroom together with their coats, scarves and handbags. As anticipated by Leah, Robert was more interested in spending the evening with his one true love and left them to it, agreeing to meet up again at the door at half past ten on the dot.

And so here they were in the Plaza. The band was playing 'Run, Rabbit, Run' and the two girls were standing by the door, optimistically hoping someone might ask them to dance.

They'd done their best to make themselves suitably appealing. Leah was dressed in a peacock blue satin frock which reached right down to her ankles and shimmered as she walked, clinging to every curve of her slender figure. With scarlet lipstick, fair hair piled high and those brilliant blue eyes, she looked as if she'd stepped straight out of the silver screen. Jess saw it as a proper, grown-up ball gown rather than the knee skimming day dress style she herself was wearing, yet felt not a trace of envy for her friend.

Leah had delved into her wardrobe and found a pale blue crêpe frock for Jess. It had a lacy collar and covered buttons all down the bodice, fastening at the waist with a neat little belt which had a gold buckle. Since Jess had point blank refused to wear a ribbon, Leah had pinned up Jess's hair into fashionable coils all about her head, then applied not only a soft pink lipstick but also powdered her nose, put rouge on her cheeks and smoothed Vaseline on her eyelashes to make them shine.

Mrs Simmons had declared herself enchanted by the result, and had generously dabbed a touch of her favourite Lily-of-the-Valley perfume behind each ear, assuring Jess she'd be the belle of the ball, after Leah of course.

Jess had never felt so glamorous in her life. It was all so exciting.

'I do hope I don't make a fool of myself,' she said, a note of anxiety in her voice. 'What if I forget the steps and everything we've learned?'

'You'll be fine. Look at you, jigging to the beat already. How could someone as musical as you not be able to dance?'

They'd hardly been standing there for five seconds before

a sailor claimed a delighted Leah in a dance, spinning her away into a fancy quickstep. Now Jess stood alone and she flattened herself back into the shadows of the entrance, heartily wishing that the ground would open up and swallow her. In the corner by the stage she could see a number of professional dancers, of both sexes, who were there to partner people like herself who had no one to dance with. Except that she couldn't afford to pay sixpence for a ticket, so she would have to remain a wallflower, probably for the entire evening while her more glamorous friend was snapped up by every man in the room.

She could feel her cheeks start to burn with the shame of it; would have escaped entirely, or crept to a chair in a corner had she been able to find one. The only seats available were placed around the small tables which circled the dance floor, generally occupied by what were obviously courting couples. Just watching them kissing and cuddling made Jess feel even more the odd one out, a reject, a failure, unwanted by anyone. She noticed that Leah was now dancing with a soldier and was waving to her over his shoulder. What on earth had possessed her to come? Mrs Simmons had given her a lovely birthday tea, wasn't that enough?

'May I have the pleasure of this dance?'

Jess almost jumped out of her skin. Someone was actually asking her to dance. He was quite skinny with ears that stuck out, a bulbous nose, dressed in an air-force uniform that looked three sizes too big. Nevertheless she graciously accepted. Jess didn't feel she was in any position to be too choosy.

From then on her luck changed, or perhaps she just looked more relaxed and smiley, but she was soon inundated with offers, never short of a partner for a single dance. There were admittedly one or two near disasters, though not through any fault of her own. There was the soldier who was so much shorter than Jess that his face came perilously close to her bosom while she could barely see more than the top of his head. The plump man who kept treading on her toes as he tried to steer her around the crowded floor, runnels of sweat streaming down his flushed face, evidently due to the concentration involved. Then there was the one who gripped her so hard she was flattened against his chest in an iron hold, while she strained to turn her face away from his tainted breath which stank strongly of pickled onions.

There was always an element of tension as a possible partner approached and each girl would wonder which of them he had his eye on. Their response could be either relief or resignation but they were never anything less than polite. Mrs Simmons would have been proud of them.

No alcohol was allowed in the dance hall but during the interval they bought a glass of lemonade each and slipped outside for a breath of fresh air. The room might be hot and overcrowded but Jess found the atmosphere magical, the crush of people intoxicating, the colourful swirl of skirts with their tantalising glimpses of suspenders and French knickers, exciting. The band was superb, and the singer seemed to float across the stage in her long white gown, her voice filling the room with achingly sweet love songs like 'A Nightingale Sang in Berkeley Square' followed by rousing numbers such as 'We're Gonna Hang Out the Washing on the Siegfried Line'.

'It's fun isn't it?' Leah said, giggling. 'I reckon I clicked with that last sailor I was dancing with. He was Welsh, called Taffy, naturally, and took quite a shine to me. Offered to marry me on the spot but I told him I had every intention of staying fancy free, thank you very much. No quick, wartime wedding for me. Not my scene boyo, I said. What do you think of the band?'

'Great. I love the sound. Three trumpets, two trombones and five sax. Brilliant!'

Leah raised her eyes in despair at the fact Jess had troubled to count. 'I was more interested in their looks. The drummer's rather dishy, don't you think? Maybe we should go and chat him up while he's on his break.'

When they returned, the band was already back on stage playing 'The Blackout Stroll' and for the next hour the two girls scarcely saw each other as they were kept busy on the dance floor.

'I don't think my feet will ever recover, not to mention these silver shoes of yours,' Jess groaned. 'They've been trodden on that much.'

Next came the Ladies' Excuse-Me. 'Come on,' said Leah. 'Now's our chance. I fancy the dishy airman dancing with that fat girl with the spotty chin. I'm sure he'd much rather have his arms about me. Which one have you got your eye on? Make your mind up quickly, then we can dance round together.'

Jess glanced frantically about, wondering if she had the courage to actually walk up to some perfect stranger and ask him to dance, or even more daring, interrupt a dance in progress and drag him away from someone else whom he might very well prefer. She could feel her cheeks burning with embarrassment at the very thought. 'I'm not sure that I can – er – want to. You go. Don't worry about me.'

'Grumpy. You're turning into a real old misery boots. No fun at all.' But Leah didn't hang around to argue as she was intent on grabbing her airman who seemed delighted to be relieved of trying to make conversation with his more ample partner.

For a moment Jess felt utterly bereft, again standing alone on the perimeter of the dance floor while everyone else seemed to be laughing and dancing, changing partners with dizzying frequency and clearly having a marvellous time. Was Leah right? Was she turning into an old misery boots? This was a whole new experience for her. She felt rather dazed by it all, overwhelmed suddenly by the reckless determination of everyone to have a good time, no matter what tomorrow might bring. Some of these young men could be flying planes straight to their own deaths; innocent young girls could be bombed in the factories where they slaved away every day making parachutes and nuts and bolts for aeroplanes, or even in their own homes while they hid under the stairs. Yet here at the Plaza, it seemed impossible to imagine that there was a war on at all. How could there be, when everyone was so happy?

Jess had just decided that she'd sit this one out when she saw him.

Her gaze homed in on him, perhaps because he was not in uniform as almost everyone else was, or because he sat huddled in a corner beside the stage, a rapt expression on his face as he concentrated entirely upon the band. He seemed so alone, so apart from the colourful swirl of dancers, the only sign of movement being the tapping of one foot, and fingers beating in time to the music. Perhaps he was deliberately hiding himself away, and Jess felt a rush of sympathy for hadn't she experienced the very same emotions herself, a resolve to appear disinterested and unavailable; as if not for a minute did he expect a gorgeous young girl to ask him to dance. Without even pausing to consider her action, she set off across the floor.

'You look like you're enjoying the music and since this is a ladies' choice, may I have the pleasure?' She really didn't know where she had found the words, or the courage to ask, and nearly turned and fled as he lifted his gaze to frown up at her. In the long silence which followed, Jess felt quite certain that he would refuse and she would have to creep away, rejected and humiliated. She could feel her heart beating wildly against her breastbone. Why was he studying her so intently?

The next instant the frown melted away and, unbelievably, he was actually smiling at her. 'I don't do fancy steps.'

'Neither do I.'

'That's OK then.'

He had a thatch of tousled, red-brown hair which looked in dire need of cutting, and the kind of face which was surely made for smiling, round and open with a seemingly permanent upward tilt to the wide mouth; hazel green eyes that sparkled with ready mischief from beneath half closed lids as he continued to consider her with a quiet scrutiny. The next instant he took her in his arms and swung her effortlessly on to the dance floor amidst the throng of dancers. He proved to be a far better dancer than he'd claimed and somehow, without any apparent effort, managed to steer her amongst the myriad of other couples without bumping into any of them, pulling her closer should there appear to be any danger of someone crashing into them. Jess rather enjoyed the sensation. She felt cherished and protected, as if she were made of delicate porcelain, perfectly at ease in his arms. When he talked, he looked directly into her eyes, giving the impression that he truly cared what she thought and that he was interested in her opinion. Jess smiled up at him, perfectly relaxed and utterly enthralled.

He told her that his name was Steve Wyman, that he worked at A.V. Roe as an aircraft engineer, a reserved occupation, and that he played in the band most evenings. 'Although tonight should be my night off.'

'So what are you doing here then?'

'I was told I might be needed, after all. Hal, the bandleader, thought there was a risk some of the lads might not show up and asked me to hang around, just in case. Waste of time. As you can see, I wasn't needed. Except it isn't a waste of time, not now that I'm dancing with you.'

The dance ended and he asked if she'd like a coffee.

Jess flushed and shook her head. 'No thanks we've just had a lemonade.' He looked disappointed and she was too naïve to realise that the offer had simply been a ruse, to keep her to himself for a while longer. The music changed, a foxtrot this time and breathlessly Jess strived to keep up with his expert steps while she asked what instrument he played.

'Sax, trumpet, cornet, comb and paper. Whatever I'm paid to play.'

'It must be marvellous to be in a band.'

He chuckled softly, negotiated a reverse and half turn and then slowed his step so they could talk more easily. 'Don't you believe it. It's hot, sweaty, and tiring work.'

'It always seems so glamorous. Don't tell me all the girls aren't desperate to get to know you,' and then remembered her own boldness in asking him to dance. No wonder he was laughing.

'You haven't told me your name, or anything about yourself. What do you do?' But before she could answer, Jess found herself elbowed out of the way by a very determined girl in WAAF uniform. 'Excuse me,' the girl said, casting Jess a bright smile of triumph. Jess caught a glimpse of regret in his hazel-eyed gaze as the pair whirled away and she could only smile ruefully before turning and going in search of Leah. It was ten-twenty, very nearly time to go. But at least she could tell Leah that she'd clicked too. Almost.

6

Going dancing with Jess became a regular part of their routine, though not always to somewhere as grand as the Plaza. Sometimes they would go to the Co-operative rooms, to various church halls, or take the bus to the ballroom at High Street Baths. Robert and his fiancée nearly always accompanied them but Muriel was growing dissatisfied over the length of time it was taking for a suitable candidate to step forward and claim her daughter's hand, at least one of which she might approve, and had therefore begun to take action herself.

Leah had just spent the better part of an hour explaining why it was she didn't care for Ambrose Gartside: that he was boring and spotty and she therefore had no intention of accepting any invitation to go to the pictures, have supper with him, go for a walk or any other ploy he could think of to get her on her own.

Muriel was unimpressed by her protest. 'How do you know he's boring if you've never spent any time with him? Ambrose might have a fascinating hobby, or wonderful plans for the future, and the poor boy will grow out of his spots in time. He's eighteen, about to start work in his father's printing business, quiet and well mannered, and comes from a very good family.'

'*Mother!*'

'Oh, I know, I know darling, you don't like me saying such things but I'm not being snobby, really I'm not. I'm simply being sensible. The Gartsides are business people, like ourselves, and believe in hard work and endeavour. Coming from a similar sort of background to your own is so very important.'

Leah knew that her lovely, charming mother was nothing if not practical. She was the kind of woman who made lists for everything. She knew to the last pickled onion what she had in her larder, the price butter was last year, when the loft had last been cleared out, or the dining room dusted, and when they would require attention again. She sent her husband's suits regularly to the dry cleaners, kept his humidor well stocked with his favourite cigars, and woe betide the tobacconist if he'd sold out just when dear Clifford needed fresh supplies.

But worse even than this concern over domestic minutiae was her obsession with her children. She had always kept a close record of their progress: first tooth, when they started walking, the dates when they'd suffered from measles, chickenpox and so on. It was now a habit that she was quite unable to break. She continued to keep a careful note of their school reports, lists and addresses of all their friends annotated with her opinions on their suitability, as well as a diary with dates such as when Robert or Leah were next due to visit the dentist, even though they were both perfectly capable of organising these matters for themselves now that they were both grown up.

'Why is it important to come from similar backgrounds?' Leah grumbled.

'I beg your pardon, dear?'

'Why should it matter? For what purpose?' Since she knew very well, Leah wondered why she bothered asking. Perhaps in yet another bid to secure her independence.

'So that you'll get along perfectly, should you wish to – to see him again.'

'You mean marry, don't you?' Leah challenged. 'Why can't you be honest with me, Mother, and say so? You're picking him out as a likely candidate for a husband, aren't you? For God's sake, I'm only just turned seventeen!'

As always at this point in the argument, Leah was beginning to feel trapped and thoroughly exasperated. Time and again they'd had this conversation which nearly always concerned some young man whom her mother happened to be currently favouring. All of them equally dreadful.

Robert had, at one time, likewise found this sort of manipulative behaviour on the part of his beloved mother particularly galling. Having failed his medical for the army because of poor eyesight and flat feet of all things, he'd been driven to working for the family firm, much against his will. Muriel had been delighted to keep her son safe at home and had taken advantage of the situation by introducing him to Sophie Winstock, the daughter of a friend from her bridge club, whose husband was a chemist of some substance in the city centre. She'd engineered various social functions between the two families in order to bring the young couple together, and now a wedding was planned for two years hence, and a new house had been built for the happy pair. Always supposing the war was over and done with by then, of course. Robert gave every appearance of being content with his lot, but occasionally would rebel about something or other, not being allowed to join the ARP for instance, and Leah sometimes wondered if her brother still yearned for an altogether different sort of life.

Now she feared that her parents were embarking upon similar action towards herself. She adored her parents and neither would ever dream of using force or any form of physical sanctions; nevertheless their immensely reasonable arguments, their gently persistent persuasion, and their intense sense of logic felt at times like psychological bullying.

What Leah feared the most was that one day she might be caught at such a low ebb that she would actually agree to go out with one of these dull young men her mother procured for her, if only for the sake of a little peace.

Perhaps this was why her tone had been sharper than she intended.

Muriel was greatly offended. 'Please don't be rude and shout, darling. And don't swear. It isn't polite. I only want what's best for you, as every good mother should. What is so wrong in that?'

'What is wrong with allowing me to grow up and please myself? For me to get a job, have fun and live a little before I start making such long-term decisions which I don't yet feel ready for?'

Muriel Simmons clicked her tongue with impatience, shaking her head in despair at her daughter while adopting the tone of voice she might have used on a six-year-old. 'Of course I don't expect you to marry for a long while yet, darling. How very silly of you to suggest it, but we must plan ahead. You can't simply allow life to happen, as if by accident.'

'Why can't I?'

'Because it isn't done. It isn't sensible.'

'Or practical.'

'Quite.'

'Well, of course one must be seen to mingle with the right people.'

'Absolutely, darling,' not recognising the irony in her daughter's tone and thinking this meant that she finally understood and agreed.

Leah sighed, knowing she was not getting her point across at all.

After every raid, the streets of Manchester would look increasingly battered as huge areas of the city were wiped out and the numbers of bombed-out buildings grew week by week. Much of the centre had gone, although here and there an historic building could still be seen protruding out of the heaps of rubble. The Old Wellington Inn stood proud next to the ruins that were once the Old Shambles. The elegant circular building that was the Central Library looked as fine as ever, though the Gaiety Theatre nearby was on the verge of collapse. Tragically, even Salford Royal Infirmary was bombed, a number of the nurses killed. And there were sandbags everywhere with not a place name in sight.

Unfazed, Mancunians soldiered on, knowing their city inside out and resolving to defend it. Roads might often be blocked and ambulances face long detours in order to reach the wounded; the local buses might look dented and very much the worse for wear from their efforts to get through, yet it didn't prevent them from trying. And as the list of casualties and fatalities grew, many were equipped with stretchers and doubled up as first-aid vehicles, or to transfer patients away from danger. The Salvation Army too somehow always managed to be there at the right moment with their mobile canteens.

'Where there's a will, there's a way,' became the oft-heard cry. Everyone determined to do their bit. Except for one or two notable exceptions. Harry Delaney, for one.

Not for one moment did he consider offering his services to the community. Harry had avoided call-up by sending his mate George Macintyre to have the medical meant for him. Since George had a dodgy ticker and carried Harry's identity papers, that had got him off the hook nicely. When it came to Bert a year later, George had gone again, this time wearing spectacles as a disguise, but it had been a different doctor so nobody had recognised him. It cost thirty quid each time but Bernie had paid and it had been worth every penny. George did all right too. He'd got a nice little business going but then Harry hadn't seen him around for ages and wondered if he'd done one too many favours and got caught.

Harry, of course, was much cleverer than George and as well as being naturally concerned with saving his own skin, he was as keen as his father to make a profit out of the war. He certainly meant to use his natural skills of subterfuge to great advantage.

Now he took one look at the loaded van standing in the yard, checked it against the docket, and came to a snap decision. The usual driver had parked it up the night before to wait for its load, but this morning had sent his wife with a note to say he was sick. More likely hung over. Harry could quite easily have found another driver to move it, but why should he? What was one small vanload of sugar? Who'd miss it? And even if they did, so long as he made sure the paperwork was up to scratch, no blame could be attached to himself. They'd assume some bugger had nipped into the yard overnight and nicked it. Happened all the time in a war.

He turned to Bert. 'We're a driver short so we'll just tek this van over to t'depot. Gerrin.'

'What, me an' all? Why d'you need me? You'll be back in a jiffy.'

'Shut yer cake 'ole and don't argue. Can't you spot an opportunity when you see one?'

Harry admired his father and had always been content to follow his lead. But he was twenty-two for God's sake and had no intention of playing second fiddle all his life. He wanted to become a big shot in his own right. There'd come a day, not too far off, when folks would have the same tone of respect in their voice with him, as they used whenever they spoke of Bernie Delaney. Harry knew he could achieve even greater heights than his father, if he put his mind to it.

He was not so cautious, for one thing; a bit of a gambler and not afraid to take risks. He enjoyed being in charge and

making decisions. He had far more sense than his brother
Bert, though admittedly that wasn't difficult, and there was
no reason why one day he shouldn't be a man to be reckoned
with. Generally speaking, folk liked him and thought him a
sociable, easy-going sort of bloke. Women certainly did,
considering him quite good-looking with his square jaw and
closely cropped fair hair. He'd never had any trouble at all in
that department, and he knew how to keep a woman happy
as well as in her place, oh indeed he did. All he needed was a
lucky break to make his mark. Perhaps this could be it. He
climbed up into the cab. 'Come on dummel-head. Shape
theesen.' Seconds later they were driving out of the loading
bay. 'Couldn't be easier. Sweet as pie.'

'Or sugar,' Bert sniggered, fidgeting up and down in his
seat as he swung this way and that to check they weren't being
followed. 'That'll show our Jess, eh? Who needs bloody
coupons? What now, Harry? Where we taking it?'

'Home to Mam, plank-head, where else? She'll be med up
wi' this lot.'

As usual during a raid, Lizzie was banged up in her cell, as
was everyone else in Strangeways. 'What if we get hit?' she
wanted to know, shaking with fear at the prospect of being
trapped and left to burn in the ruins of a burning building.

'Not even Mr Hitler would dare to hit His Majesty's
Prison,' an officer told her as she turned the key in the lock.
'This is the safest place to be. And if he does, we'll be well
out of it and you won't know what's hit you, so let's just hope
your number isn't on this one, eh?'

Lizzie could follow the progress of the officer along the
wing by the din that accompanied her, swelling like a tidal
wave as each door banged shut and the rattling of tin plates
or mugs on bars and against their beds grew to a crescendo.
Lizzie just sat with her head in her hands. Why bother? Who

was there to hear? There was no escape; no one in this hell-hole that she knew or cared about.

Most of the old lags had been released at the start of the war for service or war work, but the cells had quickly filled up again. Most women were doing time for drink offences, ration fraud or assault. One woman had attacked her soldier husband when he'd come home on leave and admitted to an affair. But then she had split his skull open. Everyone said it was a wonder he was still alive but would never go soldiering again. There were the conchies of course, some more genuine than others. Other women were in for brothel-keeping, petty pilfering or child neglect. These last two were the most despised among the prisoners, even considered worse than the conchies, and Lizzie was one of their number.

'Any woman who can leave her child locked up in a cellar during an air raid, needs to be put against a wall and shot.' This from her near neighbour, Gladys Cronshaw.

Lizzie gasped, 'How did you know?'

Gladys tapped her nose. 'We don't miss much round here. And what we don't know, we can find out. It's having a bit of a crack what keeps us going, chuck.'

Dry mouthed, Lizzie had attempted to defend herself, explaining how safe and clean the cellar was, how it had been in Jess's interest to stay there, except that no one was listening. Gladys simply turned on her heel and walked away. But on the very first morning as she was making her way down the long metal staircase carrying her slops, she met Gladys coming up and was forced to retreat back up and start all over again, only to meet Gladys's mate Hettie next time on the stairway. In the end it took five attempts before she managed to slop out. The women were allowed a chamber pot each night in their cell, which had to be washed out, dried and placed on the rack each morning. If, for any reason, they had to spend much time in their cell during the day, there was no similar concession. They just had to wait.

But then Lizzie soon discovered that the prison officers treated the women with barely disguised contempt. Elsie, a young girl in for a similar offence to her own, said it was because they were so badly paid, and had very little training. 'The best ones joined up at the start. This lot are just doing the absolute minimum, their bit for the war effort.'

Most were open to bribes, cigarettes, sweets and the like but Lizzie never dared take the risk. Besides, where would she find ten quid for a packet of fags? It was easier to nick them, even here in prison. So long as the other inmates never caught her at it, why worry? Life couldn't get any worse, now could it?

The following morning her optimism was proved to be unfounded. Life could indeed get much worse, proving more forcibly than ever why Lizzie hated being in prison. The smell of it was enough to make her gag. It stank of urine and disinfectant and too many bodies confined in stale air. And she was lonely. Many of the women had visitors which gave them something to look forward to. Bernie would never think to visit, and Lizzie had instructed Jess not to come near. The last thing she wanted was for her daughter to see how low she'd fallen. And there were things going on here that no one should ever get wind of, least of all an impressionable young girl.

For some reason Lizzie's one and only friend, Elsie, took it into her head to have an hysterical fit one morning, and started smashing up things in her cell. It happened to everyone from time to time apparently, the result of being confined for eighteen hours or more in any twenty-four. Nobody went to calm her down, or ask her what the problem was. Instead, they opened a small aperture in the cell door, inserted a hosepipe and sprayed her with water until the screams changed to sobs and then finally quietened altogether. It was all over by breakfast time and everyone went to work at the appropriate hour as if nothing untoward had taken place.

Lizzie ate her dinner alone, wondering what on earth the poor girl had done to deserve such harsh treatment as she hadn't set eyes on her all day, not since the fracas. Nor did she dare ask anyone. Best not to poke your nose into matters which didn't concern you. Few people even spoke to Lizzie which, in a way, was a relief. Lonely as she was, she didn't trust anyone, preferring to keep herself to herself. It was safer that way.

The alert sounded just as they were about to go back to work on the afternoon shift. At first it seemed a bit of a lark to snooze instead of doing their usual two hours of hard labour, sewing mailbags, scrubbing floors, peeling spuds and similar uninspiring tasks. But the all-clear sounded and no one came to let them out. Normally they worked from ten to twelve and two till four every day, and were then banged up for the night in their cells, taking their tea with them. It was almost six now yet with still no sign of release and Lizzie was desperate for a pee. She began to hammer on the door and shout.

'Hey! Anybody out there? I need to visit the netty.'

An officer's voice echoed lazily back to her. 'Everyone does Lizzie, but you'll have to hold yer water. Nobody moves till I'm good and ready.'

This brought a good deal of ribald laughter and some saucy comments from the other inmates, but Lizzie was having none of it. 'And how long might that be?'

'Who knows? Might not be till morning. Some of the officers haven't come back from after the raid yet. So how can I take the risk without sufficient staff?'

Lizzie was distraught. How was she to manage to cross her

legs till morning? She hadn't relieved herself since dinner time and the pain of being patient, or 'holding her water' as the officer so aptly described it, was already excruciating. 'But I want to go *now*! Come on, open up.'

The argument continued for some time but long after the other inmates had warned Lizzie to shut up and pee in the corner of her cell like everyone else, she was still pounding on the door with her mug and shouting for a chamber pot at least.

And then, catching her quite unawares, the door of her cell flew open. Four women wardens entered, every one of them square faced and square shouldered, their stocky bodies filling the open doorway, completely blocking any hope of exit. Lizzie recognised at once that this wasn't a rescue committee.

'I hear you've wet your knickers, FP906.'

Lizzie shook her head in furious denial, stunned into silence by the grim expressions on their faces.

'Reckon you will have before long.' She tried to hold them off but that only made matters worse as they grappled her to the floor, earning her a beating and a cut lip from a heavy bunch of keys in the process. They carried her bodily downstairs to the prison shower rooms where they flung her into a corner and played four hosepipes on her till she had indeed carried out this necessary function. Afterwards, she was handed a rough sacking nightdress to wear in place of her usual one, marched back up to her cell and locked in, shivering, cold, and soaking wet through. The rough nightdress offered little protection for what proved to be the longest, coldest night of her life. They didn't even provide her with the usual chamber pot. Long before morning, Lizzie had abandoned the last remnants of her dignity, and used the corner like everyone else.

*   *   *

Cora stood with her fists firmly clenched against her substantial waistline and looked at her two sons as if they'd run mad. 'Tha's fetched me what? A lurry load of sugar? What the bleeding 'ell am I supposed to do wi' that lot?'

'Don't worry Ma, Dad'll see to it. We just need somewhere to store it while we take the van back. And we have to look sharp afore we're missed.' Harry had the doors open and was already starting to unload, arms full of large blue bags.

'Well you can't fit a lurry load of sugar in my pantry.'

'It's a van Ma, not a lurry.'

Bert stopped juggling bags of sugar and frowned. 'She's right though, our Harry. There's not enough room in the pantry for all this lot.'

'Shurrup, muzzle-head. I know that, doan't I? I were only going to give you a few bags, Mam. To stock up like. We'll sell the rest.'

'Where? When?' Bert wanted to know, hopping from one foot to the other and sounding agitated. 'There must be tons of the stuff here. Where can we keep it all, our Harry?'

'Fer Christ sake shurrup, you. Stop asking so many flaming questions.' Storage was a complication Harry hadn't properly considered. Acting on impulse to take the van had seemed like a golden opportunity but perhaps, in retrospect, had been a touch reckless. When Bernie arrived minutes later, having been dragged from his favourite watering hole by a frantic Cora, it was to find a big black van blocking the back street, and his pantry, kitchen table, as well as the Anderson shelter in the backyard full to the brim with blue bags of sugar.

'Where are your brains, you great gobbin?' he yelled at Harry.

'I thought you'd be pleased, Dad. This sugar's worth a bleedin' fortune.'

'It's worth several months in Strangeways, if not life

imprisonment. How could you take such a risk in broad daylight? D'you want to get nicked? And yer mam's right for once, where are we supposed to put it? It'll tek us months to shift this lot, a few bags at a time.'

And so it proved, but at least the Delaney family could pander to their sweet tooth without a care in the world in future. Though what would happen at the next air raid when they needed to use the shelter, no one cared to consider.

It came sooner than anyone expected and they'd only managed to shift a fraction of the sugar, which meant there was room for only Cora, Jess and the three younger children to sit with any safety in the Anderson shelter.

'We could allus use them as sandbags,' Cora suggested, but since Bernie didn't find this the least little bit amusing, nobody else dared laugh either, although young Tommy went very red in the face for a while as he desperately held his mirth in check.

The boys and Bernie took refuge in the cellar with several bottles of beer to keep them company. As enemy aircraft droned overhead, dropping their weapons of destruction upon the city of Manchester, Cora said, 'Aren't we the lucky ones?' and in a way Jess had to agree. She'd had enough of cellars to last her a lifetime.

But the children were afraid, Sam and Seb clinging to Cora as if to their own personal lifeline, pushing their little faces into her big, fat belly for comfort and to block their ears against the dreaded sound. Sandra, wearing her usual scowl, whined, 'Mam, I'm hungry, can I have a sugar butty?'

There followed a number of raids in quick succession and Harry and Bert soon grew bored with being confined in the cellar and announced their intention of going down to the shelter on Dolefield, feeling in need of a bit of company, they explained. In truth they intended to do some scavenging in the bombed-out ruins. A bit of salvage work, as you might say. Where was the harm in that?

The backyard was already a clutter of junk: bits of old bicycles with wheels or chains missing, car tyres, lengths of timber which might come in useful one day, unused gas masks, rolls of chicken wire they'd picked up for a song. It did no harm to add to the collection. You could make a tidy profit out of selling anything these days, particularly if you hadn't paid for the stuff in the first place.

'I thought you didn't like the municipal shelter,' Bernie enquired mildly.

The two lads exchanged a quick glance, having no wish to divulge their plans at this stage. Harry was worried that Bert might blurt it out, and Bert was half convinced his father could read his mind anyway, so they both looked guilty. 'We don't like it much but it must be safer than our cellar, and the main thing protected by the Anderson is that blasted sugar.'

'I don't like the communal shelter. Can I stop at home, Bernie?' Cora asked, glancing nervously at her husband. He'd never objected before but you never could tell with Bernie.

'Course you can, love. You can keep an eye on our investment.'

Cora went happily off as usual with her brood to settle in among the heap of blue bags and Jess went along with her. It didn't seem fair to leave her aunt to cope with three children on her own.

Bernie said no more as his sons swaggered off, but his eyes narrowed with suspicion. He'd need to keep an eye on them two. They were getting a bit too big for their boots. Happen he should have encouraged them to join up after all. A bit of square bashing might have done them both a world of good. Harry in particular might like to give the impression he was obeying instructions but half the time Bernie suspected he was doing exactly as he pleased.

As for young Tommy, he wasn't even here this evening as he'd taken it into his head to volunteer his services as a fire-watcher. He'd gone along a few weeks ago with his pal Frank Roebottom to the nearest warden post where they were each given a steel helmet and an axe and told to stay awake and use their common sense. At first they'd thought it all a great adventure, a bit of a lark, messing about in the dark, sleeping in odd corners of factories and pretending they were heroes while they waited for action. But when it came, it had been a different story. They'd found themselves kicking incendiaries off the roofs of buildings, suddenly realising that war was a very serious business indeed.

This particular evening they were at a warehouse on Liverpool Road. Which was a pity in the circumstances, as they might have recognised the dull thud as the incendiary landed on the scullery roof. Nobody else heard it, or understood the nature of the sound if they did; not until the back door blew off and the roof fell in.

When the siren sounded, Leah welcomed it with heartfelt relief because it put an end to yet one more long and fruitless argument with her mother.

To most people going to the shelter might represent a restriction to their freedom, for Leah it meant escape. Down there she could talk to real people about real things, and put an end to her mother's machinations. Until the next time at least. This small victory allowed her to smile as she reached for her coat and the latest romance she'd got out of Boot's library. 'Here we go again, Mother. Grab your knitting bag. Let's go.'

Mrs Simmons disliked going down into the communal shelter. She told herself that it wasn't because of any snobby tendencies on her part, but a perfectly natural desire to be clean. The smell of those places was quite nauseating and the sight of so much human suffering, so many anxious faces, always depressed her. But knowing there was no help for it, she pressed her lips together with firm resolve, picked up her bag and followed her daughter down the back stairs and out into the street.

One glance along the lobby told Leah that the girls in the shop had already gone, no doubt quickly locking up and taking the cash box with them, as instructed. Her father, who was this evening doing his stint as an ARP Warden, had set rigid rules which he was most insistent they follow precisely. Leah quickly closed the interior lobby door and led her mother out the back way. It was only as she turned the key in the lock that Muriel remembered that she'd left her spectacles behind and began to fluster, wanting to go back for them.

'You can surely manage without them for once, Mother,' Leah protested, feeling suddenly anxious. Manchester was a prime target. It didn't do to hang around dithering.

'No, no, I need them. You know how bad my eyesight is these days. Where do you think poor Robert got it from? I can't do a thing without them and a night spent in a shelter is miserable enough without being deprived of my knitting. I simply won't be able to read the pattern.'

Leah sighed. 'You stay here then, I'll go.'

She unlocked the back door again and shot upstairs, running from room to room in a frantic search, finally unearthing the spectacles from under a cushion where her mother had tucked them. Leah pounded back downstairs, banging the door to behind her. 'Got them. Come on, we must hurry.' Grabbing her mother's arm she began to propel her along the back street.

'Did you remember to lock the door, darling?'

Leah hadn't the first idea whether she had or not. She was out of breath, hot and bothered and desperately anxious to get off the street before the raid started. Already she could hear the dreaded drone of enemy planes getting ever nearer, a sound that softened her bones to water and blotted every sensation but fear from her mind. She knew the shop door would be locked, so what did it matter about the one at the back? Most folk didn't bother to lock any doors at all on the grounds that there were far more important considerations to think of, like saving their lives. Even as she hesitated, considering the question, there came the all-too-familiar whine, cut off into an ominous silence, followed seconds later by a blast that blew them both off their feet, even though it must have come from a couple of streets away. The air was thick with dust, the smell of cordite choking their lungs and making them both cough. Winded but still in one piece, Leah dragged herself and Muriel to their feet, and even retrieved the tangle of knitting.

'I'm certainly not going back again to check. Quick, let's run for it.'

7

Leah and her mother were still safely in the shelter an hour later when the Delaney boys ambled from street to street, about their usual scavenging. As always Bert found it impossible to walk in a straight line and, whistling tunelessly, dashed to and fro peering in windows, trying doors, generally prying into every nook and cranny. They'd discovered how very careless folk were with their goods and chattels once they heard the air-raid warning. Exactly as they'd hoped.

Passing the Globe, they noticed the door standing wide open and not a soul inside. 'Hey up, someone'll be in bother,' Bert remarked. They've up and made a dash fer it wi'out bothering to lock up.'

'Useful though,' Harry commented, 'I don't know about you but these raids allus leave me fair parched.' And giving a little swagger, he wandered into the pub, calling out hello as he went, just in case. But as Bert had rightly suspected, the place was deserted.

They helped themselves to a couple of pints each, followed by several shots of whisky as a chaser, leaning contentedly on the bar counter and drinking at their leisure as if the war would be happy to wait until they were done. 'We'd best lock up when we go,' Harry said. 'Mek sure it's safe like.'

'Aye,' Bert smirked. 'Wouldn't be right for the poor barman if owt got nicked, would it?' After stuffing their pockets with a few packets of Woodbine and Craven A, the pair left, carefully locking up behind them and posting the key through the letterbox.

Several streets later they were back on Deansgate and again Bert took the lead, suggesting they take a shufty round the back of Simmons' Tea Rooms, just in case. They couldn't believe their good fortune to find the back door was indeed unlocked and didn't hesitate to go inside. First they went along the lobby and into the confectioner's shop. Ignoring the door which led into the tea room, they went straight to the counter looking for the till. They couldn't find it anywhere but the silver trays of cakes arrayed in the glass display counter looked tantalisingly delicious.

'By heck, see that custard slice. It must be three inches thick.' Bert stretched out his grubby fingers and took one, barely wiping the custard from his mouth before reaching for another, and a third after that. Harry helped himself to a wedge or two of apple pie, to which he was partial before finally coming to his senses.

'Here, what we wasting our time on this muck for. If there's no till, wheer's the bloody cash box then?' To their great disappointment they couldn't find that either. Someone had judiciously taken it with them to the shelter, so they went upstairs instead. Here they had better luck, discovering the Simmonses' identity cards and ration books in the kitchen drawer, and a wallet full of notes in the dresser.

'Who needs air-raid shelters or cellars?' Harry bragged. 'The best of it is there's no fear of being interrupted by husbands, since they're all away in the forces, and even the police we have left are a Mickey Mouse crew. Like I said, I knew it would be profitable to go out and about doing a bit of business while everyone else cowers in the shelter.'

'So long as we don't get bombed,' Bert said, his thin face creasing into a worried frown.

'No fear of that. We're indestructible,' and stuffing all of these precious treasures into their pockets, along with a cameo brooch and a pretty blue necklace that might be sapphires, which they'd found in the dressing-table drawer of the front bedroom, they let themselves out and went happily on their way, still whistling.

'Would you like a scone dear, and a refill of tea?' Jess glanced up at a kindly face framed by a blue bonnet, and smiled.

'Don't mind if I do.'

Just to see the Sally Army roll up and start serving tea, soup and sandwiches had lifted everyone's spirit. There were some who said the smile alone was worth a tanner but no money ever changed hands as they gave their services free, though they might try to sell a few copies of their magazine, *The War Cry*, later. They never enquired what denomination you were, or even if you believed in any God at all, but simply offered to 'serve and to succour', providing what they called 'the human touch', and if you discovered the answer to your spiritual needs while they tended to your physical ones, so much the better, but it was not in any way compulsory. It was really up to you.

Jess wasn't sure what she believed in. Certainly Lizzie had made no effort to instil any sense of the spiritual in her, and she wouldn't have dreamed of setting foot in a church herself, let alone take her daughter to one. At times Jess's hope for a good future was so clouded by depression over her mother, she felt a dreadful sense of bitterness. It was a hateful feeling, and one she struggled to resist. She smiled again at the girl in the blue bonnet and asked if she'd made the delicious scones herself.

She gurgled with laughter. 'No, no, we get them cheap from Simmons's because they're a bit stale. But still good, don't you think?'

'Delicious.' But then they would be if Mr Simmons or

Robert had made them. How generous that family was. How kind and thoughtful. Jess couldn't imagine Uncle Bernie doing anything which didn't bring in a decent profit for himself.

Cora and the children were certainly glad of the scones, slightly stale or not, as well as the hot tea. She'd been in a dreadful state by the time the ARP Wardens had pulled them from the rubble, anxious to find her children and check all their limbs were in good working order. Miraculously they were, but Cora had only just stopped shaking. She looked pale and vulnerable drinking the tea with her children gathered close to her side, as if she had shrunk within her comfortable layer of fat. Her usually rosy face was the colour of parchment, her wire wool hair still in curling pins and her swollen ankles spilling out over the top of the inevitable carpet slippers. As always, there was about her person an underlying, acrid scent of sweat, on this occasion mixed with plaster dust and cordite.

The house was badly damaged, with the odd door and window blown out and the back scullery flattened completely, but it could be repaired and parts of it were still habitable, or would be when the smell of smoke had gone and the water from the fire hoses had dried up. Even more amazingly, the Anderson shelter had withstood the blast intact, though with sugar spilled everywhere from the burst bags.

Bernie wasn't too pleased about this. 'There'll be little hope of selling the stuff now its full of muck and plaster.'

'Never mind, luv, it saved our lives, that sugar,' Cora told him. 'I'll never hear another word against our Harry.'

Fortunately, Bernie had managed to close the door on this damning evidence of black marketeering before any rescue party arrived, who fortunately didn't investigate too closely and even accepted, without protest, his decision not to leave the house or be checked over by the first-aid people. They warned him of possible gas leaks, and of the further risk of fire but Bernie insisted he must look for a few personal possessions, then board up the house, so they left him to it. They had far more to worry about than nutcases who wanted to poke about in smoking ruins. Besides, it happened quite often, folk wanting to root through the rubble to find family pictures or stay to guard their precious belongings.

Jess ate the second scone and drank a third mug of tea. By this time Sam and Seb were curled up on their mother's knee like a pair of puppies, fast asleep with thumbs in mouths. Sandra was snuffling and complaining about wanting to go home while Cora patted and soothed her, urging her to close her eyes and try to get some sleep.

Feeling at a loose end, and as if she didn't quite belong in this moment of family togetherness, Jess volunteered to help serve tea. Besides the young girl in the bonnet with the pretty face and bright eyes who said her name was Harriet, there was one other girl, a qualified nurse in her main job, and a man, all in Salvation Army uniform. Another batch of bombed-out victims had arrived and the three of them seemed to be run off their feet.

'You could brew a fresh pot,' Harriet readily agreed. 'This one is getting low.'

'Right you are.' Jess refilled the big urn and lit the gas beneath it. The next hour or so flew by as she filled and refilled the big brown teapots with scalding hot fresh tea time after time. Sometimes, she poured it out herself into tin mugs, seeing bowed heads lift, smiles turn up drooping mouths, and faces lined with grime and despair light up with pleasure and gratitude. At one point she took the mouth organ from her pocket and played them 'A Nightingale Sang in Berkeley Square' and everyone had a bit of a sing-song.

'Eeh luv, that were reet grand,' one old woman said, wiping tears from her eyes.

There were a few others blowing noses or wiping away

surreptitious tears, so she played a rousing version of 'She's
a Lassie from Lancashire' to cheer them all up again. It was
a good feeling. To Jess, it seemed like a worthwhile thing to
do. Better than cowering in a cellar, or even a sugar-bagged
Anderson shelter. She wondered how Lizzie was faring. Was
she having a sing-song and a mug of tea? Did they take the
prisoners down to the shelter, she wondered? Feckless as her
ma was, she really didn't deserve to be in that awful place at
all, let alone with all this going on. If only she could find
somewhere better for them when she came out.

'It's Jess Delaney, isn't it?'

Startled by this sudden interruption to her thoughts, Jess
turned to find herself being closely scrutinised by an officer
in Salvation Army uniform. He was a tall, thin man with a
waxy moustache. He wore the peaked hat square on his head,
beneath which a pair of large ears protruded. There was a
gleaming badge pinned just above the hat band, plain strips
of navy braid in horizontal lines across the front of his jacket,
as well as a brighter variety on the shoulder epaulettes. He
looked vaguely familiar to Jess, but she couldn't put a name
to him or know why he recognised her.

'I'm Sergeant Buxton, or just plain Ted if you like. I knew
your dad. How is the old codger then?'

Jess flushed with pleasure. It wasn't often she met anyone
who knew Jake, not since they'd moved out of Salford to be
nearer the rest of the family after he'd gone off to war. 'He's
overseas with the army, I think.'

'So I heard. I enjoyed your playing of the mouth organ,
which isn't as easy as it looks. Nice tone you got out of it. But
then your dad were allus musical. Right good trumpet player,
he were.'

Jess was surprised. 'Was he? I never heard him play the
trumpet. He used to play his accordion mind, all the time.'

The sergeant's eyes seemed to take on a challenging

twinkle. 'He could play pretty well any instrument he fancied, and you've inherited his talent. You're a dab hand at the trumpet yourself, eh?'

Jess laughingly shook her head. 'I've never tried to learn but I very much doubt it. All I can manage is this mouth organ.'

Sergeant Buxton frowned. 'It wasn't you then who blew that bugle last Christmas Eve?'

Jess gazed up into what had now become an alarming scrutiny and found herself at a complete loss for words. After all this time she'd thought she'd got away with it. Apparently not. Swallowing painfully, Jess knew there was no help for it but to own up. 'I'm sorry I dropped it. I was a bit startled by the noise it made. Was it badly dented? I've no money to pay for a new one just now, but I'm hoping to get a better job soon, so I could save up. Pay a bit each week towards a new one for the band. Would that do?'

The sergeant heard her out in silence, listening to every breathless utterance. When she finally stopped talking, he put back his head and started to laugh. In fact, he laughed so loud and for so long that his hat fell off and he had to pick it up before it rolled away and got trodden on. 'Eeh lass, if I'd known you were worrying so much over it, I'd have tried harder to find you. The bugle came to no harm at all, well not much anyroad. The odd dent won't matter.'

'Oh! I am glad.' Relief swept through her. Jess really didn't see how she could ever have earned enough to buy a new one, but felt she'd had to make the offer.

'I did try to find you afterwards, as a matter of fact, but you'd left the house on Back Irwell Street, and I didn't know where you'd gone. I'm glad to run into you again, though sorry about the circumstances of course, particularly since you've been worrying about that bugle all this time. Daft happorth.'

Jess smiled ruefully. She found she quite liked Sergeant Buxton, and as she poured him some tea and made him a sandwich because he was ravenous having worked half the night, they continued to chat as if they were old friends. 'Was it you that chased after me?'

'Aye, not to tell you off though, luv. I was right shook up when I heard you play that note. I'd never heard one so true, not played by a novice.'

If this surprised her, Jess was even more startled by his next words.

'And if you really don't know how to play the trumpet then you should learn. You have a natural gift.'

'Natural gift? I don't know what you mean.'

'To try to put it simply, woodwind instruments have a reed in the mouthpiece that vibrates when you blow. With brass instruments it is the shape and position of the lips you make which produces the note. But the important thing is not to strain or push the breath, which you didn't. Being relaxed is vital so that when you come to a high note you can deal with it sweetly. Course, there's still a lot to learn. Scales and such like. And it would take a lot of practice, but I could teach you. If you were interested.'

Jess gasped. '*If* I were interested?' She couldn't imagine anyone *not* wanting to make music. 'Could you really? Oh, but I don't have an instrument. Or money to pay for lessons.'

Sergeant Buxton shrugged, as if these were minor matters. 'We can always borrow one from the band and as for payment, look at what you're doing now?'

'What, pouring tea?' She handed him his potted beef sandwich and he bit into it with gratitude.

'Helping out. You could pay for your lessons by doing more of this, by working with us in the mobile canteens. We need all the help we can get. How about it? Is that a fair exchange?'

Jess could hardly believe what she was hearing. It seemed too good to be true. 'You mean in return for making tea and sandwiches, I get to play the trumpet any time I like?'

'Oh no, any time *I* like. Whenever I can find the time in between everything else I have to do. Oh, and you'll have to learn to play the bugle as well so that instead of using your hard-earned brass to pay for the dents in the one you dropped, you can play a bugle in the band instead.'

Jess was laughing too by this time, because it was all so amazing. 'Are you serious?'

'Never more so.' He held out a hand. 'Is it a deal?'

Without hesitation, she firmly shook on their agreement.

Bernie stood at the corner of Back Irwell Street with a group of his cronies looking very much as if he was waiting for the Globe to open, and watched his two elder sons swagger off along Cumberland Street, hands in pockets, whistling tunelessly. They looked so innocent they must be up to summat. As if he didn't have enough on his plate with that niece of his, obstinate little baggage, not forgetting her ineffective mother who was likely to be let out before too long. With a growing family to support, as well as an appetite for the odd each-way bet and a pint or two at the Globe here, he needed to think of some way to improve his income. Money was getting worryingly tight. What's more, it'd be a living nightmare soon with two women in the same house. He could see it coming. And right now there wasn't a damn thing he could do about it.

He certainly couldn't afford to keep two houses going.

Cora wasn't going to be the least bit happy to have Lizzie around the place, mainly because she had a suspicion that Jess wasn't his niece at all; that she was in fact Bernie's own child. He'd wondered the same himself once over, till he'd heard her play that mouth organ, then he'd known it was all a figment of his imagination. But she might well have been. He'd had a bit of a fling with Lizzie even before she married his brother. She hadn't ever been the loyal sort. Not like Cora.

His missus didn't have a bad bone in her flabby body, which was why he'd married her in the first place. He couldn't be doing with strident women, with the kind who thought they were as good as any bloke. Cora knew her place, had always shown proper respect and gratitude for the fact he'd chosen her above more glamorous possibilities. Oh aye, he'd had other irons in the fire when he were nobbut a lad, being quite the dandy in his day and not without his admirers. Only at the time, he'd been of the opinion that devotion and loyalty were vital so far as a wife was concerned, certainly in his line of trade. And he wasn't sorry he'd made that decision. Flirts and fancy pieces yielded nowt but trouble in the long run, as his brother's hasty marriage had proved.

Poor old Jake, what a shame that things had turned out so miserable for him. They'd got word just the other day that he was a POW, being held in a camp some place. Now that really did cut him up, that did. Bernie smirked with pleasure at the thought of his more fortunate brother suffering for once in his life. The smile quickly faded as he watched his sons sidle out of an alley, obviously up to no good, and in broad daylight too. What a pair of tosspots they were. He'd skelp the pair of them if they buggered up things for him. Jake had got one over on him there too, by breeding the most intelligent and decent child of the whole Delaney bunch.

Perhaps that was why Cora didn't hold it against Jess personally. She'd quite warmed to the lass but then that was Cora, generous and open hearted to a fault.

Except where her man was concerned, and then she could be like a terrier with a rat if anyone threatened to stand in her way. Bernie had never considered himself to be a faithful husband, but he'd always been discreet. He felt he owed that to Cora, at least. So God help Lizzie if she was daft enough to flaunt their liaison too brazenly when she came to live with them in Cumberland Street. The fat would really be in the fire then.

He called after his sons. 'Here, where you two off to?'

They turned, hesitated a moment before ambling reluctantly over. 'Just having a nose around. See what's doing.'

'Well, see you keep me informed.'

'Aye, course we will Dad. Don't we always?'

Bernie edged them away from the growing crowd outside the pub, lowering his voice to a whisper. 'And fetch back summat I can shift this time, as well as store easily. Not a van load of flipping sugar.'

'Right!' Both lads grinned amiably and nodded, glanced at each other then quickly away again.

Bernie caught the shifty look and inwardly groaned. Life was growing ever more complicated with these lads of his starting to spread their wings. Pickings on the black market weren't so easy as they'd once been. One or two deals had fallen through lately, let alone that blasted sugar. The authorities were growing ever more suspicious and tended to make spot raids on shops, demanding to see receipts and examine stockrooms, checking out their sources of supply. So far Bernie had been lucky and not suffered such an inspection himself, although he'd had one or two close shaves, and once lost a substantial amount of produce when a grocer's shop had been investigated by the powers that be, before the man had settled his account.

'Have they had any problems here with air raids?' Harry was asking, intruding on his thoughts and nodding in the direction of the pub doors, still fast shut.

Bernie frowned, struggling to concentrate on the implication behind the question. 'Not that I know of. What sort of problems would that be exactly?'

Bert shuffled his feet while his cheeks fired beetroot red, 'Oh you know, things going missing like. Doors not shut proper.'

Harry gave his brother a hefty kick on the ankle but daft Bert just yelled out loud in protest. 'Hey, what did you do that for, our Harry?'

'Do what?'

Bert caught the glower on his brother's face and realisation dawned. 'Oh, right. Nowt.'

Bernie said, 'What are you rattling on about, Bert?'

'Nowt, Dad. He didn't do nowt. Right, we'll be off then, shall we? And we'll remember what you said like.'

'Aye, think on. Mind what you get up to. Things aren't too easy at the moment. I don't want any problems that I can't handle.'

Harry snorted and there was the faintest note of irony in his voice. 'There's not much you can't handle, Dad. See you,' and giving a cheery wave, he thrust his hands back into his pockets, nudged his brother with one broad shoulder to make him get a move on, and the pair ambled off.

Eyes narrowing to slits, Bernie watched them vanish around the corner into Deansgate, and his shoulders drooped with weariness. His sons weren't turning out to be at all the bonus he'd hoped for, and sadly he knew why that was. Drive and ambition they might have, but they lacked imagination and any degree of common sense. They went at things like a bull in the proverbial china shop, weren't even very good at following orders, and he sensed a definite note of rebellion in the way they avoided answering his questions. Dumb insolence, you could call it.

Harry was wrong in one respect though. He could handle owt but women. They always foxed him in the end.

'Are yon thy lads?' asked one of the chaps in the queue behind him.

Bernie nodded glumly, 'I were just thinking, I've happen saved this country by not letting 'em join up.'

'Happen,' said the other chap, not disagreeing.

What was most curious about their behaviour recently though, was that they very often went out on these expeditions during an air raid. Despite their being so afraid of getting hit, they didn't seem to use the communal shelter on Dolefield very much. So where exactly did they go? Where were they heading now? What were they up to?

Damned if he'd be bested by his own sons. Bernie turned up his coat collar, shoved his hands deep in his pockets and loped off.

'Hey up, Bernie lad. Not coming in for a jar?'

'Not today mate. I've just remembered a bit of business I must see to.'

8

A day or two later, Bernie came home early from his football match one Saturday afternoon instead of going for his
usual pint at the Globe, mainly because he had a bit of business to do later and had decided to have an early tea. He
found no sign of any food on the kitchen table, only Ma
Pickles doing a bit of camping with his wife. How women
loved to gossip! He expected her to up-tail and run at sight
of him but, engrossed with a story she was evidently
enjoying telling, she made no move to go. The whole family
seemed to be riveted by her tale, Jess sitting enthralled with a
look of horror on her face, Cora leaning forward in her chair
so as not to miss a word, with Sandra clinging to her
mother's arm. Even Harry and Bert appeared eager for
every juicy detail.

'What's all this then?' Bernie asked, unable to help
himself.

'Go on,' Cora said. 'Tell him.'

Ma Pickles was more than happy to provide a résumé,
relishing running through her gory tale yet again. 'It's Cissie
Armitage, her what works at the Co-op. She were bombed
out t'other neet. And she didn't get off as lightly as you lot.
Her Jack lost both his legs in the blast. That Mr Simmons,
the ARP Warden, found one of 'em in t'back garden, but
theer's no sign of the other, not that they can stitch it back
on like.'

Cora began to look faintly green and Bernie realised the

old woman was enjoying embellishing her story. 'Get on with it, you old bag.'

Ma Pickles sniffed loudly, unfazed by his scorn. 'One of her childer were killed outright in his cot when the roof fell in and poor Cissie's a bag of nerves as a result. They took her and the other two kids down the shelter to give 'em first aid. They're reet enough, bless 'em, but she'll never be the same again. And as if she hadn't suffered enough wi' all of that lot, when she got back home there were a load of stuff missing. There's summat fishy going on, I sez to her. It's a funny sort of bomb what leaves yer handbag intact and blasts all the shillings from yer purse. And you know where yon kept her rent book, same as everyone else, on t'corner of mantel?'

Cora nodded gravely, agreeing that she understood this to be likely.

'Well it were still theer, where it should be, right next to the spills what she uses to light the fire. But the ration books and identity cards what should have been with it, were gone. Now what sort of clever bomb is that, d'you reckon, what can pick and choose which bits of paper it destroys? Clever enough as well to pick a few bits and bobs of trinkets out of Cissie's little box in her top drawer. She were reet cut up about them, I can tell thee. Even her mother's wedding ring were tekken. Bloody tykes.'

Fascinated, despite himself, by this sordid tale, Bernie slid his gaze in the direction of his two sons and realisation slowly dawned. He could see by the twin spots of colour on Harry's ghost pale cheeks, and the way Bert was fidgeting with the buttons on his overalls, just exactly what they'd been up to. He should've known. The morbid little scavengers. What kind of sons had he raised? Where was the skill, the wit, the canny judgement in picking over folks' belongings while they were in an air-raid shelter. Yet it was cunning. He could see that. Pity he hadn't thought of it himself. But then he'd have chosen a better target than bloody Cissie Armitage.

The moment Ma Pickles had gone, he jerked his head in the direction of the back door. 'A word. Outside.'

The two lads sidled out into the yard without protest, Cora and Jess watching with some trepidation as Bernie lifted the strap from the hook behind the back door.

'What's wrong now?'

'Never you mind.'

'Don't do owt you might regret, Bernie,' wailed Cora, wringing her hands together.

'Don't worry, there won't be any regrets.'

Once upon a time, when they were young lads, he might have instructed them to drop their britches. Now he flexed the strap and told them to hold out their hands instead. Bert meekly obeyed but had Bernie not been so arrogantly certain of his power, he might have noticed that at twenty-two, going on twenty-three, this was one step too far for Harry. He was inwardly steaming with anger. It came as something of a shock when his eldest son point blank refused.

'Like hell I will,' he muttered, half under his breath.

Hand still outstretched though trembling with anticipation of the blows to come, Bert said. 'What did we do, Dad?'

'You know damn' well what you did. Without any by your leave.'

'Hey, we got some good stuff. What's wrong with that?'

'What's wrong? What's wrong with that?'

Harry gave a snort of derisive laughter. 'I'll tell you what we did wrong Bert, we left him out of it. We didn't give the great Bernie Delaney, our clever Dad here, his cut. And why didn't we? Because he's past it.'

Without pausing to consider the wisdom of his action,

Bernie aimed a punch deep into his son's belly. Harry doubled over, giving a surprised grunt, yet was barely winded. When the second one came, an open-handed clout across the side of head, he staggered a bit but quickly righted himself. And still Bernie paid no attention to how his son's eyes narrowed, the expression in them hardening as a private resolve was made. Harry considered himself too old to be beaten by his father, and he certainly had no intention of allowing it to happen again. So when Bernie swung the next punch at his jaw, not only did it fail to connect, but his hand was caught in mid-air by Harry's huge fist, to be held in a crushing grip.

'You great clot-head, I'll wallop you into t'middle of next week,' Bernie gasped.

'Just try it.'

'Choose thee window and I'll chuck you through it.'

'You and who's flaming army?'

Bernie seemed to have run out of threats, and very nearly out of puff so father and son glared furiously into each other's faces, almost nose to nose, their eyes revealing all the pent-up frustration and anger each felt for the other. Then, after several more long seconds, Harry finally released the hand, knowing that he'd made his point.

Bernie flexed his bruised fingers, shocked to the core but desperately trying not to show it. When did these lads of his grow so strong? 'It's a challenge you want then, is that it?'

'It might be.'

'What, an arm wrestle, to see who's top dog?' If he couldn't control these lads with his fists any more, he'd have to think of some other way or he was done for.

Unable to resist this offer to flaunt his impressive skill in arm wrestling, Harry grinned and began to roll up his sleeve. While his attention was thus distracted, Bernie lunged at him. He grabbed hold of Harry's collar and flattened him against the backyard wall, nearly cracking his skull against the stone. 'Don't you dare to challenge me, you no good, useless lump of lard. And next time you go scavenging, don't do it anywhere near my home. Pick a better target. It's carelessness like that what could get you caught, and me along with you, once the polis start poking their flaming noses in our business. Right?'

Surprise registered briefly on Harry's face. He felt quite capable of throwing his father off but he could sense Bernie restraining himself. The reprimand was mild by past standards, and he did have a point. Happen he had been a mite careless. Nevertheless, he was determined not to give in too easily. 'How could I get caught? Everyone were in t'shelter, including the Mickey Mouse police.'

'Open thee lug-holes, I'll say it one more time so there's no mistaking you understand. Stay away from bombed-out houses *in this locality*. Go where you're not so well known, and where you don't know who you're nicking from. Is that clear? Have I drummed it into your thick skull? That way we're less likely to suffer repercussions, either by folk like Ma Pickles poking her beak in where it's not wanted, or the polis. Right?'

Bert was dancing around, almost wetting his pants with anxiety. 'Don't thump our Harry again. But we can't do that, Dad. We're demolition men now and must go where we're told.'

With a great show of reluctance, Bernie released his hold on his son. 'Demolition? What bloody rubbish is this?'

Shaking himself free and dusting down the new jacket he'd bought for himself, Harry said, 'Aye, it pays better than the docks, and there are more opportunities. Nobody asks questions of demolition workers poking about a bomb site.'

Bernie was stunned by this new information but saw at once that this might well be true. Yet it rankled that his sons should show such enterprise without even consulting him first. They were getting even more canny than he'd given them credit for. It strengthened his suspicion that they believed they could please themselves what they did, which wasn't the case at all. He was still the boss, still in charge.

'So you thought you'd cut me out of the deal, is that the way of it? Well, don't ever try to pull a fast one like that on me again, right? Anyroad, what did you collar? Money? Coupons? Whatever it is, hand it over. I'm still the boss round here and don't you two ever forget it.'

With grudging ill will, Harry pulled a few trinkets from various pockets. A couple of watches, a ring, a couple of five-pound notes, and Bert handed over a wad of petrol coupons.

'That's more like it. Right, we'll say no more on the subject. Just see that you keep me informed in future.'

It was only after Bernie had gone back inside, certain he'd re-established his position as head of the hierarchy that Harry muttered, 'Just like I told you, Bert. He's lost his nerve. And if you ever tell him we didn't give him everything, I'll wring your flaming neck.'

Jess buttoned up her best navy-blue coat against a cold north wind that was rattling the kitchen window and tugged on warm woolly gloves. The coat was too short and a bit tight about the chest since she'd grown quite a bit recently, sprouting breasts which were a great embarrassment to her. But it would have to do, much as she hated it. She certainly couldn't wear her old school gabardine. Jess felt prickly with nerves, all jittery inside, not that worrying about how she was dressed would help one bit. True to her word, Leah had asked her father about a job and Jess had been granted an interview. She'd brushed her dark brown hair till it shone, scrubbed her nails, which seemed to be important in the circumstances, and put on her only decent navy skirt and a clean white blouse. Now she could only hope and pray that she didn't look as awful as she felt.

Cora, who had come to know the girl well in these last weeks recognised the problem instantly.

'Nay, don't get in a fret, you look reet champion. Remember it's only Mr Simmons and you know him well enough. Besides, grand girl like you he'd be daft not to give you a job, assuming you want one of course.' Much as Cora admired her niece, she was a bit nonplussed by her capacity for hard work. As well as helping her with the childer, she spent most evenings working with the Sally Army on their mobile canteens. And she was still looking for a better job, as she called it, a step up from the market stall.

'Course I want it.' Working in a confectioner's shop might not have been her first choice or in any way glamorous, but at least it would put her on the road to independence, and there was always the chance of being asked to work in the tea room where there was the possibility of tips. If she saved hard, she'd soon have enough to move away from her uncle's and make a home of their own for herself and Lizzie, even if not quite in time for her release within a few weeks. But she couldn't say any of this to Aunt Cora, who'd shown her nothing but kindness. 'It's important that I make a good impression. Mr Simmons has a reputation for being a bit of a stickler for what's proper and correct. Good manners, rules, stuff like that. Deep down, Leah says, he's a fair man and a good employer, if not exactly generous, but he likes things to be done just so. He calls it running a tight ship.'

'Aye, bosses are like that,' Cora said with feeling, and wound a scarf about the girl's neck. 'See you don't hang about in the wet. We don't want you sickening for summat.'

'I won't. I promise.' She'd been invited on several occasions to stay for supper at the Simmonses' in recent months, despite her mother being in jail. No mention was ever made of Lizzie, and there were no more offerings of mince pies or similar items of home baking but, either out of pity, charity, or sheer good nature, the family had raised no objection to her continuing friendship with Leah, for which Jess was immensely grateful. Leah's friendship was all important to her. She loved going to the dances with her friend and although she'd found herself looking out for him, she'd never again spotted Steve Wyman, which left her feeling low and disappointed. Not that you could feel down for long, not with Leah chivvying her to dance with every sailor, soldier or airman who asked.

Cora said, 'Don't forget to call at the butchers on yer way back. Ask him if he has some of them nice sausages. And if you see any interesting queues, tag on behind just in case. Who knows what might be going.' She thrust a ration book into her hand and Jess stared at the unfamiliar name on the front cover.

'It's me cousin. Me other cousin. He's planning to stop with us for a few days.' Even if Cora's plump cheeks hadn't been flushed, Jess would've known it for a lie. There'd been a few too many strange happenings during the weeks of her stay. For one thing, both Cora and Bernie seemed to have two sets of identity papers, each bearing different names, which meant they also had two different sets of ration books that they used in different shops. It was becoming increasingly difficult to remember the details when Cora sent her out shopping.

More recently, Leah had complained about the Simmonses' identity cards and some money going missing while they'd been in the shelter one time. She'd been outraged to hear Ma Pickles' story the other day. It was hard to imagine anyone so heartless as to steal while an air raid was in progress. In Leah's case, they'd even taken a few trinkets from her mother's jewellery box on her dressing-table. Jess had sympathised but now a small fear kindled in the pit of her stomach. That theft couldn't have anything to do with the Delaneys, could it? Was that why Uncle Bernie had taken both lads out in the yard for a skelping? Lord, she hoped not. She wanted Mrs Simmons to go on issuing invitations so that she could continue to taste a little of normal family life, even if it wasn't her own and largely pretence. Visiting the Simmonses' house was her main sanctuary, besides the Sally Army. Mrs Simmons had once or twice allowed her to practise her trumpet while she accompanied her on the piano. Jess couldn't bear it if the Delaneys messed that up for her as well.

'Isn't it wrong for Uncle Bernie to have so many spare coupons, Aunt Cora?' Jess blurted out the question with the innocence of a young girl who still believed in the ideal that everyone should pull together, particularly during wartime; needing to be reassured that surely even the Delaneys wouldn't stoop so low as to steal from people who were fleeing for their lives.

Cora, wiser by a mile, let out a heavy sigh. 'Rationing is a blight on the poor. You don't think the rich are hidebound by it, do you? They has the money to get round it, get round owt in fact.'

'But how could they? I mean, however much money you might have, you can't buy a new frock unless you have enough clothing coupons, can you?'

'Has anyone ever told you girl, tha talks too much. If tha'd any more mouth, tha'd have no face to wash.'

'But where does he get them all from? I found a whole box of them when I was cleaning your bedroom yesterday.'

Now Cora looked thoroughly alarmed and distressed, glancing fearfully about as if she half expected her husband to appear before them as if by magic. 'Nay, don't let on to

Bernie tha's been snooping. Cleaning our bedroom, whatever next? He won't like that, not one little bit. He's a very
private man, with his own way of going about things is our
Bernie.'

'But don't you worry about him?'

Cora's tone grew sharp, with a bitter ring to it. 'Course I
worry, but I know how to keep me lip buttoned and not ask
too many questions, a skill you'd do well to learn.' Softening
her voice she stroked Jess's pale cheek. 'You has to be
careful, lass. He might seem generous to a fault, allus
fetching us good things to eat and bringing the kids new
clothes and such, but underneath he'd tek skin of yer rice
pudding if he had a greater need fer it. So don't go poking
yer nose in where you shouldn't. Leave all his cupboards
and drawers firmly shut tight, particularly under the stairs.
Got it?' And nodding meaningfully, she ladled an extra
spoonful of sugar into Jess's mug of tea. Not that Jess wanted
it, she was growing to quite dislike sugar. Besides, Cora
might be happy to sit hour after hour supping tea and having
a bit of crack with her niece, her neighbours, or her children
but Jess preferred to be out and about, living life to the full.
And this morning she was particularly anxious to be on her
way.

'I reckon I'd best be going. I don't want to be late.'

'Aye, all right love, and remember what I said. Yer a grand
lass, and Simmons's Tea Rooms will be the loser if yon chap
doesn't sign you up on the spot.' Cora was marching her
niece briskly to the door as she said all of this, smoothing the
collar of the navy blue coat, tucking in the scarf, checking
Jess had her bag and the ration book.

'I don't think it's in the tea room, Aunt Cora. I think it's
just serving bread and cakes in the shop.'

'Well, it's a start, I suppose.' Cora looked doubtful but
then a thought struck her and her face brightened. 'Here,

you might be given the odd stale loaf, tha never knows. Or some muffins, or Eccles cakes. Eeh, I do love Eccles cakes. So think on now. Chin up and best foot forward.'

Jess suddenly felt a wealth of compassion for this over-sized, big-hearted woman in her wrap-over pinny and carpet slippers and gave her a hug. How could such a caring, warm person endure living with her loathsome uncle? She'd gone from being bullied at school as a girl, to being equally bullied by her husband. Was that how it was, once a victim, always a victim? Jess had never actually seen any physical evidence that Bernie beat his wife, but she knew for a fact he was capable of such violence, had witnessed his temper with her own eyes when he'd attacked Lizzie, so he might be clever enough to inflict bruises where they didn't show. Cora was certainly afraid of him. 'Thanks. What would I have done without you these last weeks?'

'Nay, what are families for? Have you thought what you'll do when yer mam comes home?'

'I mean to look after her.'

'Course you do love, and yer welcome to stop on here, both of you. You know that, being family like.'

Jess felt tears block her throat for although Cora didn't sound overenthusiastic she knew the offer was genuine, and a generous gesture since the two women didn't get on. 'Mebbe we won't need to bother you. Happen Uncle Bernie will be able to find us some place of us own to live.' Jess felt rather anxious about what was going to happen when her mother was released. Nothing had been said about that. No plans made.

'Aye, happen so. He allus did put himself out for your mam.' There was a wealth of meaning in her tone now, which Jess thought best not to remark upon. 'Right then. Off you go, chuck, and remember, be proud of theesen, or nobody else will be.' Then she kissed Jess's cheek and gave her a little shove, as if denying she could be so soft. 'And don't forget them sausages.'

Lizzie came home at the end of March, by which time Jess had already started work in Simmons's cake shop to help with the Easter rush. She soon learned the names of all the cakes and different types of bread, found little difficulty in adding up and giving change, and the other girls she worked with were friendly enough. She liked serving in the shop, enjoyed chatting to the customers who came in and out all day long; loved the long mahogany and glass counter which was so clean and shiny and beautiful; and the cakes displayed on the glass stands in the window looked and smelled so wonderful she could hardly resist them.

'Go on, have one if you want one,' Leah would say. 'You'll soon grow tired of them, though, when you've had a few.'

Jess was shocked by the suggestion. She would never have dreamed of taking anything without asking. That would be tantamount to stealing, although the smell of the meat and potato pies and pasties, and in particular the heady aroma of a newly baked loaf hot from the oven were so tantalising they made her juices run. But only on a Friday did the shop girls treat themselves to a cake each, at trade price of course, to celebrate the end of another week. Jess looked forward to it and would debate with herself the choice that she would make for days beforehand. Would it be a custard slice, an Eccles cake or a slice of Battenberg, which they called church windows? Or even a cream horn, though perhaps it should more rightly be called a mock cream horn, rationing being what it was. Either way, it was a special treat and always delicious.

The best part of working in the shop was that she got to see her friend every day since Leah worked in the tea room full time now, despite complaining bitterly that she really wanted to be an actress or a newspaper reporter; anything in fact which had some excitement and zest to it and didn't involve being under her parents' gaze all day long.

'It's so *boring*! Half the time the tea room is empty because there aren't any customers, or else we don't have the ingredients to make enough scones and cakes. How Robert can stand working in that hot bakery day and night, juggling recipes to make something out of nothing, I really can't imagine. And I have to stand about in a frilly apron and silly cap looking like a proper Charlie, being polite to fat old ladies who shouldn't be eating cake anyway. And would you believe, even though I've finally escaped school and my horrible teachers, Mother still makes me do my piano practice *every* night, just as if I were still a child. I wouldn't mind so much if she allowed me to play anything *interesting*, but it's always scales and boring exercise pieces. It's so unfair. Oh, why doesn't something exciting *ever* happen to me, to *us*? Why must our lives be ruined by Mr Hitler.'

Her friend's vehemence always set Jess off into fits of giggles for she didn't take her complaints at all seriously. It was perfectly plain that Leah's parents adored her, and everyone knew that Ambrose Gartside was absolutely potty about her. So what did she have to worry about?

'You could always marry Ambrose, if you want to escape your parents' clutches,' Jess suggested as they sat relishing their Friday treat together. This week Jess had indeed chosen a cream horn and Leah a Cornish split.

'What? I'd rather *die*! He's so dreary, and always looks half asleep with those droopy eyelids of his, droopy everything in fact, there's so much blubber on him.'

Jess chuckled. 'You're exaggerating, he's just well built, that's all.'

'I know. Like a tank, but who wants to make love to a

tank? I shudder to think what he'd be like in bed. I bet he couldn't raise the energy to fire his guns,' and both girls burst into a fit of helpless giggles, Jess getting a blob of mock cream on her nose as a result. To hear Leah talk in such a ribald fashion always set her off because her friend had known absolutely nothing about sex until Jess had explained it all to her. Muriel Simmons had made vague mention about a wife doing her duty, given her daughter a sanitary towel and belt, and left it at that.

'Where did you learn all this stuff?' Leah had asked, listening goggle-eyes to the sordid details of procreation.

'Don't ask, I get a running commentary every breakfast, and sound effects every night, but take it from me, men are all out for what they can get. Romance doesn't come into it.'

'How heartless and cold you sound. I don't believe you for a minute. Men are gorgeous, and I mean to fall hopelessly in love with someone dark and handsome one day, and have lots of beautiful children. Don't you? Wouldn't that be the most romantic, exciting thing in the world?'

'Not unless he could give me what I most need.'

'Which is?'

'I'm not sure.' Jess licked the cream from her horn while she reflected upon this for a moment and then realised that she didn't need to think at all. What she wanted most of all was to play her music. She'd started lessons with Sergeant Ted and absolutely loved it. He called her a natural, though she wasn't, of course, since Jess practised for hours at home. Cora never minded, but her uncle was another matter. Not for a minute did he stop complaining.

'Will you stop that bloody racket,' he'd shout. Or: 'Put that bloody cat out. It sounds like it's being strangled and I can't stand the din.'

It was too much to hope for a normal, happy family life but Jess longed to be free of Uncle Bernie and the Delaneys, to have a home of her own, freedom for herself and safety for her mother. So what she needed most of all was someone to help her achieve that. 'Maybe *I* should marry Ambrose. His parents are well off and it would at least get me away from Cumberland Street and Uncle Bernie.'

'Don't even consider it. Bernie might be a rat, but Ambrose is just a – a mouse. A big *fat* mouse, but a mouse nonetheless. And who'd care to be squeaked to death? So *boring*!'

9

The joy of starting work was muted slightly for Jess by her worry over Lizzie. Her mother seemed so listless and frail, so unlike her usual self. Jess couldn't even persuade her to get up in a morning. She'd lie in bed half the day, and then spend the rest of it flopped in a chair, getting on Cora's nerves simply by being there. Jess could tell by the way her aunt compressed her lips and sniffed disapprovingly whenever Lizzie didn't appear for breakfast, or slopped about all day not lifting a finger to help, that if something didn't change soon, her patience would explode.

She'd make excuses for her, explain how Lizzie was finding it difficult adapting to life outside, or that she couldn't get a job now that she had a record.

Cora would simply mumble something to the effect that Lizzie never did like work at the best of times. But even worse than the sullen silence which was the normal state of affairs between the two women, as the weeks and months slipped by there developed a cut-throat battle for attention from the man of the house.

If Lizzie ever did stir from her chair it would be to make Bernie a cup of tea, to fetch his slippers and fuss over him, fold his evening paper or butter his bread just how he liked it; all the tasks which were normally Cora's province. She would offer to make him toad-in-the-hole or tune in his favourite programme on the wireless. He wasn't interested in the news, or the state of the war, but he did enjoy 'Stinker'

Murdoch in *Band Wagon* and 'Big-hearted' Arthur. And Lizzie always insisted on waiting up for him to come home at night, no matter how late it was, which annoyed Cora more than anything else.

'*I* never wait up for him, so why should she?'

'She means well,' Jess would say, stuck for a better answer.

'Like hecky thump she does. She means to get her feet under my table, preferably when I'm no longer sitting at it.'

One night as Lizzie settled herself in the battered old fireside chair to wait for Bernie, Cora pulled up a stool opposite, folded her ham-sized arms and made it clear she didn't intend to budge. 'Thee can bugger off to bed, I'll see to him.'

Lizzie looked confused by this show of stubbornness on Cora's part, being somewhat out of character. Wasn't her sister-in-law supposed to be meek and mild, a victim who'd been bullied and should be grateful for any consideration at all? Not be sitting there with her hair in curlers and her tatty old dressing-gown on, with an 'I'm-not-shifting' expression on her round red face. 'I would've thought you had enough on your plate during the day with all them br—, them kids o' your'n to see to, without having the energy left to stop up late. I'll look after him for you, Cora. Don't you fret.'

'He's *my* husband. *I'll* look after him. I'll be the one to do for him owt what needs doing. You get off up them apples and pears to yer bed. Happen you'll be needing to conserve your strength for when you start looking for work.'

Now this was a prospect which had never entered Lizzie's head. Thankful to at last be out of the nick and safely ensconced in Bernie's house, she had not the least intention of doing anything so reckless. 'Bernie'll look after me,' she said, pulling her lipstick from her pocket where she kept it nice and handy so as she could always look her best for him and, using the spotted mirror over the mantelpiece, carefully applied another layer to her already thickly coated lips. 'He's said as much a dozen times. He likes having me around.'

'He does buggery. He's only mekking use of thee, for convenience sake, as he does everybody what crosses his path. More fool you for doing his bidding. Says tha'd jump in t'canal if he towd thee to. He thinks you're a flaming nuisance, a thorn in his side. A dummel-head.'

'That's not true!' Lizzie had gone quite white, turning in spitting fury upon Cora and lashing out with nails like scarlet talons. The stool went flying but Cora, light on her feet despite her bulk, neatly ducked and evaded the blow and, wrapping her arms about Lizzie's waist, grappled her to the dusty, clippy rug in a style of which any rugby player would have been proud. As Lizzie screamed and kicked and attempted to rip the curlers out of her sister-in-law's hair, Cora, with the benefit of size, pinned her to the floor easily. With five sausage fingers circling Lizzie's scrawny neck, she was sorely tempted to put an end to her opponent there and then.

'I could wring yer flaming neck like the old boiler you are.'

'Hurt me and Bernie will part yer hair with a meat cleaver. Tha's nowt a pound, thee. It's me he thinks the world of, not *you*! That's why yer bleedin' jealous. Tha knows I can pinch him from under yer nose any bloody time I like.'

Lizzie might have been safer putting a match to an incendiary bomb.

Enraged by this threat to her position as wife and helpmeet, Cora picked up Lizzie as easily as if she were indeed a scrawny chicken and might well have wrung the life out of her, or tarred and feathered her, had not Sam and Seb chosen that precise moment to come downstairs to see what all the pandemonium was about. Seeing her beloved children standing there in their pyjamas crying for their mam, brought a rush of tears to her eyes and a shaft of common sense back into her brain. She gave Lizzie one final shake and reluctantly dropped her back in the chair. 'Bloody tart, see what you've med me do. Shown meself up before me childer. Gerroff to bed afore I finish t'job proper. Mek theesen scarce.'

And wisely, Lizzie did just that. A tactical withdrawal she called it. Necessary survival in order to return and fight another day.

'He's a right lummock, your dad,' Cora told her two precious darlings as she gathered them into her brawny arms. One who, despite being the champion of her youth, had proved to be less attentive as a husband than she'd hoped. She never knew a moment's peace with him, always wondering what trouble the next day might bring, jumping at every knock on the door, fearing the polis would come at any moment and cart him off to the clink. But he was her property, hers and nobody else's. He certainly didn't belong to her flaming sister-in-law.

'Can't we have our old place back?' Jess begged her uncle. When Lizzie had related this episode to her, in full graphic detail, she'd realised that the matter was far more serious than she'd thought. Not that she made any mention of the scrap to her uncle. That wouldn't do at all, not for any of them, least of all Cora, who really had all her sympathy. But something had to be done, and quickly. They couldn't all go on living together in this tiny little house, not if blue murder was to be avoided. 'A room somewhere, mebbe? We don't fit in here any more. We need our own place.'

Bernie looked sceptical. 'Oh aye, and who would pay for it? You couldn't, not with what you're earning.'

'I'm doing better now I've got a new job, and I'll work hard. I'll manage to pay the rent, I promise. Besides, Aunt Cora has enough to do looking after her own family.'

Fond as Jess was of her aunt, nobody could ever accuse Cora of being the best housekeeper in the world. She'd sit with her feet propped up on a stool reading the paper, or have a crack with her friends for hours at a time and quite happily ignore a sink full of dirty dishes and a table still littered with the remains of breakfast. She wouldn't stir to sweep or mop the filthy kitchen floor, or think to peel a potato until the very last minute before her brood started to arrive home. And then she would bully sullen Sandra into doing these various chores, the minute the poor girl walked through the door.

Jess did most of the washing and ironing, which she was quite certain wouldn't get done otherwise. Even so, Cora didn't change the beds nearly often enough to suit her, and never thought to make one.

'What's the point when you'll be getting back into them in a few hours?' she'd say and laugh at what she called Jess's pickiness.

So Jess persisted with her plea. 'If Mam had her own kitchen, she'd pay more attention to what's going on around her. She'd mebbe want to get up every morning to make breakfast, light the fire and stuff. Better than sitting about all day with nothing to do except get under me aunt's feet.'

'Cora's never said owt to me,' Bernie grumbled and Jess didn't dare answer that his wife was too afraid to object to anything, as were his three sons, for fear of unleashing that nasty temper of his.

'I'm sure it would be good for Mam. It'd liven her up no end.'

'I can find her summat useful to do if she's bored,' Bernie snapped. 'Everyone has to pull their weight round here. I'll have a word with her, make her pull herself together.' Fearful that she might have made things worse for her mother, Jess wished she'd kept her trap shut and not said anything at all.

Jess knew she should do more around the house. She always meant to help with the breakfast, just as she'd used to when she first moved in. But the noise of the bickering would steadily rise, Sandra would start her whining and, more often than not, Jess would daub a shive of bread with some Maggie-Ann, as Cora termed the margarine, pop it into her bag and escape to the shop just as fast as she could. She was more than content to sit and eat her meagre breakfast in peace and quiet on the kitchen doorstep and wait until Mr Simmons came down to open up. He never seemed surprised to see her sitting there, even when it was cold and raining; rather the reverse, believing her to be diligent and keen.

'Morning, Jess,' he would say.

'Morning, Mr Simmons.'

'You'll sweep and mop the shop and tea room through for me?'

'Glad to, Mr Simmons.' And he'd nod and go off to the bakery to see if his son had the morning loaves ready.

Jess would happily do these tasks because it was warm in the tea room, situated as it was next to the bakery, and blissfully silent until the other girls arrived. There were no raised voices, no petty squabbles over sugar or cornflakes, no spilt milk, no Cora and Lizzie going at it hammer and tongs. There was no simmering threat that fire and brimstone might explode at any moment in the shape of her uncle coming roaring down the stairs demanding to know what all the row was about, whacking Tommy or Bert across the backs of their heads simply to make his presence felt. He never touched Harry these days, strangely enough. Nor was Harry himself averse to flinging a punch at Bert if he'd helped himself to one too many of the sausages that he'd twisted the butcher's arm to supply. Jess found it a huge relief to get away from all of that.

Apart from the shop, her other main avenue of escape was the Salvation Army. Ever since the night they were bombed, she'd helped out regularly in the mobile canteen. Jess thoroughly enjoyed helping and felt she was paying something back for the regular lessons she was having with Sergeant Ted. He'd taught her the rudiments of playing the trumpet: how she must keep her lips fairly slack to produce the low notes, and could make them lower still by pressing down the valves that opened the extra lengths of tubing. Tightening her lips pushed the air in the tube onwards before it had too much time to vibrate, which made for a higher note. Thus she learned to regulate the sounds, oh and didn't she just love playing that trumpet. She really wouldn't have missed a lesson, not for the world.

She'd also started playing in the Bugle Band and, six months on, had been given a uniform to wear which made Harry and Bert laugh like drains.

'Tha's a Junior Soldier now, eh? Hasta been saved?' Harry teased.

'I think she looks reet fetching in that bonnet,' Bert sniggered.

Tommy answered for her. 'Leave t'lass alone, pair on you. She's doing a good job there. More than some I could mention. We should all try to do our bit.'

'Sez who?'

'What've you lot ever done for the war then? Go on, tell us, impress us with your patriotic fervour.'

'We bring money into the house, make no mistake about that. A deal of money, if you want to know.'

'And how did you come by it? Not honestly, I'll warrant.'

'Who the bleedin' 'ell are you calling dishonest?'

And again Jess would make her escape, leaving the brothers to their constant squabbling and bickering, which seemed to be a sad fact of life in Cumberland Street.

Harry and Bert weren't the only ones making her life a misery, Sandra too was becoming increasingly peevish and fretful, often sniping at her, resentful of anything Jess did which, in her opinion, deprived her of Cora or Bernie's attention for even a second.

'Why should our mam wait on you, hand, foot and finger? She gave you boiled ham for your tea yesterday, and only Spam for me and the twins. What makes you think you can have the best of everything?'

'I don't. She doesn't. I pay my whack, and I bring home treats from the shop. You can have the ham next time.'

'You never fetch me nowt.'

'Oh, Sandra. I brought you two scones just last week.'

Sandra snorted. 'They were both stale.'

'That's why I got them cheap. Mr Simmons doesn't give stuff away.'

'You never do owt for me. Think yer someone, you do, 'cause you play that flippin' trumpet.'

Jess's main concern was that she didn't have anywhere near enough time to keep an eye on Lizzie. Goodness knows what she got up to during the day when she was at work. But what could she do about it? It was vitally important that she keep her job. She needed to save every penny because one day, just as soon as she was old enough, and with or without her uncle's help, she meant to get them a place of their own; to gain their independence once and for all.

It was one day in the autumn of 1941 that Mr Simmons called her into his office and told her that he'd decided to give her a try as a waitress in the tea room. Jess was thrilled. Not only could she now work directly alongside Leah, but it was better pay and with the possibility of tips, which would top up her savings nicely.

Leah was thrilled too. The two friends hadn't seen quite so much of each other lately as they would have liked. Even their trips out dancing had been curtailed somewhat. Jess had been busy with the mobile canteen and her trumpet practice, while

Leah's social life seemed to be more closely regulated than ever. There was always some function or other that Mrs Simmons had arranged, a seemingly endless parade of coffee mornings and rummage sales, a Weapons Week Fund-raising Dance where Leah spent most of the night in the cloakroom rather than on the dance floor; not to mention collecting newspapers, jam jars, old woollens, and all manner of other goods in need of recycling.

Leah would wrinkle her nose in protest and Jess would suggest that she make an excuse to get out of it next time. Or perhaps one of Muriel's friends might be persuaded to go along instead, although this never quite seemed to work for some unknown reason. If Muriel ever found anyone, they always mysteriously backed out at the last moment, leaving Leah again as the only available option. Apart, that is, from Mrs Gartside, and her stalwart son.

'Never again,' Leah would say, and stubbornly refuse to be involved but at the last minute she'd feel sorry for her mother and succumb. 'Poor Ma lays such store by these affairs. It's her way of doing her bit for the war effort. If she needs help, how can I refuse? I can't leave her to struggle alone, can I?' Afterwards, she would roll her eyes and admit that Ambrose had been present too and, as suspected, her mother could have managed perfectly well without her. 'It was clearly a ploy for us to get to know each other better. It won't work, no matter what she does. I can't stand him.'

Jess would merely smile, knowing that much as Leah might object to her mother's match-making and being dragged along to her charity functions, in reality she adored and admired her. Who wouldn't? She was, in Jess's opinion, an ideal mother; the kind anyone would be pleased to have. She would happily have volunteered herself to help Mrs Simmons, but didn't like to intrude between mother and daughter.

'One day you'll agree to marry him just to please her, or because it's the most sensible, practical thing to do.'

'Never! Even I'm not so soft. I'd elope with the milkman's horse before I'd do that.'

And Leah would continue to rant and rave while Jess simply giggled at these loud protestations. It was really up to her, after all, to stand up to her parents or not, as she thought best. But in one respect at least she did agree with Leah. Jess couldn't imagine a situation which would induce anyone with sense, herself included, to marry someone they didn't love, and Leah was so full of bounce and confidence she deserved the best. 'At least now we'll both be working together and can chat during the day.'

'Ooh goody, in between serving tea and scones to fat old ladies who shouldn't be eating them at all,' Leah irreverently added. 'I do wish something exciting would happen, don't you?'

So far as Jess was concerned, it already had. If she worked in the tea room she might get tips, and if she added these to the tin box she kept under her mattress, she might all the sooner have enough savings to get her and Lizzie a place of their own.

Jess had become a great favourite with the Salvation Army band. She loved everything about it, not simply the perform-ances, sometimes at the citadel for a service, or at the Mission and on street corners where they hoped to collect a crowd and attract donations. But also she enjoyed the comradeship, the easy laughter and happy teasing, the feeling of belonging, being part of a group and of doing something worthwhile, a sensation she'd never experienced before. Nor did she mind the rehearsals, or the endless hours of practice, she didn't even object when Sergeant Ted shouted at her for playing a wrong note. She only practised all the harder to get it right.

However much fun performing for a lively crowd might be, what she really loved most of all was the feel of the instrument in her hands. She loved the pressure of the valves beneath her fingers, the wonderful sensation that flowed through her veins like liquid gold whenever she put her lips against the mouthpiece and the most marvellous sounds came out. Ted told her that she played the bugle like a dream and the trumpet with a warm, mellow sound. Jess could hear only her own imperfections and glaring mistakes. Oh, but she meant to play better one day, she really did. She must just keep practising.

Sergeant Ted insisted that she do at least an hour every day, preferably two. She must warm up by going through the fundamentals, starting with the middle register and working through to the higher. Then some long low tones followed by running through the scales and practising chord changes. And all the time Jess would be trying to improve the flexibility of her lips, making sure she blew straight out and not down, got the right tension, and worked on the exercises and pieces of music set for her. Only when she'd spent at least an hour on these would Jess allow herself to play whatever she liked, attempting to improvise, since she possessed no written music of her own.

No matter what hurdles Uncle Bernie might put in her path, however much he might shout and complain about 'having that din in my house' which often meant that she was forced to practise in the backyard, or out on a stretch of waste land down by the River Irwell, she would never give up. To Jess, it didn't matter where she was, nothing and no one would prevent her from doing what she loved most: playing the trumpet. Even if he clouted her or beat her black and blue all over as he had Lizzie, it wouldn't make any difference, she'd keep on playing.

Ted declared himself pleased with the result, was proud of his achievement in teaching her to play so well, and said she should be even more proud to be blessed with such a rare talent. 'The Good Lord doesn't give these gifts out lightly. Make proper use of it and prove his faith in you.'

Sometimes she was allowed to play for the bombed-out victims receiving tea and sympathy at the mobile canteen. She would regale them with 'We'll Meet Again', 'Mareseatoats', and her favourite, 'Don't Sit Under the Apple Tree' which was becoming almost like a signature tune. Ted said that folk often made out they were in trouble when really they just wanted to listen to the liquid notes of her music. People round about only had to hear the trumpet start up and the canteen would be full in minutes.

'We'll have to start charging,' Ted joked, 'or we'll have nothing left for the genuine needy.'

'They're all genuinely needy,' Jess would protest. 'Look at the state of their lives, screwed up by the war.'

'Aye well, whether they are or not, you pull your weight in other ways, lass.'

It was certainly true that whenever Harriet or Ted went out selling *The War Cry*, or taking round their collecting boxes to get donations to fund the work they did, they'd ask her to go along with them, just to play. That way they made twice as much money. Jess enjoyed going, not only because she loved playing her trumpet but because it got her out and about, escaping the misery of Cumberland Street for yet another evening. And she got to know a good many interesting characters along the way.

There was Molly. If she'd ever had a surname everyone had long forgotten it, as she was generally called Molly Gaum after the British Gaumont News, because she was such an old gossip. Pat, who was a female bare-knuckle fighter and could take down a grown man with a single punch. People were immensely polite to Pat and she always put a shilling in the collecting tin. 'Just as insurance, in case I ever get knocked senseless and need carrying home.'

'We're the Salvation Army not the St John Ambulance,' Jess laughed.

'For me old age then, or if I should cop it sudden like. Someone has to see I get a decent send-off.'

'You're not ready for promotion to glory yet.'

Playing 'Lili Marlene' in the pubs would be sure to bring a rattle of coins into the collecting tin and Harriet had been known to sell out of *The War Cry* if Jess should play 'Danny Boy', there not being a dry eye in the house.

Jess started to attend the citadel on a regular basis, though to her shame it was again more as a means of escape than genuine belief, at least initially. But to her surprise she found that she enjoyed it. The people were warm and friendly and made her welcome, and she particularly liked the way music was a major part of the service.

'I wouldn't have thought the Sally Army would approve of such music,' Jess said. But Harriet disagreed.

'Very early on, General William Booth who founded the movement said, "Why should the devil have all the best tunes?" and so new words were written to popular numbers. People love a good sing and why shouldn't we worship in a cheerful, happy way?'

They'd sing 'Bless His name, He set me free' to the tune of 'Champagne Charlie' with so much joy and vigour that she would sing at the top of her voice before finally accompanying them on her trusty trumpet while Harriet would bash her tambourine.

But then it wasn't really *her* trumpet at all. It didn't belong to her. It belonged to the Sally Army Bugle Band. Now, more than anything, Jess longed for an instrument of her own. But how to get one, that was the problem? She certainly didn't have any money to spare at the moment. Every penny she earned went towards paying for their keep, both for herself and Lizzie, and saving towards a better future for them both. If there ever was anything left over, which was rare as Bernie was always claiming extra expenses for this, that and the other, it went into the savings tin which she kept tucked under her mattress. This represented her one hope of escape from Cumberland Street and the tyranny of her uncle.

IO

Over supper one evening, Jess happened to casually mention how Mr Simmons had put new locks on his doors since the break-in, and bought a new till which he believed would be safer than the old cash box.

'It feels odd, really strange having to ring things up. It gives receipts and everything but we had a queue a mile long at dinner time because we kept getting in a muddle over it. People were shouting that they'd die of starvation if we didn't hurry up,' Jess related with a giggle.

It had been meant simply as an amusing story but proved to be a bad mistake. Bernie lowered his paper to listen, showing an unhealthy interest in the tale, wanting to know how the till operated, where it was kept and who locked it up. Suddenly it dawned upon Jess that he was asking far too many pertinent questions and she quickly changed the subject, talking instead about a new bread recipe the shop was trying out, which didn't use so much yeast.

'You use some of the old dough to get the new batch going. It's quite clever really, and very economical.' But Bernie wasn't interested in making bread rise, he folded up his paper and quietly slipped out in search of his usual evening pint.

A day or two later, hurrying to get ready to go to the mobile canteen, as she usually did after work, Jess couldn't find her trumpet anywhere.

Sometimes she went for a walk during her dinner break so

she could practise down a back street or by the railway
sidings, any opportunity Jess could find since Bernie made
such a fuss of her practising in the house, nor did she like to
trespass too much on Mrs Simmons' generosity. As she
grew ever more frantic, Jess became aware that Bernie was
watching her closely, almost smiling with satisfaction as he
sat in his chair by the fire, smoking his Craven A cigarettes.
From time to time Cora would cast an anxious glance in her
direction as she ran up and down stairs, pointedly saying
nothing as Jess dragged open drawers and cupboards,
banging them shut again the next minute.

Lizzie, prostrate in the chair opposite, with her eyes half
closed was taking no interest at all. In the end Jess said, 'Oh,
I give up, where did I put that trumpet, Cora? Did I take it
to the shop with me this morning? Have I left it at work?'

But it was Bernie who answered. 'No, I've pawned it.'

Jess stared at her uncle in stunned disbelief. 'You've
what?'

'We've suffered enough of that row, night after night. It's
doing my head in. I've put it in hock where it'll do nobody's
nerves any harm.'

Jess wanted to fly at him, to beat his brains out. Only the
pained anxiety in her aunt's face, and the tremor of her
plump jowls held her back. Cora silently mee-mawed at Jess,
making a pantomime of gestures with her eyes and mouth in
an effort to indicate to her niece that she shouldn't worry,
that they'd get it back in due course. Bernie spotted the performance and lashing out one hand, gave his wife a clout
across the back of her head. Curlers flew everywhere and her
cheeks went bright red but Cora made scarcely a sound by
way of protest.

Jess was instantly enraged on her behalf and leapt in front
of him, as if to protect her from further reprisals, hands
clenched into tight little fists. 'Don't you dare hit me aunt,

you big bully. I don't care if you have nicked the trumpet, but don't take it out on Cora.'

This only made him laugh all the more. 'Oh yes you do care about that trumpet. You never stop blasting us eardrums with it. Drove me bleeding crackers.'

'Well then *you* can explain to the Sally Army where it's gone, not me.'

Bernie got lazily to his feet, flexing and swelling out his ample flesh so that she was forced to take a quick step backwards or be knocked over as he moved threateningly towards her. 'I don't think so, girl, and if you bring it into this house again, I'll hammer it flat so that it'll be no more use to you than a squashed tin of beans.'

'You can't do that! You've no right. That trumpet belongs to the Salvation Army. What will Sergeant Ted say when I tell him? Oh, how can I ever repay them for losing one of their best instruments? How could you be so mean?' Jess could feel tears blocking her throat, a swell of pain in her chest. She should never have brought it home, never. What had she been thinking of?

Lizzie was sitting up now, her anxious, befuddled gaze flicking from one to other as if trying to follow events and understand what was going on. 'Don't you talk to our Bernie like that, madam. Show some gratitude for what he's done for us.'

Determined not to dissolve into tears, Jess turned on her mother. 'Gratitude? Huh! You must be joking! We owe him nothing. Nowt! He's ruined you already, and will do the same to me if I let him, the mean old . . .'

'Shurrup Jess, you owe him everything, and don't you forget it. Where would we be if he'd refused to put a roof over us head?'

'We wouldn't have lost the roof we did have if he hadn't taken you shop-lifting that Christmas.'

Lizzie was on her feet now, swaying slightly as if she'd been drinking, though she'd promised Jess faithfully that she'd never touch another drop as long as she lived. Some hope. Her eyes were flashing and her voice filled with spite. 'If I'd never had you in the first place, I wouldn't have needed to pinch stuff. I'd've been in clover, nowt to worry about at all.'

Jess felt as if she'd been punched in the face by her own mother. Why did Lizzie *always* have to turn nasty? Why couldn't she take her side for once, defend her own daughter instead of her brother-in-law? But then Jess knew why, only too well. Her mother was lacking in that normal part of human nature known as nurturing, which parents were supposed to exhibit towards their young. She didn't have it because Bernie had corrupted her with his own brand of greed and self-interest. Instead, Lizzie was the one needing to be watched over with love and care, to protect her from his evil influence.

Cora was wringing her hands, trying to put in the odd soothing word in a frantic attempt to offer comfort and cool growing tempers. 'Don't fret about it, love. Don't worry. We'll get that trumpet back somehow.'

But Jess was beyond comfort. She'd done her best not to be a nuisance, worked hard to pay for their keep while her mother lay about half the day, or prowled around shops running the risk of being arrested for shop-lifting yet again. She was filled with guilt and remorse for having brought the instrument home in the first place, frightened of admitting to her new friends at the Sally Army what had happened to it. And most dreadful of all, how on earth could she ever afford to replace it when she was saving so hard for a place of their own. Would she never be free?

Jess felt such hatred for her uncle that she simply couldn't contain her emotion. Tears were brimming over, rolling unchecked down her cheeks and it was just as if a great weight were pressing down on her chest, threatening to crush her.

'This is all your fault,' she yelled at him. 'You've ruined all our lives.'

Bernie hitched up his trousers with the thick elastic of his braces and ambled over to her. Everyone in the small, over-heated room seemed to hold their breath and although it was plain what was going to happen next, Jess stood transfixed as she watched the fist come towards her in what seemed like an endless slow motion.

It hit her full in the chest, sending her flying so that she fell so hard against the chair upon which Lizzie had earlier been sitting, that it tipped over backwards. Jess cracked her head on the sideboard and fell in a crumpled heap, one foot twisted awkwardly beneath her. Pain shot through her but she wasn't even blessed with oblivion as the room spun dizzily about her. There was something wet and sticky on her face, which she took to be blood and she could hear Cora crying, Lizzie telling her to hold her noise and didn't she realise she was only upsetting Bernie by her caterwauling.

The next instant he was standing over her, a smile on his face that could only have come from the devil himself and, for the first time, Jess felt real fear. 'Don't cross me girl. I don't like it.' Then he carefully hitched up his immaculate trousers and hunkered down beside her, pushing his face so close to hers she could smell his stinking breath, the result of too much tobacco and whisky, and days of unscrubbed teeth. 'When I ask for details, I expect to get them. Understand? This evening you'll have the details for me of the location of the new till Mr Simmons has thoughtfully provided, and where he keeps the key for it. Also, the likely day when there'll be most money in it, that is not on pay day or the day he goes to the bank. Is that clear?'

Jess somehow managed to nod because she didn't have the strength to do anything else. Satisfied that he'd at last brought his niece to heel, Bernie quietly left the room, leaving the door wide open behind him.

The moment he'd gone, Cora gathered Jess in her arms, patting and checking every part of her as she smoothed away her tears with podgy, kindly fingers. 'There, there, does this hurt? How about here? Nay, I reckon you'll live. Come and sit by t'fire while I mop that blood from yer head. It looks worse than it is but you're shivering with shock. Hutch up, Lizzie, for God's sake. She's your lass, not mine, blast you, and thee should be doing this, you great gormless trollop.'

When she was sufficiently satisfied with the state of her patient to leave her for a second, Cora ladled out steaming hot stew into a dish for Jess, as ever believing that healing depended on a good supply of food. 'Daft bugger. He's in a paddy over summat. Them big lads of ours, I shouldn't wonder. When he comes home again lass, don't you mention what's gone on here just now, and neither will he. It's by far the best way. And he'll not mek you do owt you don't want to, I'll see to that.'

Brave words which neither of them believed for a moment. As both Jess and Cora knew well enough, if Bernie said something must happen, it generally did.

'How can you live like this, Cora, always afraid to mention this, that or the other? Terrified to do anything he might not like.'

Cora glanced about her, as if desperately seeking an answer although she knew one didn't exist, then rested her gaze fondly on Sam and Seb. Completely absorbed in each other, as always, the twins appeared oblivious to everything going on around them. Harry and Bert had long since downed their supper and gone out on their demolition work or whatever they did with their time. Tommy and Sandra were in the back scullery arguing fiercely over who should wash up. If they'd heard the din above their own quarrel they'd learned not to interfere in scraps between adults. Cora said, 'Nay, I live with it because I must. I might as well make crutches for lame ducks as argue wi' that husband of mine. He dun't listen to no one, not me, not yer daft mother here. No one. And don't you try argifying with him neither. *Sandra*! Are you going to stand there all day wi' that dish cloth in yer hand or do summat useful with it?'

Jess valiantly struggled to eat half the stew then pushed it to one side, her appetite gone. What did she have left without her trumpet? How could she live without getting out? Silently, she vowed to make her escape from Cumberland Street just as soon as humanly possible.

The next morning, on her way to the shop, Bernie suddenly jumped out in front of her, just as she was walking along Cumberland Street towards Deansgate. It gave Jess such a shock that she stopped in her tracks, hand pressed to her chest, breathing hard. Nervous of inflaming his temper yet again, she remembered Cora's advice and kept silent, waiting to see what he wanted this time, though she could guess. She'd avoided his return the previous night by going to bed early but if he thought she was cowed by his bullying, he'd another think coming. Nothing would induce her to betray the Simmonses.

'I wanted to catch you afore you went off to work. I have it in mind that you didn't quite catch my drift of what it is I want from you, so I thought it best if I explain it again, nice and calm like, with no tantrums nor tears. All right by you, Poppet?'

Jess felt a chill run down her spine. Never had he used endearments towards her before. What did it mean?

Nothing good that she could think of. 'I understand perfectly what you want and as I've already told you, I can't provide any information at all about the new till. I really don't think there's anything more to be said on the matter.' She made to move past him but he blocked her way.

'Oh aye, you really don't, do you? La-di-dah all of a sudden, aren't we? Fact is, I'm not sure if you appreciate how things have been a bit tight lately, what with the war, and yer mam not being fit to work. So the truth is, I need you to contribute a bit more towards your keep.'

Jess was appalled. She already paid him a pound a week for herself and her mother, plus extras towards rent and other household bills Cora never quite seemed able to manage. 'I pay my whack. You know I can't afford to pay any more than I already do. I'm saving up for a place of us own. Anyroad, you should be helping us to do that. It's as much your responsibility as mine that Mam is in the state she is. You owe it to her, and to me, to help get her back on her feet.'

His face was as hard and cold as polished steel but his voice remained soft and wheedling. 'That's what I'm saying, luv. You do me a few favours and I'll see what I can do to help thee.' He rested one massive hand on the wall above her head as he leaned closer, thus bringing the stink of his breath to her nostrils yet again and Jess almost threw up when he started to scratch his crotch right there in front of her. What an unpleasant, despicable man he was, surely the very worst uncle a girl could possibly have.

Bernie was thinking how bonny she looked with her cheeks all flushed and her hair tied back with that baby blue ribbon. What a pity it was that they were related. How much did that matter? He weren't her dad, after all. And he'd know how to bring her in line then and take great pleasure in the doing of it. He scratched himself again as he became excited by the prospect. 'Nice young lass like you should be able to think of some way to please a chap.'

'I don't know what you mean, but if you don't let me go soon, I'll be late for work, and what good will that do either of us if I get the sack. I won't be able to pay you anything then.'

'Just one more minute, Poppet, it'll not take long. Point is, I were thinking about this reluctance of yours to give me information on this new till at Simmons's and I thought mebbe I could understand your point of view.'

Jess swallowed but said nothing, knowing she was right to be cautious.

'So instead, I thought happen you could take advantage without anybody noticing like. I mean, nobody's quite got the hang of it, have they? So I thought, instead of ringing up the exact sum, tha could happen ring up less and pocket the difference.'

Jess didn't think she could have heard him right but, apparently, she had. 'Never! You must think I'm daft.'

He smiled at her, pleased to have got a response, however negative. 'It's quite simple. If the customer spends half a crown, thee only rings up two bob and tha puts the rest in yer pocket. A few extra sixpences here and there'll add up to a tidy sum by the end of the month. Don't overdo it, mind. Be canny.'

Jess was aghast by the suggestion. 'But that's stealing!'

'Nay, think of it as a bonus on thee wages. One tha deserves for working so hard.'

'It's not a bonus, it's theft. And why on earth would I steal from Mr Simmons? He's never done me any harm. In fact he's been kindness itself.' She didn't say how he'd started unlocking the door even earlier in a morning now that summer was changing into autumn and it was so often cold or wet. How he let her warm herself in the bakery before giving her any jobs to do and, having one morning noticed the size of her breakfast, had insisted Robert give her a buttered bap from the bakery, sometimes with a bit of fried Spam to go with it. 'What do you think I am?'

'A chip off the old block.'

Jess bridled with hot fury. How dare he presume to make such a comparison? 'Just because me mam were stupid enough to do everything you told her and landed herself in jail as a result, doesn't mean that I'm as soft in the head as she is. I'm nothing like Lizzie. Anyroad, even she only stole that one time because you made her.'

Bernie laughed. 'One time? Is that what you think? Shows how little you know yer own mother.'

Some instinct told Jess that perhaps he could be right there, that Lizzie might have gone in for more petty thieving than she'd admitted to, so she shifted to another tack. 'Mr Simmons would soon spot that the money in the till didn't match what had gone off the shelves.'

'He wouldn't suspect a thing, not if you do as I say and don't ring up the full amount. And even if he did get suspicious, he'd put it down to problems with you numbskulls learning how to operate the new machine. There'd be no danger of your getting caught, or anyone suspecting you of doing owt wrong, not with that angelic face of yours, and those big brown innocent eyes. And if you think Lizzie has mended her ways then you must be soft in the head. She's still at it, even now, and she'll not listen to reason. If you don't want her back inside, it's up to thee to stop her. Who knows what might happen, otherwise?'

'Is that a threat?'

'Let's call it a timely warning.'

Jess felt a small panic start up inside. What was he suggesting? Had Lizzie really started stealing again? Surely even her trollop of a mother wouldn't be so stupid. 'You know I don't want her back in jail. Nor do I want to land in there myself, ta very much.'

He stroked a finger down her cheek, making her shudder with revulsion. 'Tha's a bonny lass, and as well as being prettier than yer ma, tha's much more intelligent, so thee has the good sense not to get caught. Just remember, I can't afford to bankroll the pair of you any longer, so tha'll have to pay her whack as well as yer own, one way or t'other.'

Jess was shaking in every limb, trembling with fear of him, yet determined not to become a victim, like her mam. 'I'll not do it. One thief in the family is enough, in my family anyroad. Yours seems to have any number.'

He flipped out a hand and clouted her across the side of her head, sending her staggering with the weight of the blow. 'Watch that glib mouth of yours, girl.'

'And you watch that fist of yours,' Jess shouted back, eyes filling with hot tears. 'Don't think you can bully me, because you can't. I've told you, *I'm not me mam*!'

He grabbed her by the shoulders then and shook her so violently that it made her head rock backwards and forwards on her slender neck. She could smell the sweet-sour stink of stale sweat on him and, screwing up her nose in distaste, Jess tried to pull away but he had too firm a grip. The pressure of his bloated stomach trapping her against the wall made her cringe with loathing, his smile one that chilled her to the bone. He was still talking and, senses reeling, she knew she must listen. '. . . so we need to come to some mutually beneficial arrangement, then yer trumpet might magically reappear. Who knows? You fetch a few sixpences, or better still, pound notes, home from that shop and I'll get that blasted instrument out of hock for you, so long as you play it outside and not in the bleedin' house. How would that be, eh? I can't say fairer than that, now can I?'

'Never!' Jess said, almost spitting in his face.

His face darkened. 'You're our Jake all over again, you. He allus had to argue the whole damned time. Nothing were ever good enough for him. Never would do as he were told.'

'If you mean that I speak my mind, yes I do, and always will. And I intend to remain honest like me dad too. I'd rather replace a hundred trumpets you steal from the Salvation Army, than give in to your nasty threats.'

Placing his mouth close against her ear, his voice dropped to a hoarse whisper. 'Look at it this way girl, it's yer mam who would benefit. If you want to keep her safe, do as I say or you'll live to regret it. If'n you refuse, I'll make you sorrier than you can imagine. I'm a patient man, but I wouldn't recommend you push me too far. Who knows what I might be forced to do.'

If she'd felt a prick of fear before, now she was paralysed by it. It drained her of all energy, making her feel limp and helpless in his massive hands. Aware suddenly of her own fragile vulnerability, Jess felt as impotent as a fly caught in a giant's fist. He could snuff her out without a second thought. Or could he? Much as he might want to, he needed her. As he said himself, Lizzie was useless, and Jess sensed in Harry and Bert the start of a quiet rebellion. They were tired of dancing to his tune and wanted to make their own way in the world. And if she let him get away with bullying her as he had Lizzie and Cora, then she was lost too. In the few seconds it took her to think this through, Jess resolved that she wouldn't allow it to happen. She lifted her chin and, looking him straight in the eye, managed to dampen down her fear sufficiently to have her say.

'Do your worst, I'm not scared of you, great bully that you are. I'm saving for a decent future for me and me mam, so don't think you can force me to do anything wrong or against the law, because you can't. I'll never give in. *Never*!'

Momentarily startled, either by her bravery or her cheek,

his hands loosened their grip, which gave Jess the chance to wrench herself free of his grasp. She swung away from him to march away up the street, head held high. And then a bark of laughter rang out. 'That's what you think girl. That's what you think.'

The sound of his raucous laughter followed her every step of the way.

11

'Buy your own trumpet and keep it well hidden from your uncle,' Leah urged Jess, as if the solution were simple.

'How? Do you know how much trumpets cost? And where could I possibly put it to keep it safely away from his grasping fingers?' Jess had made no mention to her friend about the real reason for her uncle pawning the trumpet: his insistence that she should steal from Leah's own father. It didn't seem quite appropriate, and if Mr Simmons ever got wind of it, might well result in Jess losing her job.

They were sitting on a couple of chairs in a corner of the dance hall sipping lemonade as they exchanged confidences. On this occasion they were at the Harpurhey Baths Ballroom on Rochdale Road with strict instructions not to miss the bus and be home by ten. They'd got into the regular habit of Jess always staying over at the Simmonses' house on the nights they went dancing. There were a lot of air force trainees around tonight who were stationed at Heaton Park so, as usual, neither of them had been short of partners. At that moment an airman asked Jess for a dance and, remembering Mrs Simmons's advice, she politely accepted although she was far more concerned about what to do about the loss of her trumpet and had to concentrate hard to give the young man her full attention. It was a quickstep and he didn't start off too well as he immediately trod on her foot, then let his hand slide down to her bottom as he pretended to lose his balance.

'Sorry about that. Quite a crush here tonight.'

'That's all right,' Jess said, placing his hand back on her waist.

As they danced, she scoured every face in the band as she always did, and was disappointed not to see one that she recognised. There were two trumpets, one bass, three saxes and a trombone, plus a pianist and drummer. They were good, putting lots of energy into the music but Steve Wyman was not amongst them. She became absorbed watching the trumpet players, checking their fingerwork as they played her favourite, 'Don't Sit Under the Apple Tree'.

'Am I boring you?' her partner asked, rather rudely Jess thought even as her cheeks coloured slightly with shame over her inattention. His hand felt hot and sweaty on her back, in fact it was edging around to the front, creeping up her rib-cage and Jess began to feel acutely uncomfortable. He was pushing her round in a dizzying whirl, and had again trodden on her feet a couple of times. He must be the clumsiest dancer on the floor and she couldn't help but compare him with Steve, wondering where he was playing these days.

Leah shimmied past in the arms of a sailor. 'You could always store it at our place.'

'What? Oh, absolutely not. I don't . . .'

'Accept charity, I know. What are friends for?'

'Excuse me,' said the airman, his probing fingers now squeezing the curve of her breast. 'Are you with her or me?'

'Her,' Jess said, and walked off the floor.

Jess decided that she really wasn't in the mood for dancing tonight and spent the remainder of the evening hiding away in the cloakroom, chewing over her problem. What could she do? She didn't want to give up her trumpet lessons, nor her work with the Sally Army, but she was going to have to explain to Sergeant Ted that she'd lost the instrument, somehow without creating even more problems. The last

thing she wanted was for the sergeant to come and tackle
Uncle Bernie, because she knew who would come off the
worst in any confrontation. Oh, why did Uncle Bernie have
to spoil everything for her?

Later, as they changed their shoes and collected their coats
and bags, Leah saw that her friend was still troubled and tried
to offer some comfort. 'He'll have taken it to Mr Yoffey's
pawnshop. Why don't we at least go and talk to him? We may
be able to negotiate a deal. The dear man has a heart of gold
and may let you have the trumpet back without paying a
penny.'

Jess didn't believe this to be at all likely, not for a moment,
but went along with the plan anyway. What did she have to
lose?

Abe Yoffey considered the two girls very seriously from
behind his owlish spectacles for a long time in contemplative
silence. He liked young people, having served as Treasurer
for some years in the Manchester Young Zionist Society,
now sadly in abeyance. On the other hand, he was of the
opinion that the role of the female of the species was best
confined to the home front, to nurturing, and to providing
refreshments for functions at the synagogue or, in their case,
the citadel. Playing the piano, as Miss Leah was known to do
was one thing, wanting to play a trumpet seemed to be quite
another entirely. What was the world coming to? Dear, dear,
dear. Girls were even driving trams these days. Yet he liked
to think of himself as having a generous nature, and was not
one of the narrow-minded breed who so blighted every
religion, including his own. Perhaps prejudice against
women was equally as bad.

Prejudice. He should be guilty of such a thing?

He woke every morning in a cold sweat, waiting for the
knock on his door which would bring incarceration. Early in

the war, May 1940 to be exact, most of his friends had been taken away to be interned as aliens for the duration simply because they were Jews. For some reason, perhaps because of his age, eighty-nine next birthday, and the fact that he was well liked: a childless widower who had lived in Manchester for most of his life and whose family was all dead and gone, had saved him. Abe suffered the occasional brick thrown through his window but he could live with that. He desperately longed to stay in his own home and, for now at least, a blind eye had been turned and he remained unmolested. But he had little hope of it lasting. It would be his turn next. Being a Jew anywhere, even in Britain, wasn't a good thing to be right now.

He gave an expressive shrug. 'You want for me to give you a trumpet? I'm so old and foolish I would give something away for nothing?'

'But it would only sit in the back of your shop otherwise, wouldn't it, dear Mr Yoffey?' Leah artfully pointed out.

'For ever, I should think. Don't I get better ones through my doors every day of the week?'

'Then I'm sure you wouldn't mind letting it go.'

'My uncle had no right to hock it. It didn't even belong to him, but to the Salvation Army.'

'You say that you have no money?' He lifted up his hands in a helpless gesture.

Leah wasn't for giving up. 'You could think of it as a sort of loan.'

'It's a lending library for instruments I am now? You would take advantage of an old man, a fine young girl like you, from a good home? Am I not poor enough that I live on Bismark Herrings morning, noon and night? Worn out with too much work and this endless war. Do I not deserve a rest already?'

Jess giggled. It wasn't quite polite to do so in the circumstances, but she couldn't help herself. Even as the old man was bitterly complaining and flourishing his hands about with an air of outraged disbelief, the eyes behind the spectacles were glimmering with laughter and mischief as if they were saying, I'll have some fun with these two girls before I give them what they want. 'I would take good care of it,' Jess promised in the smallest of voices.

Mr Yoffey frowned. He liked Jess Delaney although he didn't much care for the rest of the breed. And he had no quarrel at all with the Salvation Army. Sadly though, on this occasion he was unable to help. He carefully explained how he'd refused to accept the trumpet from her uncle, not believing his reassurance that it was honestly come by. 'Is it my fault that people underestimate my intelligence? I told him to put it back where he found it. He was not pleased.'

'No, he wouldn't be.'

Mr Yoffey saw the bleak expression of pain come into the soft brown eyes and almost wished that on this occasion he'd been less particular. There was something about the way she tipped down her head and allowed that wild mane of shining hair to shield her disappointment from pity that cut to the heart of him. He knew instinctively that she had suffered, could sense her courage, in every line of her too slender, young body. 'I suppose it's a musician you think you are?'

Jess gave a little shrug, still not meeting his gaze as she addressed the tattered linoleum beneath her feet. I'm trying to learn, but it isn't easy.'

'Play for him,' Leah suggested, suddenly seeing a way of winning the old man over. 'Go on, give him a tune.'

'He's just told us, Leah. He doesn't have the trumpet. Weren't you listening?'

Leah put her arm about her friend's shoulders and gave her a little squeeze as if telling her to have heart, before rewarding the old pawnbroker with her most dazzling, blue-eyed smile. 'I'll bet he doesn't know half what he's got in that cavern behind his shop. There could well be any number of trumpets back there, if he looked hard enough.'

He returned their conjoined gaze for several seconds without saying a word, and then turning on his heel, disappeared into the dark recesses of his shop. He was gone for some time, so long that the two girls grew curious and edged further into its depths, examining the weird and wonderful treasures within. A moth-eaten stuffed fox; a tarnished silver tea pot; a Victorian pianoforte complete with candelabra; a bridal wreath beneath a glass bell jar; several pairs of clogs, boots and shoes; hats, coats and dresses by the score and any number of boxes all bearing carefully printed labels to identify their contents.

Finally, he emerged out of the gloom, trumpet in hand: a shiny, graceful instrument which had clearly been properly cared for over the years, and well loved by its previous owner. Jess wondered if it had hurt very much to be forced to pawn such a wonderful item, but then forgot to worry about this unknown stranger, whoever he was, as old Mr Yoffey handed over the instrument with a reverence which seemed to indicate he'd been anxious to hear her play all along, if only she could be persuaded.

Jess gave the trumpet a quick glance over, checking all its working parts, the valves, the mouthpiece, testing the feel of it in her hands. When she felt comfortable with it, she put it to her lips and began to play. She chose 'Goodnight Sweetheart' and she could hear Leah humming softly beside her, see Mr Yoffey nodding his head in time to the beat. When she was done, the old man took off his spectacles and dabbed at his eyes with his polishing cloth, before giving his spectacles a furious wipe and setting them back on the bridge of his nose. 'So I'm a fool to myself. It has cluttered up my shop for long enough. You take it, and do what you can with it.'

Jess stared at the instrument in her hand in a daze of disbelief. 'But I honestly don't have any money to pay for it.'

He lifted his two hands in a gesture of defeat. 'I live till I'm ninety, you pay me then. I'll be hearing plenty trumpets soon enough after that anyway. But see you make good music, and don't let that uncle of yours anywhere near it.' Then he flapped his hand for her to take it away quickly before he changed his mind.

Nineteen forty-one ended in a mood of bleak austerity and the first months of nineteen forty-two seemed little better. Rationing, queues, make-do-and-mend became common practice. Cora sorted salvage into four different buckets which she kept out in the backyard: scrap metal, paper, waste food, though there was never much of that left, and one for old bones to make glue of all things. Seemed to think she could build a warplane single handed with the stuff. She nagged her family constantly to switch off the light, and spent a lot of time listening to the *The Radio Doctor*, learning which foods were good for them, and how to cook lentil roast and the dreaded Woolton Pie. 'Those who have the will to win, Cook potatoes in their skin.'

Bernie reckoned nothing to such tasteless fare. He liked his meat, his bacon and eggs, and his potatoes fried, and made sure he had the wherewithal in the way of extra points, to provide these necessities for his comfort.

Nor did he subscribe to the theory that folk should be limited to one complete set of new clothing a year. The government could devise whatever schemes they liked, using poorer materials, cutting down on turn-ups and pockets, telling folk to buy a size larger so it'll last longer. Utility they called it. Bernie didn't care for that scheme either. He agreed with Churchill for once, that 'stripping the people to the buff' was not a good thing to do. A man of substance, such as himself, deserved a bit of style. He was going up in the world, come what may, war or no war, points or no points.

Even petrol coupons were losing their value. The government had insisted you couldn't use a car unless it was for essential war purposes. With a tin box stuffed full of petrol coupons, Bernie's profits had consequently taken a nose-dive. Yet another blow to his economy. Some folk cheated, of course, and pretended to be on essential business when they weren't but most abided by the rules, much to his disgust. It was downright inconsiderate of them to be so flaming honest, and for the powers-that-be to keep changing the rules. How could a chap hope to make a decent living under such conditions?

Fortunately it wasn't Bernie's policy to follow orders, keep to rules or meekly do as the government ordered. Nor did he feel inclined to stand by and do nothing while his sons took over, or else in no time at all they'd be the ones ruling the roost.

Even that flaming niece of his was puffing herself up, quite above her station, earning more money than any young woman had a right to, off dancing twice a week and even doing her bit with the Sally Army. He thought he'd spiked her guns over that flaming trumpet but damned if she hadn't got herself another which she kept hidden some place he couldn't fathom. And she still hadn't brought him any cash home from that blasted tea room.

She needed bringing into line, that was for sure, but first of all he had to get his hands on a bit more brass, not just a few trinkets here and there or the odd ration book but something more substantial, enough to turn his life around completely. He had to hand it to them lads of his for sowing the seeds of the idea, but he reckoned he could do better. He carefully made his plans then waited for an opportunity to put them into effect. He'd show 'em who was top dog. And once he was nicely placed with a little nest-egg stowed away, then he'd tackle that little madam once and for all.

Jess called again on Mr Yoffey and the old man was delighted to see her. 'Ah, so you like coming to my shop, of your own free will? Ay, ay, ay, normally I have to do a lot of *shlepping*, which is how we Jews explain coaxing people in off the street by dragging them in by the scruffs of their collar.'

Jess giggled, 'I don't believe you have to do that at all.'

He gave one of his expressive shrugs and chuckled. 'Folk come to me because they must. They need to eat more than they need fancy suits, as do we all.'

She explained that she'd wanted to let him know how she was getting along with the trumpet he'd loaned her, and to prove she was taking care of it by keeping it in good condition. Pushing back a tangle of dark hair she cast him a sidelong glance. 'I wondered if perhaps I could pay you a little each week. I think I can manage, now that I'm making good money in tips. Then it truly would be mine one day.' Her big brown eyes looked so beseeching that, utterly captivated by her charm, he instantly agreed.

'Can I resist such limpid beauty when you use such powerful blackmail?'

On impulse, Jess gave the old man a hug. 'You are wonderful and it isn't blackmail at all. I just want to do the right thing, to pay you what the trumpet is worth.'

'It is worth nothing at the back of my shop. Besides, a *shnorrer* you are not.'

'What on earth is a *shnorrer*?'

Abe waved his hands about and made a little poofing noise by blowing out his cheeks. 'She does not know what is a *shnorrer*? It is a beggar, or as you Lancashire folk say, someone always on the scrounge. A cadger. I think you are not one of those, little one. You are pure gold, and when you play that trumpet it too turns from base metal into something magical. Besides, am I a selfish old man? I should be the one to deny the world the benefit of your talent?'

'Then you'll agree to let me pay for the trumpet?'

His eyes were twinkling. 'I agree only because you will have to call in my shop every week to make the payment and I can enjoy your company. Perhaps you would do me the honour of taking tea with me sometimes.'

'I would be delighted.'

He bowed in gratitude, like the gentleman he was. 'I shall look forward to it with pleasure.'

Taking tea with Mr Yoffey became a regular feature of her week. Jess would call every Friday evening after she'd got paid and hand over a shilling, sometimes a florin or a half crown if her tips had been good ones, which he would enter with meticulous care into a large ledger. After that, he would brew a pot of tea and they would sit in the back of the shop, Mr Yoffey with his cat on his knee, nodding wisely, interrupting only rarely as she told him about her week, about the kind of customers who came into the tea room. There were the ones who sent back the toasted tea cake because they said it was too dry or too cold when really it was perfectly acceptable; or always asked for a small tea pot for four persons and extra hot water so that it didn't cost quite so much. Or ate several cakes off the stand and then expected them to be included in the price of the standard afternoon tea they'd also consumed.

How Mr Yoffey loved to listen to her chatter.

'People are an endless source of entertainment, I think,' he agreed. When she finally stopped talking long enough to draw breath, she would accept the bagel he offered her. One particular evening Mr Yoffey said to her, 'Your trumpet practice, it is going well? You have the instrument with you? I know you wouldn't think to play it for a weary old man?'

'Of course I would.' Jess slid it out of its case, put it to her lips and began to play *Joy, freedom, peace and ceaseless blessing* to the tune of 'Swanee River'. It was a haunting melody and one she played often in the Citadel.

She'd barely played a couple of bars when the door burst open and a young man strode in. He stood stock still in the middle of the shop, glaring at her with red hot fury in his eyes.

'What the *hell* do you think you're doing with my trumpet?'

Unable to believe her eyes, Jess stared at the intruder in dawning horror. It was him. After all this time, *she'd found him at last*! But before she could gather her thoughts, Mr Yoffey stepped in front of her, redirecting the intruder's attention away from his young protégé.

'Young man, you cannot charge into my shop like a bull in the proverbial china shop and claim ownership of my property.'

'That trumpet is *my* property. I've come to redeem it.'

'Too late. Too late.' Mr Yoffey said, tutting sadly and shaking his head. 'More than a year it has sat collecting dust on my shelves. I am supposed to give it house room for ever, till you decide you might like it back?'

'Yes, dammit, that's the whole point of pawning something, isn't it?'

The old man shook his head with vigour. 'Ay, ay, ay, you think I run a charity here? You take my money. You leave your trumpet. You come back within the time it states on the ticket and pay the full amount, plus interest, you understand? Then I think you get it back. You are showing me your ticket? You are telling me you are within the time permitted?'

Had he not been scowling quite so disagreeably Jess might well have reminded him that they'd met before. But she dismissed the idea as dangerous folly. His mouth was compressed into a tight line of fury and the green eyes were blazing. Perhaps her memory had played tricks, or she'd been mistaken to think him attractive on that first occasion. It must have been the magical atmosphere of the ballroom that had gone to her head for she really couldn't find anything to like about him at all now. The collar of his blue shirt was white and the necktie all askew. Neither matched the brown suit he wore which was shabby to the point of threadbare, although to be fair, whose wasn't these days? When he'd first entered the shop he'd been carrying a small brown suitcase fastened with a leather strap, together with the sort of case which would hold a musical instrument, only something larger than a trumpet. Jess wondered what it might be. He'd placed them both on the floor and dropped a shabby trilby hat on top, that had also seen better days.

Finally Jess found her voice. 'This is your trumpet? I thought . . .'

Ignoring her completely, he suddenly began searching his many pockets, pulling out a fistful of coins and notes and slamming them on the counter. 'There you are and no, I don't have your damned ticket. I haven't a clue how long you allowed me to redeem it but here's my cash. Every penny I possess. Take it. Take it all. Just hand over that trumpet.'

'It belongs to this young lady now. She has paid for it.'

He cast scarcely a glance in Jess's direction. 'Don't talk rubbish. It's mine and I want it back this minute.'

Jess was watching and listening to all of this in stunned silence, uncertain what to say or do next. A part of her was thrilled to have found him again, while her heart was sinking over the circumstances which had brought them together. This was *his* trumpet? This precious instrument which she'd hoped would replace the one Bernie had stolen from her and disposed of she knew not how. Jess felt devastated, had never felt so uncomfortable and embarrassed in all her life. What on earth could she do? She certainly couldn't keep it, not if it still rightfully belonged to Steve Wyman.

And yet she'd already made several payments on it, had endured a long and uncomfortable half-hour explaining the whole sorry tale to Sergeant Ted who, finally, and very generously, had agreed to let the matter lie, saying it might well turn up one day, when her uncle was in a more generous mood. Was it any wonder if a part of her had no wish to meekly hand over the instrument, particularly since he was being so objectionable towards poor Mr Yoffey.

The old man was gathering up all the loose change into his hand, collecting and folding the notes. Putting them safely in an old brown envelope, he handed it back solemnly. 'The trumpet is no longer available. You are too late. As I have already explained, this young lady here has made several payments against it, and is now legally the new owner.'

The young man swung around, at last fixing his penetrating green-eyed glare exclusively upon Jess. 'I'm sure you think you've won,' he growled, 'but I'm damned if I'll let you get away with it.' And upon these words he swung on his heel and strode out of the shop.

Jess found she was trembling so much that she had to sit down rather quickly. What did he mean by that? Won what, the trumpet? 'Why did he say that, Mr Yoffey, about not allowing me to get away with it? I really don't want any trouble or unpleasantness.'

'Unpleasant that young man certainly is. Too big for his britches I think. He does not deserve so remarkable an instrument. Drink your tea, little one. Will we worry about him?' And for once in his life Mr Yoffey answered his own question. 'I do not think so.'

12

After a long period of quiet the day finally dawned when the skies were again filled with enemy bombers and Bernie knew his chance had come. He left Cora sitting under the stairs in the tin bath with Seb and Sam on her lap, Sandra squashed in beside her, which, for some reason, she'd decided was far safer than sitting in the Anderson with Lizzie and Jess. Women, he would never understand them. Then he donned the bogus ARP Warden's uniform he'd managed to acquire and went off trawling the streets, quite certain he'd find some likely pickings. There was the usual initial panic when people found they couldn't get home because craters had suddenly appeared in roads previously undamaged. They ran about, frantically calling for their loved ones, desperately searching for another way to reach them. Bernie would urge them to go to a shelter, like the diligent warden he was making himself out to be. He caught one woman running right back into the line of fire towards a blazing warehouse.

'Here, hold on, where you off to, missus?'

'I've got to go back for me insurance policies. I forgot to bring them with me. Me husband will kill me.'

'Not before Hitler's bombs kill you first. You'll be buried with them policies if you don't watch out. Get along into the shelter now.'

Oddly enough he felt as if he'd saved her life and began to see himself as a hero; next helping one old woman, complete with parrot in a cage, down into the shelter. He didn't feel in any great danger himself out in the open like this. Bernie saw himself as indestructible and was almost revelling in the excitement of it all: the massive explosions like giant fireworks, walls tumbling before his very eyes, even the screams that came from the less fortunate making him feel brave and powerful.

Besides, it was common knowledge that plenty had been killed outright in their own cellars, so nowhere was truly safe, not in this war.

But he still had his bit of business to attend to so, not wishing to have his disguise tested, he slipped away down a back alley. Nobody saw him go. The air was thick with dust; the smell and taste of fear and death almost tangible. And the streets seemed to be piled high with stuff: abandoned bicycles, chairs, tables, clocks and clothing spilling out of rooms ripped open to the four winds, like doll's houses with the fronts lifted off. He even found a fur coat in one garden, a bit moth-eaten but likely to fetch a few quid. Bernie helped himself, filling the handcart he'd brought with him and trundling his booty back to Cumberland Street. This would be the easiest money he'd ever made.

'Here, what am I supposed to do with this lot?' Cora wanted to know. 'Haven't we got enough lumber?' indicating the accumulated pile of junk that already took up half the backyard.

'Throw a tarpaulin over it. Put it in the Anderson shelter. Owt you like only keep it safe till I have time to dispose of it. It'll only arouse suspicion if I do it too quickly.'

'Oh aye, everything must be kept safe, everything 'cept yer wife.'

He flung out one hand and smacked her across the face. 'Shut yer mouth, woman. When I want your opinion, I'll ask fer it.' Seb and Sam, seeing their mother so abused, opened their twin mouths and let out a loud wail of protest. 'And shut them brats up an' all.'

He stormed off in a fury, banging the backyard door after him so hard, it rocked on its hinges. Cora took what satisfaction she could from how daft he looked in the tin helmet and ARP overalls, both of them several sizes too small for his substantial girth. Happen Jess was right and she was daft to put up with such treatment. Surely she deserved better? Then she bent to comfort her children. 'It's all right, Mam's not really hurt. Come on me little loves, how about a chip butty?' and she gathered her children to her bosom and carried them indoors.

When Jess came home she did a double-take the minute she clapped eyes on her aunt. 'What have you done to your face, Cora?'

'I walked into t'pantry door, didn't I? Never look where I'm going, me.'

Jess opened her mouth to express her disbelief at this tale, then spotted the wide, frightened eyes of the twins and thought better of it. 'Put yer feet up then, I'll make a brew.'

'Eeh, tha's a good lass.'

As she handed her the cup she hissed under her breath, 'You don't have to put up with this, you know. Tell him you'll leave him if he ever hits you again. Tell him you'll not be used as a punchbag.'

Cora gave her a blank look. 'I don't know what yer talking about luv. Eeh, is that an Eccles cake you've fetched me?'

Back at the bomb-site Bernie had hit a snag. He'd met up with a genuine ARP Warden in the form of Clifford Simmons, who would have done better to stop at home at his bakery, in Bernie's opinion. In his confusion, he took off the too small helmet, then put it back again.

'Good to see you carrying out your civic duty, Mr Delaney,' Mr Simmons said, trying to disguise the surprise in his voice.

'Aye, well, you have to do yer bit, eh?' Cornered, there seemed little else to say. Nor could he protest when Simmons, as the senior officer, took control and started issuing orders.

'Take it steady now, Delaney, anybody could be buried under this lot, and keep a sharp eye out for looters,' Mr Simmons told him. 'If you spot any, tell that sergeant over there.' He indicated a small group of soldiers picking through the rubble.

'What'll they do?' Bernie asked, though he doubted he'd much care for the answer.

'They'll clap them in t'clink, assuming they haven't dealt with them first.'

'What d'you mean, dealt with them?'

Mr Simmons lifted up his hand and forming it into the shape of a gun, pointed it at Bernie. 'Bang, bang.'

Strangely enough, Bernie didn't spot a single looter, but he did spend the rest of the afternoon and evening pulling half mangled bodies out of the rubble and learning, for the very first time, exactly what war was all about.

Bernie revised his plans and discarded the ARP uniform. Rooting among ruins for dead bodies was not his line of work at all. The very next time the siren sounded, he went to find his sister-in-law. Lizzie was on her way down to the municipal shelter. With Jess more often than not at the mobile canteen there was little pleasure in being in the Anderson on her own, nor sitting under the stairs in the tin bath with Cora who complained all the time about her smoking.

Bernie said, 'Hold on Lizzie lass, I've got a little job for you.'

'What's that, Bernie luv? You know I'd do owt for you. You only have to ask.'

'Course you would, and I think you'll enjoy this. We're going to pop out for a bit, just you and me. Do a bit of salvage work as you might say. How would you mind pretending to be my wife for the afternoon, girl? At least, that'll be our story should anyone make enquiries what we're up to?'

'Eeh, I'd like that, Bernie luv, I really would.' She didn't ask what it was they'd be up to. Lizzie was too pleased and excited to be included in his schemes, and to be called his *wife* no less!

They'd hardly reached the end of the street when the all-clear sounded. It was nothing but a false alarm after all. 'Drat!' Bernie felt the coil of anger he always seemed to have inside of him these days, tighten even more. He was so unlucky. He'd done well out of the war early on, using the profits he'd made from the sale of coupons to buy a couple of run-down properties. One a pub on Deansgate which had been badly damaged by bombs, the other a small house on Rice Street which he let out to two old dears who were terrified of him and never got behind with the rent. But the income was much less than he'd hoped and he was desperate for more brass. His pockets had grown dangerously thin of late.

'Do we have to go in the shelter now, Bernie luv?' Lizzie asked, and looking into her once lovely grey-green eyes he saw confusion there. She was no longer certain which sound meant the alert and which peace. Lovely Lizzie was losing her grip. The doc had always said the booze would be the death of her, one way or the other.

'No, we're all right luv. We can still go. Come on, shake a leg. We must be able to find some pickings somewhere, eh? If we look hard enough. And aren't you my little jackdaw with an eye to owt what glitters?'

Lizzie giggled, girlishly. 'Ooh Bernie, you say the daftest things.' She linked her arm into his and was secretly delighted that he didn't brush her off, as he so often did when they walked out together in public. Perhaps she was winning him over, after all.

Bernie would have linked arms with the devil incarnate if it guaranteed making a bit of brass.

They headed out towards Bury Old Road – which to Bernie's way of thinking seemed a more likely spot than Castlefield or Ancoats, looking for all the world like a man and his wife out for an afternoon stroll. Taking care to keep well away from the ARPs, the pair trawled several bombed-out sites, though none of them particularly recent ones. They found a bottle of hair oil, a cameo brooch, a pair of ivory cufflinks and a few packets of tea which Lizzie got very excited about. Opting on the side of caution, Bernie insisted that she weep copious tears into her hanky while they searched, just in case anybody should see them and start asking questions. If that happened, they could claim it was their house, or that it belonged to their daughter whichever seemed appropriate and they'd popped back to look for something. Of course, there was always the risk that someone who knew the real occupants of the property would happen by, but it was a chance worth taking.

In the event they weren't troubled by anyone and apart from emptying a few gas meters, found little of any value among the rubble. Compared with Harry and Bert, their success rate was low, finding more old shoes, empty handbags and battered photo frames than anything else. But then the lads had rooted round during an actual raid, while the iron was hot, as it were. Now the trail had gone cold, and they'd just have to wait for the next one.

Nor did Bernie believe, not for one moment, that his sons had handed over everything that they'd salvaged from the ruins. Young Harry was too canny by far to do owt so soft, and Bert didn't have the brains to disagree. He could only hope that Churchill didn't end the war quite as soon as he promised, so that he had enough time to make the fortune he'd promised himself.

He certainly wasn't for giving up, oh dear me no. No one could ever accuse Bernie Delaney of being a quitter.

Jess couldn't believe her bad luck. For so long she'd dreamed of seeing Steve Wyman again, and now to come across him in such circumstances was truly heartbreaking. It seemed sadly ironic that for months now, she'd been hoping against hope that she'd find him again, perhaps playing in a band at some dance hall or other that she and Leah still regularly attended, that he would ask her to dance and hold her close once more. She'd even made up exciting little conversations between them, except that this time she'd get to tell him her name, together with a carefully edited version of her life and situation. Naturally, in the dream, he found her absolutely fascinating and asked to see her again. She pictured them slowly dancing the last waltz together to the tune of 'Dancing in the Dark' with the lights in the ballroom spinning around them.

She practised harder than ever with the trumpet, trying to justify depriving him of it and 'I'll Be Seeing You' became one of her favourite tunes. Tears would roll down her cheeks as she played 'I'll be looking at the moon but I'll be seeing you'. Even now, despite their meeting going all wrong, she couldn't seem to stop thinking about him, expecting to find him around every street corner; dreaming that she would indeed see him in all the old familiar places.

The reality was that it had simply been one dance. Nothing more.

She'd been relieved when he wasn't waiting for her that

day as she'd left Mr Yoffey's shop, yet at the same time oddly disappointed. He must not have recognised her, which just showed what a poor impression she'd made on him at the dance. Though it was several months ago now, and he'd had plenty of time to forget all about her. Nor was he there the following week when again she called with payment, although old Mr Yoffey admitted he had spotted a young man hovering about outside the previous day.

'You won't tell him my name, will you?' she begged, suddenly concerned that he might still be angry with her. 'Or where I live?'

'I look like a man with no brains? Would I do such a hare-brained thing?'

Strangely, Jess felt disappointed by his vehemence when really she should be relieved. 'I've been thinking about that trumpet. Perhaps I should return it after all, since it was important enough for him to hand over all the money he possessed to get it back.'

'Poof, that young man simply likes to have his own way, I am thinking. That is how he saw it, as a game, a competition to be won. He couldn't bear to think of someone getting one over on him. I know the sort. You keep the instrument, little one. It is yours now.'

And remembering how nasty he'd been, and how Steve had threatened her before walking out, Jess tucked the trumpet under her arm and decided that Mr Yoffey was right, she'd keep it after all.

The only solution seemed to be not to think about Steve Wyman at all, but to shut him out of her mind and Jess determined to do just that. She would forget him. She would continue attending the dances as she'd always done, even though much of the pleasure seemed to have gone out of them for some reason. Even Leah had remarked upon it, telling her to cheer up and smile for goodness sake. It was with some relief therefore that one night at the Plaza Jess had spotted Tommy. His presence was like a breath of fresh air and she quickly introduced him to Leah as her favourite cousin, which he found amusing.

'I know what you mean, our Jess, but it's not strictly true that nobody can find our Harry and Bert lovable. It's hard to reckon but somebody must, as they're each walking out with a girl.'

Jess was all ears. 'Are they really? Good heavens. No wonder I haven't seen much of them lately, and what a relief that has been. They must be saints though, these girls, whoever they are.'

'Or hard up,' Tommy laughed.

As Jess saw Tommy casting shy, sidelong glances at her friend, she turned to Leah to explain. 'Tommy is the only Delaney who believes in doing his bit for the war effort. Harry and Bert are both bone idle and only out for themselves, while Tommy here is a fire-watcher.'

Tommy grinned. 'Aye, I'm the only one daft enough to put meself in the firing line, though I will be even more soon. I'm hoping to join the army by the end of the year. Can't be worse than sleeping on a camp-bed in some freezing warehouse or other, waiting to play football with incendiaries.' Then he regaled them with a funny story of trying to get water up from a bucket with a stirrup pump to put out a fire. 'It would have been quicker to chuck the bucket of water on it.'

Leah was roaring with laughter. 'Why didn't you then?'

'Regulations. Anyroad, we didn't have any more water.'

'What a war!' They were all laughing by this time, then seeing his bright, adoring gaze Leah sighed and gave one of her soft, enticing smiles. 'You can dance with me, if you want to.'

'Oh, I want to all right.'

'But you have to ask properly.'

Tommy grinned. 'Can I dance with you properly then?' Tommy took the laughing Leah on to the dance floor and Jess never clapped eyes on her again for the rest of the evening, which left her feeling more depressed than ever.

Unbeknown to Jess, the dance with Tommy lasted no more than a few moments before they were rudely interrupted. 'Hello Tommy lad, who's this little chick you've picked up? Does she know that you're only just out of short trousers?'

'Leave off, Harry. Can't you see not to push yer nose in where it's not wanted.'

'I reckon we should let your lovely partner here be the best judge of that.'

Leah found herself looking into a roguishly handsome face with a square-cut jaw, grey laughing eyes and close cropped, almost black hair with just the hint of a curl. Broad shoulders and a powerful chest gave way to slim hips and long, interesting legs. Hanging on to his arm with feverish tenacity and clawing red fingernails, was a girl with bleached blonde hair and a sulky expression on her thin, pale face. And no wonder. He exuded confidence and bonhomie. There surely wasn't a girl in the room who wouldn't have been delighted to be seen on his arm, and the way he was eyeing her up made Leah's stomach clench in a thrill of excitement. He was, to her mind, utterly gorgeous!

'Perhaps you should introduce us, Tommy.'

She could sense his reluctance as he swiftly and carelessly introduced the newcomer as his eldest brother. So this was the devilish Delaney whom Jess was constantly going on about? Obviously she didn't appreciate his potent sensual appeal, since he was her cousin. Leah found herself utterly entranced by him and put up a hand to tidy a wayward strand of hair, all of a sudden acutely aware of her own appearance. Drat it, why hadn't she worn her new blue silk with the dazzlingly low-cut neckline instead of this old green linen number. But then that might have been too daring and frightened him off, and he clearly found her attractive, judging by the way his gaze was devouring her. The butterflies in her stomach started up a clog dance in pure ecstasy. Maybe Harry here was exactly what she'd been waiting for, someone to put some zest and passion into her life, bring an edge of excitement to it.

Gripping her firmly around the waist, Tommy attempted to steer her away back into the mêlée of the other dancers. Harry, however, had taken a fancy to Leah and had no intention of letting her slip away.

'Why don't we exchange partners for this one, eh Tommy lad? You take Dotty here, and I'll give – Leah was it? What a pretty name. I'll take Leah on a merry little spin around the dance floor.'

Yes, Leah thought with wry amusement. I bet you've led many a girl a merry dance. Well, she wasn't above a little jig herself, given the opportunity. At eighteen, Leah was longing to be more grown up, to try out some of these adventures she heard the other shop girls chattering about in whispers, some of them even younger than herself. 'Sounds good to me,' she said brightly and somewhat breathlessly, trying not to feel guilty at the shaft of disappointment that flared in Tommy's eyes. Why the hell shouldn't she swop partners? Harry looked infinitely more interesting.

Once in his arms she could feel his magnetism, sensed other girls around them eyeing him up, envying her. He was, in Leah's opinion, one of the handsomest men in the room. Why had Jess never mentioned that simple fact? Was she so blind to her cousin's masculine charms? Leah suddenly felt all girlish and shy, quite unlike her normal self and absolutely lost for words. Harry had no such problem.

'So you're our Jess's friend, from the tea room, eh?'

Leah nodded, wanting to kick herself for her own silent inadequacy. Why should a man have this effect upon her just because he was good-looking? Admittedly he was a few years older than herself, and very full of himself. But then she liked a man with an air of self-assurance; a man with authority who knew where he was going in life. Clearly the bottle blonde he'd abandoned was less than pleased at being dumped on to his younger brother. Leah couldn't help but think that she'd got the best of the bargain.

'Cat got your tongue?' The charcoal grey eyes were laughing at her, even as he pulled her closer in his arms, smoothing a hand up and down her spine which sent little shivers of excitement pulsating through her.

'No, of course not. I was just thinking that I ought to be finding Jess. She'll be wondering where I've got to.'

He gave a deep, throaty chuckle. 'No you weren't thinking owt of the sort. You were wondering how quickly we could get out of this place so we could get to know each other a bit better.' Harry was thinking that if he played his cards right he'd have her up a back alley with her knickers off in no time. He imagined them as white, lacy, and very French.

'Heavens, you are full of yourself, aren't you? Why would I want to go anywhere with you when I'm quite happy dancing?'

'Because you fancy me rotten, just as I fancy you. What about a breath of fresh air. No harm in that, surely? We could go for a walk and see where it takes us.'

Leah felt a tightening in her chest. 'Hey, what are you suggesting? I'm not that kind of girl.'

'Course you're not. That's why you're intrigued by me. Because I am that kind of chap.' Harry had always found that straight talking generally worked like a charm, both with the scrubbers and with the classy sort, the ones who'd been brought up proper and overprotected. It had never failed in the past to get him a bit of how's-your-father, and he couldn't see it doing so on this occasion. Maybe not tonight, but a few carefully judged manoeuvres in the right direction could well pay dividend in the end. He moved his hand a bit closer to the swell of her pert young breast, just to test his theory and was pleased to discover that she made no protest at all. On the contrary, she was gazing up at him out of eyes that were surely dilating with desire. Drat it, if he didn't get her out of here damn quick, he'd make an exhibition of himself here and now on the bleeding dance floor.

Leah couldn't quite take in what was happening. Oh, but she was intrigued, indeed she was: by the way he regarded her through the speculative glint of narrowed eyes; the wicked twist to his wide, laughing mouth and she found herself trying to imagine what it might feel like to have him kiss her. The prospect set her pulses racing. For all she knew, Simmons's Tea Room could be bombed to smithereens tomorrow and she might die without discovering what the greatest mystery in life was all about. And what a tragedy that would be, to die a virgin, never knowing the true meaning of passion. Time suddenly seemed to be running out for her, as if she must experience everything right now, before it was too late and she'd lost the opportunity for ever.

Besides, once again this morning, she'd had words with her mother over plans for the weekend. Muriel had arranged for the Gartsides to come for tea on Sunday, and Leah was naturally expected to be present to entertain Ambrose. She couldn't seem able to get it across to her that she loathed the sight of him, that she thought him dull as ditchwater and had no intention, now or ever, of agreeing to walk out with him, let alone the possibility of matrimony, however suitable his family background. But Muriel didn't seem to be listening. She could find no fault with him, and assumed her daughter should feel the same. Whereas Leah would have cut her throat rather than allow Ambrose Gartside within ten yards of her.

Perhaps the best way to shut up her mother was to find herself a different boyfriend, and Harry looked a likely candidate. Leah very much doubted you could ever accuse a Delaney of being dull, and wouldn't that give Muriel a heart attack to see her beloved daughter roughing it? Serve her right for being so bossy and trying to interfere.

Coming to a swift decision Leah rewarded Harry with her most brilliant smile so that even he recognised, in that instant, what a very fortunate chap he was. 'Why not?' she agreed. 'A walk would be lovely, so long as we're back by nine-thirty, in time to meet up with Jess and go home.'

'No problem.' That gave him the better part of an hour. If he hadn't made his mark by then, he wasn't the man he thought he was.

Leah was pressed up hard against a brick wall down by the Irwell, dust in her hair, lipstick gone and all she could think of was what a good kisser he was. She'd never spent such an exciting half-hour in all her life.

'Where have you been all my life?' Harry said, rubbing his hand over her breast.

Dazed by his passion, with his hands going everywhere and aware the situation was running quickly out of control, Leah was reluctant to stop him. She didn't want to offend him, was in fact anxious that he not think her some silly weed of a shop girl who'd go running home to ma if he touched her where he shouldn't. She wanted him to ask to see her again. Even as she masqueraded sophistication, as she was so fond of doing, Leah felt confused. Harry Delaney was the most exciting bloke she'd ever met in all of her young life, and he was making her head spin so much that she couldn't seem to think straight. She could feel him edging up her skirt as he pushed one knee between her legs, his fingers slide beneath her stocking top and experienced a burst of panic for this was one step too far. Was she ready? Did she really want to *do it*? Not now surely, not yet. He'd think her cheap for one thing, and when she did try it, she'd want to be sure that he took proper precautions. She was no dummy.

She pulled his hand away and pushed down the hem of her skirt. 'What do you think you're doing, Harry Delaney. I think that's far enough, don't you?'

'Not for me it ain't, nor you neither sweetheart from the look on your lovely face. I can tell when a girl's begging for it. But OK, not right now, happen. I'll retire gracefully and admit defeat.' He gave her waist a little squeeze and said, 'Come on Cinderella, time I was taking you back to our Jess.'

Disappointment warred with a sense of relief that he'd given in so easily. Leah knew in her heart that it would take very little persuasion on his part to make her change her mind. 'You do like me though?' she softly enquired, taking his caution for respect instead of the canny manoeuvre it actually was.

Harry's instincts with women were much sharper than his level of intelligence would signify, and he prided himself on knowing when to draw back, and when to push a little bit more. This one needed to be hooked first. 'Course I do luv, but I don't want our Jess battering me ear lobe. She'd never let me hear the last of it if you missed your bus.'

He abandoned her the moment they were back inside the dance hall, just as if the half-hour of intense passion between them had never taken place, or he'd wiped it completely from his mind. 'See yer around then.' And he loped away with a sly grin on his face, aware he left her quivering with uncertainty, wondering whether he really did want to see her again, desperate for him to ask her out. Oh, he was an expert on women all right. Next time, she'd be eating out of his hand, panting for it, and more than willing to let him do whatever he wanted with her.

13

It was the following Wednesday evening and Jess was serving in the mobile canteen as usual when a docker walked in. He was quite a bit older than herself, in his early thirties, quite tall with brown hair slicked down with Brylcreem, long straight nose and eyebrows which had a faint look of surprise about them. He was no dreamboat by any means, being too thin and bony for her taste and his smile was a bit slow in coming, adding an air of seriousness to the oval face with its long, pointed chin.

Jess noticed how quiet he was and, unlike many who visited the canteen, he wasn't already half cut with the booze. He was well mannered, extraordinarily polite, always saying please or thank you. Thinking he looked familiar, Jess politely asked if he'd been in before and he freely admitted that he had. 'I'm on maintenance work down at the docks and whenever I get a bit of free time, I come to listen to you play. I hope you don't mind.'

'Not at all, why should I?'

He came three evenings on the trot, speaking to no one as he silently watched her going about her work. On the third occasion he said, 'You look a bit tired tonight. Couldn't you sit down for a minute and take a rest?'

'I'm supposed to be working.'

'Aren't you allowed to talk to the customers?'

'Oh yes, but not for too long. There's a lot of work to be done so I can't devote too much attention to any one person.'

'I couldn't be that lucky. I've been watching you, you're very popular here, especially with the men.'

Jess laughed. 'They like my playing.'

'So do I. You're good. You're also very lovely, with that long dark hair and sweet face. A natural beauty like yours can't be hidden, it shines forth like a beacon of pure light.'

Jess was astounded. She'd never thought of herself as anything other than ordinary and was embarrassed to be complimented in such a personal manner by a perfect stranger. It left her at a loss for words, unable to think of a sensible thing to say. Though if it had been Steve who'd said such lovely things to her . . . 'Are you on your own?' she asked. Oh dear, now he would think she was being forward and making a play for him. She started to move away but his next words, coming out all in a bluster, gave her pause.

'Sadly yes, my wife and young son died about eighteen months ago and I don't have any family left – so it's not much fun at home.'

'Oh, how terrible. I'm so sorry.' Jess wondered if it was a bomb, but didn't like to ask. Who knew what fate had befallen the poor woman and her child? Jess wondered if she should ask how he was coping but it didn't pay to pry too closely into emotions in these difficult times. Yet she couldn't simply walk away from him now, not after such a confession. She shyly cleared her throat. 'So, how are you?'

'I miss her, naturally.'

'Of course. How old was your son?'

'Only eight. I miss him even more, as we were particularly close. And I'm such an ugly old brute I'm not expecting to marry again, so I'm not likely to get the chance of another.'

He smiled at her then, such a sad, sorry sort of smile that Jess felt filled with pity for him. Poor man, to be widowed so young, and to lose an only child. 'Don't talk daft, you're not ugly at all,' she told him briskly. 'You shouldn't think so little of yourself.'

Sergeant Ted had impressed upon her how they should always find time to talk to victims, at least for a little while, so Jess brought them both a cup of what passed for coffee, being the bottled Camp variety, and sat down with him, hoping that a bit of company might cheer him up. He seemed happy to talk, keen to tell her all about his wife, how she went out one day to buy bread and simply never came home. People all too frequently vanished off the face of the earth during a war, she agreed.

'But why did she take the child with her?'

'She couldn't leave him on his own, could she?'

'Oh no, of course not.'

'So what about you? Why are you so tired and over-worked?'

'Don't worry about me. I'm fine.' It amazed her that, despite his terrible loss, he could still show a genuine interest in others, herself in particular, gently asking questions so that she began to talk too. Jess would much rather have been sharing her troubles with Steve but told herself firmly that he'd been nothing more than a fantasy and it was easier in a way to talk to a stranger, one who didn't judge. And it was good to get it all off her chest.

She told him much more about her own life than she'd intended, simply because he was such a good listener; so thoughtful and silent. Jess explained how she loved playing the trumpet, about the friends she'd made in the Sally Army and how spending time with them had saved her sanity because she so hated living with her uncle. She spoke of how desperately she missed her father; all about the family feud and the tricks that the Delaneys got up to. She even bitterly related how her mother wasn't capable of looking after her properly because she went out drinking every night, and used to leave her locked in a cellar when the bombs were dropping. She made no mention of Lizzie having been arrested and imprisoned for shop-lifting. Some things were best kept private.

As he was about to leave he asked if he could see her again and Jess experienced a flush of panic. Perhaps she'd been too encouraging, given the wrong impression and implied that she was available. She shook her head, embarrassed, and explained how busy she was working at the bakery as well as here in the mobile canteen.

'No wonder you're tired. Don't you ever get any time off?'

'Of course, but I have other interests, friends to see. Like I say, I'm pretty busy.'

'How about tomorrow?'

'I'm working.' She felt relieved about this, thinking it would surely get the message across that she wasn't available but as she cleared away the mugs, he persisted, hanging around as she washed up. She really must insist that he go. She could see Harriet glancing curiously over in their direction, wondering why one of the customers was in the kitchen area with a tea towel in his hands. Jess took the towel from him and folded it away. 'And now I have to dash off home and see if Mam's all right. It's been nice chatting with you. Good night.'

'How about the day after, or Saturday? We could go to the pictures or something. You've made me feel so much better about myself, Jess. I'd really like to get to know you better.'

Oh dear, now she'd really lumbered herself. Leah would laugh fit to bust when she heard this tale of a love-struck docker. Perhaps it would be best to let him think that she already had a boyfriend, before he got too interested, even if it wasn't true. Jess smiled kindly at him, wanting to let his hopes down lightly. 'I'm sorry, but I already have a date on both nights.'

He looked crestfallen. 'You've got a boyfriend then?' He was gazing at her with such wretchedness in his eyes that Jess could hardly bear to look at him. It filled her with guilt. She hadn't meant to give the wrong impression, or to lead him up the garden path by taking too much interest in him. Any minute now and her soft heart would be won over and she'd agree, which would never do at all.

She gave a self-deprecating little smile. 'Sort of.' No need to say that it was all fantasy, all in her dreams.

He helped her on with her coat and insisted that he walk her home at least, since accidents were rife in the blackout. Jess tried to tell him that she was quite used to that but he was adamant, insisting it was the gentlemanly thing to do and she couldn't think of a polite way to refuse, not without offending him again. She said good night to Sergeant Ted, Harriet and the rest of the volunteers, then set off home with Doug Morgan, as he'd introduced himself to her. And really, she was glad of his company when on the corner of Dolefield they came across a few drunken sailors on their way back to their ship after a night on the town. Not that they were in any way violent, only slightly merry, giving her wolf whistles and the like. Jess found it all rather amusing but Doug was less inclined to be benevolent towards them.

Taking a proprietorial grip upon her arm, he said, 'All right lads, leave the little lady alone. She's with me. You see now why you shouldn't be walking about on your own at this time of night,' he scolded her gently when they'd gone. 'You never would if you were my girlfriend.'

Long after she'd said good night and gone indoors, Doug Morgan continued to stand on the pavement silently gazing along Cumberland Street, watching the house she'd entered and reflecting upon his good fortune. He'd seen her several times at the canteen before she'd even noticed him, had been watching her for weeks in fact. This had truly been his lucky day for her to offer him coffee and sit down to chat with him, and an inspiration to come up with that tale of losing a wife and son. But then a woman with a soft heart could never resist a sob story. No need for her to know that he'd never come close to marriage, or having friends of any sort for that matter. If he could just persuade her to come out with him a time or two, he was quite sure that all his problems would be solved, and he'd never be lonely again.

It wasn't until after he'd seen Bernie arrive home, very much the worse for drink, that he finally left. Judging by the state of that uncle of hers, Doug decided, she was in dire need of rescue herself, as well as a guiding hand. He could see they were destined to be together, made for each other as you might say.

'What happened to you the other night? Did you have a lovely time with Tommy? Are you seeing him again? You didn't say much when we were going home, but you looked all dreamy. Go on, tell me everything.'

Leah shrugged, suddenly reluctant to say anything at all to Jess about what really had happened at the dance that particular evening, guessing that she certainly wouldn't approve of her going with Harry. 'Tommy's OK. Bit young for me perhaps.'

'He's about the same age as you.'

'Still, I like my men a bit older, with experience. Hey, what about you? I hear you've got a fan who comes to listen to you play every night? Chap in his thirties I believe, who saw you safely home. What a dark horse you are.'

Jess blushed. 'Who told you that?'

'Sergeant Ted. He and I were having a bit of a gossip when I came to meet you last night. So, go on, what's he like? Is he nice? Do you like older men too?'

Jess screwed up her nose. 'No, so don't read anything into

it. Not really my type. He lost his wife and child in the bombing, so I was just being kind by talking to him and letting him walk me home.'

'Oh!' A moment of silence and then, 'So what is your type? You seem to have got very picky all of a sudden. You never seem very keen to dance with any of those lovely airmen and sailors these days.'

'Maybe I'm waiting for Mr Right.'

'And would Mr Right's first name be Steve by any chance?'

'I really don't know what you're talking about.'

Days later, feeling guilty at having missed their regular tea-time meetings for a few weeks, not simply because she'd been working hard but also because she'd been nervous of meeting up with Steve again, Jess went back to Mr Yoffey's little shop to make her apologies. She also intended to hand over a final payment for the trumpet, having borrowed money from her store of savings under the mattress. She arrived to find the door locked and the blinds drawn. The dusty 'Closed' sign hung in the window gathering cobwebs. Jess clanged the bell which hung by the door, rattled the letterbox and hammered on the window to no avail. There was no sign of the old man and nothing for it but to go away again. She returned the next day to find exactly the same situation. The shop was locked up and barred, bearing an abandoned, lost, and sad sort of air. Jess felt a sickness start up deep inside. Where was he? What had happened to the old man?

'They've taken him away.' The answer seemed to come out of nowhere but, turning, she found the words had been spoken by the very person who had kept her away from his door all these weeks. Steve Wyman was frowning at her in the way she remembered only too well.

'Taken him where?' Her heart was pounding, more out of fear for poor Mr Yoffey than anything. Nothing else seemed important now.

'He's no doubt been interned in the Aliens' camp on the Isle of Man.'

'But why?'

'Quite clearly because he's considered to be a serious threat to peace,' said Steve drily.

Rage bubbled through her veins. 'That's ridiculous. Preposterous! An absolute scandal! He's an old man, not a threat to anyone. Who would do such a thing? The City Council? The Mayor, was it? Government officials? Where would I find them? I shall give them a piece of my mind.'

She set off at a brisk pace down the road, as if about to march that very minute right into the City offices and take them all on: the mayor, the corporation and the city fathers, while her blood was still boiling. Steve caught her up and grabbed her elbow.

'Jess, Jess, hold on. You're wasting your time. It has nothing to do with anyone locally. This is a government thing. The local council tried to protect him, but in the end they had no say.'

'But it's so wrong! How can they imagine Mr Yoffey of all people to be a threat to anyone, a dear old man like that? And how could you even imply that he is?'

'I was being sarcastic. I didn't mean you to take me so seriously. Oh, don't cry Jess. Please, I can't bear to see a girl cry.'

She wiped the tears from her cheeks. 'How do you know my name? I never got around to telling you that time, not at the dance, nor in the shop. And Mr Yoffey promised that he'd not tell you either.'

'For once he broke his word. Look, it's my fault, don't blame the old man. Will you let me buy you a cup of tea, then I can explain?'

*   *   *

He took her to the Ritz, to the afternoon tea dance. The stage was brightly lit, the place heaving with people as always, many in uniform and all bent on having a good time. People were laughing and talking to each other as they jigged about to the music with varying degrees of skill, finding tongues loosened on the dance floor which might otherwise be tied up with shyness. The band was playing 'The Jersey Bounce' and it was all Jess could do to resist tapping her feet. Instead, she folded her arms and put on her most disapproving expression.

Steve was looking a bit shame-faced. 'I thought this would be as convenient a place as any for us to talk as I have to go to work in a minute, or would you rather dance first?'

Jess couldn't wait to get on to the dance floor, to be held in his arms as she'd long dreamed of doing, to feel the heat of his body pressed close against hers, but not for a moment would she admit as much. She scowled furiously at him. 'Work where, at the aircraft factory?'

'Nope, up there, on stage. My spare-time job.'

For a moment she was startled by this unexpected piece of information, but obstinately didn't show it. 'You're lucky to have any spare time at all. Most of us are too busy working at a proper job as well as doing our bit for the war effort.' It was unkind, she knew it, but some devil had got inside her and she couldn't seem to stop the hurtful words from pouring out of her mouth.

'Mr Yoffey told me that you spend your spare time helping the Salvation Army. A worthy cause. Or is that how you pay for your trumpet lessons?'

'That's not why I do it at all. I just like helping. Well, in a way it is. I mean . . .' Jess felt flustered, as if he'd caught her out in an untruth. 'It sounds like you and Mr Yoffey had quite a chat. It's a wonder my ears weren't burning.'

'Sorry, but I admit to applying pressure by explaining that we were already acquainted. He was quite moved by the tale of how we were whisked apart before properly getting through the basic introductions. I assume you do remember how well we danced together on that first occasion? Which is why I thought you might wish to repeat the experience. However, I'm not the sort of chap to push myself forward where I'm not wanted.'

Jess could feel her traitorous cheeks start to burn and decided it was far safer to go on the attack. 'I rather assumed you hadn't recognised me, or you'd forgotten we'd already met, which is fine by me.'

'How could I ever forget?'

Not sure what to make of the implications behind this enigmatic statement, she hurried on, 'I take it you don't approve of women trumpet players?' thereby sharply reminding him of their differences.

He grinned happily at her. 'I don't recall saying any such thing. I do remember commenting that you had purloined my trumpet.'

Jess glanced down at the instrument case clasped in her hand, then hugged it defensively close to her chest. 'Purloined?'

He saw the gesture and chuckled. 'Borrowed then, and refused to return it. It's all right. I'm not going to steal it back. I've accepted defeat on that one. For now, anyway. Let's check it safely into the cloakroom, shall we? Neutral territory.'

Jess handed over the case reluctantly to the smiling girl, took a ticket in return and, as always, stuffed this inside her shoe so that she wouldn't lose it. Breathing deeply as she struggled to decide how to handle what could turn into a tricky situation, she told him, 'I didn't steal it. That's not how it was at all.'

'Well you certainly weren't for handing it back were you? Even though I'd brought every penny I possessed to pay for it. How would you feel if you'd been forced to hock your favourite instrument and then some idiot who thought they could play, nicked it from you?'

Jess gasped. 'I've told you, I didn't nick it! I'm not an idiot and I *can* play.'

He had the gall to laugh. 'Who told you that? Some tinpot do-gooding Salvation Army chap, I suppose. What would he know about real music?'

'A great deal, as a matter of fact. What's more if you think I'm . . .'

The wind was knocked out of their ding-dong argument as an airman grabbed hold of Jess to whisk her on to the dance floor. The band had struck up 'Boomps-a-Daisy' and soon she was bumping backsides with a perfect stranger while Steve, she couldn't help noticing, was rocking with laughter as a very fetching strawberry blonde in WRNS uniform wiggled her bottom at him.

This was followed by the hokey-cokey with a good deal of shaking of arms and legs, then the St Bernard's Waltz with much stamping of feet followed by the Gay Gordons where Jess thought her head might never stop spinning again. But how could she resist when she was having the time of her life. It was all great fun. Finally, as the music changed to the Progressive Barn Dance she found herself back with Steve, except that the moment he had her firmly in his arms, he practically frog-marched her from the dance floor.

'Right, let's get this sorted out once and for all.'

'You could at least buy me a cup of tea first.'

'It's included in the price of the ticket.'

'Which you don't even have to pay for, presumably, since you're going to play in the band.'

'At least I *can* play.'

'We'll let your audience be the judge of that.'

'And at least I didn't nick someone else's instrument.'

For a long moment Jess glared furiously at him, and then suddenly she saw the funny side of it all. They weren't getting anywhere, only going round and round in circles. She recognised a mischievous challenge in his gold-flecked hazel eyes and could hold back no longer. She began to giggle, then to laugh, and as if thankful to be relieved of the effort not to, so did he. They laughed so much that tears ran down her cheeks and she had to hold on to his arm to prevent herself from toppling over.

'Jess, that was the most fun I've had in a long time. Thank you,' and without warning, he gathered her into his arms and kissed her. She didn't protest, she couldn't possibly have done so. She felt herself melt against him, aware only of the soft warmth of his lips, the powerful strength of his hard body against hers, the magic of the moment. It felt like being welcomed home.

Jess had somehow discovered an enormous appetite, and consumed Steve's slice of cake which came with the tea, along with her own. They talked and talked, oblivious of time, right up until the moment he went on stage to play his saxophone. Jess retrieved her own instrument from the cloakroom but instead of dashing off to catch her bus, as she should, couldn't resist lingering to listen. He played 'The Way You Look Tonight' and she was utterly entranced, not least by the fact that his eyes rarely left her throughout. It was as if they were all alone in the ballroom and he was playing only for her. Jess felt privileged to be singled out amongst all the other adoring girls crowding around the stage.

He finished to rapturous applause from his adoring audience but then after whispering something to the bandleader, approached the microphone and spoke softly into it. 'Folks, we have a special treat for you today. We have with us this afternoon a young girl with a very special gift. I am reliably informed by a dear old friend of mine that she has no mean skill with a trumpet herself. So let me introduce to you, *Jess Delaney*. Come on Jess. Step up on stage and enchant us all.' And as he held out a hand towards her, everyone turned to look in the direction he pointed.

Jess felt as if she might die on the spot. She knew her cheeks were burning like fire and wanted nothing more than for the floor to open and swallow her up. She could feel the music case holding Steve's very *own* trumpet scalding her hand. Was this his revenge for her appropriating it? She could see his eyes twinkling at her and realised that he was issuing her with a challenge. This was his way of saying, so go on then, prove to me that you're worthy of owning my trumpet. Play it well or hand it back. Drat the man, if he expected her to turn and run, he'd mistaken his opponent. Hardly able to believe that her feet were actually taking her there, Jess made her way up the steps on to the stage. People were standing back to let her through, smiling and clapping, looking her over with open curiosity. Was she quite mad? Did she want to make a complete fool of herself in front of this crowd, some of them professional dancers?

Her hands were shaking as she lifted the trumpet from its case, and she was quite sure for a moment that she would drop it, perhaps even dent it as she had the Salvation Army bugle. Then Steve's hands were on her shoulders as he turned her gently to face the audience. 'Keep smiling and tell me what you want to play.'

Jess swallowed and looked about her. The bright lights were so dazzling she could scarcely see the blur of faces which seemed to spin before her eyes in an eerie, disembodied sort of way. His voice in her ear said, 'Don't look at them, they'll only make you nervous.' Then he was smiling down at her and perhaps it was just as well that his gaze was the only one that she could truly register. For a long moment Jess felt as if she were drowning in it, losing all grip on reality, and yet it seemed to fill her with a new strength, new courage and she finally answered his question.

' "I'll Be Seeing You".' She didn't even know where the words had come from, somewhere in the deep recesses of her longing.

Steve spoke quickly to the bandleader then nodded at her, smiling his encouragement. 'Go on, knock 'em dead.'

She lifted the trumpet, adjusted the tension of her lips, and blew. It was a hesitant start, shy and tremulous but confidence grew in her by the second. Jess put all her heart and soul into the number and long before she was halfway through, her audience were holding on to each other, swaying as they sang along with the music and Jess didn't need Steve, or the bandleader to tell her that it sounded good.

When she was done the room erupted. Everyone was cheering and calling for an encore but Jess couldn't move a muscle. She felt drained, exhausted and yet exhilarated and all she could do was smile in a bemused, astonished sort of way, laughing with relief as she took her bows to rapturous applause.

'Pity you're not a chap,' said Hal, the bandleader, shaking her vigorously by the hand. 'Or I'd offer you a job on the spot.'

Steve, she noticed, had suspiciously bright eyes as he led her from the stage, and then once more she was in his arms, his cheek nestled close against hers as he held her tight.

'I take back every word, Jess Delaney. My trumpet is yours. Keep it. Mr Yoffey was right to lend it you. You *can* make that instrument sing.'

14

Day after day Bernie continued with his plan, dragging a hapless Lizzie in tow. House doors were often found standing open, either because the occupants had rushed off down the shelter, or simply gone to chat with a neighbour. But it was becoming increasingly difficult to find something of value, as few people had anything left worth stealing. And if the alert didn't last very long, there was always the chance of getting caught on the job, of which Bernie was naturally wary, and so he ordered Lizzie to be the one to walk in and see what she could find, while he waited at the end of the street.

Even Lizzie balked at this plan. 'How do we know there won't be someone still inside?'

'If there is, pretend to be looking for someone.'

'Who?'

'I don't know, make up a name. Go on, girl, get on with it.'

And because she was potty about him, or threepence short to the shilling, as Bernie preferred to describe her, she would do exactly as he asked.

Sometimes they'd work the markets or small traders, or the big department stores like Lewis's which, because of the war, had too many customers and too few staff. Thanks to the ban on wrapping paper, it proved remarkably easy to pick up a few useful items here and there and secret them about their clothing. He wasn't too fussy what she got: scarves, lighters, shoes, stockings, a few fountain pens or powder compacts.

Bernie would sell them on through pawnshops and one or two dealers he knew well.

Lizzie tried not to think about the possibility of getting caught again. She knew that she was useless, that there was no hope of her getting a proper job and living a decent life like normal people, so if she could at least please Bernie, he'd see her all right. She'd be needing a few things of her own before winter set in: a warm coat, some decent gloves. How else could she get them except by nicking them? Besides, Bernie was feeding her and providing her with a roof over her head. Lizzie gave no credit to her own daughter's efforts in supplying these essentials. Bernie was the brains and the provider in her view, so wasn't it only right and proper that he shouldn't take any undue risk, that she should be the one to do the legwork? Best to go along with it and not argue, even if she did still have nightmares about getting caught again and ending up back in jail.

As with the houses, so with the shops, he always stood some distance off while she worked, so that he wasn't too conspicuous but he always made a great fuss of her when she returned. Lizzie liked that. Even if she hadn't managed to get much more than a few handkerchiefs or scarves, he nevertheless managed to say something kind. He was really very good to her.

'Never mind girl, we'll get summat for them and you'll do better next time.'

She thrived on praise, basked in his favour, needing his approval.

Inwardly, Bernie was seething. Things weren't going well for him at all. Nothing she picked up was of any great value and when he totted up his first month's 'takings' it came to little more than fifty quid. Not much for all that effort and skill.

He'd tried, like Britain, to hit back but nothing had worked out quite as he'd hoped. He no longer had the physical clout to keep his boys in line, not since they'd grown so big. He envied their strength, and their youth. He didn't care to admit, even to himself, how much he needed Harry and Bert to be on his side, working for him and not for themselves. Instead of which, the pair were doing a bit of courting and wouldn't even reveal what their latest money-making scheme was. He rather thought it had something to do with petrol coupons as he'd found his own stash had been tampered with, or else it was the result of finally selling all that dratted sugar, but Harry always seemed to have a good deal of money in his pocket.

As they grew ever stronger, he felt his own energy and effectiveness seep away, just as it had with Jake all those years ago. It was the same old story all over again. People leaned on him, depended upon his goodwill, sucked him dry and then treated him like some sort of old fool who wasn't worth the candle.

He'd begun to worry that perhaps he might be losing his grip, like poor Lizzie here, which fuelled the rage that simmered deep inside him all the more. The anger at times was almost more than he could suppress.

Why did things always go wrong for him? Why wouldn't his family do as they were damned well told? How could he possibly be losing it? Lizzie was the real problem, not him. She didn't look the part. Who would believe she was an honest woman out shopping for knick-knacks? She didn't have that air of innocence about her any more. Even in the clean new frock he'd bought for her, the neat shoes and hat with the fancy little veil, she looked what she was, a worn-out, tatty ex-con, always with a fag in her mouth. Expensive, classy shops were no longer Lizzie's forte. She'd never get a sniff of a watch or anything of real value, not looking like that. As the sad loser she undoubtedly was, no smart jeweller worth his salt would even allow her to cross his threshold. Jess, on the other hand, Bernie realised, looked entirely trustworthy and for all her protestations of honesty, she had to be made to pull her weight somehow.

Only a month or two back she'd come to him all prim and proper, nose in the air as if there were a bad smell. 'There won't be any problem with paying for our keep, in future, now that I've got a better job as a waitress. But I don't intend to stay with you and Cora for ever, even though my aunt at least has made me welcome. I mean to find Mam and me a room of us own to rent just as soon as I can, so we won't be a trouble to you any longer than absolutely necessary. We'll be out of your hair in no time.'

'Good,' Bernie had told her. 'Can't be soon enough for me.'

But he didn't want her to leave. He'd invested too much time and money into that family, too much pain and sorrow over the years. They owed him, big time. Wasn't he the brightest of the Delaneys, and the best, the one upon whom the whole bloody lot depended? Some bugger would have to pay for the fact that he was always the one to suffer. Come what may, some poor sod would have to pay. Jake had escaped, got away scot-free and turned into some sort of bloody hero, so if Lizzie was no longer any use to him, then young Jess must take her place. It was only fair. There must be some way he could make her do his bidding.

He might no longer be able to control those great idle lumps that were his sons, but surely he could manage one slip of a girl?

Following that afternoon at the Ritz life suddenly became exciting. Jess couldn't believe she'd been so daring as to actually go on stage. Those few magical moments had changed her, and she knew that the sound of the applause would live with her for ever.

What was even more exciting, Steve took to waiting for her outside of Simmons's Tea Room whenever she was on late shift. He'd take her out to supper before dashing off to some dance hall or other where he was due to play that evening. Often Jess went along with him and in the interval when some other band took the stage, he would indeed hold her close in his arms and it was even better than all her dreams. He would sing the words softly in her ear, 'I dream of you' and her heart would melt with love for him.

Sometimes, because of the distance, or Jess's commitments with the Salvation Army, it wasn't possible for her to go with him and they'd linger in the bus shelter kissing and cuddling, promising to meet the next day or the one after that. But the two of them were rarely apart. Every moment they could, they spent together. But even though Jess guessed that she was falling in love with him, not for one moment dare she allow it to go to her head. She strove to remain sensible and practical, as she always had been. This wasn't the time for dreams or romance.

Jess was sorely troubled that something odd was going on. Lizzie had suddenly taken to going out during the day and not coming back till quite late in the afternoon. Sometimes she wouldn't be there when Jess got home from the shop. Cora was naturally delighted to be free of her sister-in-law for a few hours but Jess was desperate to investigate exactly where it was she went, what Lizzie got up to and if she was drinking again. She considered following her, and might have done so if only she'd had more time. Working as she did for long hours in the tea room and bakery, her days were pretty well filled already, and whatever evenings she wasn't helping out at the Salvation Army mobile canteen, she simply couldn't resist spending with Steve. Jess rarely even saw Leah these days, who she assumed was now walking out with Tommy. Nor did she greatly mind, having neither the time nor the curiosity to enquire too deeply into her friend's affairs, being too engrossed with her own.

Jess had finally admitted to Steve the full story of why she'd wanted the trumpet and he'd been furious on her behalf, wanting to go and bop Uncle Bernie on the nose there and then. Fortunately she was able to persuade him of the fruitlessness of such an action.

'I want to protect you, and make you happy,' Steve protested.

'Oh, you do, you do. You make me so happy, you wouldn't believe how much.' For the first time in her life, Jess felt truly cherished. No doubt about it. She was in love.

'Hello, Harry,' Leah said, trying to sound casual. She'd just been coming out of the shop door and there he was, large as life and twice as handsome as she remembered. It made her knees go all wobbly just to look at him. 'Thought you'd forgotten all about me.'

'Nay, how could I ever forget a smashing bird like you? Best-looking chick around. I did mean to get in touch before now but I've been a bit tied up with business lately. Feel like coming with me to the flicks tonight?'

'Oh yes,' Leah breathed. He'd asked her out. At last! He'd actually asked her out. She felt made up. That was one in the eye for Mother and all her clever little machinations. Leah knew she was treading on dangerous ground, but she didn't care. Harry Delaney was much more fun than flabby Ambrose would ever be.

They went to see Jane Russell in *The Outlaw*, and Leah felt almost jealous as Harry was clearly slavering over the Hollywood actress, his eyes nearly popping out of his head in the stable scene when she was showing off her considerable assets in that low-cut blouse.

Perhaps that was the reason why she let him go a bit further than she'd intended, allowing him to fondle her between her legs which Leah was ashamed to find got her all excited, and even more curious about what might happen next. Maybe she would let him tonight, or was that still too soon? Once she'd given in, there was no going back and, deep down, Leah still had her doubts.

Harry was filled with optimism that he'd be quids in tonight and on their way home, took her down a suitably dark alley and got going on the kissing and cuddling. He found this part boring but girls expected it, and he was willing to oblige. It paid to humour them a bit, to grease the wheels as it were, and she was certainly responsive; gave every impression of wanting him to go all the way. But then the minute he slid his hand inside her knickers she shoved him off as if he were a bit of muck she needed to shake off her shoe. He hated her for that and had to bite back his irritation.

'No, Harry. I've told you. I'm not that sort of girl.'

He longed to mock her silly, complaining voice, but managed to remain calm and resolutely single-minded. 'But you'd like to be, eh chuck? Don't try to cod me that you aren't interested. Come on, luv, what're you afraid of?' And then light dawned. 'Bloody hell, tha's still a virgin. Is that it?'

Leah could feel her cheeks start to burn and knew she was blushing, thankful now for the blackout and the privacy of the alley. 'So what if I am? Not a crime, is it?'

'It's bloody marvellous. Sorry luv, shouldn't swear in front of a lady. It's just that a chap like me doesn't come across the likes of you very often, not in a month of Sundays.'

'I don't suppose you do. Though I'm sure you've any number of girls panting for you to have your wicked way with them.'

Harry saw that he'd made a bad mistake. She was backing off, and he was that hard and eager for the off, the pain was excruciating, 'I should be so lucky. Nay, it's the war. Everyone wants their oats before it's too late.'

But he wasn't going to get any oats, not tonight he wasn't, leastways not from this silly little bitch. She was busy tidying her hair, tucking her mouth in all prim and proper and insisting they dash to the bus stop this very minute or she'd be in trouble when she got home. 'Mother will go spare. She's most particular, and gets very anxious if I'm late in.'

Mother will go spare. Not Mam – Mother. Full of herself, she was, using fancy words all the time. 'How about next week then? Or have I put you off with being so pushy?'

Leah almost cried with relief. She'd been afraid that she had put him off, by being so prissy. She really must stop being so nervous. What was there to be afraid of anyway? Everyone was entitled to a bit of fun. There was a war on, after all. And hadn't she craved some excitement in her life? If anyone could provide that, Harry could. 'That'd be lovely,' she said, casting him a speculative, sidelong glance to make sure he was still genuinely interested and not just asking her out of pity. She really fancied him like crazy, so what was holding her back? Probably the fact that he was Jess's cousin, and her friend would not approve as the two didn't get on for some reason.

Harry rewarded her with his most charming smile in a valiant attempt to disguise his irritation. Daft cow! She obviously liked playing hard to get. She'd better be worth the wait, that's all, or he wouldn't be best pleased. 'Right, you're on then. Same time, same place.'

'I could meet you inside, if you like. I don't mind paying for myself.'

He puffed out his chest as if she'd greatly offended him. 'Nay, when Harry Delaney takes his girl out, he expects to pay the full whack. Got to keep you sweet, haven't I? And you are my girl, aren't you, Leah?' Harry wheedled, dropping his voice to a soft, husky note. He often played this card because, generally speaking, it worked like a charm every time. And tonight proved to be no exception.

Leah had heard only those two simple words. *My girl!* She could hardly believe he'd said them, or that he meant it, and couldn't resist making sure. 'Is that what I am, Harry? Your girl?'

'Course you are, luv. Would I say it if it weren't true? At least you can be, if you play yer cards right. It's rather up to you, isn't it? Hey up, here's yer bus. You'll be all right now. I can walk from here, after I've seen to a bit of business with a mate of mine.' God, he thought, I'm starting to sound like me old man.

She gave him a kiss on the cheek before quite happily climbing on to the bus, waving a cheery good night as it trundled away. The moment it turned the corner, he went straight into the nearest pub and got well bevvied up. What a waste of a night that had been, not to mention the one and six each for the flicks. Flaming scandal! There was Jane Russell getting him all fired up and nowhere to run his engine. What a let-down.

He'd never expected it to take this long to have his wicked way with her and was beginning to worry that she might simply be a tease, egging him on one minute and then pulling down the shutters the next. He'd left it two whole weeks before he'd hung around the tea room with the intention of asking her out again, to make sure she'd be desperate for him after such an agonising wait. And he could tell by how her cheeks had flushed all pink, that she'd been worried that he'd forgotten all about her, even before she blurted it out in that naïve way of hers. But then it had dawned on him quite early on that Leah Simmons wasn't half so experienced or sophisticated as she made out, for all her family fancied themselves a cut above his own. For that reason alone he should have realised that she would still be a virgin, only it had never crossed his mind because, in Harry's world, such girls were as rare as hen's teeth.

Maybe she never would cut the mustard, though she didn't seem the frigid sort. If she didn't make him so blasted randy, he'd drop her here and now, not bother with her again. But there was the added attraction that everyone knew old Cliff Simmons was bow-legged with brass. When Harry had broken into the shop that day – walked in more like, since the back door had been unlocked, he'd almost been able to smell money. There surely must be a safe in there some place, where the old chap stashed his takings. If so, Harry meant to find it. At the very least he could happen squeeze a few more interesting details out of Simmons's daughter than his dad had out of Jess. Like when the wages were made up for a start, and if there were any more interesting pieces of jewellery than the odd bits of trinkets he'd already picked up off that dressing-table. A cameo brooch and a blue necklace that had turned out to be glass with no value at all.

As he staggered home later than night, he bumped into Queenie Shaw, who used to be in his class at Atherton Street school and was very nearly as inebriated as himself. Hardly able to believe his good luck, Harry took her up a back alley off Tonman Street and found her much more amenable. He'd barely unbuttoned his flies before she was ready for him. If only all girls could be so accommodating.

Cora was avid for details about Jess's young man and today, as on so many occasions recently, she was trying to persuade her to bring him home so that she could meet him. 'Fetch him, why don't you? Let's have a shufty at him.'

Lizzie lifted her head lazily to light a fresh cigarette from the one she'd smoked down to the butt before callously remarking, 'Don't imagine it'll last. Who'd want to marry Saint Jessica? Stifle any man's lust, she would.'

The remark stung and Jess could think of no satisfactory reply. But perhaps Lizzie was right in a way. It was certainly true that she'd always had a tendency to be somewhat naïve and moral, despite her colourful upbringing. Or perhaps because of it. With a mother like Lizzie you'd be bound to go one way or the other, and being involved with the Salvation Army had made her even more so. At every meeting in the citadel they were urged to resist the temptations of sin and Jess agreed with the sentiment. If you didn't stick to the stony path of righteousness, you landed up in Strangeways like her mam.

'I have boundaries over which I'm not prepared to cross. What's so wrong with that? Better than having no boundaries at all.'

Lizzie snorted her derision. 'If that's a dig at me, it won't wash. You allus think you're so much better than everyone else, stuck up little madam.'

'I'm not stuck up. I just have morals, which you seem to have lost sight of.'

'Ooh, hark at her,' Lizzie mocked. 'Has an answer for everything. Spoil anyone's fun, she would.' She was annoyed that Jess was stubbornly arguing with her, but then the lass was forever telling her what to do these days, keenly watching her every move. Fortunately, Lizzie had managed to sneak a few swift shots of whisky this morning, though that had been before breakfast and now she was desperate for another. She'd got into the habit of taking a nip or two whenever Jess wasn't looking, or when she was out for the evening with her chap. Bernie kept her well supplied with the stuff. He was a treasure, was Bernie.

'Nay Lizzie, that's no way to talk to yer own daughter. She hasn't got a mean bone in her body.' Cora was growing increasingly weary of fending off her sister-in-law's insults, once again attempting to intervene between mother and daughter as she'd frequently been called upon to do over these last weeks. Why couldn't she leave the poor lass alone? Lizzie was the selfish one, not Jess, though generally speaking the girl seemed to have endless patience with her mother. Far more than Cora had. 'Where's the harm in a bit of hand holding, or a simple kiss and cuddle? Time enough for that other mucky business later.'

'Where's the harm? Hoity-toity madam. So lah-di-dah and full of herself! Allus looking down her nose at other folk. Go on, fetch him home, why don't you? Let's have a gander at this fella of yours. See if he's got one head or two. Or are you ashamed of him?' Lizzie hiccuped loudly and swayed back into her seat.

'Course I'm not ashamed. Have you been drinking again? Is that why you're in such a foul mood?' The prospect of allowing Steve to meet her family made Jess feel sick to her stomach. What would he think of them? Would his feelings for her change, once he'd seen her as part of such a nefarious crew?

Lizzie pushed the half bottle of whisky further under the cushion. 'What's it to you, if I have? None o' your flamin' business. I'm over twenty-one and can do as I please. And don't change the subject. Are you going to fetch him to meet yer mam, or are you ashamed of me? Or is there happen summat wrong with him? Is that it?'

'Don't talk daft.' And as Lizzie reached for yet another cigarette, Jess snatched away the cushion and whipped out the whisky bottle in a flourish of exasperation. Ignoring her mother's pitiful wail, she poured the contents down the sink.

With some trepidation, Jess brought Steve to tea the following Sunday afternoon. Lizzie said, 'By heck, no wonder she's been keeping you to herself. I wouldn't mind if yer warmed my bed any time.'

Steve laughed, saying something about understanding now where Jess got her beauty from but Jess blushed scarlet to the roots of her hair. Trust her mother to make such a crude remark.

Bernie walked in at precisely that moment and stood stock still in the doorway, startled to find a stranger on his territory. Being a man who guarded his privacy, he didn't care for unexpected callers. 'What's this then?'

Introductions were made with Bernie scowling and complaining he'd had to spend half his Sunday down at the docks trying to get a shipment of merchandise released.

'You have my sympathy, Mr Delaney. Red tape is tying us all in knots these days, issuing endless lists of instructions which I'm sure wastes far more paper than we actually salvage.'

'Tha's put thee finger right on the nail there, lad.' This seemed to thaw the ice somewhat and in no time at all the two men had launched into a mutual condemnation of the evils of bureaucracy, seeming to hit it off surprisingly well. Jess put this miracle down to Steve's supreme tact and good manners and took the opportunity to whisper a few reminders to Lizzie on how she must behave.

'I hope you haven't got another bottle tucked away some place.'

'As if I would?'

'Well see you remember what I said.' Jess had earlier issued strict instructions to Lizzie not to speak unless she had something kind, or pleasant, to say. Somehow it seemed vitally important that her mother make a good impression. 'We don't want none of your caustic comments today, Mam, so watch that waspish tongue of yours. And don't you dare mention Strangeways. We want a quiet family tea, right?'

Lizzie affected innocence, claimed not to understand her daughter's concerns, had even manufactured a few tears to win sympathy. In desperation, Jess now simply resorted to bribery. 'Just keep your trap shut and I'll bring you a lovely cream cake home from work by way of a thank you tomorrow, right?'

15

At the tea, Cora was her usual, warm, caring self, fussing about like a mother hen as she brought out a plate of pink salmon, saved for just such a special occasion. There were a few slices of cucumber to go with it, as well as lettuce and tomato, Steve tucked in with gusto as if he'd never seen such a feast.

'This is grand, Mrs Delaney. Can't remember the last time I tasted a nice bit of salmon. Living in digs as I do, I rarely get anything half so good. You must be an excellent manager. It's not easy to get hold of these days.'

Cora preened herself at the compliment. 'I've made a nice trifle to follow. I've always been known for my trifles.'

'I can't wait.' Steve even succeeded in eliciting a smile from Sandra by admiring the pretty colour of the ribbon in her hair, and had Sam and Seb giggling in no time as he plaited his handkerchief into the shape of a rabbit. Fortunately, Harry and Bert were out today, though no one was quite sure what they were up to. Jess was simply relieved not to have them around stirring up mischief. Tommy had done what he'd been threatening for so long and accepted his call-up without protest, unlike his cowardly brothers. He'd gone off the previous week to join the Manchester Regiment. Leah, Jess had noticed with interest, had been moping about with a face like a wet fortnight for ages. Tommy's sudden departure was unlikely to improve her mood.

Conversation at the table was slow and rather stilted at first, concentrated mainly upon the war, on how things had changed in and around Deansgate village and what improvements would be needed when it was finally over. 'Which it will be soon enough,' Bernie announced, as if Churchill had assured him personally of that fact.

Cora's mind was not on the future, but firmly set in the past. She was entertaining her visitor by reminiscing over going to Smithfield market on Shudehill to buy fish and vegetables when she was a girl, and seeing the barrow boys selling cherries. 'Tuppence a pound they were, though I had to have been a good girl to get even a farthing's worth. Before the war, the first one that is, my gran would buy tea from Seymour Mead every Christmas as a treat. Cost a bleedin' fortune it did. They sold lovely bacon an' all. Eeh, I did love the shops on Deansgate and Market Street,' and went on to say how she thought it was nothing short of a miracle that Barton Arcade had survived the Blitz when all the rest were tragically little more than a memory now, buried beneath a heap of rubble. 'Not that I have time to do much shopping these days. I leave all of that to Bernie, don't I love?'

Bernie cleared his throat, a warning sound which made Cora cast a nervous glance in his direction. She should watch her tongue, she was gabbing too much. 'Eeh, hark at me, rabbiting on. I'll fetch the trifle, shall I?' and leaping from the table she hastily began to clear and stack plates. Jess got up to help, while Lizzie patted her pockets for a cigarette, remembered Jess had deprived her of these too and sank into a deep sulk.

While the women worked, Bernie was closely examining their visitor, wondering whether this relationship could be turned to his advantage. He hated to miss an opportunity for using somebody and, judging by Steve Wyman's comments earlier, he was clearly a man with views. 'So what line are you in then? How come you aren't in uniform?'

'Aircraft building. Can't say too much about that, sorry. Pretty hush-hush.'

'Course it is. Leave him alone, let the lad enjoy his tea,' Cora said, placing a dish of trifle before him with a small flourish of triumph.

'My word, Mrs Delaney, that looks grand.' Steve tucked in with relish, having been previously warned by Jess not to ask how she'd got hold of the coupons, despite all the fruit and cream.

Bernie's interest had perked up considerably at talk of an aircraft factory, and wondered whether he could get his hand on a load of screws or bolts, or some such, 'I suppose security must be pretty tight at them places?' he enquired blithely.

'I'll say. Tight as a drum. We're searched going in and coming out. The pressure is immense but I let off steam by spending my evenings playing in a dance band.'

'A *dance* band?' Bernie said the word with utter contempt since he could think of no possible benefit from knowing someone in a dance band. What was there to trade from there? Sheet music was useless, and he'd not got more than a few quid for that blasted trumpet when he'd finally found someone to take it off his hands. 'Why would you do that? Does it make you much money?'

Steve laughed, shaking his head. 'Wish it did. The pay can vary, depending on the booking but no, that isn't the main reason I do it. I just love the music, and being a part of that scene.'

Bernie gave a disparaging growling sound deep in his throat. 'Our Jess took a notion into her head to play a flamin' trumpet, with the Sally Army of all people. I soon put a stop to that business. I made it plain she were not to play it any more. Daft as a brush she is, and twice as useless. I wouldn't mind if she were any good, but she's like a troop of tom cats on the prowl.'

There was a short silence at this. Sam and Seb looked about them, bemused, as if expecting a troop of tom cats to appear out of nowhere that very minute; Sandra giggled and Lizzie gave a snort of laughter which turned into a loud hiccup as a result of the snifter of gin she'd just downed in place of water.

Cora said, 'Now Bernie luv, don't start on that, not when we have visitors.'

'Start on what? I'm not starting on anything. I'm simply stating a plain fact. Having me eardrums blasted day and night with that caterwauling, wasn't my idea of domestic bliss. I put a stop to it, and quite rightly.'

'I think Jess is rather good actually,' Steve said, smiling proudly at her.

Bernie's mouth dropped open, as if no one had ever disagreed with him before, or dared to challenge his word, not in his own house at his own tea table, and he didn't quite know how to deal with it. 'What did tha say?'

Ignoring his host's nasty scowl Steve turned to Lizzie and blithely continued, 'You must be so proud of your daughter's musical talent, Mrs Delaney.'

Lizzie, unable to resist masculine charm and feeling very slightly woozy, gave a weak smile and agreed, muttering something about Jess getting it from her father who'd been quite gifted in that direction.

Jess tried to intervene and prevent what instinct told her was coming next but Steve simply grasped the hand she was flapping at him and held it firmly in his own. 'I certainly am. Very proud. She played at the Ritz the other afternoon and stunned her listeners rigid. What a talent she has. Pity we can't bottle it and sell it to the troops, we'd win this war in no time then. Vera Lynn had better watch out, or they might adopt a very different sort of forces' sweetheart.'

Bernie was staring at his niece, dumbfounded. 'Tha played at the Ritz? How did thee manage that? Didn't I get rid of that bleedin' trumpet, to make damned sure tha never played it again?'

Jess hung her head, not knowing what to say for the best, for whatever she did say would be wrong. She should've known this visit would turn into a disaster. Steve had un-wittingly dropped her right in it. Uncle Bernie would never let her hear the last of this, never.

Steve, perhaps realising some of this, said quickly. 'Oh, it was my trumpet, not hers. She borrowed the instrument from me.'

The glance of gratitude she sent him was intercepted by her uncle and all too accurately interpreted. 'Dusta think I were born yesterday? Thee *would* say that. I know a bare-faced lie when I see one. Where is it lass? Upstairs? Go and fetch it.'

'I can explain . . .'

'Go and fetch it this sodding minute.' Bernie was on his feet now, his voice raised in temper, sending the trifle dishes spinning to the floor as he slammed his fist down upon the table and glared furiously at the pair of them. 'I'll not be bested in me own home.' He jerked one thumb in the direc-tion of the door. 'And you, young man, can sling your hook. Jess is under-age and I say where she goes and what she does. If I put a stop to summat, it stays stopped. Understand? Got that? I'll have no bloody trumpet playing in this house. I had enough of that poncy, arty-farty rubbish wi' her dad. If this little madam has time on her hands, I can find a better use for it, see if I can't. Do I make meself clear?'

Steve, looking deathly pale and deeply concerned; had

half risen to his feet. Jess squeezed his hand by way of reassurance. 'It's all right. You go. I can handle this.'

'Like hell you can. I'm not leaving you to handle anything, not on your own.'

'I can manage, really I can. It won't help, your being here. It'll only make matters worse.' She was almost in tears now, urging him to go, wanting this whole scene never to have taken place. Oh, why did her uncle always have to spoil everything?

Looking Bernie straight in the eye, Steve said, 'The trumpet she has upstairs is most definitely mine, and if anything – unfortunate – should happen to it, I'm going to be very, very angry. Very angry indeed! Even more important, if any harm should come to Jess here, simply for having possession of it, or playing at the Ritz, or for any other reason for that matter, I won't be responsible for my actions. Do *I* make myself clear?' Then turning to Jess he continued more quietly, 'I'll go because you insist that I do, but I'll be back later, just to check you're all right.' And politely thanking Cora once more for entertaining him so royally, he collected his hat and made for the door.

Tears filled her eyes. Nobody had ever stood up to Bernie like that before, not so steadfastly, nor on her behalf. 'No, wait Steve. I'm coming with you.' At the door she paused to look back at her uncle sitting frozen in his seat, his face like thunder, and took a deep breath. 'I'll be back when you've calmed down a bit but I'll not give up my music for anyone. I thought I'd already made that perfectly clear. You'd do well to remember that I'm not a kid any longer and I'll do as I please.'

'Like bleedin' hell you will.' But the words went unheard as Jess and Steve escaped into the street, running off, hand in hand.

Sidling up to her father's side, Sandra said in her nasal,

whining voice, 'That little madam has got the better of you again, Dad. I'm surprised you stand for it.'

Bernie flung out a hand and knocked his daughter flying, making her howl in surprised anguish. As the twins started up in unified sympathy, and Cora rushed to shush and pet her offspring, Bernie threw the remains of the trifle to the floor then trod through the resulting mess to storm out of the house in their wake, muttering furiously to himself that Jess Delaney might have won the opening skirmish, but he'd win the flaming battle. See if he didn't.

Not too far away, across on Deansgate, Leah was making every effort to resist her mother's insistence that she play a little Beethoven to entertain the Gartsides. Muriel had invited them to tea, along with their beloved son, the ubiquitous Ambrose, and Leah was having great difficulty in maintaining the expected level of politeness which one should adopt for guests.

Perhaps her mother had been right in one respect, he no longer resembled a suet pudding, all fat and squashy with red currants pitted into his skin. He looked more like a pink slice of Spam in a sandwich as he sat on the sofa between his even more substantial parents. Admittedly his bulk was firming into the muscle of a mature man rather than a plump boy, but he still didn't interest Leah in the slightest. Nothing about him appealed to her. She could hardly bear to even look at him without feeling a huge urge to laugh, particularly since he appeared as miserable as she felt, as he stared moodily down at the floor.

His mother had spent the last hour, or perhaps longer, listing his virtues and attributes, explaining at length why it was important for her precious son to be allowed to finish his education, war or no war. How he would soon be going to university to train as a doctor, and how she was hoping this would be considered as suitable war work in place of active service. He was due his call-up soon and, like all mothers, she was terrified of losing him at the very moment he became a man.

'The war can't last for ever,' Mr Simmons assured her, clearly wishing to draw a line under this fruitless, and seemingly endless discussion. 'Even if Ambrose is called up, I doubt he'd be in any real danger. Genuine advances are being made, we're hitting factories in France, our convoys are reaching Russian waters and with the help of American armoured divisions, it won't be long now before Hitler throws in the towel.'

'Ah, but *you* can afford to take such a relaxed view since you do not have a son about to be sent into active service,' the boy's desperate mother insisted.

Cliff Simmons looked momentarily stunned, as if Robert's bravery and not his poor eyesight had been called into question. 'We are all affected by the war in some way or other, dear lady.'

Muriel stepped quickly to her husband's aid by taking her daughter's elbow and almost dragging Leah from the chair where she'd been skulking for the entire evening, 'I think, darling, we'd all appreciate being lifted out of our war gloom, perhaps with a little Beethoven?'

Leah thought this might be much more likely to depress them still further. Hadn't she suffered from years of being coerced to play whatever her mother thought suitable, but seeing how her father's brow darkened ominously, she obediently made her way over to the pianoforte. No point in making a fuss now as there'd be confrontation enough later when she'd told them all about Harry. Once her mother discovered she'd been dating a *Delaney*, for God's sake, she'd have a heart attack for sure.

Not that Leah really cared. She'd been out with him twice

more since that first date, going a little further along that dangerous road each time. They were having a marvellous time together so what did it matter if their backgrounds were slightly different? They lived only a few streets apart in Deansgate village. Their respective families were both working-class folk. There surely wasn't that much to choose between them? Except that her parents, Leah realised, would not see it that way. To Muriel, the Delaneys were the lowest of low. How could she convince her otherwise: that the son need not be tarred by the same nasty brush as his father?

Leah placed her fingers on the keys preparatory to launching into Muriel's favourite piece, 'The Moonlight Sonata', when her mother artlessly suggested that Ambrose could turn the pages for her, almost as if this were a completely spontaneous thought that had occurred to her on the spur of the moment, and had not been planned in fine detail hours earlier.

Mrs Gartside was giving her son a gentle nudge, just as if he were still five years old and she needed to encourage him to go out and play. 'Go along dear. I'm sure Leah would appreciate your assistance.'

Finding Ambrose suddenly at her side, scowling slightly yet clearly ready to behave like the good, obedient son he undoubtedly was, all Leah's nerve endings seemed to fizz with suppressed fury. Why would he imagine that she needed or wanted his help? Men were so arrogant, always believing themselves to be indispensable. He was probably peeved with her for not looking suitably grateful for his assistance. She'd largely ignored him all evening, which Leah fully intended to go on doing. What did he think he was doing, for heavens' sake? Behaving like a damned puppet while his mother pulled the strings?

But was she any better?

'You must stay in on Sunday,' her own mother had

insisted, without even enquiring whether she wished to do so or not. 'I've invited the Gartsides.' She'd then gone on to inform Leah how she would be expected to entertain them on the pianoforte, and now she was telling her to play Beethoven, knowing full well that he was a composer she disliked immensely.

Leah felt rather like some nineteenth-century young miss being asked to perform at a musical soirée. Perhaps she should be wearing a pretty Empire line gown instead of these pale blue slacks and sweater. Yet despite her resentment, here she was seated at the piano, about to do exactly as she was bid. What next? Jump in the lake? Marry Ambrose? Leah recklessly decided that if she had a choice in the matter, she'd choose the former.

But of course she had a choice! What was she thinking of? There always was a choice. She'd much rather have Harry Delaney any day, no matter what her mother might say. It was her life, not Muriel's, and she must be in control of it. Leah glanced up at Ambrose, ready to tell him, in a fit of rebellion, that she really didn't need his help and for the first time recognised a similar panic in him. For a moment Leah was so stunned that she met his gaze unflinching, instead of avoiding it as she usually did. He didn't look like a loyal son at all, more like a rabbit caught in a trap, rather as *she* must look. And it suddenly came to her in that moment that he wasn't enjoying these parental machinations any more than she was.

While chairs were being moved in preparation for the anticipated recital, lamps lit and blinds drawn Leah politely enquired if he read music, if only for the sake of something to say to fill an awkward moment.

Ambrose shook his head. 'Only a little. Not really my thing.'

'What is your thing?' For the first time, she felt a spurt of curiosity about this young man who had so little to say for himself.

'I like rugby, any sport really. And fishing. I enjoy fishing most of all.'

'Why fishing for heavens' sake?'

'I like the quiet on the canal bank.'

'Ah.' Leah nodded, struggling to understand anyone who preferred silence rather than filling their head with beautiful sounds. She lowered her voice to little above a whisper while she rifled through sheet music, apparently seeking a particular piece she needed. 'What I mean is, I know what your mother wants for you, but what do *you* want to do? Do you wish to go to university and train to be a doctor, or else become a printer like your father?'

He leaned closer so that he wouldn't be overheard, and there was almost a smile on his round face. 'Neither. I've always intended to join up just the minute they'll have me. In fact, I've already been in touch. I'll be going any day now, and I've every intention of staying in the army, war or no war. I want to become a regular soldier.'

Leah's eyes widened and she could actually feel her mouth slacken and drop open in shock. Never, in all her life, would she have imagined him wanting such a thing, or being so brave as to go ahead and do it. How amazing people were. 'And you haven't told your parents?' she whispered back in awed tones.

He shook his head.

'Your mother won't like it.'

'Neither will yours,' and suddenly he grinned and Leah gave a spurt of laughter which she quickly smothered with the flat of her hand.

'No, indeed she won't. OK, let's really give them something to think about, shall we?'

She played the opening bars of 'The Moonlight Sonata',

as directed, developing the mood of the piece nicely, aware of the hush of appreciation from the assembled company, of Ambrose seated beside her, anxiously following the notes and patiently waiting to turn the page at her signal. But then with her left hand, she placed her finger and thumb together on the lowest note she could reach and drew them swiftly up the length of the keyboard, running one note into the next in a rising crescendo of sound, before lapsing into 'Tiger Rag'.

Leah had always been more of an instinctive musician rather than one who followed notes, played chromatic scales or studied appropriate exercises. Now she simply let rip, putting all her heart and soul and energy into the music. Jazz and swing were her thing, not boring fishing, or Beethoven. Out of the corner of her eye she could see Ambrose's square fingers happily tapping out the rhythm on his knee. When she was done and the music ended in an abrupt and startled silence, he burst into lavish applause. No one else moved a muscle.

Harry's luck had changed. Later that same afternoon when the Gartsides had gone home in a flurry of embarrassment and excuses from Muriel, Leah made her apologies to her tight-lipped parents and declared herself in need of some fresh air. She escaped their frosty silence for an early evening stroll by the canal and, to her astonishment and delight, found Harry waiting for her, almost as if he'd possessed some second sight into her movements. She was not to know that he'd been keeping a watch on the house for an hour or more in the hope she might come out, Queenie Shaw not being available this afternoon.

'Was that him, your intended?' he asked, jerking his head in the direction of where the Gartsides had driven off in their little Ford motor.

Leah gave a grunt of disdain. 'He would be, if my mother had any say in the matter.'

'Which she doesn't?'

'None at all.'

'I'm glad to hear it. Feel like a stroll?'

'Can't think of anything I'd like better.'

'Can't you?' He grinned at her. 'I can think of summat we could do far more exciting than walking.'

After that, it was the easiest thing in the world to finish what he'd started all those weeks before. With practised ease Harry slid the buttons of her dress undone, kissing her soft willing mouth all the while, probing it with his tongue, giving her no time to think as he peeled the dress from her naked shoulders. Removing her brassière was soon dealt with and before she'd thought to protest about the knickers, which were indeed white, lacy, and very French, his excitement was by then at such a fever pitch that he'd ripped them off and was thrusting his way into her in seconds. And, judging by the way she moved beneath him, she wasn't complaining. True, there'd been a small startled cry as he'd entered her, which served only to inflame his passion further. And perhaps, because of her inexperience, she wasn't quite as exciting as he'd hoped although taking a virgin always had its own kick of satisfaction. In no time at all it was over and Harry felt completely vindicated by his patience. No other bloke could ever have what he'd just taken. By heck, but he was a grand, clever chap. Wasn't he just?

Ever since that afternoon at the Ritz when she'd played her trumpet in front of all those people, Jess's attitude towards her music had changed, aided and abetted by Steve's championing her in front of Bernie at the Sunday tea. She was used to entertaining bombed-out victims at the mobile canteen but saw that not only could she bring pleasure and comfort with her trumpet but also make it serve a very different purpose. If she were part of a band she could do as Steve was doing and play at dances, with the added benefit of earning money from it which, in turn, might go some way towards paying off her debts to the Salvation Army. She might even be able to buy them a new trumpet to replace the one her uncle had so cruelly disposed of. Although Ted had very kindly held no grudges over the loss of the instrument, Jess knew well enough that the band could ill afford to suffer such a blow. Yet she held little hope of persuading Uncle Bernie to return it. She'd already visited every pawnbroker in Manchester, and now with Mr Yoffey gone, could think of nowhere else it might be.

Besides all of this, it would be yet another useful way of escaping the claustrophobic four walls of the house on Cumberland Street, her miserable, complaining mother and Uncle Bernie's tyranny. The very next day after finishing work at the tea room, she screwed up all her courage and went down to the Ritz to ask Hal, the bandleader, for a job.

'Sorry love, you're good, I'll give you that. But my chaps would never wear it, not a chick in the band. Wouldn't work.'

No matter how much she protested about there being a war on and women doing all kinds of different things they'd never done before, he refused to budge. Disappointment bit deep but the ambition to play in a dance band, now she'd been given a taste for it, simply wouldn't go away. Being rejected brought all her stubbornness to the fore and Jess became more determined than ever. What had being a woman got to do with anything? She could play as well as any of the lads.

And so an idea was born.

She didn't talk to Steve about it in case he tried to put her off. He might be the sort to encourage her but she didn't want to take the risk. Look how he'd reacted to her *purloining* his trumpet, in the beginning at least. Besides, who better to share the idea with than Leah, her very best friend who, unfortunately, merely laughed.

'You're going to start what – a dance band? Have you gone soft in the head?'

'No, I'm perfectly serious. Just a small one, to start with anyway, and all female. We'd need a sax player, clarinet, maybe a cello or double bass, most certainly a drummer, which might be the most difficult to find. You could play the piano and I would play the trumpet of course.'

Leah was struggling to take in this new information, to drag her attention back from other distracting thoughts. Ever since Sunday when she and Harry had finally gone the whole way and put the seal on their growing romance, she'd been in a lather of concern. She really couldn't recall him taking any precautions, and she'd been in such a mad, reckless mood herself that day she'd never thought to ask. She'd counted on her fingers and deduced that in a couple of weeks she'd know for certain if she was safe or not. In the meantime, she was glad of anything which took her mind off the terrifying possibility that she might be pregnant, that her safe, comfortable world could collapse about her ears.

And what if it did collapse? Did she want to marry Harry? Would he even consider marrying her? Leah rather doubted it. She'd never had any desire for matrimony. Leah felt far too young and not in the least bit ready for anything so grown-up. She just wanted a good time, to put some fun and excitement into her boring, sheltered life. So she put the problem resolutely from her mind. 'Where would we play with this band?'

'At dances of course. We'd probably need to advertise although it might be worthwhile circularising all the local ballrooms and dance halls to tell them of our existence and expertise.'

Leah giggled. 'Do we have any? Expertise, I mean, and we don't exist yet, do we? So far there's only you and me.'

'A piece in the small ads of the *Manchester Guardian* could change that tomorrow. So, are you with me on this, or not?'

'Too right I am. Anything is better than playing Beethoven to Ambrose flipping Gartside.'

16

The advert brought forth fewer replies than Jess had hoped. Having got permission from Sergeant Ted to hold the auditions in a meeting room at the back of the mission hall where there was an ancient but well-tuned piano, she and Leah settled down one Saturday afternoon after the tea room had closed to wait for the hopefuls to arrive. 'We can only pray that there might be one or two last minute entries to give us some sort of choice.'

'Otherwise it's—' Leah consulted the list. 'Mary, Flossie and Lulu. Lord, the names alone put me off.'

Mary turned out to be tall and elegant and absolutely refused to play jazz. Her instrument was the violin and she'd only ever played Beethoven. She was willing to lower her standards a little, she informed them, in order to do her bit to entertain the nice soldiers, but there were limits. Leah thanked her politely for coming and Jess said that perhaps the advert had misled her, knowing full well that the wording had plainly stated that they were forming a dance band. Who, in their right minds, would choose to dance to Beethoven, worthy as that great composer was.

Flossie, as her name might suggest, was plump and over-dressed in a pink floral frock with an amazing array of frills about the hem and neck. She breathlessly agreed that she'd play anything, absolutely anything they wanted her to play. She really had no particular preferences herself, absolutely *loved* music and dancing, and was simply *desperate* to be a part of their band.

The only problem was that she couldn't – play that is. If she hit a right note on her brand new, shining clarinet, Jess freely admitted afterwards to having missed it. Leah could scarcely accompany her on the piano for giggling.

'Thank you so much. Have you been playing long?' she asked.

Flossie confessed that she hadn't. This was a recent hobby, taken up when her husband was sent overseas at Easter and he bought her the instrument as a going-away present to keep her company.

'Come and see us again then, when you've had a bit more practice and experience.' And Flossie went away quite happy, vowing to work harder at her music lessons in future, now that she had a goal in mind.

Lulu breezed into the room all fire and energy and boundless enthusiasm, sleek and shiny blonde hair cut in a stylish bob bounced upon slender shoulders seemingly with a life of its own. With lips painted a bright fuchsia and nails to match, she would clearly be a wow with all the 'nice soldiers'. She was also clearly gifted on the tenor sax. Reduced to tears by the skill with which she played 'As Time Goes By', her chosen piece, Jess offered her a job without a moment's hesitation.

'You do realise that it's on the understanding I can't pay you any money until we start earning some. This is all a bit of a gamble. I intend to make a start by advertising ourselves in the local rag, visiting ballroom managers to actively seek work, and maybe organise a dance of our own, just to get us launched.'

Lulu agreed this all sounded perfectly fair. 'Hell, why not? Life's short, let's experiment a bit and have some fun.'

'Hear, hear,' echoed Leah, and Jess cast her a sideways

glance, the fleeting thought crossing her mind that her friend seemed pale and hadn't been quite her usual smiling self recently, despite a show of bounce and superficial good humour.

There being no other candidates that day, Jess locked up and the two girls celebrated the start of their dream with fish and chips on their way home.

Next morning, Jess optimistically got on with making preparations for the dance. She arranged to hire Atherton Street School Hall and had posters printed which she and Leah stuck up a few days later, all over Deansgate village. These gave full details of the dance and announced the introduction of Delaney's All Girls Band, tickets being available at the Co-op. But she was still trying to find other band members. One trumpet, sax and a piano was nowhere near enough. Jess and Leah trawled through all the dance halls, asking around, hoping that word would spread.

'What if we don't find anyone else?' Leah dared ask one day as yet another week slid by with no further response to a second ad in the *Guardian*, or to their enquiries.

Jess brushed her concern aside. 'We will, don't worry. We've still got three weeks before the date of the dance. Plenty of time.' Privately, she felt nowhere near as confident as she sounded.

On the plus side, Steve had proved to be entirely supportive, as she should have guessed he would be from the start, in particular by helping them to find suitable pieces to play and providing some old sheet music to rehearse with. He'd even offered to fill the gaps in the band with some of the lads, if necessary. Jess expressed her gratitude but refused point-blank. She simply wouldn't hear of it.

'Absolutely not! I intend to create an all female band or nothing at all. I'll cancel the dance sooner than admit defeat.

I want to show that women are every bit as good with music
as men.'

'Independent to a fault,' he teased, shaking his head in
mock despair, all the same approving of her determination to
make the plan work.

Then just as even Jess herself had begun to give up hope,
a young girl walked in on their somewhat half-hearted
rehearsal one evening, saying she'd heard they were looking
for a clarinettist. Adele was small with shining black hair,
ruby lips and flashing dark eyes, and seemed to pulsate optimism and energy. 'I smoke, drink, have never managed to
hold down a decent job in my life because I have itchy feet
and hate to be in one place for more than five minutes. Oh,
and I'm never on time.'

'You are at least honest,' Jess said with a wry smile. 'But
you would need to be on time for rehearsals with us, and
never miss a performance. Right?'

'I'll do me best, chuck. Hey, and I also have a weakness for
Sherbet dabs. Playing this thing is all I'm any good at.' And
lifting it to her lips, she started to play 'I Got Rhythm'. She
was indeed good. Excellent in fact and Jess hired her on the
spot. She'd work on the punctuality problem later.

It was a week or two later that Bernie announced his decision
to find them a place of their own after all. Jess was so startled
by this change of heart that she was instantly suspicious and
asked what he was up to. He adopted a wounded expression,
as if she'd mortally wounded him.

'Nay, I can surely do summat for me own kith and kin. I
decided you were right, you and Lizzie do need yer own
home. It'll happen keep yer mind off this daft music business
you've got so involved with.'

What would he say if he knew that 'this daft music business' as he called it, was practically taking over her life. Every

evening when she wasn't working at the mobile canteen, Jess, together with Leah and the girls practised hard in the back room of the mission hall and she was still on the lookout for more band members. Like Steve, Sergeant Ted had been most helpful with advice and assistance and had got quite interested in their little enterprise, as had many of the regulars who came in for soup or a bed for the night. They would tap their feet in time to the music, or bang on the wall to complain if they hit too many wrong notes, which they frequently did at first.

All in all, matters were proceeding very smoothly. There'd been little interest from the ballroom managers thus far, but Jess had hopes that after they'd run a dance of their own, they might sit up and take notice. The word would soon get about if they played well.

Keeping all of this to herself, Jess frowned at her uncle and said, 'I thought you said you couldn't afford to help us. What's changed? Anyroad, if the money isn't honestly come by, I'm not sure I want anything to do with it.'

'Dusta want a knuckle buttie? There's no pleasing some folk. I'm doing thee a favour. The war can't last for ever so we have to start thinking of the future. You and that chap o'yourn will happen want to settle down and get wed one day.'

Jess flushed bright crimson and, as always, when embarrassed, instantly went on the attack. 'Nothing of the sort has been suggested. In any case, it's none of your business what we decide to do, and I can't believe you're doing this out of the kindness of your heart because you haven't got one, you nasty old bloodsucker. You must have some ulterior motive.'

'Nay, that's a mite unkind Jess, lass. I've never neglected thee have I? Allus seen you well provided for, even when yer mam were in t'clink, eh? Your well-being is my chief consideration now and ever will be,' stroking the strands of greasy hair across his bald pate and smiling at her in that sickening way he had.

He was up to something, Jess decided, and she'd have to take extra care till she found out exactly what it was.

Bernie felt he could afford to be generous since he'd recently enjoyed a stroke of good luck. On one of his scavenging missions, admittedly in a classier area on Stretford Road out Hulme way, he'd enjoyed a most profitable expedition. He'd picked up a velvet bag, released it more like from the hand of its former owner, who was still holding on to it for dear life though she'd never have call to use it again. The poor sod had obviously copped it when her house came down in ruins around her ears while dressing for some fancy do or other. Inside the bag was a little box and inside the box, he'd found a ring. The fact it was so neatly stowed away within the velvet jewellery bag convinced him that it must be valuable. Perhaps she'd been about to put it on before going out gallivanting.

'I'll give it a good home, luv,' he'd promised, shoving the ring in his pocket, together with a strand of pearls, a diamante brooch and a couple of pairs of earrings, hiding the velvet bag in the rubble to avoid harbouring incriminating evidence.

And he'd been proved right. His old friend, Bodger Smith, had identified the stone as a diamond. He'd handed over a fair sum for it, admittedly nowhere near its true value but then, as Bodger explained, he had his own expenses to account for, and he needed to find a buyer for the ring before he himself made any money out of it at all. Bernie was more than happy with the deal. The pearls and brooch fetched a tidy sum too, though the earrings weren't worth much and so Bernie decided to hang on to those. Happen he'd give a pair to Cora for her birthday, or to a more exciting woman should one happen along. He could afford to be a bit more choosy in that department if he had a bit of brass in his pocket. Lizzie didn't satisfy him any more. She was as besotted with him as ever and all he had to do was to keep her supplied with the booze and she'd stay that way, but whatever sparkling titillation she'd once provided had long since fizzled out.

He believed that the end of all his troubles was at last in sight. He'd got enough money to settle his debts, with plenty left over to expand his enterprises. With this bit of spare cash in his pocket, he was seeking an opportunity not only to rid himself of a tricky situation of having three women in one house, but also to manipulate matters to his own advantage. He felt this was his moment to branch out, to stop being a small-time crook and slide smoothly up a notch into a bigger league.

Adele announced one day that she'd been talking to her old music teacher, who played the cello like an angel apparently, and was interested in joining the band.

Miss Mona, as she liked to be called, proved to be a quiet, dignified lady of mature years with white hair and spectacles perched precariously on the bridge of her sharply pointed nose. The idea of hiring someone's music teacher sounded rather daunting to Jess. However, it was such a huge relief to have another band member signed up and, with the day of the dance drawing ever nearer, she was beginning to panic just a little.

'All we need now is a drummer.'

The lack of a drummer proved to be the least of their worries as, days before it was due to take place, Cissie Armitage, who now worked at the Co-op in order to keep a sick husband and her two remaining children, apologised to Jess that she'd sold very few tickets. 'I did me best, luv, as most folk are in need of a bit of a laugh these days but few had even heard the dance were taking place and had already made other arrangements, while others said they wouldn't touch it with the proverbial bargepole.'

'But why hadn't they heard of it? We put up posters everywhere. People love to dance, and I thought it would cheer everyone up in the middle of winter.'

Cissie went to the shop door, opened it and glanced up and down the cold, empty street as if to check they weren't being overheard. There was little that Cissie missed in this close-knit community, but she wasn't keen on other folk knowing her own business. 'It's nearly dinner time, you can go off early,' she told the young boy who helped her behind the counter. He grabbed his coat and wasted no time in doing so. A wind whistled bitingly in and she shut the door again with a bang, pulled down the blind and slid the bolt across. She nodded at Jess. 'Come through to t'back.'

Once she was satisfied that they were quite alone, Cissie continued, 'I reckon you should ask that uncle o' thine what's put folk off. If 'n you ask me, he's been using threats left, right and flipping centre, telling people to stay away if they know what's good fer them; that there's going to be trouble at the dance and he'll be the one to start it. Warned me an' all that I'd live to regret it if I sold a single ticket over this counter. I told him to sling his hook. Having lost me babby, and wi' our Tom laid up, I don't give a tuppenny damn. I've no proof but I reckon it were them two cousins o' thine what nicked me stuff that night we were bombed, so no Delaney is going to bully me. Anyroad, folk should enjoy theirselves while they can, that's my view.'

Jess listened to all of this in stunned silence. How dare he try to spike her plans? What right did he have? First he nicked her trumpet, now he was trying to ruin her future yet again, to destroy all her dreams. Presumably because she refused to give in to his threats and pass on vital information about the financial situation at the Tea Room. What a nasty piece of goods he was. Oh, but she wouldn't let him ruin everything. She really wouldn't. She'd go ahead regardless.

Undeterred, Jess asked Mr Simmons for a day off work and spent the entire time calling on friends and neighbours to tell them that the dance was going ahead regardless, and would they spread the word that tickets would now be available on the door. When the day finally arrived, Jess and her fellow band members, including Adele, all turned up on time at Atherton Street School Hall, and started to tune up. Seven o'clock approached and, apart from Cissie with one or two of her mates and Ma Pickles and her son Josh, there were a few regulars from the mobile canteen and two little boys all goggle-eyed, asking if they could get in for half price. No one else turned up. It was a complete disaster. Delaney's All Girls Band waited in vain for three quarters of an hour, then packed up their instruments and went home.

Further investigation revealed that every one of their expensively printed posters had been ripped down, so was it any wonder if few people had even heard about the dance. And none knew better than Jess how Bernie could bully even those who did know of it, to stay away. Wasn't he an expert in that department?

'We're done for,' Leah said, her eyes oddly bright, almost feverish.

Jess considered her more closely, surprised and a little hurt by her friend's negative attitude. 'Nonsense, it's not the end of the world. I, for one, am not ready to hang up my trumpet yet, not after all that trouble I had getting hold of one in the first place, and learning how to play the dratted thing. Didn't we always say that women were the stronger sex, that we weren't going to rush into marriage but live life to the full, war or no war? Hey, are you sickening for something?'

'Whatever makes you think so?'

'You look proper green about the gills. Are you missing Tommy, is that it? Don't fret. He's like a cat is our Tommy, blessed with nine lives. Nothing will happen to him.'

The colour in Leah's pretty face paled even further. 'Why would I be worried about Tommy?' Leah still hadn't owned up to the fact that it was his brother, Harry, she was dating. Jess had put two and two together and made five, and all because of their once meeting Tommy that time at a dance.

'I expect we're all just a bit strained and tired. It was a distressing evening and I didn't sleep well afterwards, did you?'

Leah could scarcely think straight but Jess's artless comments made her feel worse than ever. She'd got away with it last month, and the one before, but her period this time was two days late and the disappointment over the band was the least of her worries. It seemed as if her greatest fear was about to come true. She was terrified. What would her mother say? Muriel would crucify her for sure; throw her out of the house and tell her not to darken her doorstep again. Leah couldn't begin to imagine how she would manage to bring up a child on her own, homeless and without a father, and with the shame of illegitimacy attached. Not for one moment did she expect Harry to do the decent thing. He was far too self-centred and had never uttered any protestations of undying love. They'd just been having fun, nothing more.

She'd done her best to avoid him during these last couple of weeks, and on the one occasion she had succumbed to his pleas, she'd been more than a little frosty towards him, much to his irritation. When she'd slapped his fumbling caresses away as he'd walked her home after the pictures, he'd stormed off and left her all alone in the middle of Albert Square. Afterwards, she'd regretted being so abrupt and, to her shame, had cried herself to sleep that night. It had been their first quarrel.

What a mess she'd got herself into. It would never do for Jess to suspect. Didn't she have enough on her plate, what with her uncle being difficult, her mother sliding back into her old bad habits, and the poor girl desperately striving to find a solution to all of this through her meagre savings, as well as fulfil her own musical ambitions? Right now it was better for Jess to continue to think she was simply worried about Tommy.

The moment Jess heard Lizzie's warbling snores tune up, she dug out the old toffee tin from under her mattress and counted every carefully hoarded shilling. She couldn't do everything. Jess knew she was asking too much of herself. She couldn't repay Sergeant Ted for the trumpet Uncle Bernie had nicked, *and* save enough to set up a place of their own, *and* organise a dance. But nor could she allow her uncle to control her life and get the better of her. She had to win her independence one way or another, to somehow break free to fulfil her own ambitions and not simply become obsessed with family problems, dire though they may be. She supposed that a part of her had snatched at the idea of starting a band in the hope that it would prove to be a good investment: help her to not only replace the money she'd withdrawn from her savings, but also add more to it. What she hadn't bargained for was having to do everything twice, or for it to cost quite so much. Still, in for a penny . . .

With this in mind, Jess resolutely determined not to give in but to start from scratch all over again. Only this time she sought Cora's advice, in the hope that her aunt could give her some tips. Jess was beginning to understand that Uncle Bernie's family avoided direct confrontation with his bad temper by careful manipulation, not by pure chance at all. That's why no one ever disagreed with him. Leah had been right. They kept what they were up to as secret as possible, in order to avoid trouble.

And indeed her suspicions were proved to be correct as Cora's first reaction was to advise caution through absolute secrecy. 'Nay, don't tell him you're going to hold another, nor owt what you're up to, love, then he can't spoil it.'

'How can I keep quiet when I need to advertise the dance in order to get people to come to it?'

Cora slid a fried egg next to the chips on Jess's dinner plate as a special treat to compensate for her disappointment, and conceded that this might indeed create a difficulty. 'Well then, you'll just have to put your posters a long way from Deansgate where folk aren't scared of our Bernie.'

'But why would perfect strangers, people from another part of Manchester come to our little dance when they can go to the Ritz or somewhere nearer to home?'

Stumped for an answer to this one, Cora picked up a chip and absent-mindedly dipped it into the yolk of Jess's egg. 'Well, that's true, love. That's very true. Here, look what I'm doing. Eat yer dinner lass, afore I pinch t'food off thee plate. Eeh, that's it. That's the answer.'

'What is?' Taking her at her word, Jess began wolfing down her dinner at record rate. A fried egg was too rare a treat to share, though she didn't begrudge her aunt the odd taste.

'Food. What is it folk crave more than anything in these austere times? Good food, that's what, of which we are never short, praise be.' Cora pulled up a chair and sat down beside Jess at the table, her plump jowls quivering with excitement. 'We could make a pie and pea supper. They'd come in droves for that.'

Jess said, 'But you'd need fat, for all that pastry?'

'I've enough dripping saved to get us going, and Bernie can provide the coupons for more fat in future, and for the pork meat we'll need. That can be his contribution. Not that we'll tell him what it's for, eh? How about it? I don't mind mekking a few pies. No bother at all. I dare say Cissie would give me a hand.' They both knew Lizzie would be no use at all.

And so it was decided. New posters were done, hand-written this time since money was scarce, advertising a pie and pea supper included in the admission charge of one shilling, as well as the thrill of introducing the new Delaney's All Girls Band. Tickets available on the door or from the Co-op. The dance was to be held on Valentine's Day to make it extra special. Neighbours and friends got very excited at the prospect, word spread quickly and Cissie was soon asking for more tickets, having sold her initial bundle. Everything seemed to be progressing smoothly. They even found a drummer.

Ena Price certainly had rhythm, even if she was a Catholic who nursed a secret ambition to be a nun. 'Except that I can't quite bring meself to give up sex, to which I'm altogether quite partial, being still in me prime. You might as well know now that I've got two boyfriends, not that either of them is aware that they aren't my one and only, you understand. Jeff is in the fusiliers, and Pete on a boat somewhere in the Med. And I've no intention of giving up either one of them.'

'Suit yourself,' Leah said, with open admiration at the difficulties which must be involved in juggling two relation-ships when she couldn't even manage one properly.

She was feeling quite perky this morning, having started her period at last, overflowing with relief and happiness that her fears had been groundless all along. She'd also wisely decided not to trust Harry to take the precautions, visited the Birth Control clinic and got herself set up with proper protec-tion. Not that the doctor had approved of the fact that she was unmarried, and had delivered a long lecture on why she should marry her boyfriend forthwith, before she sank too low. Let him make an honest woman of you, had been

his unyielding advice. Leah had smilingly agreed, not taking
in a word. Of one thing she was quite certain. She didn't
know if marriage was a possibility or not, but she couldn't
possibly give up Harry. He was far too gorgeous, making her
tummy wobble just to think of him. But nor was she prepared
to go through all of that agony month after month.

Jess put her friend's change of mood down to the success
of their new venture. She didn't volunteer herself to help with
making the pies. She left all of that to Cora and her team
which comprised Cissie Armitage and Ma Pickles, who
gladly brought their rolling pins round to help so they
wouldn't miss out on all the fun, and maybe a bit of free pie
along the way. Lizzie was given a potato peeler and set to
work although she spent more time nipping out to the backyard for a quick fag, claiming she didn't want to smoke near
the pies. Jess just hoped she didn't have a bottle hidden out
there, but accepted that she was doing her best to help, in her
own way.

Between them they made half a dozen meat and potato pies
in huge basins, borrowing half her neighbours' ovens in order
to cook them all. Even Sandra agreed to watch that the mushy
peas didn't boil over, and sliced and pickled lots of onions
and red cabbage, weeping copious tears as she did so.

'Why do I allus get the rotten jobs?'

Jess devoted her time to rehearsing her new band, which
was worry enough. Adele excelled herself and wasn't late
once, although Lulu was nearly always half asleep since she
worked in a munitions factory and her days were long and
tiring.

'I need my sleep, darlings, as this is the first time I've done
any real work in my life. Eight hours a night and not a
moment less. Allow me that small indulgence, and I'll be fine
and dandy, crackling with renewed vigour, ready and willing
to work hard and do whatever is asked of me.'

'Well make sure you get plenty of sleep the night before the Valentine's Dance.'

Miss Mona was a great help, very calm and upbeat. Her vast experience included having once played in the Manchester Youth Orchestra many years ago, a spell in Vienna and several more years playing at the opera house in Prague. She now confessed to Leah that she'd actually had an affair with the conductor and got thrown out. At this stage in her life, she admitted to boredom with the classical scene and the need for something more lively. 'Before it's too late.'

'Well, you'll certainly get that with us,' Jess told her. 'So long as my nerves can hold up.'

'We have every faith in you Jess,' Leah told her, beaming with pride.

When the night of the dance finally arrived, Jess turned up early to find a queue stretching right around the block. She could hardly beilieve her eyes. Could they possibly have beaten him and won? Or did he have some other card up his sleeve, to play later when she was least expecting it? She'd just have to hope for the best and not lose her nerve. Oh, but that wasn't easy, she felt sick, the butterflies in her stomach doing a frantic clog dance. 'Lord, will you look at that. How will I face all these people without you beside me to whisper sweet words of confidence in my ear?' she said to Steve, hanging on to his arm for support.

'You'll be fine once you get up there,' he told her with a grin, 'I know you can do it.'

It did indeed prove to be a riotous success, packed to the doors with everyone having a marvellous time. The girls in the band did their part to add a touch of glamour by wearing evening dresses they'd made themselves from fabric donated by Cora, though Jess didn't dare ask how she'd come by it. Off the back of a 'lurry' no doubt. They were all looking very elegant and glamorous for all it was only a school hall, and played as they never had before. Steve did his part by agreeing to act as Master of Ceremonies, announcing the name of each dance and watching for any irregularities, that the code of etiquette on the dance floor was properly followed. Jess had been concerned to have a man around in case of trouble. In the event, there was none at all. Everyone was having far too much fun.

And they loved the music, applauded every number, whistled and shouted and showed their appreciation to the full. And since it was Valentine's night, Jess made sure that there were plenty of novelty dances to give people the chance to get acquainted, and that kissing was an integral part of most. There were kisses in the progressive barn dance, the Paul Jones, and even in a Scottish reel where couples were expected to make an arch and kiss their partner before they went through it. People loved it and were shouting out for more. All great fun! And then the lights were lowered for the romantic number 'Dancing in the Dark'.

And even though Jess had loved every moment of being on stage, of thrilling people with her music, at that moment she almost regretted not being able to take part in the dance itself. She ached to be held in Steve's arms, and to have him kiss her as all these other lovers were doing. She couldn't even see him with the lights down so low, although she was keenly aware of him standing close by, and could sense his pride in her, his joy in her success.

What's more, there was nothing but praise for the pie and peas. Cora glowed from the compliments and became a different woman for days afterwards, far removed from her usual born-to-please, down-at-heel old self. At one point she even told Bernie to 'mek his own buttie', if he was hungry, since she was too busy planning the supper for the next dance Jess had booked for the following Friday. Life had taken a huge leap forward for Cora, and she wasn't for stepping back into the dark ages, not if she could help it.

Bernie, having realised that Jess was indeed still involved with this 'daft music business' and that he'd failed to put a stop to her nonsense, sat and glowered for a long while, then stormed off in a sulk. She'd thwarted him this time, but he'd have the last laugh, see if he didn't.

17

It wasn't as easy to get the band underway as Jess had hoped. Bandleaders and ballroom managers sucked in their breath, puffed out their cheeks and accused them of not being able to withstand the physical hardships of long hours of playing. 'Women don't have the stamina that men have,' said one.

'Limited scope,' said another.

They would say that they weren't in the business of employing 'young ladies who thought it might be fun to show off on stage, however charming, genteel and accomplished they might be.' This incensed Jess and she would tell them in no uncertain terms that her girls could play 'In the Mood' every bit as well as they could play 'Greensleeves'.

One manager had the gall to say that women had no real sense of rhythm in a jam session, as they were hopeless at improvising, 'I know you lasses are doing your best, what with the conscription taking away all the men, and bands desperate for decent musicians but we're not looking for amateurs. We need the best. Women are long on looks but short on talent.'

Outraged, Jess said, 'Absolute rubbish. It's possible to be both.'

A shake of the head. 'Women aren't made to sit on a stage and blow their brains out.'

'We could blow the men right off it.'

But no bookings were forthcoming at the top ballrooms

such as the Ritz or the Plaza, or any number of others in and around the Manchester area, so they spread their net wider, checking out more modest venues. Their first professional booking was at a Lad's Club in Bury. Jess thought the manager took them on out of pity.

He didn't, however, bill them as professional musicians, but as: 'Patriotic Angels with a Big Talent'.

Adele said, 'I suppose we'll have to settle for that girls, grit our teeth and bear it. What choice do we have, except to hope maybe it'll lead to better things, and attitudes might change, in time, when they hear us play.'

'Borrow my nail varnish,' Lulu offered. 'We'll knock their eyeballs out.'

'*Then* we'll hit them with our music,' Miss Mona added quietly.

'We certainly will,' Jess said.

'Bet your sweet life.'

The lads and their sweethearts, not to mention the rest of the folk who attended the dance, thankfully did not share the manager's view. To them, it didn't seem in the least incongruous, and they were completely nonplussed by the fact that the band was comprised entirely of women. After all, if women could build ships, work in factories and buses, why not in a band? They saw them as the patriotic 'girl next door'. 'Rosie the riveter' types, who were freeing men to fight. They cheered and applauded and declared the girls played every bit as well as men.

'I wish they'd just say we played like musicians,' Ena grumbled, after one of her ear shattering drum solos.

'I want to make a career out of this,' Adele said, 'I haven't spent years learning to play the clarinet just to be thought of as a temporary replacement. A pretty wench with no talent and a good body.'

'Yeah, but folk like glamour,' Lulu reminded her. 'Go on, try the varnish. Fuchsia is just your colour, sweetie.'

'Look, I'm not tarting myself up just to get bookings,' Adele protested. 'I'm a serious musician. Don't you agree Miss Mona? Aren't I right?'

'Well, dear, we have to please the customers.'

Jess would listen to all their worries and concerns and try to steer them on a middle course, gently point out that they could do both. Look feminine and prove that they were indeed skilled musicians.

Playing at the Lad's Club became a regular booking and following this success Jess persuaded a few more managers to give them a try. But glamour was indeed considered an essential part of the gig. It was made clear to her that the public expected it. The girls were required to look good if they expected folk to listen to them play.

'The boys like to see a pretty girl. It reminds them what they're fighting for,' said one manager, and since he'd just booked them for every Friday over the next six weeks, the girls smiled and charmingly agreed. The next day Jess went to Kendals department store and bought a bolt of blue taffeta for new gowns. They were about to turn into glamour queens.

Bernie proudly announced to Jess that he'd found them a property which, he thought, was just the ticket. It had suffered considerable damage in the blitz but plainly had great potential.

Jess's first instinct was to refuse but bit back her protests. Money was still tight. Much as she longed for complete independence, she couldn't afford to be too stubborn. She decided to play for time. 'Where is it, this house?'

'It's nobbut a step away from here, a commercial property on Deansgate. I mean to open it up as a public house-cum-club for servicemen, but you and Lizzie can be the ones to live on the premises, to act as caretakers like. It'll make a nice home for the pair of you, and useful for me to have someone living in. It'll be rent free of course. Na then, I can't say fairer than that, can I?'

Bernie grinned slyly, having no intention of giving away the full details of his plans, not at this stage of the game.

Jess had mixed emotions about all of this. She was surprised by his generosity and yet because she so desperately wanted a way out, squashed down any lingering doubts about still being obliged to live on premises her uncle owned. What did it matter who supplied the roof over their heads, so long as it was separate from his own?

Bernie had his plans largely in place and had very nearly decided against involving his sons in the scheme but common sense prevailed. It was bad enough having young Tommy turn honest, at least Harry and Bert had more sense. The pair might have their faults but their expertise for quick thinking would come in handy, even if it did sometimes land them in difficulties. They'd quickly volunteered for the job of barmen, and to find a supply of booze, which was useful. You couldn't run a pub without beer. And it was Harry who'd come up with the idea of having girls to wait on and act as hostesses.

'I know one or two who might be interested. Queenie Shaw for one. Quite a looker, she is. And amenable, you know what I mean? I could check a few more out, ask around her friends like.'

'They'd need to be tasty, high-class lasses,' Bernie warned, 'fresh and young. No old scrubbers. We need to provide the right sort of tone for the place. I'm not running a flaming knocking shop.'

Harry widened his eyes in mock innocence. 'Never thought you were, Dad. Though what these girls get up to after they've served the drinks, is up to them, right?'

Bernie smirked. 'So long as I get my cut.'

'Goes without saying.'

Bernie was more than happy to leave this little matter in Harry's capable hands, and father and son did seem to be on the same wavelength for once. At one time there'd been nearly fifty brothels within easy walking distance of Cumberland Street.

He couldn't wait to see his name over the door, proudly proclaiming that he'd well and truly arrived. One up from a common-or-garden pub, Delaney's of Deansgate would be a classy sort of place where a bloke could buy a drink, enjoy a game of cards and place the odd bet (discreetly, of course, since it wouldn't be strictly legal), as well as the more usual dominoes and darts. And what with all these Yanks pouring into the city, business should be good.

A bit of flash and razzmatazz wouldn't go amiss either. Bernie felt he needed to make his mark, and Harry and Bert would make certain that no one else would try to move in on his patch.

Oh aye, they were handy lads to have around.

Jess's first view of the property did not exactly fill her with unmitigated optimism. It was situated close to the junction of Tonman Street, near Campfield Market. A busy thoroughfare and not one she would have chosen as a place to live.

The property itself looked half derelict as it had clearly been hit by a high explosive bomb at some point recently. Surprisingly, the walls remained intact, for all it lacked doors and windows, part of the roof was missing and here and there were huge gaps in the flooring. When Bernie asked her what she thought, Jess was hard put to know how to reply.

'It's very big, and in a sorry state.'

'There you go again, never showing a morsel of gratitude.' Lizzie fluffed out her stringy, hennaed hair, as if
personally affronted by the remark.

'I only said it was big and in need of attention, which is
plain to see. I didn't say I wasn't grateful. But why here?
Why this particular property? Wouldn't you get a better
clientele at the other end of Deansgate, further away from
the railway and the docks?'

'Hark at her. La-di-dah.'

'Shut yer trap, Lizzie, for God's sake,' Bernie said, then
turned to Jess with a sickly smile about his big wet mouth,
clearly still slavering with pride over the deal. 'I got it cheap
some months back, off a mate of mine. It'll be right as
ninepence when I've done it up a bit. I've organised some
chaps to start work tomorrow. You won't recognise it in a
week or two.'

Nor did she and, despite her misgivings, Jess became
quite excited by the whole project. The upper floors and
roof were soon repaired, doors and windows put back, the
whole place cleared of the heaps of old brick, plaster and
rubble. Its rebirth seemed to herald the promise of a new
beginning, a world which one day wouldn't be dominated
by war, where people would be able to dust themselves off
and start to live again. Everyone was saying that now the
Americans were in, it was all over bar the shouting.
However optimistic this might be, Jess could only hope that
they weren't too far wrong. Perhaps when the war was
finally over, and her dad came home, they would at least
have a decent place for him to come to, and perhaps even a
job waiting for him, if the pub was successful. Jess thought
that if things had been different between her and Uncle
Bernie, she might even have been persuaded to help make it
so. But no one could claim them to be on good terms, for all
his protestations of family loyalty.

By the time the work was only halfway finished, Jess was awestruck, the property seeming to grow bigger every time she saw it. There were eight bedrooms, plus living room, kitchen and bathrooms on the two upper floors, while the ground floor boasted two bar lounges and a snug. On the first floor there was also one long room which ran the full length of the building. Jess couldn't help but visualise this room as a possible venue for a dance, and wondered if she dared approach Uncle Bernie with the suggestion.

'What were you thinking of doing with that room?' she asked him, but he refused to say, only tapped the side of his nose and grinned, revealing chipped, tobacco-stained teeth.

'I don't suppose you'd consider letting us hold a dance there?'

The expression on his face was answer enough but, just in case she hadn't got the message, he told her, in no uncertain terms, that he wasn't playing silly kids' games. He meant to make some real money.

Even so, Jess couldn't resist calling in every evening on her way home from the tea room to watch in disbelief as richly patterned carpets were carried in and fitted in each and every room, save for the long one upstairs. Here, the wooden floors were stained and polished, as indeed were the rooms on the ground floor where a bar counter was also installed together with a brass foot rail around its perimeter. Next came the furniture, carried in by Harry and Bert: large beds, ornate wardrobes and dressing tables. Sofas and comfy chairs followed; together with tables of every size and shape, both for the upstairs rooms and for the ground floor. None of it utility stuff, Jess didn't care to ask how he had acquired it, but it must have cost Bernie a small fortune. She began to feel decidedly uneasy about the whole project.

*   *   *

Whether it was the glamour or the skill of their playing that paid off, it was certain that their popularity increased with every new booking. They wore halter tops and swirling taffeta skirts, or a slinky number with a thigh high slit. It made it harder to play. As Adele pointed out, playing a clarinet and trying to do battle with a strapless bra at the same time wasn't easy. The strap cut into a bare neck, and high heels were so uncomfortable to wear for any length of time, that the girls would quietly slip them off once they were safely ensconced behind their music stands. Then they could be free to wiggle their toes and stretch their aching feet, although Ena had a pair of comfy flatties handy, so she could operate her drum pedal.

They did have one sticky moment when a ballroom manager took Jess to one side and suggested she drop Miss Mona. 'She's too old, darling. No one wants to look at her tired old face, or that white hair.'

Jess took a deep breath, crossed her fingers and said, 'If Miss Mona goes, we go. I'd never find a replacement half as good.'

A long pause, and then a sigh. 'All right, sweetheart, but get her to do something about herself, a bit of lipstick would help. Or dye her hair. Something! And tell her to take those flaming spectacles off. They make her look like a schoolmarm.'

Fortunately, Miss Mona agreed to allow Lulu to 'doll her up a bit' as she put it, and the girls spent a riotous evening giving her a blue rinse and trying out different lipsticks and eye shadows. She was even persuaded to remove her specs, though she insisted on hanging them on a velvet string around her neck, just in case she forgot the music and needed to take a peep now and then.

This glamorous allure might bring in the bookings, but sometimes worked to their detriment as they would find men hanging around outside the stage door when they left. 'Clearly they see us as easy meat,' Adele complained, flashing her dark eyes and pouting her ruby lips. 'Not like little wifey waiting at home. Perhaps they consider it our patriotic duty to entertain them backstage as well.'

'I might consider taking up the odd offer,' Ena said, 'were I not already double booked with my Jeff and Pete. Two's enough I suppose.'

'I should think it is,' Jess giggled, and neatly side-stepped one goggle-eyed sailor who seemed determined to persuade her to come for a little stroll with him down by the canal.

'And kiss goodbye to your virginity on that little walk, assuming you've still got it,' Leah said with a sly wink.

'Speak for yourself,' Jess countered, laughing, and fortunately turned away at just that moment to watch Adele sign her autograph for a soldier, so didn't notice her friend's blush.

'You've decided to be friendly again asta?' Harry said, when he found Leah waiting for him, full of apologies for their quarrel and with the suggestion that he might like to come dancing, as a change from the flicks. 'Am I supposed to be grateful that you've suddenly remembered me?' He'd been so annoyed when she'd turned up her nose and refused to see him for a while that he'd told himself he'd have nothing more to do with her. But one glimpse of that shapely little body of hers, and his mouth was watering.

'I just thought you might still be interested. Sorry if I've neglected you but I've been a bit busy lately with the band. We're settling into a routine now so I could just manage to squeeze you in.' She said this with an air of indifference, as if it really were of no interest whether he agreed or not, yet inside she was quaking with fear that he might refuse.

He gave a crude, lopsided smile. 'I like the sound of that. I like a bit of a squeeze,' and Leah blushed.

In that instant she saw him for what he was, a crude, rough bloke out for what he could get. She asked herself what she thought she was doing chasing Harry Delaney and making herself look cheap and available. But then as he and Bert manhandled a piano into the new pub his father was setting up, she watched with trembling fascination and knew why. She simply couldn't resist him. The rippling muscles in the grubby vest, the way his lazy, deep-lidded gaze slid over her as if stripping every stitch off her, set her pulses racing even while she was filled with guilt over her shameless behaviour. He excited her, and really she must have him, no matter what the risks.

'I thought you might.'

Harry only had to look at her to feel randy and he glanced up and down the street, irritated suddenly by all the shoppers on Deansgate, the traffic and even the sight of a rozzer not too far off. Far too busy for a quick one. Inside, however, was another matter entirely. 'Bert, go and get yourself a pint.'

'I'm not thirsty, Harry.'

'Aye you are. Bugger off.'

Bert looked from one to other, got the message and skedaddled. Harry grabbed Leah by the arm and took her to one of the bedrooms, empty save for a large, comfortable bed, which was handy.

'It's not made up, and probably damp,' Leah protested, Muriel's training suddenly coming to the fore.

'Who needs sheets and pillows? Let's just test the merchandise, shall we? Try it for size, like.' And in no time at all, he had those fancy French knickers off and was satisfying his lust very nicely indeed.

*   *   *

'Where are you getting all this stuff from?' Jess challenged Harry a day or two later, but he only laughed and tapped the side of his nose in a fair imitation of his father.

Bert said, 'Don't worry, our Jess. There's plenty more where that came from,' which did nothing to ease her concerns. And that wasn't the only puzzle. Who were all those bedrooms for?

By the time she and Lizzie had finally moved in, setting out their few meagre possessions in the cavernous wardrobes and chests of drawers, her curiosity had reached mammoth proportions. She tried to express these concerns to her mother.

'There's just one thing, since there's only the two of us, what are we supposed to do with so many bedrooms? Is it to be a boarding house as well as a pub, do you reckon? He hasn't asked you to provide bed and breakfast for commercial travellers, or the armed forces, has he? Because you can't cook to save your life, and I already have more than enough work, ta very much.'

Lizzie shook her head in bemused ignorance. 'He hasn't said owt to me. But then I were quite happy in the old place, and would still be there if you hadn't moaned so much about it.'

Jess didn't trouble to answer the accusation, knowing it would be a waste of time to attempt to explain to Lizzie the value of privacy and independence. All her mother wanted was to be near to her beloved Bernie. Cora, on the other hand, had been delighted to see her sister-law-law finally leave, and gladly helped her to pack.

'You know where we are, Lizzie, if you feel like a natter.'

'I wouldn't set foot back in this house again if you paid me,' Lizzie had perversely responded.

When Jess returned for the last load of their belongings,

she'd had a private word with her aunt over a quick cuppa. 'What are his plans for this place, do you know? Is it to be a club, a pub, a boarding house or all three?'

Cora said, 'Nay, don't ask me. He con do owt, our Bernie, even wheel hisself in a barrow.' By which Jess took her to mean that there was no stopping him, he'd do as he pleased. And as she knew from past experience, Cora would never question him on the subject, not directly. Yet something was going on which Jess didn't understand and she, for one, intended to ask a few questions of her own.

She found him with the builders, sleeves rolled up, collar undone, though with a flat cap still in place on his head, perhaps to keep the dust out of his precious few strands of hair. He seemed to be happily putting up glass shelves which would presumably hold the liquor, while an electrician nearby was fixing lovely rose-tinted wall lights. To her intense disappointment, though not in any way a surprise, Bernie refused to answer a single one of her questions. He wouldn't say why the place was so big or what use he intended for the large upper room which seemed to increase in grandeur every time she saw it, now having sprouted chandeliers.

'You'll be told what's what, all in good time. Let's just say we have us living to earn and you'll be no exception.'

'I hope you know that me mam can't cook, and has never managed to keep a house clean in her entire life. As for me, I have a job already which I'm not eager to leave, certainly not until I know what's going on here.'

'You get more like your dratted father every day,' he said, a nasty gleam in his eye that should have warned her against further comment. 'Allus arguefying. And look what happened to him. He buggered off to fight for King and country; to be a bloody hero, and where is he now? God knows. So shut yer lip, you. You'll be kept informed, as and when,' and refusing to say another word on the subject, he hitched his trousers up by the braces, and chuckling softly to himself lumbered off, screwdriver in hand, in search of another shelf.

Jess watched him go. It always troubled her when Uncle Bernie was one minute his usual foul-mouthed self and the next sounding all happy and content. She was beginning to regret accepting his offer of accommodation. Perhaps she'd been a bit hasty. Something wasn't quite right. This was no ordinary public house, and not at all the kind of home she'd planned for herself and Lizzie. She'd wanted a two up and two down of the kind they'd occupied in Back Irwell Street. This one was sumptuous. This house was enormous. This house was a puzzle.

'I don't know what you're worrying over,' Steve said, as they walked along the canal bank on their usual Sunday afternoon stroll.

His arm was around her waist, her head tucked into his shoulder and just being with him made Jess feel supremely content. Were it not for these problems over her mother and Uncle Bernie niggling away and threatening to spoil everything, life would be quite perfect. But it was difficult to explain all of this, even to Steve. 'I don't trust him.'

'I understand how you feel, love, and he might be a bit of a chancer, your uncle, but you've got to admire his ambition. He's thinking ahead, for when the war ends. There'll be money to be made then, one way or another.'

'Yes, but how does he intend to make it? There won't be enough money to be made out of selling a bit of beer, not for Bernie Delaney. What is this property going to be exactly? He won't say.'

'Does it matter so long as you and your mam can get

away from Cumberland Street and from being at his beck and call all day. You'll be able to play your trumpet to your heart's content then. Perhaps for the customers, or even hold one of your dances there.'

'If he'll let me, which I doubt.'

'True, I could easily have clocked him one that Sunday when he insulted you over your music. What has he got against you?'

'Don't ask. It has a long history, all concerned over being jealous of my dad. Daft business. As a result, he'll make life difficult for me any way he can think of.'

Following that Sunday tea when Steve had so valiantly stood up to her uncle, she'd tried once more playing the trumpet in the house, stuffing the horn with a large handkerchief to mute the sound. Cora had listened enthralled as she'd played Gershwin's 'The Man I Love', dreamily saying how wonderful it sounded.

'Eeh love, that fair brought tears to me eyes. You have a gift, you really do.'

Bubbling with happiness, Jess had hugged the older woman, pressing close against the apple softness of her cheeks and singing in her ear, 'Someday he'll come along, the man I love,' and they'd both laughed.

'Eeh, happen he has already, love. Play some more. Go on, I could listen all day.'

And she did play more. They'd enjoyed a wonderful afternoon while Jess had played tune after tune, including 'Not For Me' from the musical *Girl Crazy*. Cora had been happily singing 'A lucky star's above, but not for me,' when Bernie had burst in from the backyard where he'd been sorting his spoils and demanded they 'Stop that bloody racket this minute.' Had it not been for Cora's intervention, Jess might once more have been deprived of an instrument.

It would certainly be a definite plus to get away from

Bernie's volatile temper, no matter what the truth about his new scheme.

Jess certainly had no intention of leaving a good job at the tea room to go and work for her uncle behind the bar of a public house, as she'd already made clear. She felt well able to stand up to his bullying in that direction at least, knowing that Mr Simmons would be loath to lose her. Her concern for Lizzie was another matter, a public house being the last place her drunken sot of a mother should be living. She remained vulnerable and if too much was expected of her, could very easily descend again into decadence and crime; had already slipped back into some of her old habits. Jess was fully aware of her secret drinking but at a complete loss to know how to prevent it. Keeping Lizzie on the straight and narrow was a full-time occupation, demanding constant vigilance, and how could she do that and work as well.

Explaining none of this to the man she loved, Jess leaned into his shoulder as she smiled ruefully up at Steve. 'I suppose you're right and I should stop worrying. I'd just like to know what Uncle Bernie's up to, that's all, but I've asked him point blank and he simply won't say.'

'Oh that's easy to understand. It's all about power.' Steve laughed, and adopting a mock Lancashire accent, continued, 'You're nobbut a lass, after all. Why should he tell you anything? It's nowt to do with you. Being a woman, you wouldn't understand business matters.'

She stopped walking to stand and stare at him. 'Why wouldn't I understand? What has being a woman got to do with anything? I've a brain in me head, same as him, same as you, same as any man in fact.'

Steve held up his hands by way of defence, 'I didn't say that was *my* opinion. It's the way *he* thinks, that men and women are different.'

'So *you* don't believe men are more intelligent than women?'

'Course they are,' ducking as she took a swing at him, then catching her in his arms and laughing more than ever at her show of temper. 'No, no, of course I don't think they're more intelligent. Except in the case of present company.'

'Drat you, Steve Wyman, I'll . . .'

'What will you do?'

'I shall – er – kiss you to death if you say one more word against women.'

'Oh well, in that case, I think they're all stupid, always did,' and the two lovers quite forgot whatever nonsense it was they'd been sparring over, including Uncle Bernie and his entrepreneurial mysteries. There were far more important matters to deal with, after all. Besides, when he kissed her, as he was doing now, all other thoughts vanished from her head. And it was there, deep in the long grasses among the heady scent of bluebells, that they made love.

When matters were quite clearly running out of control he paused only once to ask, 'Are you sure?' and, dazed with emotion, Jess was too choked to speak, could do no more than pull him closer and help him to undo her brassière which impeded their closeness.

She gave herself willingly to him because it seemed right for her to do so. She loved him, and deep inside knew that he must feel the same way about her, even though he'd never said as much. Not yet he hadn't, but he would. She was sure of it.

She put all worries about her uncle, and her mother, from her mind. Nothing else seemed to matter but that she and Steve should share and explore these feelings they had for each other in the only way possible. Jess felt exhilarated, filled with optimism for the future. She felt in her heart that she could make a success of her band, saw the world now as her oyster, and she in control of it, not Uncle Bernie. Best of all, happiness and love were being offered to her at last, after all her troubles and disappointments, and she grabbed the chance with both hands. Wasn't this what she'd always longed for? And who knew when she might find it again?

18

The club had been operational for a couple of months before Doug Morgan, disappointed over his lack success with Jess, decided to check it out. He didn't deny that he'd been intrigued and suspicious from the start. He'd heard talk of lavish bedroom fittings, rose-tinted lamps and satin sheets which could hardly be considered innocent. He didn't understand how Jess could bear to live there. She'd told him a little about it, insisted that she'd nothing at all to do with the business side of things, that she still went every day to work in the tea room, but Doug wasn't sure he believed her.

He'd become a regular at the mobile canteen and had on several occasions tried to ask her out but she'd always refused, much to his disappointment. She was a pretty girl and he'd seen how men looked at her. Couldn't keep their eyes off her when she played that trumpet. He believed that it was partly the way her breasts strained against her jacket when she raised her arms to play, eyes closed, lost in the music. Such movements were tantalising and surely even Jess must realise the effect she had upon them. She'd started that All Girls Band which, apparently, was proving to be most popular with the local dance halls. Jess Delaney fascinated and disappointed him all at the same time. Flaunting herself, yet there was still about her a certain naivety which he found irresistible.

She'd been corrupted by that senseless mother of hers. That's what it was. And she really oughtn't to be living in that dreadful place on Deansgate.

And so tonight, while Jess was doing her stint serving tea and sympathy at the mobile canteen, he'd made up his mind to visit the club and find out exactly what was going on, to see for himself if the rumours were true.

'What'll you have, just a drink or summat more like?'

Brought abruptly from his thoughts Doug looked up to find himself confronted by Harry Delaney. Glass polishing cloth in hand, eyebrows raised in quizzically polite enquiry, he looked every inch the interested barman.

Doug felt not a scrap of embarrassment. He could deal with Harry right enough, man to man. This was man's business, after all, in a man's world. Women, now they were the mystery and always had been. What his own mother would have said about all of this, he really couldn't imagine. But then he remembered that he knew very well what she would have said. She would have laughed and said that sex was a part of life, to be enjoyed by all. He felt a great anger towards her for thinking that way. A mother's love should be above corruption, not equated with sexual shenanigans. Wasn't that how it was supposed to be?

Jess too should be angry with her mother for letting her down, instead of forgiving her and constantly wanting to protect her. From what she'd told him, she'd been deprived of the joy of being nestled close in a mother's arms, of being told how much she was loved, how she was all that mattered in her world. He had enjoyed all of that, at least for a while. But then his mother had lied. He hadn't been enough for her in the end. He'd done all she'd asked of him, pleased her in every way he could think of but still she'd turned from him for a man who wasn't even her own husband, just when he'd needed her most. What sort of mother deserted her child? He still hated his mother for that, after all these years. Sometimes he was so angry with her, that it boiled up inside him, for all she was long dead and the memory of her was fading. He felt at times as if he was on fire with it, consumed by his anger. Women, in Doug's opinion, should be perfect, above such low desires and base needs.

Mothers, wives, girlfriends, they had to be taken proper care of, which was the man's task, and he meant to do precisely that, to find out the truth about this place so that he was in a better position to take care of Jess. 'What's on offer?' he asked.

'Owt, except booze. We're waiting for a new delivery. I've orange juice, of the National variety. Rum punch but that's so diluted now, there's not much fight left in it, if you catch my drift. We have other pleasures on offer, even if we are low on alcohol. From a single dance to a foxtrot if you take me meaning,' answered Harry, deliberately vague. 'Though don't take me literally. Dancing is the one thing we don't have here. What d'you fancy then? Discretion thrown in for nowt. Depends on how much you want to avail yourself of the facilities like. Why don't you start with a drink and see if owt else takes yer fancy.'

He meant if one of the girls were to take his eye, Doug thought, and deciding it would be more productive not to get embroiled in coy prevarication, said, 'Can't I just go straight upstairs?'

Harry smirked. This wasn't exactly the sort of customer he'd been told to encourage. 'Get 'em tanked up on whatever we've got, spending a lot at the bar,' that's what his father had instructed. But hell, the poor chap looked desperate. There was a fire in his eyes that needed quenching. Not that it surprised Harry. He'd seen him around, knew who he was, always following Jess and panting after her. He'd got it bad and Harry understood such feelings, knew what it felt like to be on short rations. Though he would never admit as much, there'd been a time once when, had it not been for Queenie Shaw, he'd have been in the same boat himself, reduced to paying for a bit of the other, so he felt some sympathy for the poor bugger. 'Aye, course you can. Whatever you like. The customer's allus right and all that.'

Fees were discussed, names and descriptions quietly provided before Harry handed over a key from under the counter and Doug quietly slipped through the door and up the stairs.

He located the correct room all right, but didn't attempt to go in. It was proof he needed, not physical gratification, so that he could convince Jess of what a mess she was getting into, and how he could look after her so much better.

He carefully investigated the other rooms and when he finally found one which was occupied, peeped through a crack to watch.

The girl was good, he'd give her that. Not much to look at but she knew her business. He could tell by the way she was riding the young soldier who lay beneath her, with such rollicking vigour. He certainly wasn't complaining. He was pawing at her breasts and she had her head flung back, arching her throat so that the nipples sprang willingly into his greedy hands. Doug could almost feel himself getting aroused, just watching. Oh she was good all right, and clearly enjoyed her work. But then his mother would have agreed that was essential too, in the circumstances, had she been here.

The very next day Doug suggested Jess should consider moving to other quarters. He didn't admit how he had come by his information which he claimed confirmed the reality of the rumours, but rather put his concern in a very round about sort of way, one which he felt to be appropriate for an innocent young girl of her tender years. 'You'd not want to live where the law was being broken, now would you?'

Suspicious that there was illegal gambling going on in the

long, upstairs room which she had coveted for her band, Jess assumed that this was what Doug Morgan was referring to.

'I've no control over what Uncle Bernie does, but that doesn't mean I approve, or am in any way involved.'

He could tell that she was angry. Even so, he couldn't seem able to leave well alone. 'How can you help being involved, if you live there?' He went one step further. 'I mean, what do all those girls do, for instance? Nothing respectable, I'll warrant.'

He could see at once that he'd made a bad mistake. She was furious with him. 'What are you suggesting? It isn't like that at all. Delaney's is nothing but a glorified pub with rooms, and we take no part in that side of things anyroad, beyond Mam acting as caretaker. It's our *home*! And at least it provides decent employment for Harry and Bert, which is a change for the better.'

'Folk will assume you're one of them, one of those – girls.'

'Meaning what?' Again she looked daggers at him. 'They're waitresses and barmaids. What's wrong with that?'

He could see she was near to tears, that he'd pushed her too far, and was devastated when she rushed off and left him standing outside the mobile canteen. What on earth had he done wrong? He'd only been trying to protect her.

Delaney's All Girls Band went from strength to strength. They liked to think that, because they were women, they were able to express more emotion in the music, and certainly men watching would fall in love with them on sight. But they must have also impressed with their musical skills as well as keeping up a glamorous image, because the number of bookings proliferated. They were hugely popular and increasingly successful, proving to be a serious rival to their male counterparts.

Not that you would have thought so from the reports

which appeared in the press. Photographs would be taken of them in their gorgeous gowns, smiling and holding their shining horns aloft, Leah perched provocatively on the lid of her piano, Ena with her drums. It all seemed like harmless fun, though it rankled slightly when the photographer kept calling out to them to 'show your best side, love', or 'flash a bit of leg, darling'. They would try and explain their passion for the music, how they'd trained and got started, but the reporter would be more concerned with asking for their favourite recipes, how they did their hair and what beauty tips they had for the lonely wives stuck at home.

And when the report came out it would say what fun it was for them, as if it took no serious musical effort at all. It stated how Jess had learned to play in the Salvation Army Bugle Band and spoke of her 'fresh beauty', describing how she worked in a cake shop, thus proving that she was just a fluffy little woman, with no brains or talent after all.

They didn't go on tour because they all had jobs during the day which must be kept up but they did like to play for the troops, perhaps at a local army base or hospital. They would always allow time for comforting those young soldiers who seemed in need of it, they would smile and tease, flirt with them a little to ease their fears. They'd tell them not to worry about their next tour of duty because it was more dangerous right here in Manchester.

The military were sometimes favoured with famous names such as George Formby, Joe Loss, Gracie Fields or Charlie Chester. But more often they were entertained by unknowns, like themselves, and Delaney's All Girls Band could bring the house down. At first they'd felt somewhat overwhelmed to be faced by a room full of men for the troops would go wild, whistling and cheering, stamping their feet and yelling, loving every minute of it.

They always started a gig in the same way, with Leah and

her classical piano trailing a few opening bars of some quite serious melody or other. The audience would listen in respectful silence. Then there would be a roll from the drums, a fanfare on the trumpet, the drums would answer back, cymbals crash and they'd be away, swinging into action playing 'Bugle Call Rag' or 'St Louis Blues'. Jess might do a trumpet solo or Leah improvise something on the piano, and of course everyone loved it when Ena became the focus of attraction on her drums. One night Miss Mona got so carried away, she tossed aside her bow and started plucking the strings of her cello with her fingers. The troops went wild, and she never used it ever again after that.

Once, at a function for naval officers on board a destroyer, Jess felt able to soothe the girls' nerves by reminding them that these were officers, a class above the ordinary enlisted men so there would surely be a bit more decorum. She was delighted when not only did they play terrific music that night, but looked pretty good too in new slinky gowns of gold sateen. Perhaps too good, for afterwards the Chief Petty Officer came round and invited them to 'come and mingle, so they could have a drink with the boys.'

'I'm not sure that's such a good idea,' Jess said, glancing quickly around at the others to make sure they agreed with her. She could see at once that they did, perhaps with the exception of Ena, who was already giving the Chief Petty Officer the glad eye. How that girl ever imagined she could survive in a nunnery, Jess couldn't understand.

'Come on now girls, be fair. You've got to be nice to the lads. They enjoy spending time with a pretty woman. A bit of fraternising does no harm at all. They deserve it.'

'What, exactly are you suggesting?' Adele asked, dark eyes narrowing to a dangerous slit.

'Why do you think we invited you, and not a men's band? Some of these guys might not see a woman again for months, if at all. Do them a favour, girls. Be generous. You know that it's expected. Why else would you accept the invitation?'

Lulu poked him in the chest with her sharply pointed, fuchsia-tipped finger and pushed him backwards out the door. 'Sod off, you nasty little man. We're musicians, not tarts!'

They were very careful which bookings they accepted after that. Enlisted men, they discovered, were in fact far more respectful than the officers, certainly in their experience.

Jess arrived home late one evening to find the bar full to bursting with people and a party in full swing, one that had obviously degenerated into what was generally known as a knees-up. The sound of their raucous laughter and singing met her at the door. Half opened boxes stood about on the floor, on tables, on the bar counter itself, spilling their contents over every surface. That was all she needed. She'd just had a wonderful evening with the band, playing at the Tramways Club for the conductors and drivers and had come away happy and glowing with success, only to come tumbling down to earth when she viewed the reality of her life as it truly was.

'What's going on?' she asked, of no one in particular, which was just as well since nobody was listening. Only Cissie Armitage, ever ready to drown her sorrows at someone else's expense, bothered to answer.

'Your Harry and Bert has getten a new delivery. Not that anyone's asking too many questions about which lurry it dropped off the back of.' Jess certainly knew better than to ask such a question. Bernie could lay his hands on anything, once he'd set his mind to it. He'd put out feelers, as he called them, and then send Harry and Bert to chance upon a few cases that had 'accidentally' lost their way.

Cissie explained that word had quickly spread, and folk had poured in. As a result, the place was humming.

Jess made a quick check that all the blackout curtains were safely drawn then went in search of Bernie. It was nearly midnight and if the police came by they'd be in dead trouble, likely lose their licence, assuming he had such a thing.

He saw her coming and got to his feet, swaying slightly, whisky bottle in one hand and a large glass in the other. 'Nay, dun't fret,' he told her when she relayed this possible cause for concern to him. 'Just enjoy theeself. Gin, vodka, whisky, we've got it all here.'

'So I see.'

'Tha doesn't change much, Miss Lah-di-dah. Allus so bloody righteous. How dusta like Delaneys then? Sounds grand, dun't it, to name a club after meself? I'm going up in the world at last, eh?'

From the look of him, Jess rather thought he was on his way down, not up, but didn't risk saying so. It would be far too dangerous to quarrel with him when he was in this state. Before anything more could be said, he'd lurched away and vanished in the fug, lost in the crowd at the bar.

With its dim lighting and general mêlée, Jess could barely see who was who but she spotted Ma Pickles, or rather could hear her laughing loudly after having swiftly drained her glass of milk stout. Josh, her devoted son was seated obediently by her side, as always, neither drinking nor adding a word to the lively conversation going on around him. What a life that poor man led. Would she ever allow him to grow up? Someone started singing 'Roll out the Barrel', and he didn't even join in with that. Jess could see George Macintyre, who clearly wasn't allowing a dodgy ticker to prevent him from enjoying his whisky, and Frank Roebottom, Tommy's old fire-watcher mate. Tommy himself was in Italy, and not getting much in the way of leave, but he'd written with his congratulations over the new club and Jess's success with the band. Aunt Cora was fast asleep in a corner, the children cuddled up beside her, as usual. There were a few other vaguely familiar faces including Sandra, full of her own importance at twelve, who was flirting outrageously with a sailor: fluttering her eyelashes and behaving as if she were at least eighteen. Jess went over and gently suggested that she really ought to be in bed, as should the twins.

'Would you help me gather them up and take them home? Your mam looks worn out and it's near midnight.'

Sandra gave her a scornful glance. 'Push off, you.' Then wrapping her arms around the sailor's neck, captured him in a long and passionate kiss. Jess panicked and fled, deciding she was probably making matters worse as Sandra would do anything to shock, and probably accuse her of interfering.

There were other servicemen, well gone on Bernie's booze, and quite a few girls making up to them. The place seemed mainly to be full of strangers and Jess couldn't help wondering whether, in the fug of cigarette smoke and the excitement of actually having genuine alcohol to drink, anyone was keeping a proper watch on who was paying for what. Still, it was none of her business whether Bernie made a profit or not, or what those girls were up to. Doug's words suddenly came back to her as an ominous warning and Jess made her way over to the stairs, anxious to escape to the peace of her bed, thinking that maybe he had a point. They really were no better off at all.

It was then that she saw Lizzie. And, like Bernie, she was rip-roaring drunk.

The all too familiar sense of disappointment kicked in. Ever since her mother had been released from prison, Jess had dreamed of saving Lizzie from herself, of creating a home of their own so they could be a proper family, hoping it would be the making of her; instead of which it was apparently to be her ruination. Oh, but she knew who to blame. Too right, she did. Jess felt a flare of anger towards the man who had got her mother into such a state. Only this wasn't the moment to make a fuss. Her priority must be to get Lizzie sobered up first.

'For goodness sake, Mam, what have you done to yourself? Or what has he done to you? I must have been mad agreeing to us moving in here.'

Lizzie got up from the table at which she'd been slumped and staggered over to her daughter to wave a finger in her face. Close up, the fumes from her breath nearly knocked Jess out. 'Don't start on one of yer lectures, girl. I'm having a good time, right, so shurrup.' Then she continued across the room as if unable to curb the propulsion and collapsed in a state of semi-consciousness on to a bench under a window.

Jess marched over and tried to drag her to her feet. 'Come on, let's get you upstairs. What were you thinking of to let yourself get into this condition? Where's the point in that?'

'There you go again with yer flippin' lectures. I were only having a bit of fun. What'sh wrong wi' that? Nay, yer a po-faced lump, our Jess. That Sally Army lot hash done you no good at all. No good at all. Why can't you let yer hair down and enjoy yerself like the rest of us?'

'Because one of us has to maintain some degree of common sense. And don't you insult my friends, they've supported me more than you ever have over the years.'

'*Degree of common sense!* Ooh, hark at her. La-di-dah!'

'No one else is going to show any, are they?' And somehow all her resentment came bubbling to the surface. Anger seared through her, blurring her mother's face inches from her own to a sickly oval, and the effort required not to slap it was almost overwhelming. Why had she even bothered to try and help her. She was quite beyond redemption.

How Jess had longed, all her life, for a normal sort of upbringing, for a mother who cared for her, who would make sacrifices as Mrs Simmons did for Leah by saving up to pay for music lessons, and by introducing her to nice young men. All right, Leah didn't always approve, but then maybe she didn't know when she was well off. Jess tried not to feel any envy for her friend but, deep inside, she couldn't help it because Leah had everything that Jess wanted. Security. Love. And hope for the future. Everything that Jess was having to provide for herself. 'I'm only eighteen, Mam. Why have you never looked after me, eh? Tell me that? Why couldn't you ever manage to do such a basically simple thing? No, don't sit down again, I'm not leaving you to loll about here, half-cut.'

Lizzie opened her mouth to protest but instead vomited the contents of her stomach all down the front of her daughter's clean skirt and blouse. Jess watched the performance with a strange kind of detachment and all her anger drained away, dissipating in a familiar wave of weariness and resignation.

'Want a hand?' Woken from her slumbers by the noise, or else the stink, Cora had waddled over and Jess accepted her help with gratitude.

'Best if we tek her round to mine. You can't manage her on yer own in that state. Much as I hate the silly old besom, I'll not see her choke on her own vomit. And I wouldn't care to imagine what's going on upstairs right now. Na then Lizzie, be a good girl and come home wi' me, chuck.'

Making no comment on this, Jess took hold of Lizzie's arm and the two of them began to steer her towards the door, Sam and Seb trailing on behind, clinging to their mother's skirts.

Lizzie shook Cora off with a violence and strength that was astonishing. 'Gerroff and keep yer flaming nose out of my business.'

'For goodness sake, Mam, Cora's only trying to help.'

'I don't need no help. Not from her anyroad. And I dun't need you prating on at me the whole bloody time neither, telling me what I should and shouldn't do. Shove off and leave me alone. If I want a birra fun, I'll have it, and neither you, nor po-faced Cora here, is going to flippin' stop me.'

Bernie came up behind them to see what all the hubbub was about, slurring his words, 'Aye, you leave yer mam alone, you. It'sh nowt to do wi' anyone what we gets up to. If we wants to get well bevvied, why the bleedin' hell not?'

'Because you'll destroy her. When I said I wanted a place of us own, I meant a little house, a bit of peace and quiet, not a drinker's paradise. This whole idea was a bad one, I can see that now, and we'll be moving our stuff out first thing in the morning.'

'Where to?' Cora said, her round face creasing with a new anxiety. 'I'd have you back any time Jess luv, but not her. One night, and no more. I've had enough of Lizzie here, more than I can rightly stand.'

Jess didn't wonder at it. She felt very much the same. 'We'll find somewhere, don't you worry. We won't be bothering you, nor Uncle Bernie, again. I'd live in Camp Street air-raid shelter sooner.'

'Nay lass,' Cora's eyes filled with tears. 'Don't say such things. It tears the heart out of me to see thee so cut up.' But she didn't retract a word of her declaration, Jess noticed. Instead, she half turned and shouted over her shoulder in a voice which cut through the din like a knife through butter. '*Sandra*, put that sailor down and get over here this minute. Yer needed.'

How they ever got Lizzie home that night, Jess could never afterwards remember. For all there were three of them, it took every scrap of strength and Cora's powerful arms to drag her through the dark streets and fight off her flailing fists. Jess quickly changed out of the stinking clothes then hurried to help Cora wash Lizzie's face, undress her and get her into bed. Sandra was delegated the task of putting the twins to bed while the two women dealt with Lizzie, with the firm instruction to get herself off to bed too.

'Never mind her nightie,' Cora told Jess. 'Let her sleep in her slip. That's as much of a battle as I've strength for tonight.'

Usually, Jess and Lizzie shared a bed but the stink of vomit that still lingered in the small room made Jess gag. She certainly wasn't prepared to climb in beside her mother on this night. Not in her present condition. Cora seemed to be of the same opinion.

'I'd sleep on t'settle in t'front parlour, if I were you. Don't worry about his lordship. I'll wait up for him for once, so the drunken fool doesn't bring everything crashing around his ears when he tries to get up them apples and pears. You've nowt to fear from him.'

19

It was cold in the parlour, filled with dark shadows and creeping mould up the walls. Jess doubted a fire had been lit in here since last Christmas, and even then probably only on Christmas Day itself. Seeing her start to shiver, Cora shovelled up a bit of coal from the kitchen range and set it in the empty grate. Instantly the room seemed less forbidding. 'That'll not last long but it'll help you get off.'

'What did you mean when you said you didn't care to imagine what was going on upstairs?'

'Never you mind. Me mind were happen wandering.'

'I don't think so, Cora. Doug Morgan, a docker who comes in the canteen now and then, nice quiet sort of chap, says there's something funny going on at the club, something involving those girls. I denied it, told him off, but is that right? Bernie's not told me everything, has he? I can tell by the gleeful expression in his nasty little eyes. I'd like to know what it is he's keeping to himself.'

'Aye well, you leave it to me, luv. I'll have a word with our Harry and Bert when they get in. They'll happen know summat. In the meantime, you get some sleep.' Cora covered her with a blanket, tucked back a strand of hair and kissed her cheek. Suddenly Jess caught her hand.

'You've been a better mother to me this last year or two than my own has been throughout my entire lifetime.'

Cora's eyes filled with a rush of tears. 'Nay lass, what a thing to say.'

'I mean it. It's true.'

'All I know is that it's been a pleasure to have you around. I think of you as one of me own. There now, tha'll have me skriking in a minute. Get on with thee,' and dabbing at her tears with her pinny, Cora shuffled off, her carpet slippers making a shushing sound on the lino.

After she'd gone, Jess lay on the prickly horsehair sofa, covered with the single blanket and wished she was anywhere in the world but here, in this cold, mouldy parlour. She felt as if she was no longer in control of her own life; as if Uncle Bernie had more say over it than she did. What was he up to? What was he planning? What did the future hold for them all? Perhaps because it was late, Jess felt tired and dispirited, disappointed in her mother and filled with her old insecurities.

She gazed into the flickering flames and thought about her father. Where was he? Was he safe and well? Oh, how she missed him. Jess had finally learned that he was a POW and wondered what the camp was like, and whether it was as bad as Strangeways. Sergeant Ted said POWs got regular Red Cross parcels, and the Salvation Army helped by putting families in touch with each other, so her letters should be getting through. If only he'd reply. Why didn't he write? And why did he have to be in prison too? What a family they were.

Why couldn't everything be simple, a normal life with parents who cared about her; with no war and nobody fighting one another. How marvellous that would be.

She must have fallen asleep while the tears were still wet on her cheeks because some time later Jess woke with a start to the sound of shouting. Pandemonium had broken out in the kitchen. She could hear Bernie's deep booming voice shouting that he could do what he bloody well pleased and didn't need her say so; Cora screaming her fury at him, followed by a loud thud and a crash, which sounded like something, or someone, falling amongst the fire irons behind the fender. After that came complete silence which, in a way, seemed all the more ominous.

Jess sat up quickly and rubbed the sleep from her eyes. Should she go in? Was her aunt hurt, or had it been her uncle falling in a drunken stupor? It was a wonder that Sam and Seb, or Sandra at least, hadn't come back downstairs to see what all the fresh commotion was about. Perhaps they were used to it and knew when to keep their own counsel.

While Jess was debating the wisdom of intervening between husband and wife, she heard someone fiddling with the door latch. Swiftly, she lay down again, pulling the blanket over her ears, desperately trying to keep still and quieten her breathing.

She heard the parlour door click open, footsteps approach, and there was no doubt in her mind who they belonged to as Bernie weaved an unsteady course towards the old sofa where she lay. After a moment the squeak of his shoes stopped and Jess could hear the sound of laboured breathing, smell the reek of whisky on his breath, making her keenly aware that he must be standing quite close by, watching her. It was as if his gaze was searing into her soul and she had the urge to get up and run, could hardly bear to keep still beneath his scrutiny.

After the longest moment of her life, he spoke. 'I know you're not asleep, so hearken to what I have to say. Tomorrow morning, first thing, you'll come back to t'club and start being nice to my customers. You'll do as I say, right? Neither your mam, nor Cora, and certainly not an interfering little whippersnapper like you, is going to tell Bernie Delaney what's what. I've had enough of your lip, madam. Is that clear?'

Jess longed to argue, to speak up and defend herself but

decided it was wiser to maintain her silence and persist in her pretence of being asleep, trusting that he would give up, go off to bed and leave them all in peace. Her hopes were misplaced as the blanket was suddenly stripped away and a great weight pressed down upon her, knocking all the breath from her body.

Her eyes flew open as she realised, to her utter shock and horror, that he was lying on top of her, fumbling with her clothing. Vapours of sour beer were overwhelming and Jess almost vomited. She felt suffocated, trapped beneath the malodorous bulk of him, becoming all too horribly aware that the more she shoved and pushed at him, the more aroused he became.

'Get off me, you drunken fool!'

But he only hiccuped loudly in her ear and made a grab for her breast.

Dry-mouthed with fear, tongue cleaving to the roof of her mouth, Jess could barely manage to utter anything more than tiny, frightened mewing noises as she fought desperately to free herself.

'Give us a kiss, you miserable bitch. Come on, don't be so bloody mean.'

His great, wet mouth fastened over hers and now Jess was sure that she would indeed vomit, so revolted was she by the sucking sensation. She heaved up one hand and scratched him right across his cheek, making him howl in protest.

'You little bugger, I'll fix you.' His fat face was streaked with blood yet he held her down easily with one hand while sausage-like fingers worked away at her nightdress, dragging it up her legs, poking beneath it, pulling down the knickers she'd left on to keep herself warm. As she squirmed and wriggled, desperately struggling to be free, she heard his breathing quicken as his excitement mounted. Then his fingers probed her groin and entered her, the pain excruciating as he thrust them inside her but as she opened her mouth to scream, she found another hand the size of a trapdoor clamped down tight across her mouth.

'Stop playing the coy little maid, drat you! You let that Steve touch you up, I'll warrant, and I saw you chatting up that docker in the canteen t'other night. Tha's a filthy little whore, just like thee mam. Stop fighting and open your flaming legs, blast you.'

Sick with fear, she anticipated what was coming next; could almost smell his arousal, feel the erect hardness of his penis pressing against her most private parts. She could hear him grunting with pleasure, a kind of animal satisfaction but her own screams went unheard behind the barrier of his filthy hand, still squeezing her mouth tight shut; her kicking limbs as useless as matchsticks against the thrusting violation which touched her very soul.

'That'll larn you, you dirty old bugger,' Cora said, as she struck him over the head with her rolling pin, and giving a loud, piteous groan, Bernie slid heavily to the floor.

It took a long while to calm the poor lass down from her hysterics, wash her bruised and sore body and settle her into Cora's own bed. Even then, she was afraid he'd come upstairs and attack her again.

'Nay, nay, he's out cold till morning. Drunk as the proverbial. He'll not bother you again tonight, or any night after this, mark my words.'

'How will you stop him? He thinks he can bully us all: Lizzie, you, and now me. I can't stand it, Cora, I really can't. I'm a victim too, completely in his power.' And she began to sob, utterly losing control.

'Nay, nay, don't tek on. Yer nowt of t'sort. Trust me, there'll be no more victims in this house. He'll not lay another finger on you. Nor on me neither, come to that. He'll have learnt his lesson after this, I can tell you, so come on luv, sup some hot milk. It'll help you sleep. I've put a nip of brandy in it, for the shock. I'm sure the Sally Army will forgive you a little snifter for once. You has to get over this, like it or no, it's happened.'

In a voice barely above a whisper, Jess murmured, 'How? How do you get over something like this?'

Cora tut-tutted, not knowing how to answer. Then, coming to a decision, gently asked the question she'd thus far avoided. 'Did I get him with me rolling pin quickly enough? He hadn't, you know, gone all the way, had he? The last thing we want after this nasty business, are any repercussions. Owt worse like.'

For a moment Jess looked bemused. What could be worse? He'd *raped* her! She tried the word out again in her brain, and recoiled from it. And then understanding slowly dawned: Cora was talking about a possible pregnancy – of Jess having her own uncle's child. Her face drained of colour and bile rose in her throat. 'Dear God, please don't let that happen. I'd kill myself sooner.'

'Tek it easy luv. It won't look half so bad in the morning. Now think, did he or didn't he?'

Jess swallowed painfully, then shook her head. 'I don't know. I don't think so. I did feel his . . .' She choked on the word. '. . . inside me, I'm sure of it, but I don't remember what happened after that. One minute he was pushing and shoving at me, the next he'd gone. It's all a bit of a blur.'

Cora looked anxious for a moment, and then briskly attempted to console her. 'We must hope for the best – that he didn't. He were probably too drunk to finish what he started. I'm sure he can't have got very far, love.'

Jess was shaking now, shock taking its effect upon her. 'But how do you know that? How can I be sure? I've little experience of such things. Me and Steve . . . we only once ever . . .'

Remembering the magic of their first love-making brought fresh tears springing to her eyes, to run unchecked down her cheeks. How could it ever be the same for them again?

Cora muttered under her breath what sounded very like a curse. 'Like I say, best way is to put it out of your mind luv, like it never happened. You'll get over it, in time, and you're still a lovely lass even if you're not quite as good as new. Your Steve will never know, if'n you don't tell him.'

No, Jess thought, but *I* will know. In the confusion and fear, she couldn't be certain of anything. But she couldn't simply put it to one side as Cora urged her to do. That was quite beyond her. Her own uncle had attempted to force himself upon her, and Jess didn't feel right about herself any more, no longer clean or unsullied. She felt soiled by the brutal assault, made dirty by the violation. She shuddered at the memory. How could she ever let Steve touch her after this? How could she even tell him?

The gentle weeping turned to tearing, heartbroken sobs, and for a long while Cora rocked her in her arms, tears rolling down her own plump cheeks. If she hadn't already done so, she'd lay him out cold, she surely would.

Finally, when Jess grew calm again, she pushed back her sodden hair and asked after her aunt's fate. 'He hit you, didn't he? I heard him. It woke me up. Oh no, just look at the state of you.'

Cora had done no more than slap a bit of iodine on to her own cuts and bruises. Now she gave a smile which looked more like a lopsided grimace. One eye was half closed and was going strange shades of black and purple by the second. Her lip was split, a tooth missing, and blood spilled over her several chins to drip on to her ample bosom where it made a pool of scarlet on her floral pinny. She swiped at it ineffectually with the back of her hand. 'Nowt I haven't handled a million times afore.'

Jess kissed Cora's soft flushed cheek before sipping the hot milk, as instructed. It was sweet and soothing, calming her. 'What was it you were arguing about?'

'This public house of his, or club, whatever it is.' Cora heaved a sigh. 'That docker chap were right. Do you know what sort of club it's going to be? A house of ill-repute, no less. A place for servicemen to come along and enjoy theirselves: to have a drink, chat up young girls and generally relax and have a good time. Up in that big, first-floor room, you know he's put tables for an illicit card school, well he means to deprive the punters of their hard-earned brass while they get acquainted with the girls afore slipping upstairs to avail themselves of the facilities. Them fancy bedrooms next to your little flat, in other words.' At this point Cora looked her straight in the eye. 'Lizzie was supposed to see to the girls, assuming she could manage not to get legless in the process. And you were to be the star attraction.'

'What? Playing in the band?'

'Aye, happen he might have agreed to that in the end. If 'n you were a good girl and did as you were told. But he mainly had other tricks in mind for you.'

A short pause, and then, 'Oh, my God!'

'Don't worry, luv. It'll never happen, not now. I won't let it. So don't feel any guilt over me whopping him one. Serve the old bugger right. You've been spared that at least.'

Once Jess was tucked up in Cora's own bed, quietly crying herself to sleep, Cora went back into the parlour to examine the prostrate form of her husband. She could feel a heat building up inside her, the muscles of her stomach bunching with a new fear. He was strangely quiet. Not like him to stay still for so long, drunk or no. She gave him a sharp kick in the ribs, shook him by the shoulder.

'Come on you lazy bugger. Gerrup! I can't lift you on this

sofa, not on me own, and you're not coming upstairs, not tonight. Happen not any night, after what you've done to young Jess. You and me have some settling up to do. You've gone too far this time. I've put up with your temper long enough. No more. D'you hear me?' She kicked him again and the heavy body rolled over, beady eyes staring blankly up at the ceiling.

Cora sat by the fire, making her plans. Even as she put the final points into place she heard stumbling footsteps at the back door. Them lads of hers. She could only hope they weren't too far gone in drink.

Harry and Bert tumbled into the room, arms around each other's shoulders they looked surprised to see their mother sitting there. She'd never been one to wait up, nor preach to them about their drinking habits, or any other bad habits, come to that. They were looking surprisingly smart in their best walking-out suits, Harry's a dark navy check, while Bert's was a smooth brown, both lifted from the wardrobe of a house near Philips Park. Over these they wore beige raincoats, casually unbuttoned, again from the same address. Only the trilby hats had been legitimately paid for, and which they always wore to the club in their new role as entrepreneurs. It had been worth the sacrifice of a few quid as the hats provided status, and also paid good dividends when trying to impress a woman.

'Hey up Ma, tha looks like tha's lost a bob and found a tanner.'

'Harry, Bert, am I glad to see you two. No, don't take yer coats off, I've a little job what I want you to do fer me. I were wondering if you knew of any bomb-sites what haven't been properly searched or cleared.'

'Aye, any number. Why Mam, what you up to?' Harry dug his brother in the ribs with one elbow and gave a guffaw of inebriated laughter. 'Don't tell me you're going to take up scavenging an' all.'

'I were thinking more of putting summat back, burying summat in the muck like.'

Harry took off the trilby and scratched his thatch of greasy hair. 'Have you gone off yer head, Mam? Why would you want to bury summat on a bomb-site?'

'There's been what you might call an accident here tonight. Yer dad got a bit above himself and did summat nasty to our Jess. Oh, she's all right Bert, don't look so alarmed. Not what she was, happen, but she'll live. But yer dad isn't all right. He's not right at all. I fettled him good and proper, d'you see, with me rolling pin, to get him off her.' She met their startled expressions with a calm, if rueful, smile. 'He's out cold in t'parlour, and I'd say we'll be needing that big handcart what you use when you go out on your demolition work, Harry. And happen tha'd best change after all, you don't want to mess up them new clothes.'

Losing one corpse, even one as substantial as Bernie Delaney, amongst the bombed out ruins some safe distance from Deansgate, proved to be surprisingly easy. Removing his gold watch, cufflinks, wallet and anything else which might identify their father, Harry and Bert buried him deep amongst the rubble. They hoped that if, and when, he was finally unearthed, no one would recognise him or know who he was, and would simply assume he'd copped it when the building got hit and had subsequently been overlooked by any rescue parties.

Back at the house, they quaffed a much needed jar of Guinness each as they watched the sun come up. Having heard the full, unexpurgated tale from their mother, they'd packed her off to bed and gone about their unsavoury business. Now they were contemplating the implications.

'You don't reckon Mam will be arrested, do you, our Harry? Tekken off to Strangeways and hanged.'

'Shurrup, you daft piecan. If you've nowt intelligent to say, shut thee trap. What d'you reckon we've been up to this last hour or two, if not making sure nobody suspects what took place here tonight. What we has to do now is forget all about it, right? If you open yer daft mouth and spill the beans we'll all be in the soup. The only way to keep Mam, and us, safe, is to shut yer trap and tie that loose tongue o' your'n in a knot. Got it?'

'Oh aye, Harry. I'll not say a word. You can rely on me.'

Harry gave him a withering look. That's what I'm afraid of. We've no choice but to rely on you.' He took a swallow of the rich black liquid, letting it slide down his dusty throat, wiping the froth from his mouth with the back of one hand. Then he eased off his boots and propped his feet in their sweat- and dirt-encrusted thick socks on the warm brass fender where earlier Cora had lain bleeding. 'Course, you know who's really to blame, don't you?'

'Who's that, Harry?'

'Our beloved cousin. If it weren't for her flaunting herself, Dad would never have been tempted to try his luck, and Mam wouldn't've needed to clout him one with the rolling pin.'

'Eeh, I don't think it were our Jess's fault.'

'Aye you do. I've just said so, haven't I?' Harry snapped.

'Oh, right. It must be then. If'n you say so, Harry. I were only thinking that Dad were allus one to get in a paddy over nowt.'

'Well it weren't over nowt this time, were it? It were over her not doing what she were told, not agreeing to help out at the club. Defying him, as always.'

Bert was frowning. 'We've never done what he told us neither, our Harry. Not properly. We've med out that we were, but underneath we allus went us own way.'

Harry heaved a sigh of exasperation over Bert's slowness at catching on but then allowed himself a small smile as a new thought took root. 'Aye well, that's as mebbe. We won't need to use no more subterfuge though, will we? I'm in charge now, not Dad. He's history.' He got up from the hard chair on which he'd been sitting and took what he considered to be his rightful place in the battered old fireside chair where his father had sat night after night, reading his *Sporting Chronicle*, issuing his orders. Harry settled into its dusty depths with a satisfied sigh.

He was top dog now, the one who would move up in the world, as he rightly deserved. He glanced about the shabby kitchen, at the milk jug turning sour on the battered deal table, the old Lancashire range which his mother black leaded week after week. The tiny scullery where he could just catch sight of the brown slop-stone sink where his mam did the washing every Monday, half hidden behind a strung up curtain. She deserved something better. They all did. And it was up to him to provide it now, to find them a better place to live, though not at the club where them spare bedrooms were needed for a more lucrative purpose. And mebbe he'd take a wife to give him that much needed air of respectability. Harry puffed out his chest, quite liking the idea. He reminded himself how he'd reached this exalted position, partly by his own skill, but also because of what had happened this night. He should never forget that.

'Is there any more ale in that jug? Top us up then, there's a good lad.' And as Bert rushed to do his bidding, blithely continued, 'I tell you what, we'll make her pay for this mess, see if we don't. We'll make that lass sorry she ever upset a Delaney and put our mam's life in jeopardy. She'll wish this night's business had never taken place.'

20

Jess already did wish that last night's events hadn't taken place, with heartfelt agony. She knew, deep in her heart, that she could never see Steve again. She was not fit to be his girl-friend, not after what had happened. Not fit to be anyone's girlfriend. Where was her hope for the future now? How could she bear to have a man touch her, even Steve, without bringing back painful memories which were rapidly turning into nightmares. Jess doubted she would ever feel clean again. Cora had bathed her afterwards, and again this morning at first light, Jess had crept down to the kitchen and washed herself from head to foot, striving to cleanse the filth which had penetrated her body, yet somehow it seemed to be lodged in her soul as much as in her flesh, and she simply couldn't eradicate it.

Afterwards, Cora brought her breakfast in bed, telling her to stop where she was, that everything was at sixes and sevens, Harry and Bert having had a lie-in and the twins being particularly fractious but she'd have them on their way in no time. Jess was not to worry as she'd sent a note with Sandra to Mr Simmons to say she was a bit poorly and wouldn't be in today. 'A day in bed and you'll be right as rain tomorrer, yer old self again.'

Jess knew she'd never be her old self ever again. She'd been assaulted by her own uncle, despite her determination over the years never to become one of his victims, now she too was blighted by the foulness of the man. Nor could she stay here. She'd have to go away, anywhere so long as it was as far from Uncle Bernie as possible. But for today, Cora was right. She couldn't face going away. She needed to rest, to hide under the covers once she'd washed herself yet again in the big basin of hot water her aunt had brought up.

When Jess finally did emerge downstairs later in the day, it was only because Cora had convinced her that he was nowhere around. Lizzie was sitting in her usual chair crying through a haze of cigarette smoke.

Cora took Jess's hand and led her to a stool by the fire; which blazed halfway up the chimney despite it being a warm, sunny day, making the kitchen stiflingly hot. 'Come on luv, sit yerself down and have a nice cuppa. Take no notice of yer mam. She's a bit upset over Bernie doing a moonlight flit.'

'He's left me,' Lizzie wailed, as if she were the wife and not Cora. 'Without a word, not so much as a goodbye.'

'What? You mean . . . ?' Jess could scarcely take in the import of these words. Ignoring Lizzie's wails, she turned to Cora, 'Is she saying – he's gone?'

Cora's tone was bitter. She'd been putting on an act for most of her married life, making out she was happy when really only the childer had brought her any comfort. It would be a relief to tell the truth about her marriage at last, though a few more lies would be needed to bring the matter to a satisfactory end. But if it made this lass feel better, it was all to the good. 'Aye, up and done a runner, as he allus does when things get sticky. Good riddance to bad rubbish, that's what I say. Who needs him, the rotten bugger. We can make a do without him, see if we don't. There you are luv, I've put two sugars in, since we have plenty and you need to keep yer strength up.'

'But why has he gone? And where to?'

'Nay, I wouldn't know and don't want to. He's slung his

hook, that's all that matters. He left a note on t'mantelshelf to say he'd seen the error of his ways. I'd show it to you only I flung it on t'fire.' The lies were coming thick and fast now, smooth as butter. 'He apologised for having crossed a line he shouldn't have and thought it best if he took himself off to pastures new.' This was the best explanation Cora's feeble imagination could come up with. Aware it didn't sound convincing because when had Bernie ever troubled himself about crossing lines or caring what folk thought? So she kept well away from Jess while she told her tale, busying herself getting the twins ready for bed, pouring out their nightly dose of cod liver oil. 'Keep still willta,' she complained as they deftly evaded the spoon. 'Tha's like a pair of wriggling worms.'

This sent Sam and Seb flat on the floor, wriggling about on their stomachs, giggling uproariously. Cora slammed down the spoon and shook a fist at them, the grin on her round face giving the lie to her words. 'I'll banjo you two when I catch thee.' Then she opened the back door and yelled in a voice that would carry not only to the bottom of the backyard where Sandra was sitting on the wall talking to her mates, but very likely to Salford docks as well, '*Sandra*, get inside this minute. I'll not tell you again.'

After chasing the two wriggling worms around the room, now on all fours having grown arms and legs, Cora finally captured her quarry by the scruff of their collars and placed both children at the kitchen table where they were liberally dosed. They screwed up their little faces in distaste, attempting to spit out the vile liquid while she ladled more in.

'There's good little lambs,' Cora indulgently and in-accurately remarked. Afterwards they were rewarded with a stack of thickly cut wedges of bread and dripping while she collapsed back in her chair and, through rasping gasps for breath, urged Jess not to worry. 'Tha's had a bad shock, lass. Best to tek it easy for a while. Just be glad we're shut of him. I am.'

'But I thought you adored him, Aunt Cora. Worshipped the ground he walked on.'

'True, he looked after me well enough once, but you can mebbe have too much of a good thing. Happen we'll get a bit of peace round here now.' Cora was growing desperate to change the subject, almost willing the twins to be naughty. 'Na then you two, don't eat all that bread and dripping, leave some for yer mam's supper an' all. Nay, look at the state of them hands!' Glad of the distraction, she jumped to her feet again and began applying liberal quantities of carbolic soap and water to the hands and faces of the terrible twosome.

Having slept for much of the day in a state of shock, Jess had trouble getting off to sleep that night. She huddled under the covers listening to the intermittent sobs and snores of her mother beside her, still mourning for her lost love, and thought of how things might have been so very different; how this budding romance between herself and Steve might well have developed, if life had continued as smoothly as she'd hoped. Tears rolled down her cheeks, wetting her pillow and draining her of all energy. Could it still? Could she tell him about this terrible thing that had been done to her?

If she'd known him better, if they'd been engaged, or if he'd told her that he loved her, at least had an understanding of sorts, she might have been more confident of his reaction. But their friendship was too new, too fragile and she didn't feel able to inflict it on him.

Jess became so depressed that she even convinced herself that he might not believe in her innocence, that he'd assume she'd encouraged Bernie and brought it all on herself. Men could be like that sometimes. Hadn't her mam said as much a thousand times, and perhaps, in this instance at least, Lizzie was right.

And yet she didn't want to lose him. Oh dear, what should she do?

The next morning, aching with tiredness and red-eyed through lack of sleep, Jess went to the tea room as usual, pretending she'd had a touch of flu but was quite recovered now. The other girls told her she still looked ill and should certainly be in bed. It was true in a way, she wasn't at all herself. She felt very much below par, almost as if she had indeed suffered a bad dose of influenza. Her limbs felt weak and trembling, one minute all hot and prickly, the next ice cold. Jess felt unable to show interest in anything or anyone around her, could concentrate on nothing, too haunted by the image of a life without Steve. How could she possibly survive now that she'd fallen so hopelessly in love with him?

She spent much of that day and the next, constantly sneaking off to the bakery to get warm where Robert would very kindly give her a warm scone or a mug of hot cocoa. And most nights she spent sobbing quietly into her pillow.

One afternoon towards the end of that dreadful week, Leah found her cuddled up in the airing cupboard, squeezed in beside the tea towels. 'So this is where you've got to. I thought you might have gone off home, feeling sick again. You came back to work too soon. You've not been right all week.'

Jess shook her head which had developed a dull ache, wishing for once that her friend would leave her alone. 'I'm fine, really.' But, apparently, Leah wanted to talk. She repeated the hilarious tale of the piano recital which Jess had already heard ad nauseum, how Ambrose was not the man for her but how, much to her surprise, he'd not only joined up but meant to stay and become a regular. Jess didn't trouble to listen. She still felt strangely detached from reality, only vaguely aware of Leah's voice droning on, having quite lost the thread. It was as if the world had tilted and everything was slightly out of focus.

What should she do about Steve?

Something must have caught her attention because she tuned in again to hear Leah saying, 'I haven't told Mother yet,' rolling her eyes heavenwards in mock despair. 'God knows what she'll say. Harry is a darling, quite thrilling really and very romantic, don't you think, to bring me roses and go down on one knee? I could hardly believe my eyes. Says I'll be the making of him. Isn't that lovely? But the fact he's a Delaney will count against him, I'm afraid. Ma will not be pleased, bless her. Oh dear, and she had such high hopes for me. Too high for my taste, I'm afraid. I wondered if you'd be there when I told her. I mean, you are going to stand for me, aren't you? Who else would I ask? And it would help so much if you explained how really he isn't at all like his father.'

'What did you say? Sorry, I think I've missed something. I thought for a minute you said *Harry*.'

Leah flushed, avoiding eye contact with Jess, knowing that in these past few weeks while she'd been seeing Harry, she'd deliberately misled her by letting her think it was Tommy she fancied and was pining over. 'Of course I said Harry. Who else would I mean? Aren't you listening to a word I'm saying, girl? Here's me talking about going against my better judgement and tying the knot with your delicious cousin and you aren't paying the slightest attention.'

'*Delicious cousin? Tying the knot?*' Jess regarded her friend through wide, astonished eyes, not quite able to convince herself even now that she'd heard correctly. 'That is what you said? But you can't mean with Harry. I thought it was Tommy who . . .'

'No, no, I said Harry because I meant Harry. Isn't Tommy in Italy? And it would hardly be dim Bert, would it? We've been walking out for a while, two or three months in fact, I thought you knew,' regarding Jess with a studied innocence.

Jess was not fooled, not for a moment. She knew her friend far too well. 'You deliberately didn't tell me. Didn't want me to know. I can't quite take this in. Harry isn't like our Tommy, you know. Harry is . . . Harry.' Lost for words, appalled by the idea of her dear friend doing such a reckless, crazy thing she hotly protested, 'You can't do it. You can't marry *Harry*!'

'Why can't I? Of course I can. I can marry anyone I choose. *I* being the operative word, and not my mother. He's explained to me how he's taken over the club on Deansgate, has sown his wild oats in the past but now has a great future before him as a businessman. And I do love him, you know. We have great fun together. He's a bit . . . well, wild perhaps is the word, but he excites me Jess. He believes in living life to the full, even if that involves taking risks, as I do. You know how terribly boring I found Ambrose, every other man I ever met, in point of fact. And working at the tea room nearly drove me demented at times. I was always longing for something amazing to happen. Well, it has! I'm never bored with Harry. He's the man for me.'

'You're not . . . He hasn't put you up the duff, has he?'

'Heavens, no. What do you think I am?' The bright crimson that suddenly stained her cheeks, giving the lie to this cry of innocence.

'Oh Leah, no.'

Leah was shaking her head. 'No, it's all right. I did think

I might be, for a while, but it was a false alarm. For heavens' sake, be happy for me. No doubt you and Steve will be doing the same soon, so come down off your high horse and start thinking about what you're going to wear. It's Thursday next, so you'll have to get your skates on. Not literally, of course. It isn't a wedding on ice. Oh lord, listen to me, I'm growing hysterical now. Come to tea on Sunday. *Please!* I shall tell Daddy before he goes off to his ARP duties after lunch. He might not react too badly, but you simply *have* to be there when I tell Mother. Just to make sure murder isn't done.'

'Oh Leah, what have you done?'

'I thought you, at least, would understand. It will mean that we'll be sisters – or is it cousins-in-law? Related, anyway.'

Jess put her arms about her friend and hugged her tight, her mind a turmoil of emotion. Life seemed to be hitting her with one shock after another at the moment, and it was really all too much. 'You realise you're quite mad, joining the Delaney family.'

'I understood it to be a requirement.'

'Absolutely.'

Jess's presence when Leah announced her wedding plans to her mother did not, in any way, seem to help as much as she'd hoped. Jess felt very much a spare part, an intruder between mother and daughter as, ashen faced and tight-lipped, Muriel made her feelings on the subject very plain. She did not approve of the match and never would, had no intention whatsoever of attending the forthcoming wedding and foresaw nothing but misery and disaster for the happy couple in the years ahead.

Deep down, Jess had to agree with her, had already tried to say as much but her friend wasn't listening.

'And I would remind you, Leah dear, that you are still under-age.'

Leah, glassy eyed with fury, swiftly responded. 'Fine, but don't think you can stop me. Harry and I love each other and if you won't give us permission then I'll simply go and live with him. Cora would have me, wouldn't she?' Leah asked, defiantly turning to Jess.

'I – I'm not sure. Little fazes Cora, it's true, but the house is a bit overcrowded already, what with us all doubling up because me and mam have decided to stay on with Cora to keep her company, now Uncle Bernie isn't around any more. Though that's only so long as the pair of them manage not to do blue murder to each other. For all the cause of their friction has done a bunk, they can't resist letting fly at each other at the least provocation. Mam flung her porridge at Cora the other morning at breakfast, so there's no guarantee it'll work.' From out the corner of her eye, she caught the look of horror on Muriel's face, the shudder that ran through her, and quickly strove to adopt a more positive note. 'However, I heard Harry saying the other day that you and him could move into the little flat over the club, and Bert and his girl, Maisie, have found a place on Quay Street, so it should all work out.' Jess ground to a halt in some confusion, not sure whether she'd made matters better or worse.

Leah said, 'And you and Steve will be getting married soon too, won't you?' as if this would make her own decision seem perfectly reasonable.

'Marriage? Oh, I'm not so sure about that.'

'Why? I thought you were itching to wed Steve Wyman.'

Jess didn't know what to say, how to explain her new doubts. 'For one thing, he hasn't asked me. For another, I'm far too young to even consider such a thing yet.'

Muriel stoutly informed her daughter, 'There you are,

you see. Even dear Jess isn't so stupid as to rush into matrimony. I maintain that you are far too young.'

'How can you say that when you've been trying to talk me into it for years?'

'But that was with a nice young man, one with the right sort of background, and from a decent family who could offer you security and happiness, not a *Delaney*. I can only pray that you'll have second thoughts, so please, give yourself time to think, and don't do anything stupid in the meantime.'

Jess cleared her throat. 'That's not bad advice, Leah.'

Leah cast a furious glance in her friend's direction and starkly retorted, 'Thanks for your support. Big help you've been,' and stormed from the house.

Left alone with Mrs Simmons, Jess for some reason felt obliged to apologise. 'I'm sorry. They are perhaps a bit young to go rushing into things, but at the same time Leah does have a point too. Harry is very go-ahead, and he certainly has looks, and charm.' And knows how to use it to his own advantage, Jess thought, but blundered swiftly on. 'What with Uncle Bernie having done a runner and with Leah at his side, Harry might well settle down to become an honest and upright businessman. Who knows? She could be the making of him. And the family isn't all bad. Cora's lovely, and Tommy is as nice a boy as you could ever wish to meet. He's honest and hardworking, and he clearly adores her. Bert's harmless enough, being too thick to be otherwise. I mean, if it weren't for Harry he'd never have got up to half the scrapes he has. . .' And having thus reminded Mrs Simmons that her daughter was about to marry the one Delaney who most resembled his disreputable, bullying father, she thought it politic to quietly take her leave. As Jess crept down the stairs she heard Muriel start to weep.

*　　*　　*

Back home in Cumberland Street while her mother sat up in bed smoking her 'last fag', Jess paused only briefly in the application of smoothing cold cream over her face when Lizzie remarked drily, 'That chap o' your'n come round this evening looking for you.'

'What chap?' Though the rapid beat of her heart was telling her that she knew only too well.

'That musician bloke. Steve whatever he's called.'

'What did you tell him?'

'That you were out with the God lot.'

Jess bit back the urge to take issue with this comment and simply said, 'Thanks.'

'What'll I tell him if he comes again?'

'Tell him the same. That I'm out. That I'm busy.'

'Hey up, love's young dream died the death has it?'

'What's it to you?'

'Nowt, only if you don't want him, happen you wouldn't mind if I had a crack at him meself. He's a nice looking lad.'

Jess switched off the light and slid into bed, keeping as far away from her mother as possible, paying no heed to her rasping, dry-throated laugh.

Bernie's sudden and unexpected departure seemed to benefit the entire family, strangely enough. Except for herself. Jess felt certain that she would never be able to erase the memory of what had taken place that night. Steve hadn't called again, she hadn't in fact seen him for a few weeks. He'd sent a note to say that he'd called to explain that he'd be working overtime as they had an important operation on, some hush-hush project, which was very often the case. Against all reason that part of her brain which was so obsessed by the assault, even to the extent that she refused to put a name to it in her head, believed it might be that he'd somehow heard about what had happened, and that was why he stayed away. But she didn't mind. She welcomed his absence from her life since it would give her the time she needed to think and to recover.

Jess had considered writing a note by way of reply, to tell him that it was all over between them but that had seemed too cruel, too stark. Best to wait till this project, whatever it might be, was over and done with. By which time she should have acquired the necessary strength to face him.

She had no idea whether Cora had confided in Harry and Bert; whether they knew all about the attack or not, or if they might mention it to their mates at the club after a pint or two. It made her jumpy to think of gossip spreading behind her back, as it so easily seemed to do around here. The likes of Ma Pickles, Molly Gaum, and Cissie Armitage enjoyed nothing better than relishing other people's troubles.

When two more weeks slid by without the usual appearance of her period, Jess saw that her troubles had only just begun, that there were indeed to be repercussions, as Cora had feared. Leah had got away with a false alarm but she wasn't going to be so fortunate. This was real. So if there was gossip now, it would soon get much, much worse.

Despite a genuine sense of unease over Leah's impulsive decision to marry Harry, the worst of the Delaney bunch in Jess's opinion, she still felt a spurt of envy for her friend. It hurt more than she could describe that at this, the lowest point of what, for her, had never been an easy life, it should be Leah, cherished and overprotected by her doting parents, who came up smiling every time. She'd been spared the shame and dishonour of an illegitimate child, and she would be the one celebrating a wedding, free to enjoy life and love without fear. Jess hated herself for feeling this way, but jealousy was sharp and raw in her breast.

She stared at her reflection in the spotted mirror on the wall of the bedroom, exclusively hers now that Lizzie had moved into the boys' old room, and watched tears of despair slide slowly down her pale cheeks. Her whole life seemed to lie in ruins at her feet. She couldn't bear to imagine the revulsion in Steve's face, if she ever told him about the attack and its result. Even if he stuck by her, how would she know that it wasn't simply out of pity. In the end, when he deemed it safe to do so, he'd make good his escape. No, no, best to make a clean break now before matters went any further, before any more hurt was done.

All she was left with was her music. Jess wished she could convince herself that this would be enough, that she didn't need any love in her life, nor respectability, both of which she'd craved all her young life. But she would have that at least, no matter what. Even if she was doomed to spend the rest of her life as an outcast, she would survive somehow by pouring all her energy into her music and the band. Nothing would stop her from doing that. Not even a child. A child! Just saying those words chilled her to the bone. How could she feel any love for a child foisted upon her in such an evil way?

She blamed herself for what had happened, truly believing that she'd brought about her own downfall, first by allowing Steve to make love to her, as surely no decent girl would; conveniently forgetting in her misery how very much in love they'd been and how safe she had felt with him at that time. And then she'd made matters worse by provoking her uncle into such a rage that he'd – he'd done what he'd done.

She couldn't even describe what he'd done. Couldn't say the word.

She shuddered, slapped the tears of self-pity from her face. What good did it do to mope over things that couldn't be altered? What couldn't be cured must be endured, isn't that what Cora was so fond of saying? And she would need to be tough to face whatever lay ahead for there was no escape; she would simply have to live with it, taking one day at a time. What else could she do, except hope and pray that a solution would present itself?

'Things are as they are,' she told herself sternly.

There would be no wedding for her. So be it. No love, no happiness or life of blissful contentment. Jess knew in her heart that all hope of such things were now dead because she was pregnant, and she certainly didn't have the nerve to go to Steve and tell him, because how could she even be certain that the child was his. That being the case, how could she expect him to accept one which had been forced upon her in such a revolting manner, the child of her own uncle.

21

Leah looked lovely in a blue velvet gown with pink bud roses and lilies-of-the-valley in her bouquet and on the circlet she wore in her lovely fair hair. Blue eyes shone with happiness, only occasionally clouding over when she remembered the pressure she'd had to apply in order to get permission for this wedding to take place. Neither parent had attended and there was no reception afterwards at Simmons's Tea Room. Not even her father present to give her away, that role being carried out by her brother Robert. Jess was maid of honour in a pretty, strawberries-and-cream two-piece, while Bert acted as best man to a beaming Harry, who looked particularly pleased with himself.

'They'll come round love,' he kept saying, whenever Leah glanced anxiously and hopefully towards the door. 'Even if it takes a week or two. Anyroad, they'll come fast enough when the first grandchild appears.'

'Don't be crude, our Harry,' Cora scolded, shaking a fist at him. Cora, at least, had come up trumps by providing a substantial tea of potted meat sandwiches and home-made scones and jam (since she still hadn't run short of sugar). And, of course, one of her famous trifles.

And Harry and Bert had made sure there would be enough booze for friends and family to enjoy; so plentiful that by the time the groom finally staggered to the marital bed at four in the morning, he scarcely even noticed that it was already occupied by his neglected, lonely bride. Leah lay listening to his drunken snores until every last tear had been shed and exhaustion finally claimed her.

Jess was thankful in the coming weeks for the distraction of her work at the mobile canteen, which was as hectic as ever. Manchester had taken a battering over these last two years and she couldn't help wondering if it would ever be the same again. Much of Deansgate at the far end near to the Cathedral was in ruins. Nearer to home, Young Street had gone, parts of Duke Street and Camp Street were badly damaged among countless others, including Gatrix's warehouse on Quay Street where her mother had once worked in the days when she'd taken a bit more care of herself; close to where Bert and his girlfriend, Maisie, were now living.

Harry and Leah, as agreed, had moved into the little flat above the pub, or Delaney's Club, as it was now known, where they were settling happily into married life. At least, Jess presumed they were. She'd seen little of them since the wedding as Leah had failed to show up at a couple of functions that the band had been involved with, which had left them short of a pianist. She still worked at the tea room and had been anxious to apologise, swearing that it wouldn't happen again, but there'd seemed to be so little time to chat recently, as if neither of them felt quite in the mood to exchange confidences as easily as they once had. Perhaps they were growing up: Leah wishing to keep her married life private and Jess too conscious of her own shameful secret, of which she couldn't even bear to think.

And still she hadn't seen Steve.

Keeping her mind firmly on the task in hand, she put a scraping of marg on another slice of bread and agreed with Ma Pickles, who'd just popped in to see how she was fettling, that yes, it looked as if they might be lucky and escape a raid tonight.

'Have you time for a cuppa?' Jess offered, more out of good manners than a desire to sit and chat with one of the worst gossips on Deansgate, next to Molly 'British Gaumont News' who was at this very moment sitting in the corner opposite, relating the latest additions to the list of illegitimate births.

'I'll not say no. I saw your Lizzie earlier, three sheets to the wind as usual and propping up the bar at that fancy place what your Harry runs now.'

Jess turned quickly away so that the old woman couldn't see the concern in her eyes. Nasty old maggot, she thought, so that's why she's 'popped in', to crow over Lizzie's latest fall from grace. Though just as well she isn't too interested in my state of health, not just at the moment.

Molly Gaum's voice rang out, 'Oh aye, it's a growing problem tha knows, in view of all the Yanks stationed locally,' and Jess felt quite certain that guilt must be written all over her own face, even though she hadn't been near an American GI. Hastily she picked up another slice of bread, determined not to listen to any more nasty remarks, or react to Ma Pickles' sniping.

'I thought you'd happen want to know,' Ma Pickles persisted, disappointed by the lack of response.

'Ta very much! Most kind of you, I'm sure.'

A small silence and then, 'Your Uncle Bernie not back from his travels then?' she probed, narrowing her deceptively mild gaze and edging closer so that she could focus more closely upon Jess.

'No doubt he'll turn up again one day, like a bad penny,' she replied tartly, not anxious to discuss family business with the likes of Ma Pickles. 'Now, you'll have to excuse me, we're a bit busy tonight.'

Despite there being no raids on, the place was packed with people, all apparently in need of assistance. Sergeant Ted was busily occupied taking down details of someone in need of accommodation. He kept a list of anyone prepared to offer temporary bed and board but a permanent arrangement was always more difficult as so many buildings had been damaged and rooms were in short supply. Many families were stretched to breaking point with overcrowding.

Harriet was trying to calm a woman who'd lost touch with her mother and sister. They'd got separated after their house was hit and she hadn't been able to find them since. She was desperately worried, not certain that they'd even survived. Harriet was assuring her that everything possible would be done to locate her family, by sending details through the network set up by the Salvation Army for this very purpose.

Many of their regulars had popped in simply because they sought solace from the desperate conditions at home, thankful to be free of a night spent in the air-raid shelter and while they slurped hot soup or gulped down great mugs of tea, conversation revolved around the war, as always. Everyone agreed that there was an increase in confidence, a general feeling that a corner had been turned and they were on the home straight.

'We have the planes, that's why, and the brave chaps to fly 'em. Bomber Harris has made a big difference,' one man said. 'Not least through a sustained assault on German Industry which has knocked the stuffing out of them.'

'Aye, but they've suffered too, them lads. Had the stuffing knocked out of them a few times,' said another, and went on to claim that it was the Russians capturing Stalingrad and pushing the Germans back further, which had finally done the trick.

Italy had apparently sunk into political chaos and largely given up altogether, and it was generally agreed that the North Africa campaign had ended in total victory. Finally, since the attacks on Hamburg in July, where more people had lost their lives than in the London blitz, everyone believed that the enemy was all but beaten. Yet it hardly seemed appropriate to celebrate, and Jess's heart went out to those German families caught up in this terrible war with the Nazis through no fault of their own, just as folk were here in England.

And how was her Dad surviving? She'd got one postcard with various printed sentences upon it, many crossed out, others with ticks beside them. It told her little more than that he was alive and being well taken care of. Jess didn't believe that for a minute.

'Nay, we're getting maudlin here. Play us a tune, Jess luv,' Molly Gaum urged, and she readily agreed. Anything to take her mind off her problems.

She played Kenny Baker's 'Always in My Heart', sentimental enough to bring the tears to anyone's eyes, too much for Jess so she changed to 'We'll Meet Again', 'The White Cliffs of Dover', and all the usual favourites in order to get everyone singing. But when someone called for 'I'll Be Seeing You', she shook her head and hurried into the kitchen to do the washing-up instead.

'Are you all right, Jess?' Sergeant Ted asked, his kind eyes soft and enquiring.

'Yes, I'm fine. Only, I'm a bit pushed this week at work, do you mind if I skip my lesson for once? And Mam's not been too well.'

'Course love. Whatever you like.'

She smiled, all her heart in the gaze she bestowed upon him. 'It was a lucky day for me when I dropped that bugle. Where would I have been without the Sally Army all these years? You've kept me sane.'

He patted her shoulder, only too aware of her personal difficulties at home. 'Things will buck up for you soon, love. The war won't last for ever, and you're very nearly a woman.

You'll soon be in charge of your own life. Free to make your own way.'

Jess turned away to plunge her hands into the hot soapy water, not able to bear his sympathy. 'I'll get this lot done,' she said in her brightest voice, and wisely Ted left her to it, so that he wouldn't see her tears fall. He didn't rightly know what was wrong, didn't like to enquire too closely, but something was.

Resolutely dry-eyed, Jess strove to get her emotions back under control. There was too much suffering in this world already, people who'd lost loved ones, those who'd been maimed and injured by the bombing, far worse than she had to deal with so where was the point in self-pity? And she felt proud to wear the red shield, worn by Salvationists involved in social and emergency services since the early days in the First World War. Soldiers then had been glad to see the 'Doughnut Girls' bringing sustenance and a cheerful smile, and Jess knew that many had also been gifted musicians, boosting the morale of the frontline troops, singing, praying and leaving wild flowers at the grave-sides. The canteens thought of themselves now as a 'flying squad' ready to move at a moment's notice on the home battlefront.

Sometimes, Jess worked all night long, not getting to bed until the early hours. There'd been times when she'd found this hard going, having to work at the tea room the next day but in the weeks following the assault and this knowledge of a new life within her, she welcomed it. Normal sleep seemed to be beyond her, therefore a state of exhaustion was a requirement.

Jess's wish to concentrate on her music was granted in an unexpected way. To their astonishment and delight, Delaney's All Girls Band was asked to play on the wireless. Some producer or other had seen them perform and he wanted them for a late-night show which featured new bands.

'It's on a Monday night,' Adele said, puffing frantically on the third cigarette she'd started since she'd heard the news just moments before, 'so nobody will be listening.'

Jess smiled, knowing that the thought of playing to so many people had given her an attack of the nerves. That's why she was sometimes late for a rehearsal, though she'd never yet missed the start of a performance. Her stage fright was crippling and she would often be found sitting backstage sucking sherbet dabs. Once out there in front of an audience, however, it was a different matter and she would play her heart out, loving every minute of it. 'He says they have a big audience, so I don't think we've anything to worry about there.'

Lulu was very excited. 'This could be a big thing for us. Lift us on to a whole new level.'

'Too right,' Ena said. 'Today the wireless, tomorrow the Ritz.'

'Oh, hecky-pecky thump,' Adele groaned, and silently Miss Mona handed her another sherbet dab.

On the night in question, they fumbled their way through the streets in the blackout, then into the studio with their instruments and gas masks at the ready, creeping around a bewildering array of screens and curtains so that not a glimmer of light would escape. They didn't speak, not even to console the shivering Adele as they were all nervous now, wishing they were simply doing a gig at a factory or hospital. But once inside, the atmosphere changed. They entered a brightly lit room full of jolly people, all happy to see them and anxious to make them feel relaxed and comfortable. The session went like a dream. They forgot all about being 'on air' and just enjoyed themselves. They played their socks off, and afterwards the bookings just rolled in.

They worked so hard over the next few weeks that on one occasion Jess ended up with a swollen lip and for a time it looked as if she might not be able to go on but luckily it calmed down sufficiently for her to play.

Playing on the wireless programme had given them a new confidence in themselves and they began to experiment, to 'take off' by improvising more freely, to develop their own melodic lines and chord changes. Playing the same arrangements over and over for dances can become boring, so it felt good to spice up things a little. They'd ask their audience to name their favourites and the requests would pour in, then they'd finish with some really hot swing numbers.

'We're a success! We've done it!' Leah yelled.

We certainly have, Jess thought. If only life could always be this good. She knew Steve had called round, several times in fact, but fortunately she'd always been out. He'd even written to her but she'd torn up the envelopes without opening them. Jess felt guilty about doing this but was fearful of seeing him, of saying what needed to be said.

One evening, Jess had her hands deep in a bowl of flour making Yorkshire puddings in the kitchen of the mobile canteen, when she glanced up to find Steve leaning on the door jamb, grinning at her. 'I was beginning to think you were avoiding me, now that you're famous. You weren't in whenever I called, and never answered any of my letters.'

She covered her lack of composure with as careless a tone as she could manage. 'It's not that at all. I've just been busy. Anyway, I thought you were working on some special project or other?'

'Is that all you have to say? No, hello Steve. Good to see you, Steve. I've been longing for you day after day, Steve.' He came towards her and Jess quickly went to fetch baking powder to add to the National flour she'd just sieved into a bowl. 'It's true, we've had a big job on, as I explained in my notes. You did get them, didn't you?'

'Oh yes, I got them. Er, they're around somewhere.'

'I've missed you so much. I rather hoped you might have missed me. Anyway, I came to say that as from tomorrow, I'm all yours. So you can fill me in on all your exciting news, your great success.' Hazel eyes twinkled merrily at her, trilby hat perched beguilingly at the back of his head, a thatch of unruly red-brown hair falling disarmingly over his forehead and she had an almost unbearable urge to run her fingers through it, to smother his beloved face with kisses and tell him how very much she loved him. He looked as untidy as ever in an ill-matched suit and tie but to Jess he had never looked more handsome, or his smile more enticing. She drew in a deep, calming breath.

'How have I had time to miss you? When I'm not at the tea room, I'm here. When I'm not here, I'm playing in the band some place or other. I've been run off me feet, if you want to know.'

'I should say that much is obvious,' he said, dusting flour from the tip of her nose. 'And I must say that it suits you.' He was about to slide his arm around her waist but Jess sidestepped away, neatly evading his touch as she dashed over to the cupboard to fetch a packet of dried egg. She simply couldn't have borne it if he'd touched her, not just then.

'I did intend to write to you,' she said, and then wished she could bite back the words, unspoken.

'A *billet doux* you mean? Oh yes please do, I'd really love to get one of those from you, my darling. Why didn't you? There's no need to be shy.' He caught hold of her on the way back and his arms went about her, pulling her close, nuzzling his mouth against her throat. Quite against her better judgement, Jess was melting against him, growing light-headed with her need to let him kiss her. Yet desperate not to yield to her emotion she pushed him away and turned her agonised gaze from the hurt that sprang into his eyes.

'What is it, Jess? What's happened? Someone upset you?'

'No, course not. Like I say, I'm busy, that's all. Besides, it wouldn't have been that sort of letter. I needed to tell you, to explain – I mean . . .' Oh, sweet Jesus, this was far more difficult than she'd ever imagined, even in her worst nightmares. Again she took a deep breath. The only way was simply to come right out with it. 'I think we have to stop seeing each other. It's over.'

The silence following this breathless statement was deep and profound. Jess filled it by adding reconstituted milk to the pudding mix and starting to beat very hard.

Steve put out a hand to quietly stop her. 'Would you mind repeating that, very slowly please?'

Still she didn't look at him. 'We have to end it. Now!'

'Why?'

'It doesn't feel right.'

'Pardon?'

'I'm not ready . . .'

'Ready for what? Marriage? I don't recall us getting round to discussing such things, or my asking you. Though I intended to, sweetheart. Dear God, you know that I did. I thought – believed, we had something going for us. What's changed? What in hell's name has happened to make you so cold towards me all of a sudden? It's not this damned wireless thing, is it. You haven't gone all grand on me.'

'Of course not, don't be silly.'

'Then what is it, for God's sake?' And when she didn't immediately answer, 'Talk to me, for pity's sake, Jess.'

'I can't talk now. Can't you see how busy I am. Anyway, like I say, it's over. There's nothing more to be said,' and she calmly began to pour Yorkshire pudding mixture into sizzling hot pans.

She didn't dare to glance at him, knowing his face to be all pinched and white, yet Jess was acutely aware of his eyes following her every movement in pained disbelief. And she knew to the second when he turned on his heel and walked out the door even though he made not a sound, for she felt as if he'd taken her heart with him.

Life for Leah wasn't quite so rosy as she'd hoped, though had she been thinking more clearly she would have recalled that Jess had tried to warn her, right in the beginning. Even Cora had once commented that her lads were 'an acquired taste'.

Oh, and she soon learned the truth of that right enough, certainly between the sheets. Harry was still ready and willing to prove himself the great stud he imagined himself to be, except on the nights he was somewhat the worse for wear, of course, when it was more problematic. But no one, certainly not his trusting, adoring wife, could accuse him of being romantic.

Now that he was a married man, he didn't deem it necessary to trouble himself quite so much with the preliminaries, or trying to please her. She was his wife, for heavens' sake, so why bother? It was as if he'd acquired a new toy which he could pick up and use for his own satisfaction whenever the mood took him, the rest of the time it could stay quietly tucked away, in a corner of the kitchen preferably, working on his next meal. There were no more bunches of flowers, no sweet words and soft canoodling, no teasing caresses to get her in a receptive mood. If he wanted 'a bit of the other' as he crudely described the act of love, then he took it, or rather helped himself.

Leah did try once to explain. 'Could you try a little more finesse, do you think Harry, then maybe I'd have time to enjoy it a bit more, if it lasted a bit longer?'

'Finesse? What the bleedin' hell are you talking about? I don't know such long words. Are you suggesting that I'm not capable? Women don't usually say they don't enjoy it. I've never had no complaints before.'

'I didn't mean I didn't enjoy it. Of course I do, only . . .'

'It's all right, girl. I'll not stop where I'm not wanted. There are others more appreciative,' and he'd stormed off in a sulk, banging the door after him.

Leah ran after him, sobbing that she didn't mean it, and would he please come back to bed because she loved him, but he didn't pause for a second, anxious to get back down to the club bar where there would be plenty of adoring females, not least an ever-changing parade of barmaids that he employed. For the first time, Leah experienced a sense of disquiet about the whole set-up. What had she let herself in for?

He was well kettled by the time he staggered back upstairs, but not so far gone that he didn't notice how attractive Leah was. He could see the long, slender curve of her thigh beneath the bed covers, the soft mound that was her breast as she lay half on her side, half on her back, deeply asleep and tantalisingly vulnerable. Despite having spent a most pleasant hour with one of the new girls, fresh as a peach and ripe for the picking, just looking at her lying there so inviting made him go all randy again. And she was his wife, dammit. He yanked back the sheets and quickly straddled her. 'Come on love, wake up, let's have a bit of the other, eh?'

'Harry, for heavens' sake, what are you doing? Get off me. I'm half asleep. Give me a minute, for God's sake.'

But Harry didn't have a minute. He pulled up her nightie and got on with the job. It didn't take long, him being so well bevvied before he'd reached a satisfying conclusion. A nice little extra by way of dessert, as you might say. Seconds later, he rolled off her and fell into a deep, snoring sleep, spread eagled across the bed.

Leah snatched up her dressing-gown and fled into the tiny

kitchen to make herself a cup of tea, and hope that she could cry quietly so that he wouldn't hear.

The following evening the band was playing at the Empress Ballroom in Pendleton. When they'd first started attending dances, there'd been 'No Jiving' notices up everywhere. Now, its popularity was such that jivers simply couldn't be ignored. They needed space and Jess always made a point of playing music especially for them, often a Glenn Miller number such as 'Chattanooga Choo-choo', when they could have the floor entirely to themselves. During the more regular dances, they were expected to keep to one corner. But Jess not only provided jivers with the space and the music they wanted, she also offered prizes for the best couple.

What's more, she did the same for the foxtrot, and all the other dances which were favourites with the clientele. It was one of the reasons Delaney's All Girls Band was so popular, because they were careful to please everybody and managed to create a party atmosphere.

They were booked for a guest spot at the Palais in Bury, invited by their regular musicians, and at the Broadway in Eccles. They also had bookings in Ashton, Levenshulme, the Alhambra Palais and the Savoy Ballroom in Oldham. Dyson's on Devonshire Street was a regular spot for them, usually held on a Tuesday and where the tango was a particular favourite. They were doing well, going up in the world.

Yet, despite the band's huge success, Jess wasn't sure if she had the strength to go on. It had taken every ounce of will-power to get herself out of bed that morning, knowing she'd done the deed: that she'd sent Steve away for good. Her face had felt stiff and unnatural as she'd attempted to smile at the customers throughout that long day, chatted to them about the weather and the current state of the war, desperately trying to appear as if nothing untoward had taken place and everything was perfectly normal. Inside, she felt bleak, empty, and she couldn't think of a single reason to go on living.

Leah had looked anxious all morning, obviously concerned, then had fetched coffee for them both and asked if they might have a little chat.

'Later,' Jess had said. 'We'll talk later,' walking away to avoid any further questions.

And here they were, on their rest break during the interval while a small jazz quartet kept the customers amused. Leah hadn't asked her a single question, not yet, but had sat patiently waiting to hear the reason for her very evident gloom and depression.

There was no doubt that Jess felt an urgent need to tell someone, at least the assault part of it. Cora had done her best with her homespun wisdom and advice but Jess wasn't yet ready to reveal the catastrophic result of the incident, not until she'd had time to decide what she intended to do about it. Lizzie wasn't interested in anything beyond herself of course, not unless it came out of a bottle, and Leah was as close as a sister to her, now that she was one of the family.

To her credit, Leah didn't interrupt once as Jess spilled out the whole, sordid tale. And when she finally fell silent, still with much left unsaid but lacking the will to tell it, Leah put her arms around her friend and held her close, blue eyes gleaming though whether with anger or tears over the treatment meted out by her uncle, Jess wasn't too sure. 'No wonder you've been under the weather lately, love. Cry if you like, I am.'

'I don't think I've any tears left.'

'And there was me fretting about not getting my parents' approval for my marriage. At least I am safely married if not in their eyes particularly respectably, while you've had all this to deal with.' Leah was thinking that although she couldn't pretend things were perfect between herself and Harry, or at all as she'd hoped and expected since they were clearly experiencing a few difficulties, it was surely nothing that couldn't be put right, given time and love. Jess's problem on the other hand, was the worst imaginable. *Rape!* And by her own uncle. Dear God, what could be worse than that? 'You should have belted me one to shut me up.'

'You weren't to know, and I couldn't – couldn't talk about it, not even to you.'

'I'm glad you've told me now.' Leah's blue eyes were gentle, then she gathered Jess's hand firmly between her own. 'So that's why the dreadful Uncle Bernie was notable by his absence from my wedding? And what did Steve say? I should think he'd be disappointed to miss the opportunity to knock his block off.'

Jess cleared her throat. 'Steve doesn't know. I haven't told him. Don't, in fact, ever intend to tell him. Only yesterday he came to the canteen and I explained that it was all over between us. We're finished.'

Leah gaped at her in disbelief. 'For heavens' sake, why? You *must* tell him, Jess. You can't just walk away without an explanation. That's too cruel. He adores you.'

The band of pain in her breast was like a giant fist clenching her heart. 'Don't – please. I can't bear it.'

Adele stuck her head around the door. 'Two minutes.'

'Right. We're on our way.' Jess at once got to her feet and Leah had to hurry to keep up with her as she left the dressing room and made her way back to the ballroom. 'You can't do this. You can't just wipe him out of your life as if he was of no account. This is a decision with awesome repercussions. You love him, I know you do. So if you end it all, that's it. It's over for *life*! You'll have lost him for good. Is that what you want?'

Jess had climbed back on stage, was polishing her trumpet,

rifling through sheet music preparatory to starting the second half of the dance. She really had no wish to be reminded of what she'd lost. Besides, Leah only knew half the story. Jess had made no mention of her 'delicate condition', nor had she any intention of doing so. Not just yet. 'I don't think it matters what I want. I only know that I'm not fit to be with him right now. I couldn't – can't even bear to think of being touched by any man.'

'But Steve isn't just *any* man.'

Jess wordlessly shook her head, tears spilling from her eyes and rolling down her cheeks. She slapped them ruthlessly away. 'Right girls, we'll start with "Run, Rabbit, Run", through the usual numbers to "Don't Sit Under the Apple Tree".'

Leah's face was warm with sympathy and yet with an edge of desperation to it as she put out a hand to prevent Jess from counting them in, speaking in a breathless whisper, anxious to get her point across. 'I can't begin to imagine what you're going through but I'm sure that if Steve loves you, he'll help you to get over this terrible thing. It's a natural enough feeling to want to shut out men, but it will pass, given time and his loving support.'

'I couldn't ask that of him. I couldn't let him take the risk. Not if I was frigid and couldn't be a – a proper wife to him? What then? OK, girls, one, two, three . . .'

22

Harry believed it essential that he try out each of the girls for himself, test the merchandise as it were, before selling it to the punters. Besides, he was bored with Queenie who was getting a bit well worn and predictable, and not for a moment did it cross his mind that being married required him to be faithful. That wasn't his style, any more than it had been Bernie's. His father had spread his favours wherever it had taken his fancy, and no harm had been done by it, not that Harry was aware of. What the little wife didn't know, wouldn't hurt her. Not that it would make the slightest difference if she did make a fuss. A husband was entitled to do as he pleased.

And Harry was not dissatisfied with his marriage. Leah was a likely looking lass, bonny, and sufficiently voluptuous to stir any man's loins. And he also hoped that she might bring other benefits, such as a bit more brass. Getting a new business going had proved to be far harder than he'd expected. The Yanks were always good spenders, dug deep into their pockets without a care in the world. Our own boys weren't quite so free with their money, as they were less well paid. And they were more circumspect, a pint or two of good beer coming before paying for a tart any time, preferring to get a bit of 'how's yer father' for nothing, if they could. He'd been forced to let out the rooms above the pub, accommodation being at a premium like, and to get some reliable income coming in, though he'd kept one room vacant for the club's exclusive use.

This latest girl, Honey, as she insisted on being called (although Harry seemed to remember her as Gladys at school), was a bit daft and giggly, but eager enough and willing to learn. He liked them younger himself, around fifteen or sixteen. Honey was twenty-three, only a year or two younger than himself, and therefore a bit long in the tooth for his taste.

However, she was certainly experienced, so that was a bonus.

Once she'd realised that he'd no time to waste on conversation and the preliminaries, she stroked him in all the right places, bringing him to a pitch of ecstasy that he hadn't experienced since his days as a raw adolescent behind the bike sheds. Blood pounding, and his member throbbing like a mad thing with a life of its own, Harry pushed her roughly back on to the pillows so that he could get on with it. He rather thought he'd surprised her with his vigour. There'd been a bored smirk on her face at first, which had swiftly vanished once he got going. She'd soon discovered that he wasn't a man to trifle with, had even cried out at one point when he'd turned her over and done it again.

Later, when he let himself into the small flat, their little love-nest as Leah described it, she was waiting for him with a plate of roast pork and crackling.

'By heck, that smells good.' He had to hand it to the lass, she could cook as well as the rest of her breed, and she'd done the place up champion. Put up a few pictures, bought a nice new red and beige patterned rug, he noticed. Oh, yes, she knew how to make a man comfortable, did this one.

'I've been keeping it warm for you between two plates,' she told him, and her smile brought a memory of the fun they'd once had together, making him think of other diversions they could perhaps enjoy before he got down to his dinner.

'I hope that's not all you've been keeping warm, love.' But the delicious aroma of the pork reminded him of a more mundane hunger and, a man of large appetites in every way, he wasted no time in tucking in. There'd be plenty of time later, if he was still in the mood. 'What a good idea of mine to marry a Simmons. Tha's as good a cook as thy dad.'

Leah went pink with pleasure at his praise. 'I've made rhubarb and custard to follow.'

Harry had two helpings. When he'd wiped the last dribble of custard from his chin, he said, 'Speaking of your dad, I were wondering if he'd come round a bit, now we've been wed for a while, and were warm for a bob or two.'

'If he's what?' Leah said, giving a little laugh of disbelief. She'd not sat and shared the meal with Harry because there'd been too little meat, and had settled for cheese on toast earlier. Now she began to stack the plates, happily dreaming of a cosy evening together by the fire. She'd got a smoochy Bing Crosby record on the new gramophone, all ready to play. Harry put out a hand to stop her.

'I mean, is he good for a loan, preferably without interest, naturally. When Dad did a bunk, he left me with a few unpaid bills, nothing serious you understand,' he added quickly, seeing the dismay in her face. 'But it isn't easy to get a business going, chuck, not during wartime, so I wondered since we're family now, if he'd be prepared to cough up a few quid.'

Leah was horrified. She'd known that the Delaneys were a bit rough and ready, that Harry particularly operated close to the edge, but she'd never for a moment doubted that he was a shrewd businessman, an accomplished wheeler and dealer; or suspected that the club wasn't sound. 'I thought you'd let out the rooms and that would bring in the extra income you needed.'

'I have, but it isn't quite enough, love. You know how it is these days.' He flapped a hand and gave a vague sort of shrug, not wishing to be explicit.

'Oh yes, Harry, I do. Dad's had his worries too, getting enough raw materials for the cakes and such like.' She sat down beside him, wanting to help. He was her husband after all. They were in this together. 'Why don't you ask Jess to hold a dance in the big room? That would make money, as the band is very popular now.'

Harry ground his teeth, annoyed that his stupid cousin should be making such a success of her life when his seemed to be falling to pieces, but he turned the possibility over in his head. Maybe it wasn't such a bad idea, except that he used that room for poker and blackjack. Very popular that was with the Yanks, among others. The trouble was, he tended to lose the profit as quickly as he made it because he enjoyed a game himself, and he'd had a run of bad luck lately. Nor was it his fault if he'd been forced to borrow money from some shady characters to make ends meet. Everything was so much more expensive than he'd expected. And Harry just knew that he didn't want Jess Delaney anywhere near his club, showing off and being all la-di-dah.

'Nay, a dance wouldn't make nowhere near enough brass, not unless she agrees to play for nowt, which I can't see her doing, can you?'

Leah said, 'She might, if we explain how important it is,' though she didn't sound too confident, knowing how much Jess disliked her cousin.

'Nah, best we tap your dad, he's good for a few quid,' he decided, swaggering his broad shoulders to remind himself how powerful he really was.

'I really don't think so, Harry. You know that he and

Mother didn't altogether approve of our marriage. They aren't going to take too kindly to being asked to finance your business.'

Harry looked affronted. 'I would have thought they'd be pleased to see their precious little darling well looked after. Bloody parents. No use to anybody.' His own were just as bad. What use was his poor dad to him now that he was dead. If it hadn't been for their Jess taunting him, Bernie would never have gone for her, never have been clobbered over the head by Mam, and they wouldn't have had to dump him in that old bomb-site, poor old sod. Harry suddenly came over all maudlin, forgetting how much he'd hated his father when he was alive, and had constantly challenged his authority.

And then it occurred to him, on a flash of inspiration, that he did have a lever to make Jess play for nothing. To force her to do owt he wanted. Why hadn't he realised this before now? Hadn't he said she should pay for the damage she caused? And she would, by gad, she would an' all.

Not appreciating that he was thinking things through in his head, Leah began to explain what had been on her mind ever since the wedding. She'd felt as if she and Harry were drifting apart and it had occurred to her that working together at the club might help bring them close again. 'Actually, I was thinking of giving up working at the tea room. I've never liked it particularly, and I thought I might be more use helping you here, at the club.'

'You can do that anyway, in the evenings.'

'Yes but I'd much rather . . .'

He wasn't interested in what Leah would much rather do, or what interested her. Harry was concerned only with money, and he was irritated by her lack of desire to squeeze a few quid out of her well-heeled parent, which she surely could do, if she put her mind to it. 'Where's the harm in him lending us a few quid, fifty say, or even seventy-five? He'd never miss it, well set-up chap like him. He can afford that surely? Like I say, it's all in the family anyroad.'

'I'm not sure my parents would see it in quite that way. Best we manage on our own. I have every faith in you,' and she put her arms about his neck to kiss him on the cheek. Harry shoved her off.

'Well then, if he won't agree to lend it, you'll have to borrow it without his permission.'

'I don't understand. How can I do that?'

'By helping yourself to whatever's in that fancy new till he bought, or in that safe he must have tucked away some place. I don't actually bloody care how you do it, or where you find it, nick the family jewels if you must but get me some bleeding dosh. Right?'

Leah could feel herself start to tremble. An uncomfortable thought was nudging the back of her mind, that this was the real reason he'd married her, to get his hands on her father's money. It seemed so incredible, that she almost laughed out loud. Clifford Simmons was comfortable but not what anyone would call rich, and surely no one would do such a thing, not in this day and age. And hadn't Harry been pots about her at one time, always pestering her to go out with him, wanting to make love to her? She gave a little laugh, that sounded unnatural even to her own ears. 'You surely aren't asking me to steal from my own parents?'

'You can't call it stealing. It's just getting one over, like. Me and Bert did it all the time. Anyroad, he's got that much brass, he'll never notice if a bit goes missing.'

'Don't be daft, of course he'll notice.'

'Hey, watch yer lip. Who are you calling daft? Don't you get uppity with me, girl. You're my wife now, and you'll do as I tell you.'

Leah had got up from the chair and now stood before him

with hands on hips. 'You can whistle for it. I'll not steal off my own father for you.'

Before she'd had time to guess what he was about, let alone take evading action, he flung a back-hander at her in the form of a clenched fist and knocked her flying. As she hit the floor, he tipped up the table and sent the remains of his dinner, and all the newly purchased crockery bought as wedding presents by the few friends who had come to their wedding, crashing and smashing around her.

Reaching down, he casually took hold of her arm and dragged her to her feet, then tossed her against the wall where she bounced like a cork before falling to her knees with a whimper. Even then he wasn't done with her. He was actually beginning to enjoy himself, feeling the power in his own hands that had once resided in his father's. It felt good not to be on the receiving end himself. Harry grasped the back of her neck with his fat, sausage-like fingers and pushed her face down into the remains of his dinner, now splattered all over the new rug she'd bought only the other week.

'And when tha's cleaned that lot up,' he told her, giving her a little shake to make sure he had her attention, 'tha'd do well to count your blessings and remember that you promised to honour and obey. Got that, luv, *obey*! Tomorrow, when you go into work, you won't be giving in your notice, you'll be dipping your hand into all that lovely loot your pa has stashed away, and sharing it out a bit more with your beloved husband. Got that?'

Without waiting for a reply, he picked up his trilby hat, and strolled out of the door, closing it softly behind him, to show there were no ill feelings.

On this particular evening the canteen was down by the Brunswick Basin giving the dockers a bit of cheerful sustenance. Jess was on her usual sandwich duties in the kitchen when she was interrupted by Harriet. 'There's someone to see you, Jess.'

Her heart leapt, beat painfully against her breastbone before plunging with dread. But it wasn't Steve, as she'd expected and secretly hoped for, despite the fears she held over what she needed to say to him. It was Doug Morgan.

He stood at the door, cap in hand, shuffling from one booted foot to the other and looking as shy and sheepish as ever. 'Hello, Jess. It's me.'

She smiled at him kindly, said she was glad to see him again, and instantly recalled the last occasion when he'd warned her off staying at the club. Well, she'd taken his advice, moved back in with Cora and hadn't regretted it. She gave him a carefully edited version of her decision, adding that it helped considerably that Bernie wasn't around and Harry had got married. 'We're almost civilised in Cumberland Street these days.'

'Strange that he should go off like that, just when he'd set it all up.'

Jess too found it surprising that Bernie could bear to abandon his precious new club to Harry and Bert but had no intention of discussing events of that night with Doug Morgan. He'd never struck her as a man of conscience. It was all very puzzling. Unless, of course, there was some other reason for the vanishing trick, such as someone chasing him for debt. He'd done that before today, according to Cora. 'He's gone away on a bit of business, thank goodness.' Jess knew that wherever he was he'd surely be engaged in some disreputable scheme or other.

And, of course, he could return at any time, so she should make the most of her freedom. The very idea of seeing again that mask of arrogant insolence, of recalling how that fleshy, moist mouth had attempted to kiss her, made her want to throw up.

Doug was saying, 'I'm so glad that you're back with your aunt. That club wasn't a nice place for a young lady such as yourself to be, what with all them young girls no better than they should be plying their trade.'

'That was one of Uncle Bernie's nasty schemes. It's all very above board now that Harry and Bert are in charge.' An optimistic assessment of the situation, but one she fervently hoped to be true since Leah was now residing there. He must have been mad to think she'd go along with his plan. 'It's more convenient for me to be with Cora because I can help her around the house, and with the children. Mind you, it's not perfect as you couldn't ever claim Cora and Lizzie to be the best of friends. Quite difficult at times when Lizzie has been on the razzle and . . .'

He interrupted her protracted explanation by blurting out, 'I wondered if you'd had a change of heart about that date I once mentioned. If so, I wouldn't mind taking you out somewhere nice, wherever you've a mind to go.'

He'd said it all in one breath, and Jess was filled with a rush of pity for him. She didn't imagine that he had many friends, him being so quiet and shy, but he'd shown a very proper concern for her, even if she hadn't welcomed his interference at the time. Recalling the resentment she'd felt, Jess was filled with guilt and without allowing herself a moment to think, accepted his invitation outright, saying that she'd very much like to go out with him. 'Why not? It's half-day closing at the tea room on Thursday and I could do with a bit of cheering up.'

Beaming from ear to ear Doug eagerly offered to pick her up from her home but the last thing Jess wanted was for Lizzie, or Cora for that matter, to get a glimpse of him and start asking awkward questions. Instead, she suggested they meet outside the tea room shortly after one o'clock, just as soon as the bakery closed.

She became uncomfortably aware of Harriet and Ted's combined gaze, both watching her with open curiosity, clearly wondering what had gone wrong between her and Steve. She made no effort to explain, telling herself that since there was nothing of a romantic nature between herself and Doug Morgan, it was perfectly safe for her to go out with him. And so she smiled brightly, and happily agreed that a day out would be lovely.

Leah had been edgy all day and now, as her father cashed up and prepared to lock the shop, she felt as if she might pass out at any moment, her nerves were in such a state. Would he notice that the amount of cash in the till didn't match the written total? At least there were no visible signs of the beating Harry had given her. He'd made sure of that. Her father glanced up and caught her watching him and she felt her cheeks turn crimson beneath his probing gaze, quite sure he could see the scar of guilt on her soul.

What on earth had possessed her to get involved in all of this? Even as she asked herself the question, Leah knew why. She was more afraid of her husband than she was of her father. She didn't know who she was any more, no longer in control of herself, or her own life. She'd tell Harry tonight that this was the last time. No more. She'd had enough.

'Off home now are you, love? Got something tasty for your old man's supper?'

'I thought I'd make liver and onions tonight.'

'With lots of mashed potato to soak up the gravy? Sounds delicious.' Clifford Simmons grinned, considered his daughter thoughtfully for a moment then came over to rest his hands on her shoulders. 'I'm sorry things turned out as they did. Your mother . . .'

'I know, Dad, it's all right. I understand.'

'You are happy, aren't you?'

'Of course, never more so.'

'Because if you aren't, if it was all a bad mistake, a bit of rebellion that's gone wrong, you've only to say. I'd turn heaven and earth round for you, love. You do know that.'

'I know it, Dad. But don't worry, everything's fine.' No, it isn't, screamed the voice in her head. But she couldn't tell her parents that, couldn't admit that they'd been right all along, and she'd been wrong. She'd been married for less than a month; they'd say that she hadn't given it a fair try yet, that every marriage had its teething problems and went through its sticky patches.

She'd just have to hope and pray that she could work on Harry, try to undo the damage that his father had evidently done to him over the years.

Cliff put his arms about his daughter and gave her a hug. 'Good! I know you want your mother to approve of your choice, and I'm sure Harry Delaney is a grand lad, at heart. Give her time, she'll come round.' He turned back to the till, scooped out a handful of notes, not troubling to count them as he shoved them into his pocket, although later in the evening, when he did the accounts for the day, would he then notice that there were two pound notes missing. 'Drop the sneck on your way out, love. See you tomorrow.' And dropping a kiss on her brow, he made his way wearily upstairs, tired after a long day's work, leaving Leah to switch off the lights and let herself out.

Doug took Jess to Belle Vue because there was a band concert on and he knew how much she liked music. Jess didn't care where they went but was simply thankful that it wasn't a dance. She couldn't imagine being held in anyone's arms but Steve's.

'It's very kind of you.'

'It's not kind at all. It's entirely selfish. I shall enjoy your company.'

Doug wouldn't hear of Jess paying for herself. He wouldn't even tell her how much it cost. 'Women aren't allowed to pay, not by my book anyway. Men should protect women and look after them. This is a March for Freedom display,' he told her. 'I hope it's the kind of music you like.'

'I like all kinds of music. Anything I can tap my feet to anyway.'

She had plenty of opportunity to tap her feet that afternoon as she listened, enthralled, to ten brass bands, fifteen service bands, and any number of choirs filling the sunny day with the richness of their voices. There were crowds of people watching, marching to the music, clapping and cheering and singing along with them whenever they knew the words. Jess began to feel better, the music soothing her as it always did. Afterwards, she couldn't stop talking about it. 'Didn't you just love that band who played "Fascinating Rhythm"?' or 'What was that last piece of music played by Rochdale Town Band? It was so marvellous I must tell Ted about it.'

'Who's Ted? Is he your boyfriend?'

Jess giggled. 'No, I mean Sergeant Buxton at the mobile canteen. He gives me lessons in the trumpet, for which I'm endlessly grateful.'

They had tea in the Japanese Tea Room and Jess politely thanked Doug for giving her such a wonderful afternoon. 'To think I could have been sitting at home listening to Aunt Cora grumbling about her sciatica, Lizzie in one of her drunken moods, and Sandra making sniping remarks. How blissful to enjoy a whole afternoon away from the entire Delaney crew. But I mustn't be too late home,' she said, not wanting to run the risk of him thinking this date was anything special.

'Why? Will your mother object, and not allow me to take you out again?'

'My mother doesn't care what I do.' Lord, he wanted to take her out again. Jess felt a beat of doubt about what she was getting into. She really must take care.

Doug was regarding her with some seriousness. 'You don't sound as if you much care for your family?'

'You could say that,' Jess admitted with a short laugh. 'No, that's not quite fair. Cora is a dear friend, and the twins a delight but as for the rest – well, let's say there's ample room for improvement, particularly where my uncle is concerned. The longer he stays away, the better.' She admitted then Bernie's intention to utilise her charms to attract customers to the club. The expression on his face was gratifyingly shocked. 'I don't look like a likely candidate do I, for giving servicemen a good time? Isn't that the parlance?'

'My dear Jess, you must *never* agree to it.'

She laughed. 'Don't worry, I've no intention of doing anything so stupid.'

'You must make sure, when he comes back, that he doesn't force you into it. You should find somewhere safer to live, somewhere far away from his evil influence.' His homely face brightened, making the thin planes of his cheeks grow pink and the pale, serious eyes appear almost animated for once. 'You could stay at my house if you like. I've plenty of room.'

Jess felt deeply embarrassed and just a little alarmed. She'd gone too far, told him too much, and all because of his sympathetic manner. Any minute now, she'd be spilling the beans about her pregnancy. As ever, she shut that particular problem out of her mind. 'Enough of this morbid talk. So long as I'm back by six or seven o'clock, that'll do fine. I need a bit of fun. Who doesn't, these days? Let's do something really mad and stupid.'

They queued for three quarters of an hour for a ride on the

Caterpillar. Jess was so startled when the canvas cover came over, plunging them into an eerie green darkness that she squealed in surprise.

It was then that he stole a kiss. Out of nowhere he seemed to loom over her, pressing his mouth against hers and Jess was compelled to hold her breath for quite a long while before he took it away again. She was left with a prickling sensation around her mouth, due to the roughness on his chin. Not sure how to react and wary of giving any sign of encouragement, she made no comment, pretending it had been no more than a moment's aberration on his part, a kindness because of her sudden fear. It proved to be the wrong approach for taking her silence as acquiescence, Doug put his arm round her and tried to kiss her again. As she tactfully attempted to evade capture, they bumped noses and she was the one to apologise. 'Sorry, I'm not very good at this sort of thing.'

'Sweet eighteen and never been kissed?'

Jess giggled. 'Hardly.'

His long, thin face darkened, looking more serious than ever. 'Was it that boyfriend you mentioned, who kissed you? Are you still seeing him?'

'No, no. That's over now.' It seemed amazing that since she first met Doug that day at the mobile canteen when she'd pretended to have a boyfriend, she'd started seeing Steve, fallen in love with him and now lost him for ever. How cruel life was.

'Good, I'm glad. I'm thirty-one. Does that bother you?'

Suddenly Jess wished she'd never started on this conversation. 'Why should it bother me? It's not important at all. I mean, if you don't mind me being so young, why should I mind . . . oh!'

'My being old?' He gave a hollow sort of laugh and she was mortified by her own clumsiness. She'd meant to insist that there was nothing between them, so why should their age difference be an issue but somehow it had come out all wrong. Had she offended him?

'I'm so sorry, I didn't mean . . .'

'It's of no consequence,' but he'd turned away and quietly removed his arm, much to her relief.

By the time they stepped down from their ride, a dance band was playing and she saw that open-air dancing had started. A platform had recently been opened for that very purpose with fairy lights strung all around, and it looked so romantic that Jess felt a deep ache in her heart. If only it were Steve here beside her on this lovely, mellow September evening. 'I love dancing, don't you?' she remarked dreamily, still thinking of Steve. What could be more blissful than to lay her cheek against his, to close her eyes and give herself up to the wonder of being in his arms? He was the only man for her, the one she should be kissing in the green darkness of the caterpillar ride, yet never would. Oh my own darling, how will I survive without you?

Doug said, 'I don't think a nice girl like you should be seen dancing in a place like this. Far too public.'

She was startled. 'Why? What's wrong with dancing outside? It all seems perfectly respectable to me.' Jess looked about her at laughing couples obviously enjoying themselves as they danced a quickstep to 'Little Brown Jug', at lovers kissing and cuddling under the guise of innocent dance steps. She felt annoyed by the dismissive remark, as if he were criticising her personally for enjoying dancing so much. 'For goodness sake, it's harmless enough. It certainly looks as if everyone here is having great fun.'

Seeing his mistake, Doug hastened to rectify it. 'If you'd like to dance, Jess, I'd be happy to partner you.'

Now she'd done it. How could she refuse after making such a fuss? 'Well, all right, if you don't mind,' she said, rather testily, and followed him on to the dance floor, striving to appear normal and hide her reluctance.

When he put his arms about her she made sure that she kept her distance, not at all as she would have danced with Steve, no cheek to cheek, no hand clenched tight against his heart, thigh pressing against thigh. This was utterly decorous and very proper. Even so, it felt uncomfortable, almost embarrassing. Entirely wrong! The rough fabric of his suit felt alien to her touch, even the unmistakable smell of tar and rope and the docks emanating from him made her feel strangely nauseous. She could feel his eyes on her face, was desperately searching her mind for something witty or amusing to say, something frothy to lighten the heavy atmosphere. And then as Doug spun her round in a clumsy manoeuvre, only just managing not to tread on her toes, that's when she saw him.

He was playing in the band. She hadn't noticed him at first, not until they'd circled the dance floor once and come closer to the small stage. Now she looked up straight into his eyes, almost as if she'd known he was there all along. He was playing the saxophone and she sensed the wrong note he played, even without hearing it. His gaze seemed to burn into hers, searing into her soul and all she could think was: Oh, why did he have to be here? Why did Steve have to see her like this, in the arms of another man? She felt giddy with misery, trembling in every limb so that she missed a step and would have stumbled had not Doug caught her, taking the opportunity to draw her closer into his arms.

'Are you tired? Would you like to rest?'

She said that she would and they left the floor, Jess gladly accepting the lemonade he bought for her. 'It's probably the heat, almost an Indian summer.'

'Would you like to go home?'

Jess shook her head. 'No, no, I'm fine now. Let's dance

again.' A sort of recklessness had come over her. No matter how difficult, she really mustn't run away. Perhaps it was no bad thing that Steve had seen her with Doug. If she could get through the next ten minutes or so, it might finally convince him that it was over between them and leave her alone. After that, it would surely get easier. Even broken hearts mended eventually, didn't they?

And then he was there beside her. Having abandoned his saxophone to come looking for her, he was telling a red-faced, angry-looking Doug that this was an Excuse-Me and it was his turn now to dance with Jess.

He'd fixed the dance deliberately, Jess knew it. Fortunately, this thought didn't occur to Doug and he graciously, if reluctantly, relinquished her.

It was as if she'd been waiting for him. They came together with an ease that was heartbreaking. Her hand captured warmly against his chest, his arm about her waist where it seemed to fit perfectly, holding her close so that she could follow every fluid movement of his body, anticipate his next step as every good dancer should. She could feel his warm breath against her cheek, match every beat of his heart.

'Is that him, the bloke you've dumped me for?'

'It's not like that at all.'

'Are you saying we can get back together? You know, of course, that I love you.'

She could hardly see him for the shimmer of tears in her eyes. *He loved her!* He'd said those precious words which she had so longed to hear. But it was too late. Far, far too late. Bernie Delaney had made sure of that. She shook her head in numb misery.

'I can't let you go, Jess.'

'You must,' and suddenly she realised the band was playing 'I'll Be Seeing You'.

Steve pulled her close in his arms and began humming the

words softly into her ear. 'In all the old, familiar places, that my heart and mind embraces, all day through . . . I'll be seeing you in every lovely summer's day . . . I'll always think of you that way. I'll find you in the morning sun and when the night is through, I'll be looking at the moon, but I'll be seeing you.'

Jess could bear no more, she tore herself away and ran blindly from the floor, not pausing for a second even when he called out her name causing heads to turn, and the other dancers to watch her departure in open-mouthed wonder and dismay.

23

It was Doug who caught up with her at the bus stop, most insistent that she tell him what had caused her distress. 'Did he hurt you? He was in the band, wasn't he? Musicians are the lowest of the low, I've always thought. Didn't I say it wasn't a respectable place for you to be?'

'Don't say such things, Doug. I'm a musician too, remember? And I'm OK. Really I am. It wasn't anything Steve did, it was me. I suddenly came over all funny again. The heat under all those lights, I expect.'

'All women get in a state. They need a man to sort them out. Only remember I'll always be here to look after you, if you want me to. Don't you fret none about that.'

Jess flushed, alarmed by his proprietorial air, and this over-simplification of love. It was Steve she needed, not Doug Morgan. And Steve she'd just walked out on.

Jess could take no more. Her mind was spinning, her heart physically aching, just as if someone were squeezing all the life out of it. 'Take me home please?' And she ran up the steps of the bus on to the top deck and sat mute throughout the entire journey, cooling her forehead against the bus window.

Oh, why couldn't it have been Steve who had followed her to the bus stop? she thought, knowing she was being unreasonable. She'd left him stunned and hurt on the dance floor, where he would have to go back on stage and play the next number as if nothing amiss had taken place at all.

By the time she parted from Doug at the corner of

Deansgate, guilt over her coolness towards him that evening
was already beginning to surface and when he told her he
planned to buy tickets to take her to the Hallé Orchestra the
following Sunday to hear them play Verdi's Requiem at
the King's Hall, she felt quite unable to refuse. It had been
unkind and foolish of her to dance with Steve when she was
supposed to be with Doug, and stupidly dangerous. She
politely accepted the invitation and quite genuinely
expressed her gratitude for a delightful afternoon, struggling
to look pleased and happy, as if she were thrilled by his offer,
although she really didn't care one way or the other. It was
Steve Wyman she wanted. But if she couldn't have Steve,
what did it matter where she went or who she went with?

Leah had convinced herself that it would be a temporary situation, that she would eventually be able to make Harry see
the error of his ways. She'd tried, on several occasions, to
resist, sometimes objecting quite strongly. At other times
she'd talked to him with quiet reason, or playfully attempted
to tease him into seeing sense. She'd tried desperately to show
him how wrong it was to steal, while doing her utmost not to
upset him. None of her ploys had had any effect. He would
either storm off in a fury and, she suspected, take his revenge
by sleeping with one of the barmaids, or he would lash out
and hit her. She saw now that all Jess had told her about
Bernie Delaney must have been true since his son was every
bit as bad, the worst of the lot as Jess had said. If only she'd
known before she'd agreed to marry him, or rather, if only
she'd listened to Jess's sound advice.

Leah kept hoping that she could change him, that because
of his love for her, he would treat her better. But he never did.

There was a madness in him, a sickness almost, a part of
him that she couldn't reach. It was as though he had to
destroy everything that came his way, and her with it. Leah

knew she'd changed. She was no longer the carefree, adventure-loving girl she'd once been. Now she felt tired and depressed all the time, jumpy and nervous. She weighed every word before she uttered it, was careful not to anger him with a joke when he wasn't in the mood for laughing, or any comment he might construe as criticism. She always made sure that she looked nice when he came upstairs to the flat for his supper. Today, the minute she arrived home from work, Leah dashed around tidying up the place, straightening cushions, wiping every speck of dust away because Harry was oddly fastidious, considering his background and how untidy Cora was. And she wanted it all to be lovely, for him to smile and appreciate her efforts to please him. To be happy and kind to her, to be the man she thought she'd married.

'Do you like my new dress?' she asked, when he walked through the door an hour later expecting his tea to be ready and waiting on the dot of six. Leah knew she looked good, with her hair all freshly washed and shining, she'd even managed to buy a new pink lipstick on Campfield Market, and Harry himself had provided the silk stockings.

He had a glass in his hand which he didn't set down, even when she put her arms about his neck to give him a kiss. 'Did you get it?' he asked.

'Did I get what?' She drew away, knowing exactly what he was referring to. Leah kept hoping that one of these days he might forget to ask, or think better of his scheme and agree that she didn't have to steal any more. So far, she must have taken well over fifty pounds from her father's shop, little by little, and he hadn't even noticed. At least, not a word had been said. Every day when she arrived at the tea room, she half expected him to angrily confront her with the knowledge of her betrayal, almost wished that he would, so that she could tell Harry the game was up, and this terrible nightmare would be over at last.

Harry was watching her with eyes like flint, a part of him irritated that she stubbornly continued to defy him, there being more days when she brought nothing at all home, than the days when she did. At the same time he was savouring the scent of her soft, fair hair, noticing how her breast rose and fell in breathless little gasps. Was keenly aware of the sway of her hips against his crotch when she'd kissed him. He pulled her roughly towards him, lifted her skirt and slid his fingers down inside her stocking top, stroking her leg, enjoying how her eyelids fluttered closed as his circling progress homed closer to their target.

'I can mek you do owt I want.'

'Oh yes, Harry, you can, you can.' It was always best to agree with him. However much she might loathe herself for it afterwards, it was safer that way.

'And you like it, don't you? I know you do. Go on, say that you like me to give the orders. Go on, say it!'

'I like you giving the orders, Harry.' A voice in her head shouted that this wasn't true. She hated being used by him. Hated it. Hated *him*! Tell him you'll not do as he asks ever again. But he was pushing her down on to the rug, ripping her new dress in his eagerness to remove it, and Leah was deeply afraid.

Later, when he'd enjoyed her to the full and she'd handed over two crisp white five-pound notes, as instructed, Harry decided that all things considered he was really very pleased with himself, and his marriage. Not only did he have full control of a delightful, obedient little wife, but also had a hold over his dear cousin, which he could put into effect at any time that he chose.

In her desperation, Leah went to see Cora to ask for advice, explaining at length about the sorry state of the club, and pouring out all her troubles. 'I mean, I know he says money's tight and apparently there are debts, but surely there must be some other way. He's let out all the rooms, save for one which he uses for drunken customers who are incapable of getting home. But that's not enough, he says. I suggested he ask Jess to hold a dance there, but he won't hear of it. How can I make him see that it's wrong to ask me to steal from my own parents?'

'Nay, our Harry won't see it in that light. Your pa has plenty, and he's family, so why shouldn't it be shared round a bit like? Anyroad, I've been trying all me life to do the self-same thing. He's a lost cause is our Harry. I can do nowt. I wouldn't know what to suggest.' Cora scratched her head in puzzlement, the grey strands of wiry hair tightly bound in their usual curling pins, obviously in preparation for some future event which never seemed to arrive. Yet she was taking greater pride in herself these days, since her suppers had proved to be such a feature at Jess's dances. Though that didn't quite extend to personal hygiene. There still emanated from her the sour smell of sweat, or, as Cora herself dubbed it, 'honest toil'.

Leah gazed at her mother-in-law, horrified, and not quite able to take in that Harry's own mother was apparently going to sit back and do nothing to help. 'Why didn't anyone tell me all of this before?'

'Would you have listened? Folk generally don't, once they've made up their minds to do summat. I didn't, and I were warned about Bernie by everyone who knew him. Didn't our Jess say owt?'

'She said he was the worst of the lot.'

Cora cackled with laughter, which Leah thought astonishing, considering it was her own son they were talking about. 'Aye, that about sums up our Harry. Tha'll have to get canny, as we've all learned to do. Pretend yer doing as he says, but actually please theeself. That were generally the answer wi' our Bernie.'

'And where is he, your Bernie? No sign of him yet?' Leah asked, sighing with exasperation as she realised she was getting absolutely nowhere. Cora didn't understand at all about Harry. He was a very difficult man to refuse anything, partly because she was coming to fear his temper, and also, to her shame, because she loved him and still hoped that she could change his nasty ways. She hated having to come and beg for help like this, hated the sour smells in this house, the pile of dirty dishes in the sink. How could Jess tolerate living here? And in the front room, comatose on the horsehair sofa, was Lizzie, her drunken sot of a mother. What a household!

'Nay, the longer he stays away the better,' Cora said, then levering herself out of her chair grabbed the kettle and offered another cuppa, though they'd had two already.

'No thanks, I'd best be on my way, Harry doesn't like me to be late home. You won't say anything about our little chat, will you? Promise?'

'If there's one thing I've learned, living in this family all these years, it's to hold me tongue.'

The trip to the orchestral concert did not start off particularly well. To begin with Doug failed to acquire tickets for the Hallé and took her instead to a comic operetta put on by a local amateur operatic group. It wasn't entirely to Jess's taste but not for a moment did she say as much. She steadfastly sat through an hour and a half of the dullest music imaginable delivered by buxom middle-aged ladies who really shouldn't be attempting to reach those high notes. Just before the interval Jess began to feel slightly queasy and slipped out to the powder room for a cool glass of water. By the time she returned, Doug had bought her a brandy, certain that she was in need of one and quite put out when she refused.

'No, no, I can't – I mustn't. I don't drink spirits, thank you all the same.'

'You still look very much below par to me,' he told her. 'Perhaps you shouldn't have come. Is it something you've eaten, do you think?'

'I expect so.'

'Women are so delicate, aren't they? You really should take better care of yourself.'

Jess bridled. 'I'm not in the least bit delicate,' she protested, stoutly ignoring the small, chiding voice at the back of her head. 'Anyone can be ill, men as well as women. In fact, a man always namby-pambies himself much more than a woman does.'

'Oh no, men are much stronger, bound to be, since they have to earn an honest crust by the sweat of their brow in order to keep their families.'

'I really don't see it that way at all. There's no reason on earth why women shouldn't do exactly the same thing, as they are doing every day in this war.'

'Well yes, but only because they have to. It's easier for men as they do it so much better. They're more savvy, and once the war is over, the women will be able to relax and return to the hearth, where they belong.' He smiled at her as if he had just offered her the key to paradise.

One look into her fierce brown eyes told Doug he'd made a bad mistake, yet finding it difficult to back-track and still stick to his principles, he dug himself deeper into the pit that opened before him. 'Men know what's what, do you see? Been out in the world longer, protecting their womenfolk. Had the better education, generally speaking, and so they're the ones who must make all the decisions.'

'And it's the role of women to go along with those decisions, is it?' Jess was already suffering from a surfeit of guilt at having reacted so strongly to his typically male comments which really meant nothing at all. Hadn't she heard very much the same sort of piffle time and again from Harry, Bert and even Tommy. It really wasn't important, yet for some reason she couldn't bring herself to back down.

Doug saw only that the expression on her face had become thunderous and the chasm yawned wider, a pit into which he might fall if he took one more step along this path. Dangerous territory when he was doing his utmost to please her. There'd be time enough later to smooth the edges from her temper and teach her to see things in the proper way. She was young yet. 'I didn't mean to upset you, sweetheart. Don't let's quarrel. The second act is about to begin and I never meant to spoil the evening for you. Will you forgive me?'

'Of course, it was only a silly difference of opinion. Only please don't call me sweetheart, I don't like it. All right?'

'Whatever you say, sweetheart. Whatever you say.'

Leah watched, appalled, as her father rolled up the notes and thrust them into his pocket, his face so set with anger it made her shake. 'No, Leah, it's no good. I've paid her what wages she's owed, though she doesn't deserve them, and she's been given her marching orders. There's an end to the matter.'

'But how can you be sure that she's guilty?'

He slammed the till drawer shut, causing it to give a loud, startled ring. 'Because I never had any problems with money going missing until that girl started working for us. I've told her that I won't employ anyone dishonest, any little madam who thinks she can help herself by dipping her greedy, grubby little fingers into my till.'

Only Leah knew for certain that the new girl, little more than sixteen and at this precise moment running off down Deansgate in floods of tears having been sacked on the spot, dismissed without a reference, was entirely innocent.

'This can't go on,' she told Harry when he came in later for his supper. 'It must stop. Now! An innocent young girl has lost her job because of me, because of you and your greed. I'll not steal for you again. Ever!'

Harry glowered at her, his jaw tightening with fury, a white line of anger forming about his compressed mouth. 'You'll do as you're bloody told. You're my wife and I'm in charge here.'

'No, you damn well aren't,' she screamed back at him. 'I've told you. It's over. I love my dad. God knows why I stole from him in the first place, but now it's over. Got that? Finished!' For a brief instant she felt good. Jubilant! Perhaps if she'd stood up to him before now, things wouldn't have got so bad.

And then he hit her.

Leah fended off his blows as best she could, getting to her feet every time he knocked her down, only to get up again, determined to defy him, and yet desperately trying to protect herself while he rained punches on her. But finally she stayed down, lay curled in a tight, protective ball while he gave her what he called 'a good puncing' with his big heavy boots. They both knew that in future she would do exactly as he instructed, steal whatever he told her to steal, once he'd knocked all the fight out of her.

Jess saw Doug quite often after that and he proved to be a pleasant enough companion, a kind man doing his utmost to please her. She should be grateful. She was grateful. He'd quite taken her out of herself, taken her mind off her longing for Steve. It seemed an age since she'd seen him that last time at Belle Vue, though it could only be a few weeks.

'You're very good to me. I'm sorry if I'm not quite myself at the moment,' she said one evening as they turned from Bridge Street down Dolefield towards Cumberland Street. They'd been to the Odeon to see Gene Kelly in *For Me and*

My Gal and Jess had simply loved the music. She couldn't wait to try out 'After You've Gone' on her trumpet, though she thought 'Beautiful Doll' mightn't be so easy to play. She'd even allowed Doug to hold her hand throughout in an effort not to think of Steve. A ploy which hadn't quite been the success she'd hoped for as she'd sat there wishing things could be different and not in this dreadful mess.

Time was passing, and she still hadn't resolved a thing.

When she'd first found out about the baby, she hadn't been able to take it in. It hadn't seemed real. Now she felt sick all the time and, try as she might, couldn't seem to get the problem out of her mind as fear struck to the heart of her. What on earth was she going to do? Never in her wildest imaginings had she seen herself as the mother of an illegitimate child. The finger of scorn had always followed Lizzie. Jess had never meant to suffer in the same way, let alone be in a worse situation. She might scold herself for not making practical arrangements, for not finding some sort of solution, whatever that might be, but the truth was that she didn't want this baby. She loathed the very thought of it. How could she possibly feel happy about it when it had been foisted upon her in such a dreadful way.

But she certainly wasn't going to make herself feel any better by ignoring Doug. She should be paying proper attention to her escort, out of good manners, if nothing else. 'I enjoyed this evening very much. Gene Kelly is a marvellous dancer, isn't he? I got so engrossed in the film, I quite forgot to talk to you, which is unforgivable. You've told me so little about yourself, apart from the fact you lost your wife and child, that is. I mean, have you always worked on the docks, for instance?'

He looked pleased by her interest. 'Oh no, I've moved about a bit: worked in the parcel office on Exchange station, been a coalman, rent collector, and a driver for Burgess's

Dairy once over. But I was looking for something better, summat with good prospects, and that's where I found it, at the docks. I shan't be moving again, even when the war's over. I don't much care for change.'

'What about parents? I've heard you mention your mother, is she . . . ?'

'She's dead, me father too.'

'Oh, I'm so sorry to hear it. I hope, when the war's over, that my dad will come home safe and sound. He's a POW you know. I write to him all the time, though I'm not sure if he gets any of my letters. I can't wait to see him again, I do miss him so very much. He's someone to turn to in times of trouble, isn't he, a dad?' A rush of tears filled her eyes and ran, unchecked, down her face. What on earth was wrong with her, blubbing like this?

Doug tutted and patted her hand, pulled a clean, white handkerchief from his pocket and handed it to her with great deference. 'There, there, you don't need yer dad, sweetheart, you've got me. I'll take care of you.'

'You're so good to me, Doug, so kind and gentle.' Jess wiped away the tears, blew her nose vigorously and tried to smile. 'You make me feel so safe. That's why I like you, I suppose.'

'Aye, course it is.' He gave such a shy, sad smile that all her natural, warm sympathy came to the fore. 'You can give me a good night kiss, if you like.'

He looked momentarily flustered, strangely wrong-footed by the suggestion, as if she'd offered to take off her clothes and dance naked before him in the street. 'I don't think that would be quite right, do you? I mean we're not walking out, or engaged or anything?'

'Does one need to be engaged, for one good night kiss?' Jess asked, giving a little giggle and already wishing the words unsaid. What had she been thinking of to make such a suggestion? She must have gone soft in the head, but he looked so pathetic, so very much the small boy in need of petting by a loving mother. 'No further, mind,' she teased, giving him a sly wink. 'I'm not that sort of girl.'

'Oh, you don't know how pleased I am to hear you say so,' he said with some fervour. Then his face brightened and he looked more keenly at her. 'Would you like to get engaged? I could buy you a ring tomorrow.'

Now Jess was the one who felt wrong-footed. How had a mild flirtation to allow him to kiss her good night turn into something far more serious? She tried a little laugh, hoping to diffuse the situation. 'My word, that's quite a leap, don't you think? How did we reach that stage? It's a little early to talk of engagements after only one kiss. And before a man buys a girl a ring, it's customary for him to ask her to marry him.' She'd said the words flippantly, a teasing light in her eye. But she saw at once that she had compounded her mistake.

His face was alight, so full of eagerness that for one dreadful moment she half expected him to go down on one knee and propose to her there and then in the mud and dust of the gutter. Instead he said, 'I will ask you, if you like. May I?'

Perversely, Jess felt a burst of irritation that he should think to ask her permission instead of simply declaring his undying love and sweeping her off her feet, as a man should. His diffidence somehow made it seem as if *she* had failed a test, not him at all. Yet what did it matter? She wasn't seeking either love or passion, and certainly not from Doug Morgan. Those were what you found on the shelves of Boot's library, not in real life, not for her, not any more. 'I know that you're not serious, Doug, that this is some sort of silly game we're playing, but just so that you *will* know in future, you must never ask a girl if you *may* propose to her, for how can she answer?' She smiled at him fondly. 'Do you see, it would be tantamount to accepting the offer before ever you made it.'

'Oh yes, I see. I hadn't thought of that.'

'Anyway, the answer is no, I don't want you to ask me, thank you very much. As I said, we hardly know each other. It's much too soon. Anyroad, I'm not sure if I shall ever marry.'

But I'm having a baby. I need a husband. Desperately!

He looked nonplussed and frowned, as if she'd said something that didn't quite make sense. 'But all women must marry. That's their role in life, isn't it?'

Jess looked at him askance for a moment, wondering if he truly believed in what he was saying or was again simply trying to tease her. 'I think women are good for one or two other things as well, besides marriage.'

'Course they are,' Doug added quickly, seeing the pit yawn before him once more. 'But we'd be good together, you and me, Jess. I'd give you everything you ever dreamed of: nice clothes, children, a home of your own that you didn't have to share with your hated uncle, or your feckless mother for that matter.'

'Uncle Bernie is one thing, and I loathe the sight of him, but Lizzie is still my mam and I am responsible for her,' Jess said, eyes flashing.

'Course you are. I didn't mean to suggest otherwise. Sorry, sweetheart.' By heck, but she was a prickly one and no mistake. He'd really have to take care if he was ever to win her over.

'And I've told you before, don't call me sweetheart,' Jess responded sharply and began to walk away, annoyed that somehow the evening had gone wrong yet again.

Appalled by his own clumsiness, Doug set off after her at a lumbering trot. He was going to have to watch his step or he'd lose her. He called to her, begging her to stop and wait for him which, thankfully, she did, albeit with a weary sigh of resignation. Just as well since there was a limit to which even he was prepared to suffer humiliation, and running after a woman certainly came into that category.

'Don't be angry, sw—, er, I'm sorry if I've caused offence, love. You mean the world to me, you know. What would I do without you? I'd be lost.'

'Would you?'

He smiled at her warily, rubbed the sweat from his palms and grasped her small hands between his own, giving them a little pat. 'Course I would. I love you, Jess. I'd do anything to make you happy. You've only to ask. I didn't mean it about your mam. She could come and live with us, if you like. How would that be? Just say the word and I'll spend the rest of me life being a good husband to you.'

Her eyes filled with tears again, so touched was she by the genuine kindness in his tone. Wasn't this what she needed, someone to care, someone to look after her? 'You'd do that for me?' she asked. 'You'd take on my mother too?'

'If it meant you'd be happy, course I would, love.' Doug was secretly hoping it never came to that. Lizzie was a wild card, a difficult woman as well as a feckless layabout and a drunk. But if that's what it took to catch her daughter, that's what he'd do. Anyway, it needn't be permanent. Not that he expected her to accept for one moment. He couldn't be that lucky. And then Doug became aware that she was saying something else, something of even greater importance.

They were seated now on a rough bit of planking down by the Irwell, and somewhere in the distance they heard the hoot of a ship, perhaps saying farewell as it went off to war. It was almost pitch black and a mist hung low over the river, some-times parting to show the glistening black of dirty water below, sometimes enveloping them in swathes of fog. Jess could see no sign of Irwell Street Bridge she knew to be just a few yards upriver, could scarcely make out Doug seated beside her, let alone the expression on his face. Yet in a way, this was an advantage and she kept her gaze fixed on her own clenched hands as she launched into her tale. 'What if I asked you for more than that, to provide a home for more than my mother? What if I asked you to take on someone else as well?'

'Someone else?' Surely not this Aunt Cora as well, not her whole family, he thought. What had he let himself in for? 'Who?'

'A child.'

Doug turned over these two, rather surprising words, in his brain for several moments. 'I'm not sure I quite understand. I thought you were an only child, with no brothers and sisters.'

'No, not a child of that sort. I meant . . . my own child.'

'What, yours and mine you mean? Oh but I've already said . . .'

'No, not yours and mine.' Jess took a deep breath and told him, as gently and calmly as she could, about her uncle raping her, using the word out loud for the first time, and how she believed herself to be pregnant as a result. It couldn't have taken more than a few moments but she felt exhausted when she was done, drained of all energy.

A silence stretched endlessly between them. Doug was disappointed. He'd wanted her to be pure, chaste as the driven snow. Yet he was afraid to show it, for fear of losing her. At length he said: 'I am honoured that you should share this information with me. It couldn't have been easy for you.'

'N-no, it wasn't easy at all. It was a terrible thing to happen to me, to any girl.'

She'd made no mention of Steve, of their earlier lovemaking, because Jess had put all hope of a life with him out of her mind. That was behind her now, lost for ever. But even though they'd quarrelled a little, she'd enjoyed the time she'd spent with Doug, and it had made her see that she needed someone in her life. She didn't want to spend it alone, with everyone pointing the finger and calling her child a bastard. So, if he could accept her conditions, what did she have to lose?

'The only thing is – and I must be honest with you, Doug, that I doubt I could be much of a wife to you. Being – assaulted in that way, tends to put one off – that sort of thing. To put it bluntly, it would be a marriage in name only. I very much doubt that I could ever – that I would ever *want* to have sex, with you or – or anyone.'

He kept his expression carefully neutral and passive, giving no indication of how much she'd startled him. This was the last thing he'd expected and yet – did it really matter? What good had sex ever done for him, or for his own mother who had given it freely outside of a respectable marriage? She'd used sex as a weapon against his father, chosen it in preference to her own son. No, no, he would willingly live without it, if necessary. That other boyfriend of hers, Steve, the musician character whom she'd danced with at Belle Vue only the other week, had obviously let her down. He might well be the father of this child, and this tale of being raped by her uncle all a lie, a fantasy she'd made up to make him feel sorry for her.

But he would never let her down. One word from him and Jess was his for the taking, more than he'd ever hoped for; what he'd dreamed of for so long and never believed he could achieve. He would keep her like a princess in an ivory tower, all to himself. She would be entirely his.

He touched her hand very gently and smiled kindly at her. 'All right, Jess love. I'll agree to that, and right gladly. I'll look after you and the babby.'

Jess felt deeply moved by the kindness so evident in his

gaze and found herself revealing even more about herself. 'I'm not sure how I shall feel about the baby. I'm not sure I even want it, do you see? Because of the circumstances.'

'Don't worry about that now. You could always have it adopted.' He had no wish to be a father, particularly of another man's child, but fortunately she didn't enquire into his feelings on this, and he didn't offer an opinion. 'Whatever your problems are, I'll take care of you. I'm a simple man but harmless, as they say. I'll certainly not hurt you, sweetheart. Quite the opposite. I shall deem it a privilege, an honour to have you as my wife.' He smiled sheepishly at her, all too aware of her soft heart. 'I do love you, Jess, and will cherish you. If you will have me.'

He looked so incredibly earnest that Jess found herself smiling in response and accepting his offer without the slightest hesitation. She saw him as a good, kind man, lonely and sad, who'd already experienced the pain of losing a wife and a beloved child. This war had destroyed too many lives. Didn't Doug Morgan deserve some compassion, a little loving, just like everyone else? Didn't she? Not forgetting the child that her uncle had saddled her with. If this good man was prepared to take on such a burden, what possible reason could she have for refusing him?

1945

24

The sun was shining and new life unfurling in the buds on the trees, a beautiful spring day right in the heart of Manchester, outshone only by the delight and happiness on the hundreds of faces that thronged Albert Square, all of them beaming suns in their own right. Wreathed in laughter and smiles, they reflected hearts filled with new life and hope for a new tomorrow.

'Manchester Salutes the Allies' declared the hoardings, words emblazoned over a giant V for victory sign. The war was over at last. Germany had surrendered, the Third Reich was defeated.

Flags of the United Nations were flown, King George VI's broadcast relayed to his loyal subjects. There were flags and bunting everywhere, pictures of Winston Churchill propped up on backyard walls. The streets of Manchester rang with music and laughter, singing and dancing. People danced everywhere, even on top of the air-raid shelters, cocking a snook at the hours they'd spent confined in the musty misery within, over so many long years. Bonfires blazed, fireworks exploded and people took rides on gloriously decorated trams just so they could see all the fun.

Later in the day, or certainly by the next morning, reality would show that nothing had changed. Admittedly the blackout, even the dim-out that had recently replaced it was now over for good. Lights were on again in Manchester, but there were still long queues for food, even bread. Restrictions continued, though no one was complaining as they were too used to the 4, 3, 2, 1. Four ounces of bacon, three of cheese, two ounces of tea and one egg a week, if available. One shilling and twopence could be spent on meat, plus another twopence on corned beef. They were all bored sick with Spam. And even Cora was having trouble finding enough coupons these days to provide the extra fat she needed to make pies for the dances that Jess still held each month at some local venue or other.

'Not sure which they like best, my prata pies or your music but you keep playing and I'll keep cooking, luv.'

Jess believed that it was the dances and her beloved trumpet which had kept her sane over these long months. If it hadn't been for them, she thought she might well have gone mad. Right now she was playing with all her heart and soul, while the women picked up their skirts and danced, finishing with a conga from Albert Square, all along John Dalton Street and down Deansgate, singing at the tops of their voices: 'I'm Looking Over a Four Leaf Clover'. It was a day to be happy, a day to rejoice and look forward, not back; no matter what problems may lie beneath the surface of their superficially contented lives. If nothing had quite turned out as either of them had expected, at least they had survived, could breathe in the fresh air and freedom, the glorious sunshine of this precious day.

Cora was with them, as she so often was, minding the babies. Leah had a baby girl, Susie, who was ten months old. Adored by her mother, the pair were practically inseparable and Leah had given up working at the tea room in order to devote her attention entirely to Susie's welfare, though she still helped out at the club. Much to the surprise of everyone, particularly his wife, even Harry had come to dote upon his daughter, and could often be found dangling her upon his knee. He had even been spotted proudly walking the baby out in her pram on Deansgate, basking in the comments of doting matrons who stopped to admire this delightfully pretty child.

Jess too had given up her job, at Doug's insistence, and even the Salvation Army had little need of her now. But she was content to devote her days, at least, to her child although nothing would prevent her from playing in her precious band.

Despite being a good, kind and caring man, Doug had been a huge disappointment to her, spending as little time as possible with John, or little Johnny as he'd come to be called, the child who had brought them together. It was apparently the mother he'd wanted, not the baby, had even suggested that she give him up for adoption. But then why should he love a child who wasn't his own son?

Jess sympathised, understood a little of how he felt. After being in labour for almost twenty-five hours of seemingly unendurable agony, they'd finally put her child in her arms and she'd felt nothing; had looked down upon him with in-difference, her heart turned to stone. Family and friends had come to peer at him, make comments over who they thought he most resembled, and if there was a moment when she'd looked at her baby and imagined that she saw Steve in the round, bright-eyed features, and in the shaggy red-brown hair then she quickly dismissed it as wishful thinking. She and Cora knew better.

She certainly hadn't expected to love him. How could she? A child born out of violence. Even when Jess had finally brought him home, two weeks later, she'd felt utterly in-adequate as a mother, could hardly bear to look at him, let alone pick him up. She would leave him in his cot for hours at a time where he would contentedly sleep, or gurgle and talk to himself, everyone saying what a good, happy baby he was.

Sometimes she would simply sit and look at him and marvel that he existed at all, wondering who he was.

But even if she couldn't manage to love him as she should, not for the world did she wish him any harm. She did her best to care for him, would get up at night without complaint to feed, change and burp him, and walked him out in his pram every afternoon.

Lizzie had come to live with them, as Doug had agreed that she could, but it hadn't worked out quite as Jess had hoped. Any normal mother would have helped with the new baby, but Lizzie was not, and never had been a normal mother. She required too much care on her own account. At first Jess had been pleased, believing that being part of a proper family, having a grandchild would keep her off the booze. But, thanks to Harry, there was no shortage of that commodity and on too many occasions Jess had returned home to find her mother senseless. On one, never-to-be-forgotten occasion, when little Johnny was just a few months old, Jess had agreed to let her hold him, while Jess pegged out the washing.

She must have wandered off upstairs in search of a quick nip of gin, because Jess suddenly heard a piercing scream and came running in to find that her mother had fallen down the stairs. Her heart had very nearly stopped beating on the spot, until she realised that she'd left the baby up there, lying safely in the middle of her bed, having forgotten that she'd taken him up in the first place.

'Thank God, you could have killed him if you'd fallen with him in your arms. What were you thinking of?'

But of course Lizzie hadn't been thinking at all. Lizzie was beyond thought, beyond feelings, beyond anything which didn't come in the shape of a bottle.

Finally, Doug convinced her that she should move back in with her sister-in-law; that Jess had enough on her plate, looking after a new baby. And so had come the end of a dream.

Jess depended entirely upon Cora's support during those first few months, learning the skills of baby care from her aunt which her own mother did not possess. The times when Cora was occupied with her own family and she was left alone with the child, were difficult. She felt trapped and very slightly resentful of this small, demanding infant who had destroyed her life.

To her shame, Jess realised that this was exactly how Lizzie must have felt when she'd found herself in a similar situation. Not that it was quite the same. Lizzie had at least got pregnant through a normal, loving relationship, unlike herself.

But then something happened which changed everything.

Cora it was who first noticed that something was wrong with the baby. She kept saying that he wasn't developing properly; should be eating better, sitting up by now, trying to crawl, and suddenly Jess too began to worry about him. She grew strangely protective.

She even spoke of her fears to Doug. 'Cora says there's something wrong with the baby.'

'Nonsense. It's your own inadequacies as a mother that are at fault. You haven't even breastfed him, giving him that dreadful National Dried Baby Food, no wonder the child isn't thriving. You could well have hurt him by your neglect.'

'Neglect? What are you suggesting? I would never do anything to harm him.'

'Well, you're certainly not a normal mother, not like my own, for instance. Wonderful woman, my mother. You could have learned a lot from her.'

Jess listened to her husband's criticisms, issued in what she'd come to recognise as that quiet, patronising voice of his and could hardly breathe as her throat constricted with unshed tears. Was she an unnatural mother? Was it even true that she didn't love her baby? Looking down at where he lay, strangely immobile in his cot, she felt a shaft of such love and fear for him that it was as if someone had punched her in the chest. She would never hurt him, never!

Very gently, she picked up her baby and held his rigid little body against her breast, tears rolling down her cheeks, splashing on to one tiny, clenched fist. It came to her then, in a blinding flash, that he was in pain. That was why he wasn't thriving. Something *was* hurting him, very badly.

She took him to the doctor where it was discovered that he had a dislocated hip, which had knitted together all wrong.

'But how did that happen? He's scarcely been out of his cot?'

Tests were made but it was finally decided that nothing intrinsic was wrong. His bones were otherwise normal, so it had probably happened during the long and difficult birth. He was given an operation where the joint was broken and re-set, and then put in plaster, almost from waist to toe, save for his little bottom. Jess experienced every part of the agony with him. She sat for hour upon hour, day after day, unable to do or think of anything but wait for news, first during the long operation, and then sitting by his bed waiting for him to wake up and later to slowly recover, with only Cora or Leah's occasional visits to keep up her spirits. The nurses tried to insist that she go home, that they had set visiting hours but Jess refused to budge.

'I'm his mother. Don't you realise that? I'm all he has. I should be here,' and something in the set of her face, in the pained resolution of her tone, made them leave her in peace.

Cora said, 'Didn't I say summat were wrong?'

'I'm very grateful, Cora, for your perception. How would I manage without you?'

'It's all your fault,' Doug told her when he was finally shamed into visiting the baby. 'You realise he could have been disabled. As if the poor kid doesn't have problems enough.'

'What problems does the poor kid have?'

'You know very well. Being – who, what he is.'

'You mean the child of rape – of incest?'

Doug looked about the crowded hospital ward in dismay, then hissed at her under his breath. 'Don't use such nasty words in so public a place. I'm only saying that if you hadn't tried to disguise the fact you were pregnant, no doubt by strapping yourself in with corsets, then his hip wouldn't have got damaged in the first place. You must have hurt him while he was still in your womb, or why would he be this way?'

'Utter rubbish. I never wear corsets. The doctor doesn't blame me. He says its just one of those things, an accident at birth.'

'Well he doesn't know you as I do. Or else you didn't pay proper attention to what the midwife was telling you at the time, and that's how he got damaged. Either way, you're the one responsible. You really have been a useless mother to that child, right from the start. You should have given him up, given him to someone who knows how to look after a child.'

Jess gaped at him. 'Given him up? I could never do that. Never! I can't think why you say such horrible things.'

'That's what you said you'd do once over, when you were first pregnant.'

'I must have been mad. Anyroad, he's here now, so I feel entirely different about him. And what about you? What kind of father have you been?'

'Aye, but I'm not his father, am I? So he's not my responsibility.'

'No, thank God, you're not!'

Today, as she jiggled him in his pram in Albert Square, watching him laugh as she tooted on her trumpet for him, it was Leah who asked, 'When does the plaster come off?'

He was sitting up all bright eyed and alert, delighting as much as she in the excitement of the day with not a sign of lethargy or pain in him, and Jess fully believed that soon he would indeed be walking. Oh, she did hope so, for didn't she love the bones of him, as the saying went, only in her case she meant it literally. Nursing Johnny through his long illness had brought them together, mother and son, as nothing else could. She loved him now more than she could say, more than life itself. 'Oh, not for a few months yet. Even then we mustn't rush him to try and walk. It will take a while before he's strong enough. But it'll come, all in good time.'

'Poor little mite. I wonder how it happened.'

'Don't you start. I have enough of that at home with Doug. He's a very quiet man, my husband, but he knows how to make his disapproval felt, with a silence you could cut with a blunt knife.'

Leah started suddenly. 'Heavens, look at the time. I must fly or there'll be no tea waiting for Harry when he gets in.' And she began desperately to look around for Cora, who had taken little Susie out of her pram to give her a walk around on her short, chubby legs.

'It is OK for Saturday I hope?'

Leah's face held an expression of momentary panic, one Jess had seen many times and which never ceased to bring a nudge of unease, despite the fact that these concerns were nearly always shrugged off or rebuffed. 'Lord, I'd forgotten about that. I think so, yes – I expect it'll be OK. So long as Harry hasn't fixed up for me to work behind the bar.'

'Tell him to find someone else for once. Don't let him bully you.' Jess regarded her friend for a moment out of narrowed eyes. 'You don't, do you?'

Keeping her head down as she strapped the baby into her harness, all too aware of her mother-in-law's curious gaze upon her, Leah brightly responded, 'No, course I don't. As if he'd dare. I'm fine, it's just that trade hasn't been too good recently and he's short of the readies, so he's cut back on staff.'

'Well then, he won't object to your earning a few bob by tinkling the ivories for me.'

'No, course he won't. Give my love to Doug. See you on Saturday.' Then Leah was breathlessly running down Deansgate anxious not to be late home, or else Harry would never let her hear the last of it. He'd flay her alive.

Leah really didn't know why she put up with it. At first she had stayed because she'd still loved him and had hoped that he would change. And then out of pride, because she'd married him in defiance of her parents, despite their disapproval, and couldn't for shame admit that she'd made a mistake. Now she was too afraid to leave, knowing he'd find her and bring her back, and because she had nowhere else to go. Nowhere she could be certain of being safe.

She had once tried packing her bags and going home to her mother. Muriel had taken one look at her daughter standing forlornly on the doorstep, two suitcases at her feet and a brand new baby on her hip, and rolled her eyes in despair.

'What did I say? Didn't I predict this would happen, that it would all go terribly wrong? If you'd listened to me, you could have married Ambrose, who is doing splendidly I understand, a Sergeant-Major no less, with a long and distinguished career ahead of him in the regular army. Well, don't think you can come back home with your tail between your legs. Your father is retiring. Robert is taking over the business and we are moving out to the Fylde coast to relax and enjoy whatever years we have left, without work or worry of any kind.'

Leah had been flabbergasted, unable to believe her ears. 'Are you saying that you won't help me? That you won't even give me a bed for the night, your own daughter and grand-daughter?'

'You made your bed, Leah, so lie on it.'

She hadn't ever gone back again. On that occasion she'd ended up at Cora's, trailing round there in tears, the baby screaming her head off. Harry had been summoned to his mother's house and been given a thorough talking to, accompanied by a clip around the ear. It had been an almost comical sight to see the diminutive, if somewhat round and solid Cora, laying into a son so big and brawny he could have flattened her with one hand, had he been of a mind to do so. But, in the end, with Harry's promises ringing in her ears that he would behave better in future, Leah had happily gone home with him, feeling quite optimistic that everything would be different.

She was soon put right on that score.

The minute she'd put Susie down in her cot, Harry had locked the door of the little flat and taken his strap to her, 'for broadcasting our private affairs to all and sundry'. He'd whipped her till her back bled and her blouse was in ribbons on her emaciated body. She'd never risked leaving him again.

Since then, she'd learned to toe the line, to do as she was told to the letter, without thought or argument. Life was easier that way, with less pain and fewer arguments. And she always tried to look on the bright side. She had Susie, who was all the world to her. And at least, unlike Doug, Harry had never objected to her playing in the band, as he needed the money she earned from it. No marriage was perfect, after all, and there were still times when Harry could be funny and sweet, shower her with presents or take his wife and child out for a special treat, particularly if he'd had a win on the cards. And Leah kept telling herself that once he'd got these money problems with the club sorted out, he'd be nice as pie again. She simply had to be patient.

Jess and Doug spent the following Saturday afternoon in Philips Park. It had become their custom to take little Johnny somewhere special at the weekend, instead of his usual perambulation down by the canal. This was Doug's weekly effort at fatherhood, to prove to the neighbours who saw him walk out with his child on his day off, what a very fine man he was. It was all show, since once out of their sight, he would ignore the child completely, almost as if he weren't even there, but Jess accepted the charade as better than nothing. For Jess the afternoon trip was an attempt to show her child a world beyond the muck and grime of the docks, particularly since Johnny's play was so restricted. And she believed that the fresh air would do him good.

As they sat on the park bench, as usual, Doug was lost in a world of his own thoughts. He sat with his hands on the knees of his best tweed suit, bowler hat set square on his head, only a small frown creasing his brow revealing any emotion on his unsmiling face. Jess did not interrupt this inner scrutiny of his private thoughts. She had learned that if he wanted to reveal them, then he would do so. If he did not, then nothing she could say would persuade him otherwise.

Jess jiggled the pram and mentally went over the tunes she meant the band to play this evening. They were playing at the Ritz, amazing when she remembered how nervous she'd felt when she'd first gone there with Leah right at the start of the war. She was in truth itching for the walk to be over, then she could get over to the ballroom and take the girls through a quick rehearsal, leaving little Johnny with Cora, as she always did.

Doug suddenly broke into her thoughts with, 'Tonight will be the last dance then? Good place to finish, at the Ritz.'

'Finish? Last dance? What are you taking about?'

He cleared his throat, sat up a little straighter, long bony wrists sticking out from the sleeves of his jacket. 'I've been thinking, Jess, that now hostilities are over, this dance craze of yours will have to come to an end, and a good thing too.'

'I beg your pardon? Why should it come to an end?'

'Because there won't be the servicemen around any more, looking to pick up partners. Husbands will be returning home, wives to the fireside, as is only right and proper. So no more dances which, as I say, is perhaps just as well.' He would have her home every evening then, all to himself, and about time too. 'Give you the time you need to be a mother to little Johnny here and a proper wife to me. I've given the matter a great deal of serious consideration and I've decided that it's time for you to stop all of this nonsense, to hang up your trumpet and put an end to this little hobby of yours.'

Jess was struck dumb for several long seconds before she found her voice. 'Little hobby? I can't believe I'm hearing you right. *You've* decided that I stop. What about me? Don't I have any say in the matter?'

'Now, my dear, don't I always know what's best for you? And I've worried about you going out and about on your own. I do like to know that you're safe.' Before she could interrupt again, he rushed on to remind her of when they'd first started walking out together, of how shy and awkward he'd been. 'You must have thought me a proper lemon. But then, you were so angry with the world, so full of bitterness.'

'That's not quite fair. I was distressed, by what had happened to me.'

'Of course you were. But I believe I've been a good husband to you. I mean, I took you on when nobody else would have done, didn't I? Despite your being soiled goods.'

Jess winced, wishing he wouldn't refer to her in that way. She was quite certain that he did it only to bolster his own ego, but it made her feel shoddy and used, fuelling her sense of failure and inadequacy as a wife.

'Of course you've been a good husband. I've never complained.'

'And you are happy?'

'Yes, I am happy.' Even as she said the words, Jess struggled to disguise the irritation in her tone. It had become so common for him to seek these sort of reassurances, that she inwardly groaned whenever he did so. He seemed to be in constant need of her praise.

'Then do try to smile a bit more, love. I like to see you always happy.'

'Nobody can be *always* happy. Life is too full of sadness for that.'

Then I must try harder to remove the sadness from it. What more can I do? Is it me? Is it my fault? Do I make you sad?'

'No, no, of course you don't. I'm fine. For goodness sake, Doug, stop fussing. Not everything comes down to fault and blame, yours or mine. Sometimes it's just life, or what other people have done. Fate. I don't know.'

She saw the flare of hurt in his eyes and could have bitten off her tongue. How easy it was to offend him, to make him look like a whipped dog.

After a lengthy pause, he turned to her and gave her hand a little pat, just as if she were a child who had suffered a tantrum. 'On second thoughts, perhaps it would be best if we stopped it right now. It's obviously causing you great strain. Looking after the child through its illness has exhausted you, and you clearly aren't yourself, all wrought up and highly distressed, not fit to go anywhere tonight. Besides, the town

will be rowdy and full of drunks, following the VE Day cele-
brations. You must send your apologies instead.'

Jess looked at him in disbelief. 'Send my apologies? What
in God's name are you talking about? I can't simply not turn
up. What about the other girls? I'm the bandleader, how
could they manage without me?'

'They'll manage if they must. Nobody is indispensable, my
love. You'd best stop at home.' He always addressed her in
this way, calling her his love, his treasure, even his *dearest
dear*, in a fond, over-dramatic tone. At least he'd stopped
using sweetheart, which was what she had been to Steve,
never to Doug.

'And why the hell should I?'

He looked at her then, the faintest hint of surprise and a
great deal of reproval in his steady gaze. 'Because I ask
you to.'

The moment they arrived back home, he went to put on
the kettle for their afternoon tea while Jess dashed upstairs.
In ten minutes flat she was washed and changed, had
collected the baby's overnight bag, and was flying downstairs
and out of the house before he had chance to come from the
kitchen to check what had caused the front door to bang so
loudly.

The Saturday night dance was the most fun Jess could
remember. She loved playing at the Ritz, which was always
a thrill. They were not the star attraction but the second band
on, even so it was a tremendous achievement, of which she
was justly proud. The Ritz Ballroom had a two-tier band-
stand, one on top of the other, which made the changeover
smooth, with scarcely a break in the dancing.

And Delaney's All Girls Band were being very well paid,
Jess never letting on that she loved it so much, she would
happily have played for nothing. Nevertheless it was

wonderful to be making more money than she ever had in her life, still saving hard out of habit rather than necessity, and she'd been able to make Lizzie comfortable at least, even though she and Cora were still occupying the same house in Cumberland Street with a sort of armed truce between them.

Tonight, peace having been declared, everyone was in a good mood, singing and laughing and yet underneath lingered an echo of sadness. As if an era were coming to a close and no one quite knew what tomorrow might bring. As usual, the place was full of American GIs or Yankee-Doodle dandies as they were known. It was no wonder that the ball-room had become known as the forty-ninth state. Whitworth Street was chock-a-block with jeeps; with red MP armbands and batons much in evidence, worn by chunky service policemen representing Uncle Sam whose task was to deal with miscreants who stepped out of line. Not that many did, they were having too good a time, and the MPs were particularly tolerant this evening.

Jess still had her own crew intact. They stood up one by one to take their bows as she introduced them. Lulu on sax, blonde page-boy bob swinging suggestively back and forth as she played; Adele with the flashing dark eyes on clarinet. Miss Mona on double bass and Ena the sexy drummer, still vowing to head for a nunnery, once the war was over and temptation banished from her life. A joke which always brought a good laugh from the customers. Leah on piano of course, and last but not least, herself, Jess Delaney on trumpet.

'Take it away girls. *One, two, three . . .*' And the band struck up with 'Don't sit under the apple tree with anyone else but me . . .'

As well as servicemen, Brits still out-numbering the Yanks, if only just, the place was thronged with excited, giggling girls. Hollywood movies being popular throughout the war, many of them had spent it seeking out their own personal

Humphrey Bogart, and those who had succeeded would be heading out West soon. Jess watched their happy young faces as she played, wondering which of them would be fortunate enough to have their dreams come true. Hers certainly hadn't.

She was trying not to think about Doug's ultimatum, hoping that she could work on him to change his mind. He wasn't an unreasonable man, just far more proper and correct than she'd expected, a man of standards that must be followed to the letter. So far he'd stood by their agreement. They occupied separate bedrooms in the small terraced house he'd found for them on Gartside Street, though how she would manage to survive an entire married life without intimacy, Jess didn't care to question too closely. It didn't seem normal.

Sadly, his kisses could not be compared with those magical, romantic moments she'd once enjoyed with Steve. How could they? She'd loved Steve, perhaps still did, whereas Doug was simply – what? A convenience? A good friend? Someone safe to keep her from being alone and an outcast from society.

Oh dear, that sounded dreadful, if painfully true. And it could all have been so very different.

It was still second nature for her to keep an eye out for a shabbily dressed sax player. She only needed to catch a glimpse of a shaggy red-brown haircut, or a tie askew, for her heart to skip a beat. Not that she'd been fortunate in that respect for well over eighteen months. Tonight was to be no exception. Wherever he was, it couldn't be in Manchester. Somehow, Jess knew that if Steve were still here in the city, he would have come to her by now. He wouldn't have been able to stay away, not on VE Day. She didn't know why she thought that, having no reason to believe he still cared, but somehow she just did.

25

Cora had always made it a policy not to get involved in her children's affairs. Or her husband's, for that matter. Bernie was no more than a distant memory, one of the many unidentified corpses dug out of the ruins of Manchester. Cora had no regrets about that. He'd got what he deserved, what he had coming to him.

What she did regret was the effect his dirty interfering had had upon that poor lass's life. Ruined it all for her, he had. If anyone had asked Cora's opinion, she would have said without a moment's hesitation that young Johnny was the child of that musician, Steve Wyman, the love of Jess's life. Same red-brown hair, same cheeky expression, and no resemblance at all to any of her own childer, which surely he would have had if he'd really been one of Bernie's by-blows.

She'd tried to convince Jess of this at one time, but she wouldn't have it. Cora supposed that she'd so banished the thought of him from her mind, that it was too much for the poor lass to bear. If it could be proved that little Johnny was indeed Steve's child after all, then giving him up, and her hasty marriage to Doug would all have been a complete waste of time. Cora believed it to be worse than that, nothing less than a disaster. He had no feelings at all that man, not a scrap of humanity in him, save for an unhealthy and over-riding obsession with her niece. But she held her own counsel on that one. As she told herself day after day, morning, noon and night whenever something happened with one of her grown-up children. Don't interfere, girl. Nowt to do with you. And she thought of Jess as one of her own, oh indeed she did. The poor lass needed someone on her side. She'd certainly never got any help from her own mother.

As if on cue, Lizzie herself came shuffling into the kitchen. 'Is t'kettle on? Is there owt to eat? I'm fair clemmed.'

'By heck, arta ever anything else? If you're not pouring booze down yer throat, it's pints of tea. And I rarely see you lift the kettle.'

As the two women sat in their accustomed stony silence over breakfast, Lizzie nibbling at a slice of bread and marg while enjoying her third cigarette of the day, Cora sharing a large pan of porridge with the ten-year-old twins, she asked if she'd seen Jess lately. Lizzie looked blank for a moment, as if she hadn't the first idea who she was talking about.

'Your daughter, Jess. Remember her? By heck, yer losing it girl, I'll swear you are. Do you never think to go round to hers, to see how the poor lass is fettling? What sort of mother are you? Never do a hand's turn for that girl, you don't, I can't think why she's allus asking after you, why she still cares. When she did have you to stay, you were nowt but a liability to her. Come to think of it, that's all you are to me. Why do I put up with you, eh? You're no flaming use. Never so much as lift a pot towel.'

'You wanting to get rid of me?'

'You could say that. Aye, bugger off. Sling thee hook.'

'And what if Bernie comes home? What'll he have to say about you flinging me out into the gutter?'

'He'd probably say that were where you come from in't fost place. But he isn't coming back. He's gone for good. I've told you, he's probably got himself another woman some-where, more childer happen. Who knows? Who cares? I bloody don't.'

Cora had related these fantasies so often, that she'd almost come to believe them herself. She could picture Bernie living with this imagined mistress of his, running a pub somewhere nice, happen in the Ribble Valley, dandling a new babby on his knee. He always did enjoy his family, she'd give him that. It almost came as a shock to her that he'd never written to ask how they were getting on, these great lads of his. But then how could he? He wasn't in the Ribble Valley at all. He was a heap of old bones in an unmarked grave somewhere.

She could have told him that Bert was happily settled with his Maisie, married with a little lad of his own. Sandra, at fourteen, quite the little madam and eyeing up boys as if they'd just come into fashion. And her lovely Tommy would be home soon, for good this time. Except that he'd fallen for a WAAF and would no doubt be tripping down the aisle with her and going off to pastures new himself, pretty soon.

Cora sighed as she rinsed her cup out under the tap to make herself another brew. You only got to keep your children for such a short time, borrowed them for a bit like, and then they walked away from your door with scarcely a backward glance. All that agony, all that worrying was supposed to stop then. But it didn't. Cora was beginning to think that it never would stop.

She was certainly still worried about Harry. He never stopped complaining about being hard up and had asked her, of all people, to help. Cora had to laugh at his cheek. What could she do? She didn't even get a proper pension, not being able to prove that her husband was dead. She was forced to get by on hand-outs from her sons. But she didn't like the way Harry was behaving at all, bullying that pretty little wife of his, throwing his brass about like a man with three arms. It would all come to grief, if she was any judge.

'Why don't you ever worry about her, that lass o' thine?' she demanded of Lizzie, now busily lighting a fourth cigarette from the stub of the third. 'Can't you see how unhappy she is? Couldn't you help a bit with that lovely little lad she's got? Take an interest at least. Daughters are precious tha knows. They should be appreciated.'

Lizzie gazed at Cora out of unfocused eyes. 'When you go down the market, slip in t'club and ask your Harry for another bottle of gin. I've run out.'

'Ask him yourself. I'm not yer flippin' slave,' and Cora tipped all the breakfast dishes into the sink then went to the bottom of the stairs to shout in her loudest voice, 'If you don't get down here this minute, Sandra Delaney, I'm coming up to drag you down wi' t'scruff of yer bleeding neck.'

'I'm disappointed in you, Jess. You were a very naughty girl.'

It was the following afternoon and they were once more seated on the bench in the park, and yet again Doug was gently scolding her for her disobedience, treating her like a recalcitrant child.

'If you mean last night at the Ritz, it was a brilliant occasion, absolutely wonderful. If you'd been there, you'd have seen for yourself what a great success Delaney's All Girls Band was, and you would be pleased for me. Proud even.'

'I thought I'd made it clear that you were not to attend. I hate it when you go against my wishes, my love. Have I ever let you down? Don't we do all right together, you and I? We shunt along very well, I've always thought.'

'Yes, of course we do, only . . . I can't give up the band. I really can't. Don't ask me to, Doug.'

'You're depressed because of your worries over the child. That's all it is. We'll talk about it later.'

This was another of his more irritating habits: how he always put off any unpleasantness until another time. 'Why not now? Let's have it out and clear the air.'

'Shall I kiss you? Will that cheer you up?'

Jess sighed, the bubbles of excitement she'd experienced the night before, as heady as champagne, had all popped and quite fizzled out. Streamers had been thrown across the ballroom, people had sung 'Auld Lang Syne' with tears of happiness in their eyes, had clung to each other and sobbed for those they had lost who would never return to know this glorious peace.

And all her husband could do was to remain aloof from it all, and to criticise; to deprive her of the one thing which brought her happiness, her music. As if a silly kiss could make up for all of that. And *why* did he always have to ask? Couldn't he see that his tiptoeing around her, his polite requests to touch her, kiss her, even to hold her hand, had only strengthened the barrier she'd built up around herself. She told herself that he was being kind and considerate, sweet and polite, so very much the gentleman.

He leaned closer and placed his mouth upon hers, letting his hand creep beneath the shelter of her coat to cup her breast and give it a little squeeze. She closed her eyes, imagining a different face, another pair of lips altogether, as if clinging to her dreams could help her to cope. Sometimes she ached for Steve so much, it was like a knife twisting in her heart. While she held her breath, waiting for the kiss to be over, the fondling to stop, she overheard one or two rude comments from a middle-aged couple as they walked briskly by, words like 'shameful behaviour' and 'at their age'. Doug seemed to find these amusing, even titillating, and his eyes took on a feverish cast as he chuckled softly, as if seeing himself suddenly as a fine rogue.

'There's a good girl,' he said, when he was done, and she half expected him to pat her kindly on the head by way of gratitude.

The trouble was that whenever Doug's mouth came down over hers, she felt a tide of revulsion sweep through her and she longed to push him away. She never did, of course, she never needed to. He was far too well mannered, far too carefully schooled in his emotions to need reminding of their agreement. Perversely, Jess always felt disappointed that she sensed no passion in him, nothing more than a slight tremor and a strange grunting sound that he made deep in his throat.

And why here? she thought, where there were Sunday afternoon strollers, in the sort of public place he claimed to abhor? This was another of his idiosyncrasies. If it wasn't right for a discussion, how could it be appropriate for him to kiss her? For all he was highly principled and correct, he would choose the oddest places for an embrace, albeit in a furtive fashion.

Once, on the top deck of a crowded number 54 bus, he'd undone the top four buttons of her frock, leaning over her and fondling her breast for almost the entire journey's length. Jess had been trembling with outrage and only his constant reassurance that no one was paying them the slightest attention, not to mention the guilt she lived with constantly at denying him his rights, prevented her from slapping his hand away and screaming for him to stop. But she'd been scarlet with mortification, even more so to discover that in her haste to adjust her dress before disembarking, she'd buttoned it up all wrong.

Perhaps she really had no wish to be kissed by anyone, not even her own husband. As she'd always feared that she might, she'd turned into one of those frigid women who couldn't bear to have sex, or even be touched by a man. Understandable, in the circumstances but most unpleasant to live with. She'd thought, when Uncle Bernie had never reappeared, that the fear would leave her, but rather the reverse.

Jess realised now that it had been a mistake to marry, wrong to involve Doug in her problems. She told herself that he was a good man and a caring husband, even if not the best of fathers. Surely those things counted for more than mere passing pleasure. But by allowing him to provide the respectability she'd always craved for herself, and later for her child, she'd compelled them both to live a sterile existence.

He was stroking her arm, smiling at her in quiet satisfaction, as if he'd scored a victory of his own. 'The baby is thirteen months old, Jess. And I've been patient, no one can say otherwise. You've had time enough, I think. We'll leave it for now. But later, perhaps this evening or some other suitable occasion, we'll try again, shall we, and trust that you'll be better able to relax.'

It sounded ominously like a threat.

It was Cora who called in on Jess one Tuesday morning when she went down the market. Lizzie, as always, worn out from the effort of eating breakfast, had gone back to bed. 'How you fettling, chuck? How's my little man?' She picked up the baby to give him a cuddle, his little legs in the plaster cast encasing him from hips to toes stuck out at an odd angle in a permanent sitting position, so that she had to straddle him against her substantial waistline while she gurgled baby-talk at him. 'By heck, but yer a reet champion. Look at that smile, fair warms the cockles of yer heart, dun't it?'

Jess laughingly agreed that the baby could charm the birds out of the trees with that rapturous smile of his. Despite all his problems, all the pain he'd suffered and the restrictions placed upon him through the plaster cast, he was a remarkably cheerful child. Nothing seemed to trouble him at all, and he'd readily smile at anyone. No wonder everybody loves him, she thought. Everyone, that is, except Doug, the man who'd agreed to be a father to him.

As the two women walked around Campfield Market, glad

to be out of a blustering wind, it felt like stepping into another world, one filled with interesting aromas from the mounds of fruit and veg, cuts of pink pork meat and red polony sausages on display. Cora bought a little wooden toy train for Johnny, and Jess scolded her for not being able to afford such treats, now she'd no regular income coming in.

'Nay, my lads slip me a bit when they can. Our Bert's very generous, and even Tommy sends me summat now and then, though he's saving up to be wed, so that's tailing off now. And our Harry's been a bit short lately. Has Leah said owt?'

Jess shook her head, frowning slightly. 'She says very little about Harry, or about what goes on at that club. She's become much quieter these last few months, not at all the bubbly personality I used to know. I do worry about her, but she won't talk about it, not a word. Do you think they're having problems, her and Harry, with the club? Or with their marriage?'

Cora sucked in her breath, wondering how much she should tell. She, of all people, could guess what was going on behind them closed doors, and so could Jess if she put her mind to it. Maybe she didn't want to know, liked to think that everything was hunky-dory for her friend, for all she'd got herself mixed up with the dreadful Delaneys. 'I don't reckon trade's too bright, and it'll get worse now the Yanks are going back home.'

'I suppose so.'

'You're doing well though, with that band.' Cora cast her a sideways glance. Don't interfere, said the familiar, chiding voice at the back of her head. Never did no good to poke yer nose into Harry's business. Except, happen, for once, she might give it a try. That wife of his looked thin as a drink of water, and somebody needed to do something before she slipped through a crack in t'pavement. 'It's none of my business, and I don't like to pry, but I suppose you do pay Leah summat for playing in it?'

Jess had been choosing a few rosy apples for Johnny as a treat, now she paused, money in hand, surprised by the question. 'Of course I do. We all earn good money from the band. It's an equal partnership.'

'Then what d'you reckon she does with it? She doesn't put it on her back, though that kiddy doesn't go short of owt.'

'Harry dotes on her, I think he's always buying her presents.'

The market holder said, 'I thowt you were buying them apples, but happen not.'

'Oh, sorry.' Jess abstractedly handed over a few pennies, still frowning at Cora. 'But you're right, Leah gets very little for herself these days. I wonder why? Perhaps she's saving it, like me, for a rainy day.'

'If it rains much more on that lass, she'll flaming drown.'

Jess abruptly stopped walking, causing the woman behind to bump into her, full tilt. 'Sorry,' she hastily apologised yet again, then quickly turned back to Cora. 'What do you know, that I don't? What's going on? Come on Cora, get it off your chest.'

Cora stared at her in wide-eyed innocence. 'What would I know?'

'Quite a lot, I should imagine.'

'Well, I'm saying nowt.'

'Yes you are. We're going into Old Ma Greenwood's Café here and I'm going to buy you pie and peas and *you're* going to tell me all you know about Harry and Leah.'

Having tied Johnny to a chair, his bib neatly in place with a dish of peas before him, and once Cora had satisfied herself that the pie was nowhere near as good as her own, she finally spoke of her fears; the plump, homely face creased with concern so that for the first time she looked like an old woman. She told of how she thought Harry was beating hell out of the poor lass. 'Can't you tell by how thin and scraggy looking she's gone lately.'

Jess went deathly pale. She should have known, should have realised what was going on. Like father, like son. Somehow, she felt as if she had personally let Leah down, by not being there to protect her. 'I thought – I hoped, that was just from running around after the new baby.'

Cora shook her head dolefully. 'And she's allus bleating on about money. Same as our Harry is. He says Bernie left them with debts. I'm not sure whether that's true or not but I were wondering, what with you doing so nicely with that band o'yourn, whether you couldn't lend him a bob or two.'

'You want *me* to give Harry money?'

'I said *lend*. A loan, for your friend's sake. It'll happen get them out of whatever hole they're in, and it might persuade him to stop tekkin it out on yon lass, to stop bullying her into nicking from her dad.'

Jess went whiter still at this, putting down her knife and fork, her appetite quite gone. 'Oh Cora, no, not that as well.'

'Aye, 'fraid so. She told me not to say owt and I haven't, all this time, but she needs help. And she's too proud to beg for it from her folks, not after what she's done to them. He give one lass the sack over it, and Leah had to go more careful after that but Harry wouldn't let her stop. Once he's got the flaming bit between his teeth, there's no budging him.'

'I won't lend him a penny, not while I live and breathe. I'll help Leah any day, but not him. I know he's your lad, Cora, but so help me, he's more his father's son than yours. He's Bernie all over again, come back to haunt me.'

Words which proved to be more prophetic than she could ever have imagined. The very next time that the band were playing, Jess took the opportunity to speak to Leah, asking her how she was, remarking on how thin she'd got and would a bit more money help?

'It went down like a barrage balloon,' Jess told Cora afterwards. 'Wouldn't hear of a loan, or even a rise. Said she was just fine, thank you very much and what gossip had I been listening to?'

Cora groaned, 'I hope you didn't say it were me.'

'Course I didn't. I'm not entirely stupid.' The two women chewed the problem over for a little longer, but in the end decided that they could do nothing more at present except keep a close watch on events.

In any case, Jess had problems of her own to deal with. Doug was still proving obstinate about the band. Having got it into his head that she was being deliberately perverse by carrying on with it, just to plague him, he'd now instructed her to close it down completely. But the more he insisted that she should give it up, the more determined Jess became to go on. 'That band is my life,' she told him.

'No,' he stubbornly responded. '*I* am your life. Me and that child of yours.'

'You mean Johnny. He's not "that child"! Why won't you even say his name?'

Harry was a worried man. He'd taken risks to get where he was today, as had his father before him: nicking booze, running an illegal card school, using girls for what he thought girls did best. Another was getting involved with Jimmy Doyle, generally known as Little Jimmy since he was the brother of Big Pat, the female all-in wrestler. A small, stocky man with gentle Irish eyes, despite his diminutive size, he was not a man to cross wasn't Little Jimmy, not least because if he ever did find himself in a spot of bother, he called Pat in to help.

Harry hadn't given this association too much consideration in the past, simply because taking risks was par for the course, for a Delaney. A couple of unexpected visitors to his establishment one day in early June, were to change his mind on that score.

Setting up the club had strained even Harry's powers of imagination, and the gaming school had been one step too far. Bernie had done the renovations but equipping it all, putting in those chandeliers which gave the place such taste, for instance, had been Harry's idea. When Bernie's money had run out, Harry had borrowed a few quid from Jimmy, who'd shown early interest in the project. Thus it hadn't been his father who'd run up the debts, as he'd claimed, but Harry himself. And he'd always been aware that one day, Jimmy Doyle would call in the debt.

So when two of Jimmy's sidekicks turned up at his door, Harry was studiously polite to them, ever circumspect when it came to saving his own skin, and gave them a free chaser with the beers they ordered.

'It's good to see you appreciate what Mr Doyle has done for you,' said one.

Harry hastened to assure them just how very grateful he was.

'And were you considering showing this gratitude in a concrete way, any time soon?' asked the other, an altogether nastier piece of goods in Harry's opinion, with that twisted leer and a cast in one eye.

'Indeed, indeed, I shall be making another substantial repayment by the end of next week.' Harry knew that he hadn't a hope in hell of doing any such thing, not unless his luck changed overnight. He'd always believed that the owner of a card school was the one who made all the profit, but he'd discovered to his cost that wasn't the case at all. By the time he'd paid staff, barmen, cleaners, a couple of heavies to watch the punters didn't cheat him too much, there was precious little left to go into his own pocket. He got his cut from the girls and from the tenants he found to occupy the other rooms above the club, but that barely covered the cost of maintaining this establishment, which was huge. It was all very worrying.

'Next Saturday, first thing,' he said again, reassuring himself as much as them, and pouring second whiskies all round.

'This Friday would be better.'

Harry swallowed carefully, still smiling. 'This Friday it is then.'

If I don't do summat quick, I'll be a goner by Saturday week, he thought. Maybe it was time to call in a few debts of his own.

Jess had taken to calling round to see Leah more often than she had previously, trying on several occasions to persuade Leah to confide in her, though so far her efforts had been fruitless. Her friend remained steadfastly silent about her troubles, maintaining that all was well with her marriage, that nothing was wrong, nothing she couldn't cope with anyway.

These visits hadn't gone down too well with Harry who started complaining she was like a bad smell around the place. And then one afternoon while she was waiting for her friend to get changed, he came up the stairs to the flat, glass in hand as usual, sprawled in his chair and, quite out of the blue, asked point blank how much she was making out of the band.

Jess was caught unawares. 'What? I think that's my business, don't you?'

'No, I don't, as a matter of fact, not if my wife is playing in it.'

'She gets her fair share, as we all do. Leah would be the first to tell you that.'

'Let's put it this way,' Harry said with what might pass for a smile. 'It isn't enough. We need more. And you owe it to us.'

'I owe you nothing. As a matter of fact I recently offered Leah a loan, because I thought she looked so sad and care-worn, and she refused. Said she was fine, thank you very much, and she'd let me know if and when she needed anything but that she was well looked after by her loving husband. Perhaps you don't appreciate how ridiculously loyal she is to you. Loyal to a fault, some might say.'

'You haven't changed a bit, you. Still the same lippy cow you ever were.' He got up from his chair, carefully set down his half drunk beer and came to stand threateningly close, leaning over her with his hands resting on each arm of the chair in which she sat, effectively trapping her within it. 'But you do owe me. Quite a lot, in fact. Had it not been for your provoking my dad, Mam would never have needed to lay him out cold, and then me and Bert wouldn't have had to bury our own father in that bomb-site. Have you any idea how that makes a chap feel? It's not very nice, I can tell you that much for nowt.'

Jess felt as if the room were retreating, as if all sounds and images were coming from some great distance, and she was floating above it all, drifting backwards into the realm of nightmares. 'I – I'm not sure I understand what you're saying.'

'Aye you do. You understand well enough. When our mam clocked him one, she finished old Bernie off for good. Happen it were a hefty rolling pin, or else he had a thin skull, either way because of you, she's a murderess. Do you hear? Our mam is a murderess and could be hanged for knocking off her old man. *Now* try saying that you owe me nowt.' He pushed his big face close up to hers, spittle forming at the corners of his mouth. 'You get me some hard cash, luv, or happen it'll all have to come out in the open. Only the way I'll tell the story, it'll be you doing time, not our mam. Got that chuck? Loud and clear?'

Jess knew she was trembling with shock, but desperately tried not to let it show. She wouldn't give Harry the satisfaction. 'That sounds very much like blackmail.'

'Call it whatever fancy word you choose but make no mistake – I mean business. We can discuss the amount later, but a nice tidy sum, eh?'

'Never! Do your worst, I don't care what happens to me.'

It was pure bravado, and he knew it. 'Aye you do.' He gave a bark of laughter before going back to his own chair to pick up his glass and finish his beer in one long swallow, then wiped the froth from a mouth twisted into a sneer. It made him look more than ever like his father. 'Tha's got yon child to think of. What would happen to him if you were incarcerated, as yer mam once were?'

Jess went sick at the thought.

'Besides, once the polis start asking questions, who knows where it'll end up? And you don't want owt to happen to our lovely Cora either, now do you?'

'You wouldn't risk anything happening to Aunt Cora, not your own mother?'

Harry's smile was wintry as he replied calmly. 'She killed my dad. Happen I'm not too bothered either way which of you cops it, so long as somebody pays up. Preferably in cash.'

Jess thought this was a nightmare from which she might never wake. She felt quite unable to fully take in what Harry had said. Cora had killed Bernie? Dear God, what a mess! So that was why they hadn't seen hide nor hair of him in all this time. What had Harry said? That they'd buried him in some bombsite, and the rescue services had done the rest. A nightmare indeed.

'Is it true?' She had to ask Cora. Worried as she was over how to deal with the matter, she couldn't seem to let it lie.

Cora barely paused in the rolling of pastry for yet another prata pie as she calmly replied, 'Whatever he got, he had it coming. Not fit to lick your boots, the nasty bugger.'

Jess sat staring at her, dazed, and she couldn't help wondering if that was the self-same implement that she'd used on him. 'Cora, tell me straight. Did you really do for him with that rolling pin?'

'Happen I'm stronger than I look.' She looked like an all-in wrestler, someone who could go more than the expected three rounds with Big Pat herself. 'But like I say, he asked for it, great bully that he was. He'd no right to interfere with you in that way, no matter how drunk he were, or how far he managed to go – you know what I meant – it were too far. I had to save thee, lass, what else could I do?'

'Oh Cora, what can I say?'

'Tha could say good riddance to bad rubbish, I do.' And by the determined set of her several chins, she clearly meant it. 'Put it behind you. You've got a new life now, not the one you intended to have, happen, but there's not a blind bit of good moping about such things. That's the way it is, so live with it. What can't be cured . . .' And as if this settled the matter, she rolled up the pastry lid onto the wooden pin and spread it neatly over the pie dish, before trimming away the excess dough with a very sharp knife.

26

Jess did her utmost to follow Cora's wise advice to put the whole sorry tale behind her, but it wasn't easy. Bernie's image did indeed come back to haunt her. Night after night she would see his round, sneering face, feel his big wet slobbering mouth on hers, see the glisten of his greasy hair over his bald head, and she'd waken in a cold sweat. She couldn't feel sorry that he was dead, any more than his own wife did. He'd brought little joy into anyone's life, not even to his own sons, if they could so easily dispose of his remains.

And if Jess thought too closely about what he had cost her, the price she had paid for his interference in her own life, she truly would go mad. Not only had he been the reason for Lizzie being sent to jail, for all she remained the only one to mourn him, but Jess would never have lost Steve had it not been for Bernie Delaney. She wished she could agree with Cora that Johnny was Steve's child, but she just couldn't, however much as she might long to think so.

Not that it mattered. Not any more. She picked up the baby and gave him a cuddle, as if to reassure him of this important fact. Beaming happily, Little Johnny bobbed his nose against hers in an imitation of the Eskimo kiss she liked to give him, making Jess laugh out loud.

How could she ever have not wanted him, have deprived him of her love when he'd first been born? She must have been mad, or sick in the head. Wallowing in self-pity and where was the point in that? What happened wasn't the baby's fault. He was the innocent in all of this mess. And he was *her* child, a part of her, and yet already a little person in his own right. Whoever his father was, she loved him to bits, more than life itself.

'Let's play music and be happy,' Jess told him, and she sat Johnny in his chair, picked up her trumpet and began to play. He banged his spoon with perfect rhythm, proving he was indeed her child. But it brought tears to her eyes as she was transported back to a time when everything had seemed so straightforward, when she'd dreamed of marrying Steve, and of being the next Ivy Benson. A time when she'd been young, filled with hope for the future, and the joy of loving. If now all of those dreams were gone, she must make the best of what she had left. At least she had her lovely child and her music.

Harry now was the big worry, a chip off the old block as you might say, and not a man who liked to be ignored. What was she going to do about Harry?

'All we can do is concentrate on looking after Leah and little Susie,' Jess had said to Cora, who had sadly nodded. But privately, Jess believed that more definite action would be required. Harry wasn't one to let go, not once he'd made up his mind.

A few days later, Harry came round one afternoon and since Jess was out, spoke to Doug, asking if she'd left a package for him.

'What sort of package?' Doug asked, bemused. 'Don't you see Jess every day at the club, when she comes round to gossip with your Leah?'

Harry mumbled something about her always having forgotten it, claiming to have left it at home, so he thought he'd come round and save her the trouble. 'It's summat that she keeps promising me, probably in an envelope, a big one.'

Doug made a show of looking for it but was able to

honestly say he knew nothing about any envelope and sent Harry packing.

Harry had managed to wangle an extension from Jimmy Doyle, in view of a promise that he had some money owing to him, but he wasn't so naïve as to think he'd be patient for too long. It wasn't Big Pat who troubled him so much, for all she had muscles on her the size of hams because she was merely a woman, and Harry was quite sure he could handle himself, if push came to shove. What he didn't relish was the prospect of open warfare with Little Jimmy's army. Who knew how many other ex-squaddies he had waiting in the wings, just itching to have a go at him.

Wanting an outlet for his frustration, Harry went straight round to his brother and dragged him out for a drink at the Crown. Settled in a corner with a couple of beers before them, Harry came straight to the point. 'We have to do summat about that bloody cousin of ours, Bert,' he raged. 'Choose how.'

'Like what, our Harry? What has our Jess done to upset you?' Bert was a contented man these days, with a wife and family he adored, and felt some reluctance to return to the old days of being forever under his brother's thumb. He had a job down at the docks that paid good money, and was legit. Harry had refused him a partnership in the club, done nowt but bossed him around and Maisie had made him see that he was worth more, should have more pride in himself. She had a lot of common sense did Maisie. Bert trusted her, and he'd never been more happy in his life, which was saying a great deal.

'We have to make her sorry for what she did to us, and to our dad.'

'I thought it were me mum what did for him, and you were glad to see t'back of the old bugger. Made you into a big man, right?'

'Flaming hell, Bert.' Harry flashed a startled glance about the crowded public bar. 'Has thee still not learned to shut thee gob? Who knows what ears might be flapping round here. What I'm saying is that we still haven't paid her that lesson what we promised her. And I've decided that it's time we did. She's rolling in brass from that band of hers, and I don't know about you but a bit extra would come in very handy.'

'Is she going to lend you some, our Harry?'

'Lend? Who said owt about lend? Let's say she's going to make a large donation to the Keep-Harry-Alive-Fund. I've got a bit of a problem with Jimmy Doyle, and it needs sorting.'

Bert went ash white, 'Did you say Jimmy Doyle? Little Jimmy, Big Pat's brother?'

'Aye, asta gone deaf all of a sudden? Na then, all I need you to do, is make her see that it's in her own interest to pay up. Right? Got that into yer thick skull?'

Bert was looking more and more alarmed as he thought of the implications for him, if he got involved with the likes of Jimmy Doyle. 'Me? Why me? You want *me* to ask our Jess for some brass?'

'She doesn't need asking. I've already told her to pay up, and explained in careful detail what'll happen to her if she doesn't. I don't think she's keen to see the inside of a prison cell, or to get hanged for a murder she didn't commit.' Harry seemed to find this amusing, and began to laugh. 'So you shouldn't have any bother. None at all. All you have to do, is to collect what's due to us, see that she's a good girl and pays up in full.'

Bert thought of his lovely Maisie, of his fine little son, and the next one due in just a few months. Life was turning out to be pretty good for him, and even if money was tight and they weren't very well off, they were content. What's more, Maisie didn't make him feel like a witless fool the whole time.

He drained his glass and stood up. 'Nay, Harry, I don't think I fancy getting involved. I reckon you'd best find someone else to do your dirty work. Besides, I've allus rather liked our Jess. She's got spunk, that lass, and my Maisie says that she depends on me to keep on the straight and narrow, or we'll all be in t'pig swill, what with a new babby coming. So, count me out of it, right?'

Harry shouted after him, even offered to buy another round, but Bert didn't so much as glance back over his shoulder as he hurried off to his precious Maisie. Harry was so furious that when he got home he took out his ill temper, as he always did, on his wife.

Jess went to Harry to put a suggestion to him, one she'd given careful thought to over a number of days. She chose late afternoon when the club was closed, knowing he'd be there, polishing the glasses, counting his winnings. As soon as he saw her through the glass of the door, he went eagerly to let her in, even offered her a small sherry on the assumption she'd brought him his money.

'I knew you'd come round, that you'd see the sense in my request since you, of all people, wouldn't want to risk incarceration, let alone being hanged for summat you didn't do.' He smirked at her, well pleased with himself.

Jess took the seat he offered at a small table and Harry sat opposite, quaffing beer in a self-satisfied way while she sipped quietly at her sherry. Eventually, Jess said, 'How would it be if I bought the place off you?'

He put down his glass. 'What did tha say?'

'If you're not managing to make a go of the club, I'll buy it off you, take it off your hands. We'll agree a fair price. Get it independently valued with everything above board. I'll settle your debts, get whoever's putting pressure on you off your back, and you'll have enough left over to start again somewhere else.' That way, Jess hoped, free of debt and fear, he might behave better towards his long-suffering wife. She could think of no other way to help her dearest friend, since Leah refused to admit there was even a problem.

But Harry was looking at her as if she'd grown two heads, had gone mad or something. His eyes were dilated with shock, probably because he'd never imagined she was quite so well placed. His next words confirmed that. 'By heck, you like to throw yer brass about. So you have made more money out of that bloody band than Leah?'

'No, I've told you, we took fair shares but I've saved mine whereas her earnings have been wasted by you. So, what do you say? It's a fair offer.'

'And what would you do with a club?' he sneered.

'I'd smarten it up, run dances here. Turn it into a decent place to visit instead of the dive it currently is. And I'd have nothing to do with the kind of low-life you get involved with.' Jess dropped an envelope on the table. It lay between them, like a gauntlet; a challenge. 'That's a down payment, to show good faith. It will no doubt take some time to get the legal wheels moving, so that'll help pacify whoever's pressing you for payment.' Jess, was no fool. She understood her cousin too well for that. He'd kept quiet all these long months about his father's fate so that if he were ever in a tight spot, he could use it to his advantage. Besides which, she'd had a quiet word with Bert, got herself filled in on the details.

Harry picked up the packet and weighed it in his hands. 'It's not enough.'

'It's all you're getting, for now. Get the place valued. Speak to your solicitor, if you can find one prepared to work for you, and you'll get the balance in the fullness of time. In the meantime' – and here she leaned across the small table that separated them to look him directly in the eye – 'leave Leah alone. If I ever hear of you laying another finger on her, the deal's off, and Jimmy Doyle and his squaddies can have you for dinner. Got that?' Whereupon, she got to her feet and walked calmly from the room, leaving Harry shouting and yelling after her that she couldn't talk to him like that.

'I just did.'

Doug couldn't understand why Jess wouldn't do as he asked. She was still playing her trumpet, still going to rehearsals, and obstinately planning yet another dance next Saturday night, this time at the Co-operative rooms. He knew this for certain since he'd followed her on one or two occasions, just to check on where she was going and what she was up to. And to add insult to injury, one of the posters advertising it was stuck up on the side of the wharf warehouse, a real slap in the face that was. Even his workmates were making fun, teasing him for having such a talented wife.

'How do you know what she gets up to at all these gigs she does?' one asked.

Another said, 'I wouldn't let my wife loose with all of these Yanks still around, not that any of them would have my missus given in a Christmas cracker. Face on her like backside of a cow, not like your lass.'

'Aye, I'd lock her up tight, if she were mine. Right bobby-dazzler, she is, your Jess,' agreed his mate.

Doug protested that the Americans wouldn't be around for much longer; and Jess was too busy playing in the band to dance with anyone.

'What about the interval, when they change the band? Nay, I'd watch it if I were you.'

In his heart, he agreed with them. She shouldn't be parading herself in such a fashion. It was all right for a young, unmarried woman but not for a wife and mother. It wasn't seemly. He'd been quite certain, in his own mind, that he could put a stop to this business long before now: first when the baby was born, and later when he'd finally persuaded her to give up working at the tea room. She could play the trumpet at home, for him. He'd no objection to that. And hadn't he done his best for her? Why wasn't he good enough? It was his own mother, all over again. Never satisfied. You simply couldn't trust a woman. Ever! It made him so angry to find himself in exactly the same situation as his own father, and he'd expected Jess to be more obedient, extra-loving, out of sheer gratitude for him having saved her from disgrace.

Was she taking advantage because he didn't make a fuss about the lack of intimacy in their marriage? Was that the reason? Perhaps he should press a bit harder in that direction, if he could just work out the best way to go about it. He found it easier to touch her when there were folk around, oddly enough, because she wouldn't be expecting too much of him then, in a public place. On their own, in the privacy of a bedroom, was another matter entirely.

Doug wasn't absolutely certain that he could perform well enough to satisfy her in that department, so preferred to avoid the issue altogether. But he did expect her utter devotion in other ways. Oh dear me, yes. Didn't he deserve that, at least?

He decided to have it out with her yet again, to make his feelings on the subject plain. But she was rarely in the house more than five minutes together over the next few days. What with rehearsals every evening, and popping in on her friend Leah where they apparently spent hours together in the flat over the club, happily sewing, out of the remnants of parachute silk, new dresses for the girls in the band.

'Will this be the last one then?' was all he managed to ask one morning at breakfast, as she scooped cereal into little Johnny's mouth.

She sighed and refused to discuss it. 'Not now, Doug,

please. I've enough on my plate right at this minute. Don't take my music away from me, there's a dear.'

But he persisted, asking what problems she could possibly have? She was his wife, for goodness sake. Didn't he take care of everything for her? She only shook her head in that exasperating way she had when irritated with him, and claimed that this particular problem was none of his concern.

'It's a private matter which I'll sort out in my own way, am already in the process of doing so. Thanks all the same.'

Doug was shocked by her attitude. 'How can a wife possibly have any privacy, any matter of which her husband is unaware?'

She simply looked up at him, startled for a moment, and then laughed out loud. 'Oh Doug, you're such an old fuddy-duddy. This is the twentieth century, for goodness sake. Of course a wife is entitled to her privacy. Now do stop fussing. You're going to be late for work.'

It was a week or two later that, to Doug's utter surprise and dismay, Jess announced that the band was going on tour, *without even asking his permission.*

'Cora will be looking after Johnny of course, as usual. But since you're on late shift this week, could you mind him for a few hours please, and take him round to her later?' To Jess, it seemed strange that she even had to ask her husband to do this small thing for her, but that was the way things were with him. He never volunteered to help with Johnny. 'She has to take Sam and Seb to the dentist this morning so she won't be back till around dinner time, and we've got to catch the ten-thirty bus as the first gig is in Birmingham, so we've a long journey ahead. After that we go on to Leicester, Wolverhampton, Rhyl, then back up to Preston. Ena has made the bookings and we're all thrilled to bits. Our first real tour. Exciting! But don't worry, we'll be back by Thursday.'

'*Thursday!*' He'd protested, naturally, firmly insisted that it simply wasn't possible, that she must stay home and behave as a good wife should. She'd listened patiently to his outburst, then kissed him on the nose, patted his cheek and reminded him not to forget to wear his scarf when he went off to work, as the mornings were turning quite nippy now.

Minutes later, she was gone and he was alone in the kitchen with the child. *Her* child, the one he'd had to accept as part of the bargain, in order to get her.

He glared at it, sitting there in sublime ignorance, grinning good-naturedly as it happily banged a spoon on the table of the high chair. Be damned if he'd wet nurse the bastard for her. The child was definitely not his responsibility. That wasn't part of the bargain. He'd expected her to give it up, to have it adopted as she'd said she would before the creature was born. But then she'd changed her mind, insisted on keeping it and doing her duty, even though at the time she'd shown not a scrap of love for the child.

Doug had been furious and had decided that she needed a little more persuasion.

It had proved easy to dislocate the child's hip. Like snapping a match. He'd been quite certain that having a deformed and disabled child would appal her, that she would see him then for what he was: the product of evil, finally see sense and let him go. Instead of which, the opposite had happened. Nosy old Cora had spotted there was a problem and before you knew it, the doctor had been called in and Jess had started doting on the creature, rarely leaving him alone for a second. There was really no accounting for women. Utterly perverse.

Doug simply couldn't understand it, it was utterly illogical. Why would she wish to be constantly reminded of that unspeakable thing which had happened to her? He'd certainly no wish to venture into intimacy with a woman sullied and despoiled by her own uncle. Respectability, a marriage in name only was what he'd offered, what they'd agreed upon, which suited him perfectly. Why didn't it suit her? Why did she need so much more, this music of hers, for instance, which gave her far too much independence.

For he did like to keep Jess close by his side each and every day: to see her lovely face, watch the way she moved, feel the softness of her breasts, hear her laughter and touch the soft cloud of her hair. He could scarcely believe that she remained obstinately determined to hang on to a way of life which should have ended with the war. It was one thing to play for the Salvation Army, quite another to make an exhibition of herself in front of all those men.

He really wasn't having it.

In no time at all, Doug had Johnny dressed in his coat and strapped into his perambulator, and was walking him round to Cumberland Street.

As Jess had predicted there was no sign of Cora. The kitchen was empty save for Lizzie, who sat with her skinny legs dangling over the arm of her battered old chair, smoking one of her endless cigarettes. He could tell by the glazed look in her eye that she'd had a few, even he hadn't noticed the bottle poking out from under the cushion beside her. The room, as ever, was suffocatingly hot with a fire halfway up the chimney and an all-pervading sour smell of boiled cabbage and human sweat. Doug wheeled in the pram, parked it beside her and said in a loud voice, as if addressing an idiot, 'I've fetched the child, as arranged. Cora knows all about it. I've got one or two jobs to do before I go off to work, so I'll leave him with you, right?'

Minutes later he was out in the street, a free man. And if it wasn't for him needing Jess Delaney so much, he thought he'd have been better off staying that way.

*　　*　　*

The tour was going well. They were playing in ballrooms where the great Joe Loss himself had played, plus other illustrious names such as Oscar Rabin and Jack Parnell. Jess idolised famous bandleaders such as Benny Goodman, Tommy Dorsey and Ivy Benson, hoping to follow in their successful footsteps. Ena had already got them a substantial booking in the Isle of Man for the summer, and another in Brighton over Christmas, which wouldn't please Doug one bit, but was so exciting. Jess couldn't understand why he was being so difficult, yet was determined not to let him get her down. The war was over and this was a new beginning for them all. Who knew what they might achieve?

All the girls were equally thrilled with their success, looking forward to their first tour with eager anticipation. They didn't mind if the digs were a bit seedy, if ration books and points were still the order of the day. There was a great optimism in the air and even Miss Mona, thumping out the rhythm on her double bass with gusto would cry, 'Today Manchester. Tomorrow, the world.'

Tonight was a big dance contest. There'd already been sections for the Quickstep, Foxtrot, Samba and Tango so far. Delaney's All Girls Band were currently playing for the Jive section, starting with 'Jukebox Saturday Night', followed by a couple of Glenn Miller numbers. They played for half an hour before being replaced by another band who instantly changed the tempo to 'Tooraloora Loora', in order to conclude the competition with the Waltz. Jess could only marvel at the sureness of step, the smooth confidence and expertise of the dancers, all cheered on and applauded by an enthusiastic crowd, eager to watch and learn so they could emulate these skills later when the floor was opened up for all. Jess became so engrossed watching the dizzying, spinning steps of the waltzers that, for once, she paid little attention to the band.

But then the music changed to 'Now is the Hour' and

something in the distinctive tones of a saxophone brought her head up sharply, and there he was. She could hardly believe her eyes, although she would have known that sound anywhere. There was something in the unique way he played a sax, in the manner with which he held the instrument, instinctively lifting his head as he brought forth the most magical notes imaginable. She whispered his name, allowing it to slip over her lips as if by saying it, new life was breathed into her. *Steve. Oh, Steve!* She alone knew how much she had missed him, how she had ached for his touch, but now, as she regarded him in the flesh, she realised even she had under-estimated that need.

He didn't see her. She was huddled in the shadows with Adele, Lulu and the other girls. She could slip away and hide in the dressing room until it was time for them to go on again, except that she couldn't bring herself to move. Jess simply stood there, drinking in the sight of him, as if needing to quench a great thirst. The music changed again, this time to 'I'll Be Seeing You', and she could bear it no longer. With memories of the last dance they'd ever had together ringing in her head, Jess turned on her heels and fled.

Outside, she drew in great gulps of clear night air, desperately trying to calm herself, to block out the potent images. Leah came up beside her and rested a hand on her shoulder. 'He plays that instrument like it's a part of him. He looked so good standing up there tonight. No wonder you loved him. Why on earth did you ever let him go?'

Jess shook her head, quite unable to speak. '*I can't let you go, Jess.*' That's what he'd said to her. But he had. She'd given him no choice in the matter.

'Life is so unfair, isn't it? We came all through the war unscathed, only to ruin our lives with a stupid decision. You to give up Steve, who adored you, and all because of that dreadful attack by Bernie, and me to marry Bernie's equally awful son. What a mess we made of our lives.' Leah wrapped her arms about her dear friend and the two girls sat on a cold stone wall and wept silent tears together.

'We weren't to know,' Jess said at last, quietly sobbing into her handkerchief. 'I did what I thought was for the best. I honestly believed that I could never be a proper wife to him. And I didn't want him to take me on out of pity.'

'I know luv. And I was potty about handsome Harry. Couldn't keep my hands off him. You at least married a gentleman, which is more than can be said for your nasty cousin.'

'Oh Leah, you don't know the half of it. How was I to know that good, kind Doug would so take against little Johnny? Oh, what am I to do?'

Leah looked at her sadly, gently stroked her arm. 'He's Steve's son, isn't he? Go on, you can say it because, deep down, you know it's true. Doug certainly does, because that's the real reason why he loathes the poor little mite. I could have told you it was you he wanted, not a replacement son. As could Cora. It was obvious to everyone. But then, why should you listen to sense? I never did. I was so determined to marry Harry Delaney that nobody could talk me out of it, not my mother, not Dad or Robert, who both did their best to make me see what I was letting myself in for. I wouldn't even listen to you, my very best friend. Is it any wonder that it's all gone horribly wrong?'

'Do you realise Leah, the Delaneys have ruined both our lives.'

'It would seem so.'

There was a small silence while both girls absorbed this fact. 'Is Harry very mean to you?'

Leah's eyes, which she'd only just mopped dry, filled again with a rush of tears. 'Serves me right if he is.'

'Serves us both right. No, you mustn't say such a thing. Neither of us should. It isn't your fault at all, any more than it's mine. We can't have Harry treat you like that. We must do something to stop him. I've tried, by offering to buy the club off him, to settle his debts that way.'

'Huh! He'll never agree to that. He loves to be in control too much.'

'Then tell me, what else can I do? How can I help?'

'What would you suggest? Giving him a good talking to? Cora's tried that already.'

'You could leave him.'

'Where could I go, and how could I stop him from bringing me back and punishing me for showing him up? He might not love me but he needs me around, and he adores Susie. He'd never let me take her from him. I'd have to go right away where he couldn't ever find me, then I'd lose you, and the band, and probably my mind.' Leah's tone was bleak and again they clung together, weeping all the more, for what could they do? They seemed to be powerless.

'Jess? Is that you?' The sound of the familiar voice made both girls jump. Leah was the first to react, leaping to her feet and slapping the tears from her cheeks, she mumbled something about needing a drink and had gone before ever Jess thought to stop her. He came towards her and she could see him more clearly now. His face looked tired, drawn and sad, and yet his eyes were alight, burning into her as if he too couldn't quite believe what he was seeing. 'I never even noticed your band was playing here tonight, till you got up on that stage and played like an angel. If it's possible, Jess, you've got even better. And you're still playing my trumpet. I felt so proud. Then later, one of the other blokes in the band saw you dash out. Were you running away from me, Jess?'

She shook her head but could find no words, couldn't even seem to find her own voice. Just hearing him speak her name, knowing he was right here beside her, that she could reach out and touch him and yet was not permitted to do so, was almost more than she could bear. He took another tentative step towards her, said her name again, barely more than a whisper this time but it was enough. Somehow she was in his arms, he was kissing her and it was the most wonderful moment in her life.

'I've missed you, Jess. God, you'll never know how much.'

She didn't care then about Doug, forgot all about being married to another man. All that mattered was that she was in Steve's arms, and he was telling her that he still loved her.

She had only ever loved a man once, this very same man who lay beside her now in this too small bed. They'd made love as if they'd never been apart, as if it were the most natural thing in the world for them to be together even though to Jess it seemed like a miracle. Why had she ever imagined that Bernie's assault could come between them, or that it would make her less of a woman? She must have been mad. Certainly not thinking clearly. Or else Steve's very great love for her had cured her of the horrors of that night.

This night of love was wonderful, at first tender and hesitant, each afraid of making a mistake. At first they'd been content to simply sit and look at each other, quite unable to stop smiling, delighted to be together.

Growing bolder, they'd blissfully begun to explore these newly awakened emotions which later had grown ever more powerful and intense. There was no guilt, no shame. Perhaps there ought to have been, but Jess could feel only joy and a beautiful, burgeoning happiness. They belonged together, always had and always would.

Later still, as they became more relaxed together, their emotions sated, it had simply become fun. Yes, they'd cried together over being so long separated, driven apart by events, but they'd laughed too. Steve's single bed proved to be quite inadequate for its purpose on this night and soon, covers and pillow were tossed aside, or slid of their own accord to the floor, and then Steve himself followed them as he fell asleep in her arms and rolled over into nothingness. Waking up with a bump, the young lovers laughed till the tears rolled once more and, with senses stirred, they couldn't resist touching and kissing, and making love all over again till finally they fell into a deep sleep of ecstasy and fulfilled contentment, arms and legs entwined about each other, clinging on tight.

Only Leah knew where to find her, had been quietly informed that she meant to spend the night with Steve at his digs, so it was her old friend who brought Jess the news. Leah woke her from this blissful reunion with a rude hammering on the door. As Steve staggered from the bed to fling it open, she stood framed within it, fighting for breath and quite unable to speak. Not that she needed to. Her face said it all.

27

Jess felt quite certain that she would never forgive herself, no matter how long she lived. She didn't deserve to be forgiven, or to have been blessed with such a wonderful child. How could she have been so stupid as to trust Doug with her precious son, when she knew only too well how little he cared about him? How could she so selfishly put her music before her son? And now her baby was in hospital, fighting for his life.

'Will he be all right? Will he live?' Jess asked of the well-meaning nurse for the hundredth time that night as she came to report on little Johnny's progress. It was all she could say, the one thought in her head, for if her baby died, what reason would she have to go on? 'Tell me he's going to get better.'

'We're doing our best, Mrs Morgan.'

'But you must remember how delicate he is, how he suffered a dislocated hip as a young baby. Please, take good care of him.'

'We will, dear, don't fret. But you must keep calm. The doctors can do a great deal these days, with burns. That's one good thing that has come out of this terrible war.'

Jess felt sick at the thought of her tiny baby suffering, as all those poor pilots had done. And yet in a strange kind of way, the nurse was saying that their sacrifice would help him, and others like him. She could only pray this was true. She prayed a great deal: for the doctor, for her child, for all the nurses; prayed as she had never prayed before. She bargained with God, sobbed and pleaded, promising to be a much better wife and mother in the future, if only he would save her son.

And then she heard the full, unexpurgated story of the accident and her distress turned to anger. She could feel the rage boiling up inside her like a furnace, or a volcano about to explode. She heard how Doug had left the boy with Lizzie and, growing quickly bored with the lack of attention, little Johnny had leaned closer to the old Lancashire range where the stock pan sat simmering on the metal hob before the fire. Cora boiled the goodness from bones in there, and added vegetables from time to time. Perhaps fascinated by the steam as it rose from the boiling water, he'd made a grab for the handle and pulled the pan and its contents all over himself.

The doctors had told her he was fortunate that he still had the plaster encasing his legs, or it could have been much, much worse. But his poor little feet, his hands and arms, and much of his chest were badly scalded and would need expert treatment, perhaps skin grafts eventually. He was being given expert care, put on plenty of fluids but she'd been told that the shock alone could kill him. All they could do now was wait, and hope for the best.

'How could you have been so unmindful of his well-being to leave him with Lizzie? Don't you know well enough what a feckless, useless drunkard she is? She can't look after herself properly, let alone a child. How could you be so *stupid*?'

For once Doug could think of nothing to say. The accident had shocked him to the core, left him shaken and stunned by events. He reminded himself that he'd never wanted the child in the first place, had wanted Jess all to himself. What was so wrong with that? She was his wife after all. He stood ashen-faced before her and Jess could see by the stubborn way he compressed his mouth into a thin, hard line that he resented the accusation. His first words confirmed that fear. 'If you'd been at home where you belong, there wouldn't have been a problem.'

'But you only needed to mind him till dinner time. Was that too much to ask? Why couldn't you at least do that for me?'

Doug turned his head away and sat down with his arms folded, obstinately determined not to offer any sort of apology which might indicate that he accepted blame.

Even in the depths of her despair, Jess couldn't help comparing him with Steve, who had been denied the opportunity to be with her at this terrible time. He'd wanted to come when they'd first been told the news, but she wouldn't hear of it.

'It wouldn't be right. Not you and Doug together. No, no, it would be like putting a match to tinder.' She'd been distraught, not even certain what she was going to find when she and Leah got to the hospital yet thinking clearly enough to know that having the two men meet was more than she could cope with right then.

'But you're telling me that little Johnny is *my* son!' Somehow, keeping the baby a secret from him, had no longer seemed important. Mere trivia in the face of their child's dangerous condition.

'He could be, yes. I've denied it until now, but yes, I think he is.'

'Then for God's sake Jess, we need to talk about this. I need to be there.'

'No, no, it would only make the situation worse. I'll ring you here, at the dance hall, as soon as I have any news. Be patient, my love, please.'

Jess felt such bitterness, such terrible resentment towards this woman who had so blighted her life. She could clearly remember the cold dampness of the cellar, the fear of being buried alive. And as if ruining her own young life wasn't bad enough, Lizzie had now damaged her beloved child as well. Unable to help herself, she railed at her mother and it was as if a lifetime of complaints bubbled to the surface.

'What kind of useless woman are you, that you can't take care of your own grandchild? I expect you were drunk, as usual. Don't you ever think of anyone or anything besides yourself? So help me, I'll swing for you one day, I swear it. When have you ever been anything but a useless . . .'

Leah rushed to soothe her, hushing and shushing Jess in a desperate bid to calm her growing hysterics, understandable though they may be in the circumstances. She grasped Jess's hands to pull her away from Lizzie, fearful of what the two women might do to each other. She'd never seen her friend so distressed, seemingly oblivious to the tears coursing down her face, to anyone else's feelings but her own, and all because of the terrible fear growing inside that she was about to lose her son. Leah spoke in her calmest, gentlest voice, 'Sit down Jess love. Relax. This isn't the moment to be casting blame. Let's wait till we hear what the doctors have to say, shall we? I'll fetch you a nice, sweet cup of tea.'

And so they waited, all night long they waited. Jess, Doug, Leah, Cora, and even Sandra, who'd loved her little cousin to bits, she said, choking back tears.

Lizzie had been the one to call for help from the neighbours, although it had taken Ma Pickles' son, Josh, to run and phone for an ambulance, Lizzie herself being far too inebriated to cope. Ma Pickles had not accompanied them to the hospital as she'd been left to wait in for Cora, and later had stayed on to care for Sam and Seb. For the first time in her life, Cora gave no thought to her own children, nor did she attempt to solve the problem by providing food for everyone. This was all quite beyond her. She sat in silent contemplation, eyes deep and fathomless, holding on tight to Jess's hand.

For hours Lizzie had sat in silence too, eyes wide and blank as if trying to comprehend exactly what was going on, or even where she was. But then for no apparent reason, she began whimpering like an injured kitten, a sound which gradually increased in volume as the night wore on and she grew ever more restless, perhaps more in need of a drink, till finally she launched into a full-throated wail.

'Can't you shut her up?' Doug asked of Jess, clearly embarrassed by his mother-in-law's wild behaviour. He'd never wanted either the child or this woman, and he'd be damned if he'd put up with any more disruption to his calm and quiet life. 'What good are we all doing, sitting about here? Get your coat on, Jess. It's time we went home.'

'You go, if you must, I'm staying here. My child needs me.'

Lizzie swivelled about and screamed at Jess, lashing out at her with her fingernails. 'You're not my child, you're the devil's spawn. *Get out of my sight! I don't want you! Bane of my life you are. Go, go, go!*'

A plump little nurse came hurrying along the corridor like a steam train to inform them in furiously hushed tones how, if they didn't keep Lizzie quiet and make her behave, they would all have to leave. She pointed out forcibly what a huge favour the hospital was doing allowing them to stay at all, all due to the kind heart of the doctor.

In the end, far from being able to shut her up, Lizzie's wails grew to fever pitch, and she began wandering down the corridor, frantically knocking and scrabbling at doors, even opening them, as if seeking something or someone, though no one could be sure what or who it was. Each of them attempted to stop her, to coax her back with bribes of tea and biscuits, of wine gums and mint imperials, anything to keep her in her seat. All to no avail. Two seconds later she would jump to her feet and be off again, wailing like the proverbial banshee, growing more and more demented. She didn't seem to understand where she was, or why she had come here in the first place.

And then she began shrieking, 'Where's Bernie? He's here, I know he is. Where is he?' Fighting off Jess's frantic attempt to lead her once more back to her seat. 'Where've you put him? You're keeping him away from me, but I'll find him, see if I don't. You can't have him, he's mine, child or no child. I'm his wife, I'll have you know.'

'By heck,' Cora said. 'She has lost it this time.'

The nurse obviously agreed and Lizzie was gently rounded up like a stray cat and taken away to some nether region of the hospital where 'she would get the proper care that she needs'.

'By which they mean knock-out drops of the non-alcoholic variety,' said Cora, drily. 'Happen we can all get a bit of peace now.'

Several other friends called in during the course of that long night, including the girls from the band, and Harriet and Sergeant Ted on their way home from the mission. They all in turn offered what comfort they could, paced the floor with Jess for a while, or simply held her close in a silent hug.

Jess felt numb, as if she'd slipped from reality into another world, from where she could observe the shell of her former self going through these pointless motions, walking up and down the hospital corridor, sipping tea or leaving it till it went cold and then accepting a fresh one in its place. Or she would simply sit and stare into the abyss of guilt and fear, for deep down she knew there was only one person to blame. Herself. Johnny was her child, hers and Steve's, as Cora had insisted all along. Certainly not Bernie's. It had been wrong of her to expect Doug to care for him. He was her responsibility entirely, hers alone. And if he died, she could blame no one but herself.

By morning, baby Johnny was showing definite signs of improvement but it was carefully explained to Jess that the burns would take time to heal and there was always the risk of infection. It would be some weeks before they knew for certain that he was out of danger.

When Leah reached home in the late morning, Harry was waiting for her.

'Have you been seeing a fancy man too? Is that where you've been?'

'No, that is not where I've been. I've been with Jess at the hospital.' She began to tell him about little Johnny's accident, but he wasn't listening. He carried on shouting and roaring at her and Leah turned from him in disgust. Worn out and tired from the long bus journey, traumatised by the long night of waiting and drained from helping Jess cope with the guarded optimism of the hospital, all she wanted to do now was drop into bed and sleep.

Harry followed her into the bedroom, still yelling, 'I heard all about that Steve character having it off with Jess.'

Leah was surprised. 'How did you hear?'

'It's common knowledge. The gossip is all over the pub. Cheap little tart. Is that what you get up to on these gigs? Shaming us all.' He'd been furious that Jess had turned the tables on him by insisting she only give him money in return for ownership of the club. Why wasn't she scared of him like everyone else? It didn't make sense. How dare the trollop defy him in that way? True, the down-payment, as she termed it, had allowed him to fend off Little Jimmy for a bit but he couldn't go on in this fashion. He was going to have to accept her terms, or go under. The electricity board were threatening to cut off the electricity and the phone had already been disconnected. How could a chap do business with such problems on his hands? And Little Jimmy would be back tomorrow, or the day after, demanding the rest of his dosh.

To add insult to injury, now his wife had turned up late, and she too hadn't even got paid for the best part of a week's work away from home. Some tale about Jess not having time to think of it. All excuses, in Harry's opinion. God knows what the little tarts got up to. He was having none of it.

'What kind of a mother are you?' he shouted, pleased to see that she, at least, cowered away from him, recognising that he still held the power. Perhaps now was the moment to reinforce that fact.

Harry hadn't allowed her to take baby Susie on tour with her, insisting that he could look after his daughter very well himself. Now he made it clear that if she transgressed, she'd never see her child again.

Leah began to tremble, knowing that whatever else he might be, Harry was a devoted father. And the thought of losing Susie didn't bear thinking about. That must never happen. She attempted a reassuring smile, usually the best way to placate him when he was in one of his bad moods since he hated tears. 'Don't be silly, of course I haven't been seeing anyone.'

'So you say.'

'As if I would! Jess and Steve are old friends. I thought she might marry him at one time, but that has nothing at all to do with me. Why would I want to have a fancy man when I've got you, and little Susie? I wouldn't take the risk of losing her, you can be sure of that, Harry, if nothing else.'

Sometimes it didn't seem to matter what she did or what she said: whether she pleaded, teased or begged, he seemed to be beyond reason, his course of action as unstoppable as an express train. So it was on this occasion. He punched her anyway, with his fist, right in the stomach; a favourite spot since no one could see the bruises, then pushed her face down on the bed, ripped off her clothes and drove into her with the kind of unremitting force that had nothing at all to do with love.

'That'll teach you not to make a cuckold of me.'

'But I didn't . . .'

'Shut yer lip. That's what you'll get if you ever do.'

Apparently satisfied that he'd brought her to heel and properly subdued her, he stormed out of the little flat, and it wasn't hard to guess where he was going.

So this was married life. Little more than two years into it, and the mere prospect of spending the rest of her life with this brute, was driving her to the brink of insanity.

Lying weeping on the bed, nursing the latest in a long line of sores and bruises, Leah wondered what on earth she'd ever seen in him? What had happened to the handsome, teasing, flirtatious man she'd married? Where was the love, the care, the cheerful banter, the excitement and fun they'd once enjoyed together? It had all gone, or else had never existed in the first place and he'd tricked her, been playing a game till he had her in his thrall, able to do with her what he willed.

Leah had known for quite a while about the other girls, about Queenie and her little empire of tarts who came and went with dizzying regularity in the club below. She'd gone looking for him one night and found him in bed with a young girl who still looked as if she should be in school. At first she'd been upset, screamed and railed at him, feeling betrayed and degraded at sharing her husband with a prostitute. 'Don't think you can come to me, after you've slept with such creatures,' she'd shrieked at him, but Harry had only laughed.

'Why would it matter? They don't object to you.'

'I'm your *wife*! I deserve better.'

'You should be thankful for what you get. I'm considered

quite a catch round here. Anyroad, don't worry, love, I'll not see you go short.' And he'd slammed her up against the wall, ripped open her blouse, pushed up her skirt to take her there and then on the top landing, in full view of the silly little whore.

'Whoops, spare my blushes,' the girl had said, and gone off giggling.

Leah had ceased to care what he did after that. At least while Harry was tasting their favours, he was leaving her alone.

All Harry thought about now – perhaps all he'd ever cared about – was the club, apart from himself, that is. And all he ever talked about was money. How he could get more. What he would spend it on when he did.

And Leah knew that in fact he spent it as quickly as he made it. Cash dribbled through his fingers like water. Now that the blackout had been lifted, he left the lights on all the time and ran up huge electricity bills. He gave the tenants too much time to pay their rents because they were often his only customers in the bar, and he needed them around. And the illegal card school met less frequently these days, now that so many of the GIs were returning home. They'd never been particularly troubled about rules and regulations, not during the war, perfectly willing to take a risk for the sake of a bit of fun to liven their dull lives. Other servicemen had joined in for the same reason, along with more nefarious characters, the kind Harry would have been wiser not to have in the club at all.

Now everything was changing. Men were going home to their families, trying to take up life where they'd left off six years earlier, or start new ones. They were busy finding themselves new jobs, opening businesses, thrilled by the prospect of peace and filled with hope for the future. This left Harry with the dross, not only making less profit but also with the kind of customer who didn't like to wait to get paid, if money was due to them. Leah knew that her husband was more and more finding himself in a tight corner, with gambling and liquor bills to pay and not enough money coming in. Which made him a loose cannon, and who knew what he might do next?

Jess sat by her son's bedside day after day, week after week for as long and as often as she was allowed, frequently defying the nurses whenever they tried to shoo her out and send her home.

'Hospital rules are hospital rules. They have to be kept,' the stern, plump nurse would say. 'We don't want little Johnny to get an infection, now do we? Visiting is two o'clock until three each day, not a minute more. Now you must go home, Mrs Morgan, and get some rest yourself.'

In Jess's opinion she no longer had a home to go to. Her one, all-consuming desire was for little Johnny to get well again. What would happen after that, she didn't know, and really didn't care. And so she went to Cora, pacing her floor for a change, paying no attention to the comings and goings of children in the little house, refusing to eat, growing thinner by the day in her anguish, till finally, alerted by Cora to her plight, Steve came for her and took charge.

'You're wasting away, Jess. What good will you be then to Johnny? Come with me, love. Let me take care of you.' And, with deep and loving thankfulness, she did.

It was, in fact, six weeks before the baby was allowed home, by which time Jess's marriage was over. She'd left Doug, given up all pretence of their being a happy couple, and moved in with Steve. If this was wrong, then so be it. To Jess's way of thinking, they belonged together and who better to care for the pair of them, than Johnny's own father.

To see father and son together at last, filled her with an

indescribable joy. How on earth she could have believed that this precious boy was anyone's son but Steve's, Jess really couldn't imagine. How very foolish she'd been. Just seeing them together told her instantly that Cora had been right all along. Johnny was clearly Steve's son, same hair, same smile, even the tilt of their head. And it was wonderful to see them taking such delight in each other.

'Forget the past,' Steve told her. 'We can put all those mistakes behind us and begin again.'

'What about Doug? I'm still married, don't forget.'

'I love you. We're together. That's all that counts.'

And best of all, Johnny was on the mend, the end of the poor little boy's misery was at last in sight. His scars would take a little time to heal but the plaster was off, his little legs looked pale and thin but strong and straight and firm, and it was all too evident that he was eager to walk. He was constantly trying to pull himself up by the table leg or a chair arm.

Even so, Jess remained consumed by guilt and she lost interest in everything, including her precious band. Where both Bernie and Doug had tried, for different reasons, to stop her playing her trumpet, her son's accident succeeded. She locked it away and declared that she would never pick it up again. 'No more music. If I hadn't put the needs of the band before those of my own child, then he wouldn't be in the condition he's in now.'

Everyone: Cora, Leah, Steve, all the girls in the band, insisted that this was nonsense, that she was not to blame. But she refused to listen. From now on she meant to be a full-time mother. Jess wanted to put everything right. If there was to be a new beginning, she wanted it to be as perfect as possible. She longed to be free to marry Steve. Besides, she hadn't told him yet, but she rather thought that she was pregnant again.

She went to see Doug, began by apologising for the un-
happiness she had caused him, and for blaming him for the
accident. 'I should never have agreed to marry you in the first
place when I was in love with someone else, and had even
borne his child. I'm so sorry. My only excuse is that at the
time, I still believed that Johnny might be Bernie's, a result of
the rape. I can see now that he couldn't possibly be. He isn't
in the least bit like him. It's Steve he resembles. Seeing them
together, there is absolutely no doubt in my mind. He's
clearly his son, and having found each other again, we both
know that we can't risk it happening a second time. We want
to marry, to be a proper family, so I'm asking you to release
me from my promise, and to give me my freedom.'

Doug looked at her for a long moment, then he smiled and
said, 'Of course I forgive you for blaming me. I realise you
were upset, Jess, so there really is no need for you to apologise at all. I won't even bear you any grudge for this silly little
fling you've had with that dreadful musician. You're still my
wife and, so far as I'm concerned, always will be, so there's
absolutely no necessity for you to consider leaving. You, and
– little Johnny – are welcome and always will be. This is your
rightful home, after all. Now, what are you making me for
my tea, love?'

Jess stared at him, aghast. 'You haven't heard a word I've
said, you can't even say my child's name without stumbling
over it,' and she walked out the door. Divorce or no divorce,
she'd no intention of ever going back.

Leah dragged herself out of bed just before midnight, and
went to make herself a mug of hot milk. Harry was either out,
or sleeping with one of his girls, as usual. She never asked
what he was doing or where he'd been, as she really didn't
want to know. But the tiny flat felt empty and silent, deeply
depressing. She went and checked on baby Susie, fast asleep

flat on her stomach in her crib, and Leah's heart softened with love for her child. If only there were some way of getting right away from Harry Delaney, an escape, a place to go where he wouldn't ever find her.

The trouble was, she didn't have any money, which galled her somewhat as she'd earned plenty from the band but was forced to hand over every penny to her husband. A thought struck her. There was no safe, so perhaps he hid it somewhere. Surely he didn't gamble it all away. If she could find enough money tucked away some place, she'd take Susie and run. They could go to Liverpool, catch the ferry to Ireland. Somewhere far away from Harry Delaney, where he would never think to look. No matter what the cost, she couldn't go on like this any longer.

Leah began searching drawers, tugging them out and riffling through them at reckless speed, frequently glancing over her shoulder, afraid that he might return at any moment and catch her in the act of plundering his belongings. She went through every pocket of his suits, even climbed up and examined the top of the wardrobe, but could find nothing. It was as she stood on the stool looking down at her own bedroom from this interesting and unusual angle, that she saw it. She noticed that one of the floorboards just under the bed was a slightly different colour from all the rest and not quite so neatly fitted.

Quickly, she jumped down, tossed aside a pegged rug which partially obscured it and tried to prise it up with her fingernails. It took a kitchen knife and finally a screwdriver which she fetched from Harry's toolbox before she'd managed to lift out a small oblong cut into the full length of the board. Beneath, was a box hidden in the dusty depths, quite small and square. Pulling it out, Leah flung open the lid to stare in surprise and horror at the contents. A cameo brooch and a pretty blue necklace. She recognised it at once as one which an aunt had brought her back from Madeira many years ago. Items which had been stolen during that terrible air raid.

'What the bleedin' hell do you think you're doing?'

When he hit her this time, she didn't get up.

Harry was quite certain that he'd killed her. And if he had, he'd ruined everything. There was no way that Jess would give in to his demands if he had, not if he'd done for her best friend. In which case he'd be forced to hand over the club, else how would he settle his debts with Little Jimmy? He couldn't even use this flaming jewellery to get him out of the shit. He'd already been offered a derisory sum for the brooch, and the necklace was glass, a worthless trinket, its only value pure sentiment. He again looked down with open contempt at the inert body of his wife.

'Hardly worth dying for, you stupid cow.'

It was then that it finally sank in that paying off his debts was the least of his worries. Harry really had no wish to feel the hangman's rope about his own neck. In the circumstances, he did the only logical thing. He ran.

1947

28

The lights were turned down low. Outside, snow was softly falling in what was proving to be the coldest winter on record, but here in a warm, cosy room on Deansgate, Delaney's All Girls Band were playing a medley of their most requested numbers. They'd begun, as always with 'Don't Sit Under the Apple Tree', wandered down memory lane through all the old wartime hits such as 'Wish Me Luck', and 'Bye, Bye Blackbird'. Then rip-roared their way through several more old favourites including 'Pennsylvania 6-5000' and 'Chattanooga Choo-Choo', and the customers were now smooching to 'In The Mood' as the girls put all their hearts and souls into the number.

As always on the nights when he wasn't on stage himself in some dance hall or other, Steve was seated at the back with his arm about Jess. 'They're good, your girls, but with the best will in the world they don't play nearly as well without you. It just doesn't sound right.'

Jess had kept to the vow she'd made and not touched her trumpet since the day Johnny had been scalded. Steve, along with the other band members, friends and family, had tried every way they could think of to persuade her to play. Steve tried again now.

'Think of the waste. What would Mr Yoffey have to say about you neglecting such a God-given talent?' They both still remembered with great affection, the old man who had sadly ended his days in the Isle-of-Man Aliens' camp but at least had lived a long and happy life until then, and been instrumental in bringing them together.

Jess remained adamant. 'Talented or not, there's no reason why I should play. Look at the damage it caused.'

Steve patiently reminded her that their son was not only fully recovered but a lively youngster who never sat still for a minute, tearing around the place as if to make up for all those sedentary, painful months he'd spent as a baby. His young sister, Jo, clearly adored him and at twenty-one months was desperately trying to catch up.

'Yes, but look at Lizzie. Look what it did to her, having to spend all those months incarcerated in a mental institution where they fed her pills and potions, gave her cold baths and goodness knows what electro-therapy treatment. It doesn't bear thinking of. No wonder she went off her head, raving like a maniac wanting to get out, or else slumped in depression. The poor woman didn't know where she was, or why she was there. I know what it feels like to be locked up, and so does she, having served time in jail. Hadn't she suffered enough?'

'It probably saved her life, Jess. She'd have died of alcohol poisoning otherwise. You know she would.'

Steve gave up the argument, as he usually did, and called out for the girls to play his all-time favourite, 'I'll Be Seeing You'. 'That was the night I first told you that I loved you, and you responded by running away and marrying another man.'

They were considered to be quite a Bohemian couple, both musicians, with two children, living together and running what was quickly developing into one of Manchester's favourite night-spots, and yet still unwed.

Jess had never again gone, cap in hand, to beg Doug for a divorce. Once was enough. She'd sent letters, both from herself personally, and via her solicitor. All had been ignored. In the end, she'd given up the campaign and settled for what she'd got. She and Steve were happy, they had a family they adored, so what did marriage matter? It was only a piece of paper, after all. Deep down Jess knew that it did still matter, very much, but events had somehow overtaken them and there had been more important issues to deal with at the time. She'd been pregnant with Jo, and Leah had suffered two broken ribs and a broken cheekbone, spending weeks in hospital and needing two operations on her face before they were certain she'd even be able to see again. Jess had sworn never to speak to Harry ever again, were she so unfortunate as to run across him.

The word was that, like his father before him, he'd done a runner. Only Cora, Bert and Jess knew the truth, that Bernie hadn't run anywhere. Had they known the true facts, they might have said that his son had been luckier. Harry had at least survived.

They'd learned that he hadn't got very far. As luck would have it, Big Pat had had a match on that evening, at the Donkey on the corner of Hardman Street. She'd just stepped outside to take a breath of smoke-encrusted air when who should hurtle around the corner but the very bloke who owed her brother a deal of brass. Never one to let an opportunity slip by, Big Pat had lifted him in a powerful bear-hug, bounced him off a couple of walls, then pinned him to the ground in a scissors hold that threatened to detach his head from his body.

No one was quite certain about what happened after that, but knowing Big Pat's style, she'd probably have been satisfied that she'd made her point. She certainly always liked to win but never bore anyone a grudge. No doubt she picked up Harry, dusted him down, added a few deft words of her own inimitable advice and sent him on his way.

If he had managed to get over the shame and humiliation of being beaten by a woman, he certainly didn't hang around to prove his case. Harry Delaney hadn't been sighted in Deansgate Village from that day to this. Legend had it that he never did pay his debts, that Little Jimmy and his brigade of ex-squaddies were still keeping an eye open for him, just in case he ever ventured back on their territory. Strangely enough, none of his family had gone looking for him, not even his wife or his mother, so, as folk said when they discussed this juicy titbit on street corners, he couldn't have been much missed.

Quite the contrary, for just as when Bernie had vanished off the face of the earth, the rest of the family all curiously seemed to benefit as a result.

Jess and Steve paid off all the debts, moved into the flat and took over the club. They sacked the girls, completely refurbished the place and due to much hard work and endeavour, it was now thriving. Leah, having made a good recovery from her dreadful injuries, occupied two of the best rooms above the club, together with her daughter, Susie. Lizzie was said to occupy a third as a bedsit. A shadow of her former self, rumour had it that she never touched a drop of the hard stuff these days. Didn't dare, for fear Jess would turn her out in the street. Although they were said to be largely reconciled, Lizzie wasn't taking any chances.

Cora remained contentedly in Cumberland Street with her children: the twins, as self-contained as ever, never far from her side. Sandra, now a young woman of sixteen was causing her mother endless bother. And if Harry had gone, young Tommy was back in the fold, with his new wife in tow happily expecting their first child. Cora could hardly wait for the new addition to the Delaney flock as she was always ready and willing to mind Jess or Leah's children for an hour or two, and was a frequent visitor to her son Bert's house where his wife Maisie had recently been delivered of her third son. She was in seventh heaven. The Delaneys, she thought, were going from strength to strength.

As always when the band was working, Cora had spent much of the evening upstairs minding the children, but she'd slipped down for a few minutes with her sister-in-law and long-standing enemy, Lizzie, to enjoy the music while Maisie took charge for a bit. 'Give you a break, Mum,' she'd said. A good-hearted girl if ever there was one.

'Eeh, but I'm that blessed with my childer,' Cora declared, heaving her rolls of fat into a comfortable position on a too small chair while humming the familiar bars of 'The Blackout Stroll', which she remembered Joe Loss used to play, once over.

Lizzie was saying, 'Particularly those what belong to other people, like our Jess, and poor overworked Maisie.' As usual, they were indulging in their favourite pastime of what was politely termed in these parts, a bit of argy-bargy.

'Nay, Maisie's a Trojan and not in the least overworked. Our Bert wouldn't hear of it. He worships ground she walks on. Eeh, they're reet grand, these girls. They fair get my feet tapping. If only yon lass o' thine would get up there and join them. Why don't you try talking to her? What's a mother for, if not to support her kids?'

For once there was no fierce response. Lizzie wasn't even listening to her. She was staring, wide-eyed, at the door.

Cora fished in her cardigan pocket for her glasses, so that she could better see who she was looking at.

'Nay, I don't believe it.' Lizzie was on her feet now, while Cora was looking frantically across at Jess, to see if she'd noticed. She had.

Jess too was standing, with one hand on Steve's shoulder as if for support. 'What is it, love?' he asked. Cora saw him mouth the words but Jess made no attempt to answer. She was moving slowly forward, her face chalk white, as if she were seeing a ghost. And, in a way, she was.

'Dad? Daddy, is that you?' The man in the door turned when he heard the sound of her voice, and a smile lit his face, crinkling his eyes in that old familiar way she loved so much, though the face was one in which the bones stood out sharply, ravaged by starvation and the result of an incarceration neither his wife, nor a loving daughter would ever understand.

'Jess love, how are you?' Jake wrapped his arms about his daughter and held her as tightly as he could, blessing the angels who had guarded him all these years, just so he could return and see his child's lovely face again. Tears flowed but neither father nor daughter suffered any embarrassment from it, or paid any heed to the sighs and whispers of their audience. They clung to each other and laughed, and sobbed, then stood back and marvelled.

'I can't believe it's really you.'

'It's me all right. And you look a right little cracker. Always knew you'd turn out that way. Eeh, hello Lizzie, luv. You're looking – well.' Only Jess noticed the pause and the look of shock in his eyes.

Lizzie herself appeared utterly stunned by the return of her husband, and almost as worn out by time as he, if for a different reason. But Jake's attention was back with his daughter who was now introducing him excitedly to Steve, telling him of her children asleep upstairs, asking how he'd found her. And Jake was laughing at this deluge of information.

'Nay, I found you because this club of yours bears my name. And I understood that this was your band, so why aren't you up there, playing in it?'

Jess looked at him in wonder for another half minute, vaguely aware of Steve's voice softly remarking, 'Good question. Why aren't you up there, Jess?'

And suddenly Jess knew that she must play. For him, for the man who had first taught her the beauty and magic of music. Her fingers were itching to touch the valves, her lips poised to coax liquid gold from her precious instrument. But where was it? Where had she put it all those years ago?

'Where's my trumpet?'

'Whose trumpet?'

'All right, *your* trumpet. Where is it? Please, please, may I borrow your trumpet one more time.'

'With pleasure,' Steve grinned, bringing it from behind his back and handing it to her, rather like a magician pulling a rabbit from a hat.

Jess couldn't help but laugh, before kissing him with her thanks. 'You've had it waiting every time the girls went on stage, haven't you?'

'I certainly have. Waiting for the day you saw sense, the day you would finally erase the last of the scars.'

And so Jess took her rightful place on stage. 'This is for my dad,' she told her startled audience. 'He's been away a long time, like many of you here tonight he's been kept from these shores against his will. But he's back home, has travelled right across an ocean especially to hear me play. I might be a bit rusty but if I can remember which button to press on this thing, I'll give it a go.' She sent one radiant smile to the two men in her life, and then lifted the trumpet to her lips and began to play: 'I'll Be Seeing You, in all the old familiar places' . . . till there wasn't a dry eye in the house.

Jess Delaney had been reborn.